MARIE FERRARELLA

writes scintillating, heartwarming stories
with a unique, effervescent style that makes
readers bubble with joy. In *Crazy for You*,
Silhouette Books brings you
three compelling stories of women who
gamble with their hearts—and vow to win
the men of their dreams!

BUYER BEWARE
She has to clear his name—because she could
never live without his love!

GRAND THEFT: HEART
He's her prime suspect—for committing love in
the first degree....

A WOMAN OF INTEGRITY
Risk taking is her profession—but dare she
chance her heart?

"Ms. Ferrarella finds just the right balance of
love, laughter, charm and passion."
—*Romantic Times Magazine*

MARIE FERRARELLA

Prolific romance author Marie Ferrarella swears she was born writing, "which must have made the delivery especially hard for my mother."

Born in West Germany of Polish parents, she came to America when she was four years of age. For an entire year, Marie and her family explored the eastern half of the country before finally settling in New York. It was there that she was to meet the man she would marry, truly her first love. Marie was only fourteen when she first laid eyes on her future husband, Charles Ferrarella.

She scribbled off and on, while dreaming of a career as an actress. During her days at Queens College, acting started to lose its glamour as Marie spent more and more time writing. When she received her English degree, specializing in Shakespearean comedy, Marie and her family moved to Southern California, where she still resides.

After an interminable seven weeks apart, Charles decided he couldn't live without her and came out to California to marry his childhood sweetheart.

Ever practical, Marie was married in a wash-and-wear wedding dress that she sewed herself, appliqués and all. "'Be prepared' has always been my motto," the author jokes.

This motto has been stretched considerably by her two children, "but basically, it still applies," she says.

Marie, who has written over a hundred novels, including more than ninety with Silhouette Books, has one goal—to entertain, to make people laugh and feel good. "That's what makes me happy," she confesses. "That, and a really good romantic evening with my husband."

MARIE FERRARELLA

Crazy for You

Published by Silhouette Books

America's Publisher of Contemporary Romance

 SILHOUETTE BOOKS

ISBN 0-373-20167-2

by Request

CRAZY FOR YOU

Copyright © 1999 by Harlequin Books S.A.

The publisher acknowledges the copyright holder of the individual works as follows:

BUYER BEWARE
Copyright © 1984 by Marie Nicole

GRAND THEFT: HEART
Copyright © 1985 by Marie Rydzynski

A WOMAN OF INTEGRITY
Copyright © 1985 by Marie Nicole

Visit us at www.romance.net

Printed in U.S.A.

CONTENTS

Dearest Reader,

I can't tell you how excited I am about the book you are now holding in your hands. Within these pages are three of my earlier novels. I can vividly remember something special about working on each one of them. *Buyer Beware* evolved out of my husband's then passion (for something other than me) for coin collecting and my love for a good mystery. *Grand Theft: Heart* was the first story I ever set near my hometown. The title came about via eavesdropping while pumping gas (the conversation was about grand theft auto, but I made a few minor changes). It also was the very first book I typed on a computer. The computer ate chapters 3-6 twice, turning me into a nervous wreck and making me wonder if perhaps another intelligent life form was trying to make an editorial comment on the content of said chapters. Luckily for me and for the computer industry at large, my third attempt took. I've been enamored with computers ever since.

Grand Theft: Heart was also my first book about a law enforcement agent. In this case it was a lady police officer involved with a private investigator, two vocations I have returned to again and again. To me, they are as romantic as cowboys, and I have always loved cowboys.

As for *A Woman of Integrity*, that represents my own dear love. I am a movie buff inside and out, and I have always been in awe of stunt people. I thought it might be fun to follow one into a romance.

Thank you for coming along with me on this nostalgic peek into my past. I can't think of anyone I'd rather take with me. I hope you like reading these stories half as much as I liked writing them.

Love,

Marie Ferrarella

BUYER BEWARE

To
Michael and Mark

Struggle makes the success
seem sweeter—
even if it doesn't seem so
at the time

One

"I thought you people always delivered!" sputtered the fleshy-faced, well-dressed man, his voice booming through the spartanly furnished office of the Postal Service's Consumer Protection Division. There were no rugs to absorb the irritating sound, and the metal bookshelves and desks bounced the noise off one another, amplifying it.

"Let me put this as simply as possible, Mr. Dennenberg. This is a governmental agency," Casey Bennett replied dryly, trying very hard not to lose her temper. Her green eyes scanned the complaint form that the gray-haired man had finally been convinced to fill out, though he had muttered about strangulating red tape all the while. "These things take time. If it makes you feel any better, you're not alone with your problem."

"It doesn't make me feel a damn bit better!" he

shouted. "And how much time?" he wanted to know, pounding on her neatly arranged desk and sending that morning's reports colliding into the next week's projects.

Casey pressed her lips together as she picked up the scattered sheets and quickly returned them to their designated places. Out of the corner of her eye she saw her assistant, Millie, looking at her questioningly, ready to offer any help she could. But Casey prided herself on being able to handle things, even a pompous, difficult man who seemed bent on overwhelming her with noise alone.

"I've been placed in charge of this investigation, Mr. Dennenberg," Casey said, her words slow and measured. "In the past month we've received a number of complaints concerning mail order fraud involving Ashford and Ashford. The Division is quite aware of the mental anguish you've gone through," she said, hoping that her words would placate him somewhat. "Now, let me get a few things straight...."

Elliot Dennenberg deposited his considerable bulk onto the chair opposite Casey's desk. "About time," he grumbled audibly enough for the people in the next office to hear.

"You say that you purchased several coins alleged to be in mint condition."

"Alleged?" the man barked, leaning forward. "Young woman, it said so in black and white!"

Casey went on reading his form as if he hadn't interrupted. "You sent them a twenty-five thousand dollar check and received the coins back in the mail...."

"And they weren't in mint condition. Sliders. They

were sliders!'' he announced, triumphantly finishing the story for her. ''Sliders are...''

''...coins that have been circulated for a short period of time. Yes, I know,'' she said, happy to interrupt him for a change. She saw the man's shaggy brows rise inquisitively. ''You see, I collect coins, too,'' she said, smiling sweetly. ''On a more modest scale, of course,'' she added dryly, looking back at the amount Dennenberg had paid. Although twenty-five thousand dollars was not an uncommon sum to spend on a coin, even through the mails, it did take Casey's breath away for a moment. You'd think people would exercise the utmost caution before throwing that kind of money around. But it was done frequently.

'Well, there's nothing modest about twenty-five thousand dollars!'' Dennenberg growled, apparently wanting the conversation to get back to him.

''No, there isn't,'' Casey agreed. ''But it says here that you had the customary four weeks to return the coins if they weren't satisfactory....''

''I was busy!'' he told her imperially. ''My business won't run itself.''

''I quite appreciate that. Nevertheless, you did have an option you didn't take and...''

''What about decency?'' he thundered.

Wasn't he ever going to let her finish a sentence? She wondered, suddenly feeling very weary. It was Friday afternoon, her head ached, she felt a cold threatening to break over her and she was not in the mood to spar verbally with a man who wouldn't take no for an answer.

''Decency's a very nice term, Mr. Dennenberg,''

she said tersely, "but I believe King Arthur found that it didn't work too well in the real world."

"I don't want lectures!" Craning his neck and surveying the room, Dennenberg asked, "Isn't there a man around?"

That piqued Casey's temper. She didn't like his clear insinuation that a man could handle the situation better than she could. "I think there's a men's room attendant on the floor," she said sarcastically.

That seemed to cool him off slightly, she noted, glancing back down at the report. There wasn't much there to go on.

"I take it you tried to get in contact with the company," she said.

In answer Dennenberg pulled out a handful of letters and threw them on her desk. "These are copies of my letters," he announced. "This is all it got me!" From another pocket he produced a single sheet and waved it in the air. "A letter of denial."

Casey shook her head. Just like all the other stories. "Go on," she urged.

A look of satisfaction came over Dennenberg's round face as he continued. "I wrote directly to the president of the firm, and he told me that after looking into the matter he couldn't find any record of my transaction. Nothing!" he spat.

"Are you a new collector?" she asked mildly, jotting down information on her pad. When there was no response, she looked up.

Dennenberg was bristling slightly, shifting in his seat, obviously annoyed with the question and the fact that he must appear to be a novice. "Yes," he admitted grudgingly. "I wanted another area in which to concentrate my assets. Coins seemed to be a likely place. I did a lot of reading on the subject," he added, his voice crescendoing once again.

"It seems that wasn't enough," Casey commented, more to herself than to him. "If you were new at this, why didn't you have the coins appraised as soon as you received them?" she asked. It was beyond her how some people could be so gullible. She had always been blessed with a suspicious mind. She supposed all New Yorkers were that way, and was pleased to be able to count herself among them, even though she wasn't a native.

"I already told you, I didn't have the time. Besides, the man's firm was reputable. *That* I did check out. When I did take them to be appraised," he said with an angry sigh, mentioning the name of a well-known organization that specialized in appraisals, "they told me that the coins had actually been circulated. Now, what do you propose to do about it?" he demanded, once more on the offensive.

Casey sighed. It was time to wrap this session up. Millie had already left the office, on her way home for the weekend. It was time to start her own weekend. Way past time. "Mr. Dennenberg, I'll try to do all I can for you, but as I said, this will take time. I've recorded your complaint and...."

"I don't want it recorded. I want it acted on!" he said, interrupting again.

Casey wondered if the man were married, and pitied his wife if he was. The poor woman probably never got a chance to talk at all.

"Government agencies," he sniffed dismissively. "You're all alike. Just sit back on your rumps and live off our taxes while we're getting fleeced."

"I have no intention of sitting on my—my rump,

Mr. Dennenberg!'' Casey snapped, her temper momentarily getting the better of her.

"Good!" Dennenberg declaimed. "Then do something! Look," he said, pulling a newspaper out of a deep jacket pocket and tossing it on top of the letters he had produced as evidence. "He's here," he told her in the kind of voice one used to announce the arrival of a dangerous criminal. "Right here in town for a rare coin auction."

Casey's eyes scanned the page and reached the spot where Dennenberg's stubby finger was pointing. Along with the lengthy story concerning the auction there was a picture of some of the people who would be attending it. The photo showed a collection of wizened-looking men all standing about in dignified camaraderie—except for the man at the end. She raised her eyes questioningly at Dennenberg, who nodded his shaggy head. "That's him! That's the scoundrel! Even tells you where he's staying."

Dennenberg's next words were lost on Casey as some of her tiredness melted away and she forgot about her headache. She studied the picture. In spite of the poor quality of the reproduction, Casey could see that this was an exceptionally good-looking man.

"This is...?" she wanted to hear him say it.

"Can't you read?" Dennenberg demanded, pointing to the words beneath the picture. "Simon Ashford."

"The company president?" she asked, wanting to make perfectly sure. Despite all the information she had managed to gather while working on related cases, she certainly hadn't pictured a culprit who looked like this.

"The con artist," Dennenberg pronounced. "And

see, it tells you where he's staying," he said, his voice getting more excited. "Will you go confront him?" he asked.

Casey licked her lips, sorely tempted by the picture she saw. It would be a bit unorthodox to confront the man now, before a full case was prepared. But perhaps seeing him might help pull the matter together, her mind argued. And he was right here....

"It's not the money, you understand," Dennenberg was saying rather haughtily. "It's the principle."

"Be happy that you're in a position to say something like that," Casey told him, thinking of all the mail fraud victims who couldn't afford to lose the money they had spent on some venture or other.

"Knew I should have talked to a man," Dennenberg grouched, rising. He reached out to take his papers back, but Casey stayed his hand. The shaggy brows rose as the little pig eyes questioned her.

"I said I was handling the case, and handle it I will, Mr. Dennenberg. In my own way," she concluded. She thought it prudent not to add that intent to defraud was going to be hard, if not impossible, to prove.

"Here's my card," Dennenberg said, producing it happily. "And that scoundrel's staying at the Hilton Hotel."

Which was how Casey came to be at the Hilton two hours later instead of curled up in front of her television set, watching the Friday night movie. Usually she felt some sort of compassion for the people who came to her with their tales of woe. In this case, though, she almost felt that Dennenberg had had it coming to him—but then, no one should be defrauded of his money, no matter how obnoxious he was, she chided herself. As far as this matter went, she wished that this Ashford person had come to her and been the one taken in by the likes of Dennenberg. *That* she could have believed. No, on second thought, she considered, glancing into her shoulder bag again to take one more look at the handsome man in the newspaper clipping, if she were any judge of character, the person who belonged to that face wouldn't easily be taken in by anyone or anything.

"Yes?" the desk clerk asked her solicitously.

"Mr. Simon Ashford's room number, please," Casey said casually, as if this whole thing were all quite natural.

"Ah yes, of course," he murmured, skimming his finger down a list in his large guest book.

Of course? Why? Did the man have a parade of people asking him? She thought of the recent complaints she was in the process of investigating and wondered if one of those people had decided to beard the lion in his den.

"Room 1040," the clerk told her, giving her a pleasant smile.

Casey nodded and followed the ornately lettered signs that led the way to the nearest set of elevators, her high heels practically vanishing into the lush, mauve carpet that seemed to stretch on forever.

This isn't the way it's supposed to be done, Casey, her conscience nagged. There are rules and procedures to follow.... Ah, but there came a time to break rules, even for people who'd lived by them staunchly all their lives, she thought, the way she had. Besides, it wasn't every day that an opportunity to confront someone as intriguing as Simon Ashford came along.

Casey got off on the tenth floor and, after following the long hallway through twists and turns, finally found Room 1040. But before she knocked on the door something prompted her to pull out her small compact mirror and check her appearance. Normally she would have confidently forged ahead, knowing that her appearance was more than just satisfactory. Casey Bennett was blessed with a complexion and figure that needed no camouflaging cosmetics or vigorous exercise. Everything just naturally fell into place, and fell into place well.

Although Casey did belong to a gym, she attended more out of a sense of fun and a desire for companionship than she did out of a driving need to slave to keep the inches off and the pounds at bay. Casey's high-geared metabolism allowed her to eat whatever she pleased without having to wear it as embarrassing testimony to poor willpower. Her porcelain-smooth skin was just the right shade for her abundant copper-colored hair and luminous green eyes. She had been born picture perfect, which allowed her to tread in places where angels at times feared to go. Men almost always began by listening indulgently to a pretty woman.

Her most valued asset, though, as far as she was concerned, was her mind, honed at Harvard. "Beauty with brains" her boss had called her after she had proven herself to him on her very first assignment.

But this time her confidence had dipped a little below its regular level. After straightening her form-fitting dark green dress, Casey raised her hand to knock, then stopped.

What was she? Crazy? Her zeal and whimsy had momentarily caused her to abandon her normally strong vein of common sense. What she was proposing to do might blow the entire case before there was one. She couldn't come right out and ask him questions. If he were culpable, this would put him on the alert. No, this was all wrong. She dropped her hand.

But since she was there, she rationalized, trying to bail herself out, it would do no harm to see the man at a distance, would it? She abruptly decided to attend the auction instead.

Casey retraced her steps down the richly wallpapered hallway until she reached the elevators again. After returning to the ground floor, Casey found a location map on the wall. It was highlighted by a large arrow and the words "You are here."

"Terrific," she murmured. "How do I get 'there'?" she wondered out loud, pondering the floor plan for a few seconds before locating the Ambassador Room. She had never been very good at finding her way around and had only recently become comfortable with her adopted city—and even then only with the heart of Manhattan, where the streets were obligingly numbered rather than named. Numbers she could rationally deal with, she thought. But names...? There was never any order to them. There ought to be a law that, at the very least, streets should be alphabetical if they couldn't be numbered.

Tapping a pink polished nail on the plexiglass that covered the map, Casey made a mental note of her destination, then turned to head in the direction indicated. It led her into a less well-lit area, which was actually a maze of small hotel shops. It totally confused Casey, but she kept on walking, hoping that she was making the correct turns. When she passed the coffee shop for the third time she realized that she was definitely not going in the right direction.

As she passed the glass doors of the shop she heard a resonant voice ask, "Can I help you, or are you just circling before landing?"

She was about to say something flippant in response when she turned to look at the owner of the deep tones. There, flashing a row of gleaming teeth set in a sensual mouth and smiling at her from the doorway, was Simon Ashford, her quarry.

For a moment Casey was unsure of her next move. Standing so close to him was breath-taking. The newspaper picture hadn't begun to do him justice. Well, so much for watching him from a discreet distance, she thought, her mind searching frantically for a solution. Why hadn't she plotted this out logically, the way she normally did? She thought of the auction. That was it; she'd pretend to be attending the auction as an interested coin collector.

"Circling for a landing?" she asked sweetly, putting on her most innocent smile.

"I've watched you circle the shop three times," Simon told her, edging closer to her as a couple left the shop, forcing him to shift to one side.

She could smell the cologne he used. Its deep aroma seduced her senses, arousing a pleasant feeling within her.

"I'm flattered," she said, casting her eyes down for effect.

"I'm sure a beautiful woman like you must be used to having men watch her," he said, and the words sounded positively seductive, due, she supposed, to his sexy southern drawl.

How many times had she heard that line? Maybe

the man truly was a con artist, she thought. If he was, he undoubtedly had a great disguise in that suave, smooth exterior. But it wouldn't be the first time that appearances had proven to be deceiving.

"I was on my way to the coin auction being held here," she said. "But I'm having a terrible time finding the Ambassador Room," she confessed.

She saw a warm light come into his incredibly liquid blue-gray eyes. "What a small world; so was I. Allow me to lead you there," he said, offering her his arm.

Gingerly she placed her hand on it, feeling the rock hard muscle beneath her light touch. Heat drifted tantalizingly through her. Con artists, her mind announced in big, glaring red lights. Part of his trade. She made an effort to distance herself mentally.

"Are you a coin dealer?" he asked, as he led her down the left hallway. How could she have missed that sign? She wondered, staring at the gold letters on the ruby red placard. It boldly proclaimed: The Ambassador Room. A dramatic arrow pointed out the direction.

"Um, no," she replied hastily, realizing that he was waiting for an answer.

"A coin collector, then?"

Her smile broadened. "Yes, as a matter of fact; I am." She could see Simon's interest mounting as they approached the door of the Ambassador Room. But there before her was another obstacle to be surmounted. Since she had only made up her mind to come to this auction a few minutes ago, Casey hadn't pre-registered and, so far as she knew, one couldn't just waltz into a coin auction off the street. At least, that had been her experience.

Apprehensively, she eyed the two harried women who were checking everyone's I.D.s against a long list of names. Her mind raced, trying to think of something to say when they challenged her presence, as she was sure they were about to do.

But her fears evaporated when Simon simply smiled at the women and said hello. No, his greeting actually sounded more like a throaty purr. The direct result of that was that both he and Casey walked in right past them. Did they think she was his date? She wondered. The idea tickled her, despite the mission she told herself she was on.

Simon ushered her over to one of the folding chairs that had been set up to accommodate the crowd attending the auction. From her seat, Casey could see a small stage with a panel of four people at a long table. A podium was set up in the center of the stage, with a microphone attached to it. The room was three-quarters filled with well dressed people, predominantly men, all holding programs in their hands. Out of the corner of her eye she could see that Simon had pulled out his.

"Excuse me for a moment," he said, making a few last minute marks on the list, then glancing at Casey. "Don't you have a program?" he asked, curious.

"Misplaced it," she murmured, after making a show of looking for it in her purse. Think quick, her mind nagged her. "Actually, I wasn't planning on bidding tonight. I just came to watch. The coins I'm interested in are being offered tomorrow," she concluded, hoping he wouldn't ask any further questions.

"Here, we can share mine," Simon told her, shifting in his seat and moving closer to her.

Casey could feel his leg pressed against hers. Her

eyes jumped to his face, and she could see his comfortable smile. Was he trying to unnerve her? She wondered. Well, she had been "operated" on by the best, she thought confidently. Whatever his ploy might be, it wasn't going to work. She was growing more and more determined to get to the bottom of Dennenberg's allegations.

"I don't intend to bid for a while," Simon told her. "I'm only after the best," he said significantly, as he let his eyes savor her.

A few noises from the front of the room and the high-pitched wail of the microphone which was being tested told Casey that the event was about to start.

Casey looked back at the expensively-attired man on her right. Something warned her that she was getting in over her head, even though she had been at her job for four years. During that time she had handled some pretty strange cases, but it never ceased to amaze her how terribly gullible people were, sending money products from fly-by-night mail order companies that were nothing more than post-office boxes. Surprisingly, it sometimes got a little boring.

But she wasn't bored now. Not by a long shot. Covertly she snuck another look at Simon's ruggedly handsome face. God, that was probably the man's stock and trade, living off his face and manners—if indeed he was what Dennenberg and the others claimed him to be. Innocent until proven guilty, she reminded herself as she looked quickly down at the program when Simon caught her staring.

No, not that face. The man definitely wasn't the innocent type. Many a woman must have been done in by those eyes, Casey decided, feeling a wave of nervousness herself as once again Simon's eyes turned toward her, enveloping her in a smile.

"You're staring," he said, leaning over and whispering to her. His breath tickled the side of her neck.

She tried to shake herself free of the feeling that was getting a grip on her. "No, I'm not," she protested. The couple in front of them turned to glare in her direction, and Casey realized that her voice had been competing with the staccato trill of the auctioneer. "No, I'm not," she repeated softly.

But Simon merely smiled. "I don't mind," he told her, ignoring her protest. "After the auction we'll go somewhere and I'll tell you anything you want to know," he promised.

Goose bumps threatened to break out all over her body, especially when Simon squeezed her hand to seal his promise.

Two

It amazed Casey with what ease large amounts of money were tossed through the air. The vastly accelerated voice of the auctioneer ran through one lot of coins after another. Suddenly Casey became aware of Simon's newly alert attitude. Up to then he had been laid back, somewhat like a panther lazing in the noonday sun. But now they had apparently reached the coins which he was interested in. His dark head was up, at attention. His eyes gleamed as he took the measure of the other bidders who would be after the same coins he was. Casey got a mental image of Sir Lancelot girding up for battle. From different parts of the room bidders' fingers went up, signaling vouchers for thousands of dollars. They sprang up as easily as flowers in a meadow, seeking favor from the sun.

"How can they afford it?" Casey marveled to herself without realizing that her words were audible.

"Most of them are dealers," Simon interjected softly. "They're working with their organizations' money."

Casey wondered how good Simon was at working with other people's money, and if it were all done honestly.

No more words were forthcoming from Simon as a lot he had underlined in his program came up and he paid strict attention to the bids.

Glancing at the figures scribbled in the program Casey could see that Simon was willing to bid as high as eight thousand dollars for the single 1829 Quarter Eagle that was being presented. She took another look at the man at her side. Could someone who looked like him actually be involved in swindling people? But just because he looked like the real thing, it didn't meant that he couldn't have a false heart beneath the designer clothing he wore with such style and grace, Casey told herself.

Her eyes strayed over his frame, taking it all in at leisure, since he was still absorbed in the bidding. His thick, dark hair brushed against the back of his collar, tempting her fingers to reach up and touch it. Each strand lay perfectly in place, as if by a mandate from God. The bright blue of Simon's silk shirt accentuated his eyes to such an extent that each time he looked at her, Casey felt a magnetic tug. His long, sooty lashes completed a picture of smoldering sexuality.

"Hold my hand for luck," Simon said to her suddenly.

She roused herself from her mental wanderings. "What?"

"Hold my hand for luck," he repeated as the auctioneer paused to sip a glass of water. "Here comes the big one,'' Simon whispered, taking her hand. ''I really want this one,'' he said with the voice a big game hunter might use when stalking an elusive lion whose head he longed to hang on his study wall.

Simon's deeply tanned fingers curled about hers, holding Casey's hand as familiarly as if they had been friends—or more—for years, not as if they had just accidentally bumped into one another outside a hotel coffee shop.

Casey liked the feel of his hand against hers, liked the increased tension she felt as the bidding intensified. She was swept into the momentum of the event by the pressure of his hand, his excitement transmitting itself to her. Casey drew her own breath in a fraction of a moment after Simon had done the same.

''Do I hear fifteen five?'' the auctioneer asked. ''Yes. The gentleman there.'' He indicated an area to Simon's far right with his gravel. ''Fifteen seven? Fifteen seven.''

Rapidly, the amounts escalated higher and higher, sending Casey's head spinning. With each bid that did not come from Simon, she felt him squeeze her hand a little tighter. It was the only indication that he was tense. On the surface he appeared exceedingly calm.

The bidding for the single coin went up to nineteen-eight before the other bidders all bowed out, leaving the victory to Simon. A look of total satisfaction curved his generous lips.

''C'mon,'' he said to her as the next round began.

Obediently, if somewhat confused, Casey followed him silently to the double doors and then out into the hallway.

''Why are you leaving?'' she asked as the doors shut away the droning sound of the auctioneer.

"The other coins don't interest me tonight," he told her. "I've suddenly got something far more pressing on my mind," he said, his eyes telling her the rest of his thoughts.

Casey felt a flush of excitement lightly dance through her veins. But the words "buyer, beware" flashed through her brain. Steady, Case, this man is a pro, she told herself.

"Shouldn't you pick up your coins first?" she asked, trying to sound slightly aloof. She was there doing a job, righting a wrong, remember? From the look in Simon's eyes, he was intent on wronging a few rights, if she were any judge of virility.

In reply, he smiled. "That's not normal procedure," he said, eyeing her carefully—or was that her imagination?

His words hung in the air. She had forgotten that. He made her forget a lot of things, she thought. "Oh, of course," she murmured. "How silly of me. I suppose I got caught up in the excitement of the moment," she said.

"Did you now?" Simon asked, his eyes caressing her face, as if memorizing each of the classic, aristocratic lines and striking planes.

"Would you care to come up to my room and see my coins?" he asked huskily, taking her arm once more and leading her down the hallway. The dimly lit old fashioned lamps that lined the walls cast romantic shadows on every part of him, and it took all Casey's willpower to keep her wits about her.

"Is that tantamount to coming up and seeing your etchings?" she asked archly.

Simon laughed softly. "My, but you're a suspicious lady."

"I'm a New Yorker," she reminded him.

"Funny, you don't sound like a New Yorker. I always thought they were cold, hard, aloof people. You," he continued pointedly, his eyes exploring her even if his free hand did not, "on the other hand, appear warm and vibrant, like a sparkling bottle of white wine that's been saved for a very, very special occasion."

God, he was good, she thought, still trying to keep a mental space between herself and this man who was deeply assaulting her senses just with his presence.

He looked at her soulfully. "Are you going to prove me right?"

"That depends," Casey replied.

"On what?"

"On what it costs me," she murmured.

The husky laugh made every part of her body lean toward him almost yearningly. "Dinner. Will you join me for dinner to celebrate my latest triumph?"

"Which one?" she asked skeptically.

"Why, the one at the auction, of course," he told her innocently. But his countenance belied his words.

"Isn't it a little late for dinner?" Casey asked, feeling a bit safer now that they had walked into the lobby, where there were other people.

"I haven't eaten yet," he told her. "I never eat before an auction. It dulls my senses."

"I see, and now your senses could use some dulling?" she asked dryly.

"In their present state, exposed to what they're drinking in at the moment, nothing could dull them," Simon answered, slipping an arm about her shoulders as he led her through the main lobby to the front entrance, where a well padded doorman stood dressed in an eye-opening scarlet uniform. The man came buoyantly to attention as they drew near him.

"Taxi, sir?" he inquired tactfully.

"Please," Simon said with a nod of his head, as if it were the greatest favor the doorman could render him.

Within moments one of the city's multitude of cabs materialized next to the doorman.

"Where to, Mac?" asked the cab driver, chewing on a toothpick and starting the meter before Simon had even managed to help Casey to slide in onto the cracked vinyl upholstery.

"The Club Mandan, please," Simon instructed.

"Now, wait just a minute here," Casey said, putting a restraining hand on Simon's arm. The Club Mandan was a posh night club, equally famous for its food and jet-setting patrons. Casey wasn't at all sure she was up to something like that. "You're going a mile a minute."

"Lady, I ain't even started the car yet," the cab driver protested, annoyed.

"Not you," she said, looking into the beady eyes that stared at her in the rearview mirror. "You," she said accusingly to Simon. "I haven't even accepted your invitation yet, and already you're whisking me off to some club before I can catch my breath."

"That, dear lady," said Simon, coming close and all but brushing her cheek with his lips, "is the whole idea. You wouldn't deprive a stranger to your fair city of some warm hospitality..."

"Oh, brother," the driver muttered. Casey glimpsed his forehead wrinkling up in a smirk as he watched them both in his mirror, the meter ticking, the cab not moving.

Casey sighed. "Well, we'd better go somewhere before you wind up paying the highest fare recorded for never leaving the curb," she said, nodding to the cabbie.

"You two resolved your problem?" the man queried in a rough voice, turning only slightly in their direction.

"Yes," said Simon, taking hold of Casey's hand once again. "The Club Mandan," he repeated.

The lights from passing cars sent occasional bursts of light to interrupt the sensual darkness that otherwise filled the back seat of the cab. Casey wasn't sure which made her feel more uneasy, the harsh lights that jangled her nerves, or the darkness which seemed to cocoon her with this tall, dark, handsome stranger she had brought into her life.

They made the trip in silence, and it wasn't a comfortable silence, at least not for Casey. She was wondering if this was a very good idea after all. Normally her sense of adventure, aided and abetted by the catalyst of wanting to set at least small wrongs right, made her forge ahead with this sort of thing. But truthfully, she had never encountered "this sort of thing" before. She had never felt herself so instantaneously attracted to anyone before in her life. Simon Ashford, who could pay thousands of dollars for a coin without batting an eye, who suavely took a woman's arm and charmed her out of her very soul, was a little larger than life. At least, larger than the life that Casey was used to. Casey couldn't help wondering whether he were spoiled and used to getting his own way—especially with women.

She reined in her mind once again, annoyed with herself for letting it stray in his direction. She was supposed to be a professional and not to let her feelings get in the way. If Simon was a "charming bum," if he truly was a swindler, then it was her duty to at least try to prove it and bring the matter to the attention of the proper authorities.

The thought left a bitter taste in her mouth.

"You're awfully quiet," Simon commented just then.

"A quiet dame. Count yourself lucky, mister," the cab driver shot over his shoulder.

Casey bristled at the comment, but Simon suppressed a laugh. "Are all New York cab drivers this philosophical?" he asked Casey.

The smile brought out a lone dimple in his right cheek, highlighted by the headlights of a car edging past them on the right. Casey fought to draw her eyes away from his profile and address his question.

"We call it something else," she said, casting a hard look at the back of the cab driver's balding head. "And, to answer your other question," she said as the cab screeched to a stop in front of the club entrance that welcomed all comers—for a fee, "I was thinking."

"I could tell," Simon told her, leaning forward to pay the driver.

"Oh?" Casey asked. Was he a mind reader, as well?

Simon got out and held the door open for Casey. "You were frowning," he answered, touching the area just above the bridge of her small, straight nose.

Casey felt a slight burning sensation where he had touched her. Heat slipped into her cheeks and coursed down her breasts. She was certainly grateful that she had refused to see his coins, she thought. She had the strong feeling that despite her original intentions, Simon would be intently investigating something entirely different right now if she had accepted his invitation and gone to his room. The man, she thought, using a phrase that her mother had been fond of, was an operator.

"Right now, you're probably wondering what the evening has in store for you," he said, slipping his arm about her shoulders. For a second he bent his face close to hers. "Only what you want it to," he concluded, whispering the words in the confidential tone of an intimate soulmate.

But he wasn't her soulmate. He was a stranger, someone whose picture had beckoned to her only a few hours ago. An alleged criminal. If not for Mr. Dennenberg and his pounding fist, Simon and Casey might never have encountered one another. She would have lived out her life not knowing that a man with such irresistible charms ever existed.

"That would be dinner, then," Casey clipped, keeping a smile on her lips.

"If that's really what you want," Simon replied. The look he gave her seemed to say that he could detect every racing of her pulse, every throbbing response that welled up in her whenever he bent close.

Casey held her head high, the thought of being read like a book irritating her. Deliberately she started toward the huge ebony doors of the club.

But Simon took the lead very quickly, stepping up to the attendant at the door and exchanging a few words. Casey thought that was funny. Here she had lived in New York for several years and had never even been near the club, while Simon, a self-proclaimed stranger knew his way around as if he were a native.

Once they got inside Casey felt swallowed up by a fast-paced swirl of lights and dancing bodies. A deeply pulsating beat enveloped her. It was like stepping into another world. She glanced questioningly at Simon, who took her hand once again and steered her toward the back, and another massive door. Was he taking her to the alley? She suddenly thought.

She hadn't even noticed until now that they were being led by a bored-looking, trimly dressed maître d' who appeared oblivious to the netherworld they were stepping into as he held open the second door.

This room was nearly black, the only illumination coming from subdued lights which cast romantic outlines all about her. The hectic whirl that existed just a few feet away dissolved into nothingness as the huge, soundproof door shut once again.

The waiter brought them to a cozy booth—there seemed to be nothing but cozy booths in this room—and handed them each a menu after they sat down, sharing one side. After that he appeared to vanish from the face of the earth.

"You come here often?" Casey asked softly and Simon shook his head, not in response to her question, but to indicate that he hadn't heard her whispered words. Feeling compelled not to raise her voice in such a hushed atmosphere, Casey edged closer to him in the booth.

He did the same, and Casey felt slightly threatened, but also very, very exhilarated. She had never felt that way around a man before and tried to examine her response for a moment, but she was unable to deal with it objectively.

"You were saying?" he almost purred, his left arm somehow managing to get behind her so he could gently stroke her spine, sending shivers all through her. She struggled not to show any reaction to this and wondered if she succeeded.

"Do you come here often?" she repeated, the words taking considerable effort on her part. How could she think when her body was taking on a life of its own? What did uncovering a mail fraud have to do with what she was feeling? Uncovering something else, maybe... Her eyes grew wide at the sudden thought, and she pulled her control about her like a cloak.

"Whenever I'm in town," Simon replied.

"Which is...?" she asked, trying not to sound as interested in the answer as she was. The unobtrusive waiter returned with two tall glasses of wine. "Um, thank you," she said as Simon placed a glass in her hand. "When did you order this?" she asked, surprised.

"You have to be fast here," Simon informed her. "And I come into town whenever there's an auction or something else that interests me." His manner indicated that he was at that very moment sitting next to something that interested him. "Such as now," he said, raising his glass to her in tribute.

Awkwardly Casey took a sip of her wine, then remembered that in her haste to get to the hotel after work she had only taken two quick bites of a cold, leftover Spanish omelet that had been the only edible thing in her half-empty refrigerator. Lunch seemed a million light years away as the wine seduced her senses. Simon's touch affected her in much the same way. She set her glass back down on the table with a firm determination.

"It doesn't please you?" Simon asked, cocking his head ever so slightly. Was there any angle that this man assumed that didn't make him look even more appealing than his last stance? She wondered.

"Oh, it's fine," she murmured, but she didn't pick the glass back up. She did keep her eyes on it, though, feeling it safer to do so than to look at Simon. "But I'm afraid it might make me light-headed."

"In that case, I'll have them send over a bottle," he said with an endearing grin, pretending to call over the waiter.

She grabbed his arm before she knew what she was doing. "No," she cried in alarm, then lowered her voice, looking over her shoulder to see if anyone else had heard the panic in her voice. "Dinner first," she said, regaining her composure as she let go of his sleeve. "You promised," she added accusingly.

"And I never renege on a promise," he told her.

She arched a brow. "Is that so?" She wondered if it were simply a trite phrase or if he truly meant it.

"Try me," he breathed against her face. The words were heavy with a meaning that Casey didn't feel herself equipped to handle at that moment.

She drew back a little. "Dinner," she reminded him.

"Dinner it is," he acquiesced, signaling the waiter.

As if by magic, even though Casey had seen neither hide nor hair of him a moment ago, the waiter materialized again, pad in hand, ready to take their orders.

Casey grappled with her oversized menu, realizing that she hadn't even opened it yet and had no idea what she was going to order. But Simon put his hand over hers.

"Allow me," he said. "I know what you want."

His words both intrigued and startled her. "Okay," she said wryly. "Show me."

And show her he did. First he ordered *spaghetti della casa*, which turned out to be spaghetti with chopped fresh shrimp sauteed in butter. Capers and shallots were blended in, with a touch of cream and tomato added for good measure. That was followed by an order of fresh sand dabs in a sauce of mustard, cream and cognac. As Casey's head swam with amazement, Simon went on to order a veal dish topped with prosciutto and cheese. Dessert promised to be a luscious combination of Italiana pastries.

Casey waited until after the waiter left. "Okay, how did you know I liked Italian food?" she wanted to know. If she had her choice, Casey thought, she would live on nothing else but, since calories were meaningless to her body. But the frozen offerings in the grocery stores left a lot to be desired, and she was usually too tired or too busy to whip up her own renditions.

"Easy," Simon told her casually. Once more his eyes pulled her away from her surroundings and into a very private, unnerving world that was populated only by him and her—and exotic, delicious emotions. "You look like the type to enjoy Italian food."

"Why? Are there tomato stains evident somewhere?" she asked humorously, pretending to glance down at her chic outfit.

Very deliberately Simon placed a finger beneath her chin and raised her head until she was forced to meet his eyes. Casey felt dizzier than when she had

taken her first sip of wine. "No, sensual people like
Italian food," he told her very, very quietly. "It
reaches out and speaks to a soul that's not afraid of
letting go and enjoying a gastronomical extravaganza.
Eating Italian food is like a love affair. You give
yourself over to it entirely, let it consume all your
senses. You close your eyes and savor each morsel."
His eyes danced as he repeated, "Like a love affair."

Casey became aware of the fact that she had been
holding her breath as he spoke. She was either going
to pass out or melt, and she was determined to do
neither, so she took a deep breath and pulled her head
back before she was totally beguiled by this man and
his magic.

"I also like French bread," she told him drolly.
"What would you like to make out of that?"

In response Simon threw back his head and
laughed, apparently delighted by her wit.

The man was a total mystery.

Three

Dinner had been a strange affair Casey thought the next day as she sat in the small nook that served as her kitchen and nursed a cup of coffee that had gone from steaming to lukewarm. She went over the whole thing carefully in her mind, as if uncertain that it had all happened—or at least that it had all happened to her.

After the meal, which had been very, very good, Simon had taken her dancing, and that too had been very, very good. Too good. His body had fit against hers as if they were two halves of a whole, and the feeling frightened Casey. Not because she feared a relationship, she told herself, catching her reflection in the small kitchen window that was just inches away, its gay daffodil café curtains pulled back. It was just that she feared a relationship with *this* man. There were too many complicating factors to contemplate living happily ever after—or even happily into next month. After all, she thought, mentally ticking off points on her fingers, he might be a thief. One did not contemplate a relationship of any sort with a confidence man who might run off with the family jewels in the middle of the night, no matter how sexy he was.

And if there were an explanation as to why Dennenberg and the others had been bilked out of their money—and off hand she couldn't think of one, much as she wanted to—there was still the problem that she herself presented. Simon might not be lying but she was. She was posing as something she wasn't. And why? For the sole purpose of "investigating" him. Men might like being studied, she told herself, but not in the light of being a possible thief or swindler. No, this was definitely not the kind of "undercover work" that a man like Simon would approve of.

This did not bode well, any of it. She rose and began to pace the tiny hall that led from her kitchen to her living room. On the coffee table her purse lay where it had fallen open the night before. A matchbook from the restaurant had slipped out, a reminder of all that had happened.

Casey sighed, lowering herself onto her cinnamon colored sofa. What an evening she had had. She hadn't felt so stimulated, so interested, so *alive* in a long time. They had danced, rubbing elbows with people she had only read about. No one had seemed to have a care in the world and for a while, neither had she. All the petty problems that crossed her desk five days a week had slipped into limbo for the space of the evening, and she had allowed herself to be swept up in the spirit of abandonment that seemed to pervade the room.

Dancing with Simon had been like borrowing a little piece of heaven. He danced divinely. She was sure he did everything divinely.

"The man probably brushes his teeth divinely," she murmured aloud.

A cold shower, that was what she needed. An ice cold shower that would attack her body with pins and needles and drive away the warm, steamy thoughts that were enveloping her like a well-fitting glove.

She marched into her pink and white bathroom and turned the water on full blast. But once she had stepped into the frosted-glass enclosure, she was reluctant to turn the handle from hot to cold. And as her body was covered with the soothing hot water, her mind once again slipped back to the previous night. Simon had been a perfect gentleman all evening. It was only beneath his words that she had sensed what he was driving at—what a part of her was also driving at, if the truth were known. She sighed. Her eyes closed as she relived every lovely second once again.

"Thank you for making this an exhilarating evening," Simon had said, not letting go of her hand after he had given her back her keys at her door.

"I thought getting the coins at the auction did that for you," she told him. She was being coy, her mind protested. What had come over her? Coy was for Southern belles with hoop skirts and gentlemen callers. She was too honest and up-front for that. Honest. Right, Mata Hari, she chided herself. Who are you kidding?

"That was just a prelude," Simon told her, drawing her ever so slowly into his arms. Casey made no effort to forestall the action, even though her instincts fairly cried, Mayday!

"I'll be in town for a few more days," he whispered into her hair. "Spend them with me?" he urged, his breath wafting lightly over her face.

She swallowed hard, feeling like an awkward teenager instead of a twenty-six-year-old so-called liberated woman. "What do you have in mind?" she heard herself asking.

"Lunch tomorrow, for openers," he said, humor evident in his eyes. Was he laughing *at* her or *with* her? Was *she* laughing? Her usually clear mind was getting very, very muddled. "We still haven't gotten to know one another," he told her. "There are a lot of things I'd like to know about you," he murmured seductively, his hand caressing her cheek.

There are a lot of things I want to know about you, too, her mind echoed. Like, are you married? Do you swindle people regularly? How many women have drowned in your eyes?

"And the evening is still young," he went on. She could see him eyeing the door to her apartment.

"Only in Bangkok," she quipped, recognizing the danger he represented. "I need my rest, and something tells me that I'd get precious little of it if I invited you in." Too late, she realized that her words could be taken two ways.

Obviously, from his seductive smile, Simon was taking them in a way she hadn't meant—or had she?

"Little rest, perhaps, but many memories to savor," he said, his forefinger gliding along the outline of her face, tracing her jawline until she fairly trembled beneath his expert touch. It halted at the point of her chin—was it too pointy? She worried. How absurd. She had never given the shape of her chin a second thought before. And then his finger languidly continued down to the hollow of her throat and stopped at her neckline. Her breathing must have been audible to him, she thought. It was almost deafening to her.

Simon tilted her head toward him and bent his own down to sample the sweetness of her lips. Casey felt herself trembling inside and willed her knees not to buckle.

What kind of a kiss had she been expecting. She no longer remembered, but whatever it had been, it hadn't begun to approximate what actually happened. His kiss, warm and pliant, urgent yet gentle, blotted out everything else in the hallway? It blotted out New York, all five boroughs. She had never experienced anything like it before, as if all her senses were suddenly loosened and set free, running pell mell, turning into a hurricane. She felt aroused and alive, dizzy and giddy.

The pressure of his mouth grew, opening her lips, giving admittance to his lightly probing tongue. Casey's breath grew louder still, drowned out only by the pounding of her heart as Simon's tongue deftly explored her mouth. The man smelled and tasted heavenly. You sound like a commercial, her mind told her from a million miles away.

Casey was utterly enthralled by what was happening to her. She was suspended somewhere in eternity—yet she was totally aware of everything that was happening, every detail, every movement. She was conscious of feeling him press his body against her, feeling the hard, exciting contours of his masculinity. She had caused that, she thought, a heady power coming over her. In her own, unintentional, unassuming way, she had brought about this reaction from him. The thought heightened her own excitement.

Simon's hands massaged her as he pulled her closer still, sending a prickling feeling along her spine until there wasn't a shred of her left that wasn't reacting to him.

The kiss went on for an eternity, and yet it was over much too soon. Had Simon been unscrupulous or even aggressively forceful, Casey knew that he would have just pushed her door open and somehow floated her into her apartment. In her weakened state, she thought, looking back on it, she wouldn't have stopped him. Or wanted to. It would have been a mistake, of course, but she had been completely unable to resist him.

But for some reason Simon had graciously pulled back, and after he had kissed away her common sense, he had merely held her face in his hands for a moment, staring down into it with a strange smile playing on his lips.

"Tomorrow?" he had finally asked.

"Yes," she had managed to get out. "It's tomorrow." Her brain wasn't tallying things quite right.

The smile spread, parting the sensuous lips that had set her on fire. "No, I mean will I see you tomorrow? Today," he amended.

Was there any other answer to be given but "yes"? She remembered standing there like a bobble-headed doll, nodding her answer as well as saying it. "Yes." Her voice had been hoarse. Some sophisticate, her mind had taunted her.

No, she hadn't been sophisticated. Awestruck was more the word for it. And now in the light of day,

she was still awestruck. She sighed. Admit it, Case.
The man reduces you to mush, and there's no future
in any of this. She took the body brush and scrubbed
herself hard in an effort to snap out of her frame of
mind.

All she got for her effort was red skin. She turned
the water off and stood for a moment in the abundant
mist. There was probably less fog on the coast than
there was in her bathroom, she thought, stepping out
of the shower stall. Cold shower indeed. She was
working against herself even in the bathroom, she
thought, wiping off a circle on her medicine cabinet
mirror and looking at herself sternly.

Get with it, Case. You're acting like some moony
kid instead of a professional. You're supposed to be
working on a case. If it happens to take you to a nice
restaurant or two, so be it, but don't lose sight of your
goal....

Which was what? Arresting him? Turning up
enough evidence against him to bring a case to trial?
Abruptly she stopped applying her facial at the
thought. No, there had to be some sort of an explanation.... Yes, there was. The man had used his charm
on her to make her more vulnerable to his schemes.

Casey felt the cream on her face harden, and she
willed herself not to frown. She pulled the terrycloth
robe about her and leaned against the sink, thinking.
One step at a time, she cautioned herself. There was
definitely something going on, something in need of
unraveling, and she wasn't doing herself, Simon or
the Bureau any good by getting emotionally swept
away. She was going about the case in an unorthodox
fashion. So what? She was going to have lunch with
the man, ply him with a few subtle questions and

maybe get to the bottom of this thing faster. As she finished her facial, she concluded, what was the harm?

If there were no harm, she said to herself at noon, why was her pulse racing like a car in the Indianapolis 500? She'd had luncheon dates before. Lots of them. Had she ever eyed the clock impatiently before? Had she ever worried that for some reason her date wouldn't show up? Not date, suspect, she corrected herself. No, that wasn't the correct term for him, either, she thought, glancing in the gilt mirror that hung next to the door, patting down her hair and checking the two silver combs she had pushed into it.

What *was* Simon?

Magnificent, a tiny voice inside her whispered.

Also late, she thought, picking up a magazine, then letting it drop back on the coffee table. Perhaps he had changed his mind. Perhaps he had found another pigeon to fleece, she thought, recalling Dennenberg.

Casey put a hand to her forehead. This was giving her a headache. She had started for the kitchen to unearth an aspirin when there was a knock on her door.

Magically, her headache disappeared.

She looked once more into the mirror, checking to see that the skirt and blouse ensemble she wore still looked as pleasing now as it had when she had pulled it out of her closet earlier. She wondered if maybe, for some reason, Simon didn't like green. This was the second deep green outfit he was seeing her in and....

Priorities, Casey, priorities, she reminded herself, and put her unaccustomed insecurity out of the way.

She opened the door and greeted Simon with a

wide smile. "Simon, hi," she said, opening the door further, inviting him in.

But he stood quite immobile in the doorway, a smile barely lifting his lips as he looked at her, his eyes going from her hair to her toes, and pausing at places in between.

That's it, he doesn't like green, she concluded.

"I've got a cab waiting," he told her, his voice a little clipped.

"Fine," she replied, faltering just a bit. "I'll get my jacket." She reached inside to take up her suede jacket and grabbed her small black shoulderbag.

As she came out into the hallway and turned to lock the door behind her, Simon walked on ahead, hurrying back to the elevator, and leaving her standing in the hall, awkwardly holding her jacket. She had expected him to help her on with it.

Women's lib, she reminded herself, slipping first one arm into a roomy sleeve and then the other. After all, she was quite capable of putting on her own jacket.

Still, she couldn't get over the slight twinge of disappointment. She glanced at Simon's rather stern face as they rode down in her elevator. "I was beginning to think you weren't coming."

"Traffic," he replied in the same tone he had used before.

"I see," she murmured. Was this the exciting conversationalist she had met last night? Why was he being so quiet and uncommunicative? Pensively she studied his rigid profile.

Not another word was spoken as the doors of the elevator yawned open and Simon led the way out into the street. At least he didn't close the heavy wrought-iron front door in her face, she thought, stealing another look at him as she passed him. He looked the same.

Or did he?

He made no effort to take her arm, she noted, though he did hold the cab door open for her. She slid in as gracefully as she could manage. She felt the torn plastic seat cover tug at her pantyhose as a run took off down the back of her right leg. So far, this date wasn't going to well.

Simon crowded her slightly as he got in, and she pushed her way further into the musty smelling cab.

"Fish," announced the cab driver, apparently seeing her wrinkle her nose as he turned his head. He at least, looked clearly impressed with the figure she cut.

"What?" she asked, confused.

"My last fare had a big package of fish he was taking to a friend. The smell," he indicated.

"Oh."

After that the cabbie turned his attention to his driving and didn't choose to interrupt the conversation.

Not that there was any to speak of.

Casey tried. She looked at Simon, wishing he would take her hand the way he had last night, then chiding herself that this coolness was far better for her purpose.

"Where are we going?" she asked.

"To a restaurant," came the monotone answer.

Casey turned to stare closely at the man at her elbow. What was wrong? Had she done something, said something? Not done something? That was it! She hadn't pulled him into her apartment after that soul-melting kiss and he was insulted. Well, if that was the way he was going to be about it, she was doubly glad that fate or her guardian angel or whatever had interceded and Simon hadn't spent the night. She wanted no part of a man who sulked.

But he didn't seem to be sulking. He just didn't seem interested, that was all. The magic that lit up the previous night was definitely missing.

"What restaurant?" she asked.

"The Food Palace, I think it's called."

"That's the name you gave me," the driver chimed in. So he was listening, Casey thought. He must really be bored.

"Isn't that the new place run by the famous singer-turned-restauranteur?" Casey pressed.

The broad shoulders shrugged. "I think so," Simon said.

Well, he might look the same as he had the night before, but he certainly didn't sound the same. What was more, she realized, the tingling sensation was gone. Her nerve endings weren't dancing wildly. The electrical charge that had existed by night was clearly not present in the light of day. Maybe he didn't wear well, she thought, trying to analyze this strange turn of events. He was still impeccably dressed. His bone structure was still as magnificent as it had been last night, bathed in the flashing lights of the Club Mandan, but something was missing.

A feeling of dismay seized Casey. Maybe she had been coming down with something. A twenty-four hour virus. She was obviously better now, fully in control of herself and aware of the fact that although the man at her side was indeed quite handsome, stunning even, he had no intoxicating effect on her.

So much the better to do your work, she said to

herself. Well, last night had been lovely. Unreal, now that she examined it closely, but lovely. Now, back to work.

"Did you go back to the hotel last night?" she asked, trying again to make conversation.

"Hmm? Oh, of course. That's where I'm staying," he said. He appeared to be busy watching the sea of people worm their way across the wide avenue. "Are there always this many people out?" he asked, turning toward her for a moment. "They all seem to be fighting one another to get to where they're going."

Casey smiled, knowing how the city must look to an out-of-towner. "This is light. You should see it at noon during the week. It's a wonder anyone gets to where they're going," she commented.

"It's a wonder why they bother," he replied, his voice flat.

"What?" she asked.

"It's so dirty and over-crowded. I'm surprised that people venture out at all—or live here."

She felt slightly offended, a protective feeling for New York coming to the fore. "Last night you thought this was an exciting city," she reminded him.

"I don't think I said that," he said, a strange glint in his eyes.

"Yes, you did." Was she going crazy? Last night Simon had seemed to be drinking in every part of New York. More than that, he had seemed to be adding to it—at least for her. Today he was looking down his nose at it. Was she going to lunch with a person with a personality disorder? She had read somewhere that schizophrenics behaved this way.

"I should know what I said," Simon insisted.

"Yes, you should," Casey fairly snapped. If this

was some kind of a joke, she didn't appreciate it one bit.

But there was no smile on Simon's lips to confirm this fleeting hope. Then the cab came to a halt before the West Side food emporium.

Resolutely, Casey got out, ignoring Simon's hand, which he took back as if he'd hardly noticed her action.

"This way," he said, letting her close her own door behind her.

Inside, the décor strove to approximate the wonderful delicatessens Casey had come to love. The diverse smells vied for her attention, tempting her taste buds and reminding her that all she had had so far today was a cup of coffee, and that she was starving.

A waiter led them through a maze of hanging salamis and pastramis to a round table that could seat three. The chairs that surrounded it looked as if they would be more at home in an old fashioned candy store, Casey thought.

"Quaint," Casey commented, tongue in cheek.

"If you like this sort of thing," Simon said, sitting down beside her.

She was getting more confused by the minute. "Then why are we here?" she wanted to know. If he didn't like the atmosphere, he could have taken her somewhere else.

"To eat, I suppose," he replied, looking around.

She stared at him in disbelief. "But you picked this place," she reminded him. "If you don't like it, why are we here?" she asked again. She was becoming convinced that Dennenberg's story was indeed on the level and that Simon wasn't so much a con artist as he was crazy.

Her hand slid to her purse on the table, ready to pick it up and leave. She had had just about enough.

As she picked up her purse she saw that Simon was waving at someone. Oh, no, she was in no mood to turn this thing into a threesome. Simon was bad enough.

She had risen to go when a voice stopped her in her tracks.

"Hi. Sorry I'm late."

She turned slowly. Standing there before her, his eyes drooping seductively as he appraised her outfit, was Simon's double.

Four

Four

Casey's green eyes opened wide. She looked from the man seated on her right to the man standing in front of her. Except for the different suits, they were identical.

"There are two of you," she gasped in disbelief.

"That's how twins usually come," said the man before her. The words were spoken in that same sexy voice that she had heard the previous evening. It was the same sexy voice that had seductively woven itself through her dreams last night.

"Simon?" she asked cautiously.

He nodded, then seated himself on her left. He looked as if he were slightly puzzled himself. "I didn't think you'd look this bewildered. Ethan...?" he said, looking at his brother. "Didn't you tell her you weren't me?"

Ethan was now grinning from ear to ear, clearly

enjoying the joke he had played at Casey's expense. "The subject never arose," he replied innocently.

Casey turned her head in Ethan's direction. He had been laughing at her all the way here. What a fool she must have looked. "I don't usually check I.D.'s when I meet someone for the second time," she said icily. "Now, if you two have had your little joke..." She left the sentence unfinished as she turned to leave.

Simon took her hand. Beneath the heat of her momentarily flaring anger was the heat of another emotion. Yes, her body told her, this was definitely Simon. The reaction she had to him had nothing to do with moonlight or wine.

"No joke, Casey," he assured her. "At least, none intended on my part. I should have realized that Ethan might indulge his whim for practical jokes and called you ahead of time to explain. I'm sorry. It's all my fault."

So what could she do with an apology like that? she wondered. Casey sat down again, very aware of the fact that Simon still hadn't let go of her hand.

"Better," he murmured, smiling into her eyes. "Sorry I'm late. I had a little unexpected business to attend to. A call from an anxious buyer," he explained.

The term "buyer beware" suddenly floated through her mind as Casey nodded in response to his apology. The warning, she realized, applied to her as well.

Several women were being shown to the table behind them. Casey could almost see the thought telegraphed across their faces: How did Casey rate *two* such magnificent specimens? Well, she didn't want two.... You're not even supposed to want one, remember? She admonished herself.

"You didn't tell me you had a twin," she said accusingly, still smarting from being the butt of Ethan's joke.

"As I recall," Simon said wryly, signaling for the waiter, "you didn't ask if there were any more at home like me."

The waiter appeared instantly. The man must have a magic power over waiters, Casey thought distantly, as she noted another table vainly trying to capture the short, tired man's attention. The waiter had walked right past them twice.

"*Like* you?" she repeated in surprise. "He looks like a carbon copy," Casey said, staring at Ethan.

"Three glasses of red wine, please," Simon told the waiter, then turned his attention back to Casey. "Actually, I'm the copy. Ethan is older."

"By three minutes," Ethan added, glancing up from the menu he was perusing with distaste.

Now that she listened, Casey could detect a slight difference in their voices. Ethan's tones were slightly flatter than Simon's. And Simon had more of a Southern accent, a lovely, sexy drawl that curled around each word.

"Hey," Simon said suddenly, raising his eyebrows mischievously, "You're not one of those people who likes to collect one of a kind examples, are you?"

The remark caught her by surprise, but she managed to keep a telltale, embarrassed blush at bay. "The only things I collect," she informed him, trying to put him in his place, "are coins."

"Lucky for me," Simon said, a husky tone in his voice.

We'll see about that, Casey thought, taking a sip from her water glass.

"Don't waste your time with that," Simon told her as the waiter arrived with the three glasses balanced none-too-steadily on his small tray. Casey wondered if the harried man had been at this profession long. "This is far better." Simon presented her with her glass.

"You can see through *it*," Ethan added, tapping disparagingly on the glass of water before him. "Unlike this."

Casey looked his way, taking umbrage at his condescending remark. "New York water has body," she said in a clipped tone.

"Whose?" Simon teased.

Casey turned back to him. She felt as if she were sitting between two mirror images. "Just because it gets a little cloudy when you first pour it..." she began to protest.

Simon laughed, holding up one hand as if attempting to call a truce. "Boy, you New Yorkers are touchy."

Surprisingly, she wasn't offended by his words. Simon had a knack, she thought, of being able to say irritating things and somehow take the sting out of them. Ethan, on the other hand, had no such ability.

"We just don't like having fun poked at us," Casey said, looking pointedly at Ethan. Her meaning was not missed.

"No more 'poking,'" Simon promised her. "Just gentle stroking." His words made her feel as if she were already being stroked.

Casey, who wasn't about to explore that statement, was at a loss for words. Luckily the sound of crashing glass and dishware rescued her and brought all eyes in the restaurant toward the back. Casey's suspicions about the waiter were confirmed as she saw him standing behind a pile of broken glasses and dishes, mixed in with different parts of pastrami sandwiches. Miscellaneous pieces of lettuce were scattered in a jagged semi-circle about his feet. He stood with a silly grin on his face and an empty tray still held aloft over his shoulder. The tray was tilted at a forty-five degree angle.

"I think it might be a long time before we get lunch," Casey commented dryly.

"I have all the time in the world," Simon told her, leaning his chin on his upturned palm. His eyes captured her, drawing her out of her surroundings. She felt like the proverbial moth being pulled toward the flame.

Ethan's voice broke the spell. "Well, I don't," he said. She could hear a touch of annoyance in his voice.

"Door's that way, Ethan," Simon said easily, nodding behind is brother. "I wouldn't want to keep you against your will."

Casey looked from one brother to the other, this time studying them objectively. Ethan appeared to really want to leave, but something was apparently holding him back. What? And why?

"The lovely lady might take offense if I leave," he said.

Somehow the sort of suave words that came so smoothly from Simon's tongue fell awkwardly from Ethan's. Besides, she thought she detected a hint of sarcasm in his tone. You're prejudiced, she told herself.

"No offense at all," she heard herself saying. "As a matter of fact, I feel a little strange having lunch with bookends."

Simon laughed at her comment. Ethan didn't.

"C'mon, Ethan, where's your sense of humor?" Simon asked as the moment turned slightly awkward.

"In Houston," Ethan replied, his voice deadly serious.

"Why don't you join it?" Casey asked mildly. She knew she was being witchy, but she felt that Ethan deserved it.

"Match and set," Simon said, acting as referee. "Game's over." Beneath the banter, his voice had an underlying note of seriousness.

"I'm agreed," Casey replied serenely, deliberately lifting her water instead of her wine.

Ethan picked up his own wineglass and lifted it aloft. "To each his own," he proposed as a toast.

It was one that went over well with all three of them. Casey smiled, at ease again. At least she was at ease until Simon's fingers spread themselves over her hand, covering it and making her nerve endings tingle again.

The waiter approached them, looking more harried than ever. He had just helped a busboy sweep away the last bit of evidence attesting to his incompetence. He held a pad and pencil before him like a shield and sword. "What'll you folks have?" he snapped. Casey discerned the slightest tremor in his voice and hid a smile.

"Hope you're wearing something washable," Ethan remarked as he rose. The waiter shot him a scathing look.

"You're going?" Casey asked. Now that a truce

of sorts had been reached, she wanted to get to know this other brother a little better—as if she knew either one at all, she thought ruefully. Who knew, maybe Ethan was the key to the complaints that had come into her office. Her smile brightened without her realizing it. She liked that explanation *much* better.

"I'm leaving Simon a clear path before he kicks my shins to pieces," Ethan said with a touch of sarcasm.

Casey glanced covertly at Simon. He wasn't the type to kick anyone's shins. A good swift kick in the tail, maybe. But waste his time with shins? She doubted it. That seemed to be more Ethan's speed. Obviously Ethan was trying to tear into his brother's veneer of confidence. But with Simon, Casey judged, that so-called veneer went clear to the bone.

Simon seemed unaffected by Ethan's comment. "See you later, Ethan."

The waiter stood, tapping his pencil against his pad as Ethan took his leave. "Did you people come here to eat or talk?" he wanted to know impatiently.

"Both," Simon replied with a cool smile that made the waiter visibly cringe. He hunched his shoulders a little more and seemed to grow shorter right in front of Casey's eyes. Simon turned to Casey. "What's your pleasure?" he asked.

"You mean you're not going to order for me?" she asked in mock surprise.

A chicly-dressed, exceedingly thin woman glared at Casey as she walked by. "It's women like you who've set back the progress of the women's movement," she snapped as she continued walking.

Casey had to press her lips together to keep from laughing out loud.

"See?" Simon said innocently. "I was just offering to liberate you—as long as you celebrate your freedom with me."

"You can celebrate all you want, as long as you tell me what you want to eat," the waiter squeaked at them, highly irritated.

"A pastrami sandwich on Italian bread," Casey said, surrendering her menu. "With lots of mustard," she added emphatically. The waiter almost pulled the menu out of her hand, as if to fend off any second thoughts she might have.

"And you?" he asked, turning to Simon.

"The same," Simon said, closing the menu. "Except skip the mustard."

The waiter looked at Simon as if he had come from some strange planet. To some extent Casey could understand his feelings. "No mustard?" she echoed once the waiter had left.

Simon shook his head. "Why? Is that so odd?"

"Odd? You're missing the best part of the sandwich," she told him. "When I was a little girl, I used to make mustard sandwiches."

"Tell me all about yourself," he coaxed disarmingly. "What was that 'little girl' like?"

His effect on her nervous system was far more potent than any truth serum, she thought. She was going to have to be very careful what she said to him.

"Not much to tell on my part," she said almost self-consciously, glancing down at her hands.

"Meaning there is on my part?" he asked, picking up her meaning.

"Well, you're the one with a twin. It must be a weird feeling, having someone around who looks just like you. I bet you two played your share of practical jokes.''

"You're not still upset about Ethan, are you?" he asked kindly. When he talked to her like that, his soothing tone caressing all her senses, she couldn't be upset about anything. "Actually," Simon went on, his eyes stroking her, "I'm a bit surprised he did that. Lately Ethan's been awfully straitlaced. If it hadn't been you he tricked, I would have been happy that he indulged himself in a little joke.''

She shrugged. "Maybe I overreacted," she conceded. "I don't particularly like being made fun of.''

"I can't picture anyone making fun of you," Simon told her.

"Your brother just did," she pointed out.

"It wasn't you he was making fun of," Simon assured her. "He was just…" He paused for a moment, searching for the right word. "Having fun." Simon reached out and touched one wayward copper strand of hair that had fallen into her face, brushing it back and touching her skin in an intimate gesture. "I, of course, have a different definition of 'fun.'''

Casey knew exactly what kind of "fun" he was talking about. Something inside her moved closer toward him, as if warming itself in the heat of the fire he was fanning. The logical part of her mind had no luck in extinguishing it.

For a moment they just looked at one another, his eyes saying wondrous things to her in the ensuing silence. And then Simon's lips lifted in amusement. "I think that's part of the entertainment," he said unexpectedly, pointing behind her.

Casey turned in the direction he indicated. Their waiter was trying, unsuccessfully, it appeared, to fish two fat dill pickles out of a huge barrel located in the center of the restaurant. The barrel reminded her of those she had seen in grocery stores when she was a child. But yesterday's memories conflicted with the aroused feelings she was experiencing today. These were no girlish emotions fluttering hard and fast through her as she turned back to look directly into those mesmerizing blue-gray eyes.

"It'll only be entertaining if he falls in," she quipped.

"Wait," Simon laughed. "Give him time. He just might."

Casey had never met anyone who seemed to enjoy himself so much or appeared so self-assured and relaxed as Simon was. Of course, making money swindling people—and getting away with it—could make anyone quite happy indeed, she realized. Casey remembered her reason for coming to lunch in the first place and tried to act accordingly. But it was hard.

"Does Ethan make life difficult for you?" she asked as their waiter approached, shuffling across the sawdust-covered floor. He managed to kick some of it over her shoes as he placed their orders before them.

"I don't let anyone make life hard for me," Simon replied.

He sounded as if he meant that. Forceful, dynamic, handsome, and obviously well-off, he had all the qualifications for a perfect catch, at least according to everything her mother had ever drummed into her head when she was growing up. Wouldn't it be wonderful if Dennenberg's accusations were untrue? But what about all the other complaints that lay in a manila folder on her desk? her little voice queried, playing devil's advocate.

"You look preoccupied," Simon said, his velvety accent cutting into the distressing thoughts that were surrounding her.

She stared down at the huge pickle that graced her plate, taking up almost as much room as her sandwich, which oozed mustard out of every pore. "I am," she muttered in response, then looked up to catch him studying her. Quickly she asked, "Do you have any distinguishing birthmarks to help me tell you apart from Ethan?" It was the first thing she could think of in a pinch.

"Not that I know of, except that I'm the good-looking one," Simon quipped. "Of course," he went on to say more intimately, leaning forward, "you might like to look me over for any birthmarks that I might not be able to see on my own."

Some people had bedroom eyes, Casey thought. This man had a whole bedroom countenance. What was worse, she was yearning to follow him there. In self-defense, Casey did the only thing she could think of. She took a large bite of her sandwich. It tasted heavenly; it was crammed full of remarkably lean pastrami and spicy mustard. But there was nothing lean, she had noted earlier, about the price of this delicious fare.

Casey took another bite. If she kept her mouth full of food, she reasoned, no self-incriminating words were liable to slip out of her mouth, though some just might slip out of his.

But she sincerely hoped they wouldn't.

Very objective, Casey, she chided herself. Great work, so far.

Casey saw Simon glance at his watch and wondered if he had an appointment with someone. She felt a pang at the fact that she would soon be losing his company. His possible guilt notwithstanding, Casey truly enjoyed being with Simon. She liked everything about him, not just his looks. That was obvious to her now that she had met his exact double. Being in Ethan's company was like being in the company of a well-tailored, exquisite-looking mannequin; he aroused the same kinds of feelings in her that she might feel looking at a page in a fashion magazine. He appeared to have as much personality as a fashion model, as well. At least that was her initial impression. But Simon…Simon was a feast for her heart and senses. He was a delight to the eye; she loved the very scent of him, she thought, discreetly trying to take in a deeper whiff of his aftershave. His deep voice was music to her ears. The evening before, her mouth had reveled in the taste of him. His narcotically sweet lips made her heart beat faster. The effect of his touch on her skin, well, that went without saying. She had to fight back the pins and needles sensation he constantly evoked. Yes, a feast, a glorious feast—even if it was without mustard.

She grinned.

Simon grinned back, picking up a napkin and dabbing at the right corner of her mouth.

"Sloppy?" she asked, embarrassed.

"Never. The word 'sloppy' doesn't apply to you." He put the napkin down. "If we weren't in public, I'd have licked it off," he told her. The blood in her temples beat a wild tune, and sudden warmth spread to the tips of her fingers, toes and breasts. "I've acquired a sudden fondness for mustard," he confessed.

Where had this man been all her life? In Houston, defrauding people. Damn her professional mind. It was struggling to regain control. But this new, sensuous side of her was certainly holding its own.

He glanced again at his watch. "I think we'd better hurry," he said.

So he did have an appointment, she thought unhappily. "Another buyer?" she couldn't help asking. Did he think she was trying to find out if he was meeting another woman? She wasn't...so why was the thought suddenly there? She asked herself accusingly.

Simon shook his head. "Not unless you'd like to buy a few of my coins," he told her.

"I might," she said evasively. I might also buy the Brooklyn Bridge from you if you tried to sell it to me, she added, to herself.

He didn't seem very interested in selling her any coins. "I have tickets for a matinee," he went on.

She blinked. "Matinee?" she repeated, puzzled. "To a play," he told her. "I thought you might enjoy seeing a play. *Once More with Love.* They're holding a special Saturday matinee," he explained. "It's a comedy."

"Yes, I know." The words sounded mechanical as she tried to keep her wits about her. This man worked fast. Usually Casey resented things like that. This time, she seemed to love it. Her independent side, normally quite formidable, was highly annoyed with her mental fumbling.

"I don't like sad, heavy plays," he was telling her. "I like things to be light and happy."

"And no strings." Now where had that popped out from?

"Only on packages," he said. "And things of my own choosing."

There it was again, a veiled promise of things that might be. He was really good at making non-promises that sounded a whole lot like promises, she thought.

This is your man, her inner voice said. But she wasn't sure just how to take that.

"I hope you like comedies," he said suddenly, although his manner indicated that he was sure she did.

"Is your expert judgment of people suddenly failing you?" she asked teasingly. The pickle she had just bitten into spilled its juices unceremoniously down her chin, and she made a quick grab for her napkin. She made a mental note not to eat pickles around Simon again. Again? Just how many times did she expect to be eating with him? Forever, her soul breathed. Fat chance, the rest of her cynically retorted.

"No," Simon said firmly. "You like comedies, sparkling champagne, Italian food and romance."

"And mustard."

"And mustard," he added with an indulgent smile. "For spice," he added.

"For spice," she said, "I seem to have acquired you."

"I hope so," he said. From him, it didn't sound like a line. But she'd be a fool if she believed that.

Part of her was rooting for the fool.

"I'm finished," she announced, tossing down her napkin as if she were flinging down a gauntlet. It landed on top of the pickle and a corner of it turned a deeper shade, absorbing the puddle of juice it found there.

"I thought you liked pickles," Simon reminded

her, making no move to rise. "And we still have some time."

But she shook her head. "Too big for me to handle," she explained.

Simon chivalrously did not comment. But the smile on his lips said it all. In one graceful movement he was out of his chair and standing behind hers, helping her out. Her chair scraped along the floor, drawing a path through the sawdust. "In that case, let's take a leisurely walk to the theater," he proposed, taking her hand in his as she stood to join him.

He led the way to the cashier. Despite the growing crescendo of noise around them, Casey heard the click of her heels on the floor. It was the kind of sound the sheriff made walking into the saloon just before he confronted the bad guy at high noon. She couldn't help wondering if she were soon to approach her own high-noon shoot-out, and if she would be left standing once the smoke cleared away....

Five

The day was wonderful.

Casey and Simon made the matinee in plenty of time, and the play was every bit as funny and entertaining as all the zesty little ads in the newspapers had promised it would be.

As they emerged from the theater with a throng of people, Casey thought that Simon was going to take her home. Instead he insisted on doing a bit of sightseeing before he took her out to dinner. So they wound up at the top of the Empire State Building, looking down on a city that was preparing itself for its nighttime routine. From the observation deck New York looked like a model metropolis. Up there, there were no scattered newspapers gliding on the wings of a wayward wind, no debris marred the city's enchantment. Here and there skyscraper lights were going on prematurely, twinkling like tiny jewels in the rays of the setting sun.

Casey liked New York, liked its excitement, its vitality. She stole a glance at Simon to see if the city's magic had crept over him as well, but he was looking at her. Thinking, no doubt, of a different sort of magic, she surmised, a magic that was much more intimate.

His suggestion of dinner awakened her appetite. She was starved again. That basic sensation had gotten lost amid the other emotions churning through her. She found herself being whisked away—if traveling in a New York cab at five-thirty in the afternoon could possibly be called being whisked—to Rockefeller Center for dinner.

"This is a typical tourist thing to do," Casey said to Simon as they took their seats inside a glass-enclosed restaurant that bordered the edges of the Center. A few short weeks ago the Center had been the site of an ice-skating rink, sparkling and white, spread very much like an altar before the huge bronze statue of the Greek fire god, Prometheus. Now the same area was filled with folded tables and chairs, in preparation for the summer season. Just above them was a display of flags from all over the world, snapping madly in the wind.

Simon smiled at Casey's comment and replied, "Sometimes, I like doing 'typical' things."

Like wooing a woman, Casey thought. He did that very well.

She tried in vain to draw him out about himself, trying to edge closer to the questions in her mind. Trying to keep herself from being engulfed by his charm and his mere presence, Casey kept forming questions in her head that she could use to feel out his possible involvement in the coin fraud.

Somehow the conversation never managed to shift in that direction. She did learn a lot of personal things about him. He liked to ride horses bareback, and walk barefoot in tall grass and rise early to see the sun come up. She learned that he and his brother had been orphaned at an early age and taken in by "Uncle Jack," who wasn't an uncle at all, just a very good friend of the family. Casey's heart went out to Simon as she thought of him as a small boy, deprived of the comfort of a mother's love.

She also learned that it was Uncle Jack's coin business that Simon and Ethan had eventually gotten involved in and taken over with the older man's blessings, because Uncle Jack had no family of his own. And that was as close as Casey got to the subject of coins until after dinner.

"Ready to go to the auction?" Simon asked after a sinfully caloric ice cream concoction had disappeared between Casey's lips. She was now so full that she felt there wasn't any space left within her.

The auction. She had completely forgotten about it. She panicked when she remembered that she had told him that she was interested in coins that were coming up for bidding that night. If there had been any room left in her stomach it would have been taken over by butterflies.

She sighed, letting her eyes droop a little. "I feel so tired and sluggish after all that wine and food, I'm not sure my head is clear enough for something like that. I've never been on a marathon date before," she said with a smile.

"I'd like to do a lot of things with you that you've

never done before," Simon said in a seductive whisper. Casey's mind began to wander, fantasizing about what those things might be. "But I'd really feel terrible being responsible for your missing the auction."

"Are you going?" she asked.

He shook his head. "Not if you don't intend to. The coins I've been commissioned to buy come up in tomorrow's session." He peered into her face. "Are you sure you don't want to go?"

Don't raise his suspicions, she cautioned herself. Yet, on the other hand, she had no idea what coins were being offered and had no way of finding out. It would be ridiculous for her to sit through a session that might contain only very high-priced coins. There would be no way for her to cover any bid she might come up with. Casey could just picture herself being hounded to the end of her days by the auction house, waiting for her to make good her bid. What to do? The answer came to her in a flash.

"I'm sure," she assured Simon. "You could probably obtain the coins I'm interested in, and I'd much rather give you my business. All the high tension that's involved in the bidding is too much for me. I don't like competition."

"Neither do I," Simon murmured. "And I'd be glad to take your business—all your business," he emphasized. He looked around for the waitress. The smartly-uniformed girl—Casey judged that she couldn't be more than nineteen—appeared almost immediately, weaving her way between the small tables for two that lined the bay windows.

"Anything else?" the waitress asked Simon. Casey could see the girl's deep appreciation for the handsome man shining in her eyes. The phrase "coffee, tea, or me?" flashed through Casey's mind. Oh, why did he have to have this hint of fraud hanging over him? If not for that, Simon Ashford could very possibly have been the greatest thing ever to have happened to her.

"No, just the check, please," Simon said, flashing the waitress one of his bright smiles.

He certainly did smile a lot, Casey thought. But she didn't have any time to take another inventory of all his assets. Simon had taken her arm and was leading her out the door, though not before leaving the waitress a very healthy tip.

"Where to now?" he asked.

Casey sighed with relief. He wasn't going to take her to the auction. Or, she hoped, on any more sightseeing hops, she added as her feet complained after a few steps. They had done an awful lot of walking that day.

"My apartment?" What better place to get him to talk freely? And talking was all she had in mind. Wasn't it?

From the look that came into Simon's eyes, Casey knew she couldn't have come up with a better suggestion as far as he was concerned. As far as she was concerned, too, her mind added as a postscript.

Questions. She *had* to ply him with questions or else her nagging doubts would never let her enjoy his company, she told herself.

"Perfect," Simon said, responding to her suggestion.

Perfect for surrender, her inner voice called to her. She told herself she would handle that when the time came. Ah…but would she *want* to handle it? Enough

of this inner war, she thought, trying to shut the lid
on her emotions. She didn't have time for this. She
had to be mentally alert at all times around Simon.

"We're not going to walk there, are we?" Casey
asked, the ache in her feet coursing up her legs. She
didn't feel up to walking all the way to Third Avenue
and Eighty-third Street.

"Walking's good for you," Simon told her with a
grin.

"You should try it wearing high heels," she said
as the wind picked up again, playing with some of
the gathered dirt on the ground and swirling it upward. Casey closed her eyes until the gust passed.

"I don't think heels would do much for my image," Simon bantered. "I could carry you in my
arms," he offered teasingly, "if you're too tired to
walk."

"A cab would be far less conspicuous."

"The lady's right again," Simon laughed, stepping
off the curb in the middle of the block and waving
his hand at a passing taxi that just kept on passing.

Casey took hold of his arm. "You'll have more
luck at the corner," she advised, pointing toward the
end of the block. Briskly they walked past Radio City
Music Hall, with its photographs of comely Rock-
ettes. Sixth Avenue was alive with traffic.

Simon shook his head. "How do they keep accidents from happening?" he marveled, looking at the
sea of bumper to bumper cars.

"Simple," Casey quipped. "They only move three
feet an hour. Maybe we had better walk," she recon-
sidered, although her feet hated her for it.

"No, the lady wants to ride, and the lady will ride.
I wouldn't want you to think we Texans are unfeel-

ing.'' He hailed another cab. The driver didn't look as if he had a prayer of getting over to the curb, so Simon grabbed Casey's hand and they dashed toward the yellow vehicle which was stopped for a red light.

Because of the traffic, the trip to Casey's apartment took a long time. When they finally arrived she felt exhausted, and it showed on her face.

''Maybe we should have worked our way up to a marathon date slowly,'' Simon commented as they came to her door.

Casey wondered if that meant that he intended to see more of her. He had said he was only going to be in town for a few more days, and she had taken that to mean that he would stay until the end of the auction. It ended on Monday night. Two days away.

''I'm a lot heartier than I look,'' she assured him, not feeling at all hearty. Casey fished out her key and opened the door.

'' 'Hearty' is not exactly the word I'd be inclined to use if I were describing you,'' Simon said as they walked in and Casey switched on a soft light. It made the living room look warm and cozy.

''Oh?'' she asked, turning around to face him. ''What word would you use?''

She was being coy again, and she knew it, but for one moment she wanted to indulge herself. Simon's compliments had the effect of enveloping all of her like a wonderful, hot bubble bath.

'' 'Delicious' was one word that crossed my mind,'' Simon said, taking the strap of her purse off her shoulder and slipping it down her arm in a slow, deliberate motion that made her feel as if she were being totally undressed. He kissed the lobe of one ear, and

Casey fought hard to keep a shiver from running all through her body.

"So," she said with a bit too much enthusiasm as she moved a little out of his reach, "you'd be willing to guide me in purchasing coins for my collection." She reached over and turned on one of the long-necked lamps that flanked her sofa. More light was definitely prudent if she were going to get any answers to anything.

Simon looked a little surprised that she would pick that moment to discuss her coin collection, but he nodded as he sat down on the sofa, making himself at home. "That's my business," he told her.

"Mind you," Casey continued a bit nervously, trying to gather her scattered thoughts as well as figure out what to do with her hands, "I don't expect any discounts because we're...friends," she said after hunting for the word. Was that really her, hinting so clumsily at their budding relationship—or whatever it was that was budding here? Usually she sounded so self-assured, so confident of her purpose.

She knew what her purpose was, all right, but somehow it was getting terribly clouded over at the moment. Casey took a deep breath and sat down on the sofa herself, then turned to face him. She took care not to sit too close to him, though. She positioned herself at the other end of the couch and tucked one foot beneath her.

"I don't exchange favors for special coins," Simon told her. "All my customers get the very best I can offer them."

"Do they, now?" she wondered archly, remembering Dennenberg and his pounding fist.

"Of course," Simon allowed, moving in closer to her, "I do accept tokens of gratitude."

"I'll keep that in mind," she replied. Keep it in mind? There was almost nothing else on her mind. Duty was having a terrible time holding her attention.

"What do you collect?" Simon asked, not sounding as if he were really all that interested in her coins. Other things about her obviously interested him a great deal more—like the nape of her neck. Casey felt his breath as he leaned over to give her a kiss that would have brushed against a very sensitive part of her neck had she let it land.

But she moved forward, stopping the kiss in middescent. Never had a maneuver been executed so reluctantly and its success accepted so sadly, she thought. "Pennies," she declared, then corrected herself, using the proper terminology. "I collect small and large cents. It all started," she began, warming to her subject gradually, "when I was very young. I used to save pennies in a jar. My brother and I played poker for pennies. I did a lot of losing, so I had to do a lot of collecting. Eventually, I got better at gambling," she said proudly, fondly recalling those days, "and at collecting. I started taking note of the dates and mint marks, and before I knew it, I was hooked."

"I know what you mean," Simon concurred, but she wasn't quite sure if he were talking about collecting coins or not.

"My mother bought me a coin folder, and I began trying to fill all the slots with circulated specimens. Whenever I could, I'd go to the bank with several dollars and exchange them for rolls of Lincoln cents. I'd cull the rolls for the dates I wanted, then fill the rolls back up and take them to the local grocery store, where they'd exchange them for dollars and I'd start all over again."

Simon laughed. "I had it a lot easier in that respect. I got to see them all looking over Uncle Jack's shoulder."

"Were you as surprised as I was when I finally realized the enormous price difference between nicely worn, circulated coins and their uncirculated, pristine counterparts?" she asked, watching him carefully as she pushed on, building to the point she really wanted to make.

He shrugged. "Not really, I guess. It dawned on me rather gradually, but you're right, it's the difference between night and day," he agreed.

She sat up a little straighter as she got to the heart of the matter. "You know, what really bothered me, and still does—I guess it's what's kept me from collecting anything really expensive—is that I have trouble differentiating between the various conditions that a coin can be in. I felt that any unscrupulous coin dealer could sell me a lesser grade of coin than I was actually paying for and thought I was getting. After all," she said, watching his face for a reaction, "the kind of money that could be made on 'oversights' like that could be very tempting, even to an honest dealer."

If she were looking for a telltale blush or an evasive air, she didn't get it. On the contrary, Simon seemed to heartily agree with her. "When you get involved with the really high-priced coins, you really have to know what you're doing. I think," he said, running his finger along the outline of her jaw. "You're doing the right thing, putting yourself entirely in my hands."

If he were intent on defrauding her, that would be the perfect thing to say. And if he were intent on disarming her defenses romantically, he was still proceeding on the right path. In either case, she felt doomed.

"Anyway," she said, continuing in a voice that was beginning to quiver. "I *have* put together a collection of cents from the eighteenth century to the present. Worn cents that have been touched by people all through history. I think it's fascinating that a coin I have might have been touched by George Washington, don't you?"

"Fascinating," Simon murmured, not taking his eyes off her face.

"That's the added benefit of collecting worn coins. You can touch them without spoiling their value. I enjoy touching and holding things I like."

"So do I," Simon agreed. The light in his eyes touched her then and made her ache to be held and caressed. But in the interest of her job Casey pressed on, turning her face away from him so as not to fall prey to the hypnotic gleam in his eyes.

"But lately I've been thinking of looking into coins as an investment and not just a hobby." It was getting increasingly more difficult for Casey to form her words. Simon was sitting so close to her now that she felt the outline of his body against hers. As she spoke he was delivering a kiss to her shoulder. The material between his lips and her skin seemed to dissolve.

"Very wise of you," Simon was saying. Another kiss to her shoulder, another burst of fire. "How much money would you be thinking of investing?" he asked casually.

He sounded so nonchalant that she couldn't be sure

if he were interested in the matter at all. Or was he just being clever? "Oh, forty, fifty thousand," she said, letting the words drift out easily.

Simon stopped what he was doing for a moment and glanced at her quizzically, clearly surprised. "That's an awful lot of money," he commented.

She had him, she thought...so why didn't she feel triumphant?

"Not really?" she replied loftily, the lies growing more elaborate as she embellished her story. "You see, I have an inheritance coming when I turn thirty. My grandmother left me a great deal of money. I've been living on the interest," she explained, covertly watching his face to see how he was taking this piece of news. Like any other man who thought he found a rich pigeon, she'd wager. "At thirty I get the principal, as well. But I don't want to wait until I hit thirty to start looking into investments. I have a nice sum saved already," she added. There, that should bait the whole trap, she thought.

"Well, I'll do my best to help you," Simon told her.

I bet you will, she thought sadly. "That makes me feel a lot better," she said in a confidential voice, beginning to play the role to the hilt. She ran her hand along the lapel of his jacket. "I've always been afraid of being sold 'whizzed' coins," she said, referring to coins that were specially treated by dealers in an attempt to pass them off as uncirculated. Only an expert could tell the difference.

He put his finger beneath her chin and lifted her face toward his. "You deserve only the best, uncirculated types," he assured her.

Was he promising himself to her, as well? She

wondered. Steady, Casey, you're getting carried away here.

"Don't worry, little lady, I'll keep you safe and warm," Simon drawled softly.

What was she getting into? The possibility of a successful romance was receding rapidly. At the end of this trail of deception and pseudo-spying lay nothing but disappointment. One part of Casey cautioned her to break away now, to thank him for a lovely evening and push him out the door—fast. The other part, the part that was dissolving, cried, "Grab your moments while you can, never mind the outcome." Men like Simon Ashford did not rain down like pennies from heaven.

In the next moment Casey lost any opportunity she might have had to draw back. Simon had cut off their conversation by finding something else for her lips to be doing.

He was kissing her. And that was an understatement. It was like saying that Mount Everest was just another hill. Simon Ashford was performing magic by simply pressing his flesh against hers. Dennenberg, coin fraud and the sofa vanished into a misty netherworld as Simon's kisses became more and more urgent, their sweetness almost unbearably tantalizing. His lips consumed her until there seemed to be nothing left of her except her trembling knees and her eager hands which circled his neck and pulled him closer.

She tried just once to push him away, to cling to the remaining shreds of her reason before it was too late. "I've only known you for twenty-four hours," she tried to protest, the words sinking into his mouth, because their lips still touched.

"That's an entire lifetime for a Mayfly," he told her, once more claiming what was already his.

The battle had been lost without the firing of a single shot, she thought as she lost herself in his kiss.

Simon drew her onto his lap, and she leaned comfortably against his chest as his arms held her captive. His kisses continued to tantalize and torment her, blazing a path to the point of her chin, then down to the sensitive hollow of her throat.

Then they went further, parting the sides of her blouse, which had somehow become undone without her knowledge. For a moment Simon paused, nibbling on the tiny flower decoration that was all that held her bra together. Then the flower was plucked, and the material began to slide away from her breasts a fraction of an inch at a time, helped by Simon, who nuzzled his face into the deep valley between her breasts.

With teasing slowness Simon's lips trailed a line of tiny, sensual kisses from one breast to another, forging lower and lower each time until his tongue just barely touched the tips of her nipples, which strained outward to receive more of his delectable touch. A savoring moan came from deep within Casey's throat as her eyes fluttered closed and she drank in the delicious sensations that danced within her body.

More. She wanted more. Needed more. She was crazy, she knew, doing this to herself, leaving herself this open for the heartache that she knew was going to come one way or another. It would be born, at the very least, in the tangled web of lies she had spun. But she didn't care, not at this moment. All she wanted, all she craved, was the loving touch of this man. She had never felt like this before and she would, she thought, never feel like this again. Just one taste of heaven, that was all she wanted. One wondrously shared moment of paradise with a man whose eyes had bought her soul.

Without thinking she tugged at his jacket, wanting nothing to be between them. In the next timeless moment his jacket and shirt were both gone, and all that existed between her flesh and his was a silken layer of soft, dark hair. It rubbed against her nipples and brought her excitement to a higher plateau. She wanted to kiss him, tantalize him, please him the way no other woman ever had. Never mind everything else. The world could burn in the flames of the passion she felt. Everything could be discarded until all that remained was a man and a woman, needing one another not just for passion's sake, but for their souls' sake, as well.

Casey felt his fingers slipping beneath the waistband of her skirt, stretching the elastic to allow his hand to slide softly down the sensitive skin of her belly. His fingertips traced a circle around her navel. Casey sucked in her breath, but it finally burst free when Simon's hand found its destination beneath the lacy perimeter of her underwear. The area was languidly scouted out, every motion familiarizing the hunter with his prey. But she was not his prey. She was a willing offering, a victim who desired only to be made one with him.

Casey moved her hips so that the skirt would slide off easily, and she found herself sinking into the deep cushions of the sofa where she had sat a scant eight hours before, wondering if Simon was going to show up. And now he was there, and the anticipation was enough to make her bite her lip.

Once again, Simon kissed her, kissed every part that was free of clothing, and soon that meant everything. He deftly removed her panties, at first kissing her vulnerable skin through the filmy material, then tugging it away from her with his teeth. The throbbing within her body grew to enormous proportions until Casey didn't think she could live without him for another instant.

Simon rose over her, finding her eager mouth again, kissing her with more passion than she had ever dreamed possible. Instead of holding him to her the way she craved, Casey trembled as she reached down to undo his belt and rid him of the last maddening articles of his clothing. She had gone too far, had let herself slip away too fast, to stop now. She couldn't even begin to recognize herself as rapture threatened to explode inside her.

Simon lifted his hips to make her progress easier as Casey pulled at the trousers. Her hands quivered as she removed his briefs. Simon kissed her eyelids tenderly, then touched his lips to the bridge of her nose, before once more capturing her mouth with his, scorching it with the hot flood of his desire.

Casey felt the wild rhythm of passion growing stronger and stronger as she rocked against him, their bodies fusing together, becoming the single whole that nature had intended. For one glorious moment Casey had found her other half, and she clung to it with the determination of someone who was clinging to a life preserver.

Melting. She felt herself dissolving into Simon, being taken by Simon. But not just taken. She was joining him on a journey that lived elusively in the fires of love and passion, flickering all too briefly before it died away.

Earth. Reality. Dennenberg. They all gnawed slowly, purposefully, at the outer edges of her mind, encroaching into her consciousness and destroying the euphoria that Simon had created for her. Casey felt the warmth of his body over her and squeezed her eyes shut, trying vainly to keep everything at bay, trying only to relish what had happened to her in the past half hour, when one lone candle of love had been lit somewhere in the darkness.

Six

They had gone out for breakfast together. Her refrigerator had failed to come up with anything remotely tempting early Sunday morning, and they had settled for a coffee shop near her apartment. The man behind the counter looked like an ex-merchant marine who had been on one too many voyages. His hair had only a nodding acquaintance with shampoo and hadn't seen a comb that morning, possibly that week. Casey settled for coffee and a danish. Simon asked for an English muffin, lightly toasted. He got an English muffin, lightly burned. But he didn't seem to notice as he gazed into Casey's face.

"What are you thinking?" Simon asked, noting the frown tugging at the corners of Casey's mouth.

She hadn't been able to put the bittersweet sadness growing within her into words. He was going home the day after tomorrow. And today, after breakfast, he had to get back to "business as usual." He had appointments with several of his New York customers, he had told her. She looked down at her danish, which was stale.

"Nothing," she said. "I'm just wondering if this is one of the original danishes the guy bought when he opened this place." Her words were hardly audible.

Simon reached over and lightly tapped the pastry's glazed top with his coffee spoon. "I'd hazard a guess that this is one of the original danishes, period. Want to go to my hotel for breakfast?" he offered, glancing at his watch.

"No, you're in a hurry, and I'd only get in your way," she said, hoping, unrealistically, that he'd demur and invite her along on his appointments. It would afford her the opportunity, she thought, of seeing him in action with his clients. It would also give her the opportunity of just seeing him.

But no such invitation was forthcoming. Instead he said, "You'd never be in my way," and left it at that.

And so ends a lovely interlude, she told herself, lifting the danish to her mouth.

Simon's sooty lashes lifted, and he looked at her for a long moment, as if debating something with himself. She wondered if he were looking for the right way to say good-bye. Something like "Here's looking at you, kid," might have fit the occasion, she thought dryly.

Casey raised her cup of coffee and took a sip, hiding behind the rim for lack of something to say. The coffee was so strong that it made her open her eyes wide. Simon's next statement made her open them even wider.

"Come to Houston with me. Spend a week."

The words cut through the foul taste of the coffee. She choked a little. "What?" Her eyes watered. Was it from the coffee or from her happiness? Steady, Case, she told herself. The man might just want a seven-night stand instead of a one-nighter.

The sexy smile on Simon's lips warmed her heart as he repeated, "Come to Houston with me. Stay the week." For a moment Casey was at a loss for words. Simon seemed to interpret that silence as indecision. He reached out and curled his tanned fingers over her hand. "I know this is a little unorthodox."

There was that word again, she thought. Everything connected with Simon was unorthodox.

"But as a future investor, I thought you might want to see what my operations are like."

A perfect opportunity, she thought. The closer she got to Simon's operations, the better. The closer she got to Simon, the better, her cynical little voice chimed in.

"Besides," Simon continued, "I'm not quite willing to let you go yet."

Yet. Did that mean that someday—someday soon? Men don't plight their troth just because they tumble into bed with you these days, Casey. Women don't either, she reminded herself. But it did no good. Women might not, but she did. A part of her would always belong to those mischievous eyes, she realized.

"Is that how you hold on to your clientele?" she asked roguishly.

"No," he answered, "but it might be an interesting approach. I'll have to mention it to Ethan."

"Ethan?" she echoed.

Simon nodded. "He's in charge of sales—the paperwork end, actually. He's much more serious about things like that than I am."

"Is that why he plays practical jokes?" she asked, remembering her first meeting with his brother.

"Believe it or not, most of the time. Ethan is a worrier," Simon said, giving up on his muffin. It settled back onto his plate, half eaten.

"Oh?" Casey asked, becoming alert. "What does he have to worry about?" she asked, trying to sound casual.

Simon paused, as if regretting his words. "Nothing for you to concern yourself with," he said evasively. "Business matters. Well, will you come?" he asked again, his expression growing seductively persuasive.

Was he asking her because he wanted her—or was he asking her because he wanted the money she had told him she had? Lord, what a dilemma she had gotten herself into.

"Sure," she replied lightly. "I'd like to learn all about your business. I'll go home and pack my checkbook," she said glibly.

Simon leaned forward, taking her hand. "Just be sure you pack you," he told her.

Butterflies the size of 747's thundered into her stomach as they left the diner.

"So, how are you progressing with the coin case? Millie tells me that when she left here Friday night you were stuck with some irate dupe demanding this Ashford person's head on a platter."

Casey stood before Harold Steele's desk. An extremely bright Monday morning sun was nudging itself into her consciousness. It made her feel as if she

were standing alone on a stage, engulfed by a spotlight. She moved toward the side of her supervisor's
desk, away from the glare.

"Very well, as a matter of fact," she heard herself
say. The words rasped against her dry throat. "Mr.
Dennenberg—our irate dupe—" she clarified when
her fifty-year-old boss raised one inquisitive eyebrow
at the mention of the name, "told me that Sim…Mr.
Ashford," she corrected herself, wondering if Steele
had noticed the slip, "was in town. I met him."

Met him. God, had she ever met him! Her skin
prickled with excitement when she just thought of
their meeting. Since Saturday night her mind had
drifted back to that wondrous memory countless
times. Each time the sensations were as alive as they
had been originally. Even now she could feel Simon's
arms about her, feel his hands caressing every part of
her.

After their initial lovemaking, she had been horrified at what had happened. Twenty-four hours. That
was all she had known him. Just twenty-four hours.
She had never done anything like that before, made
love to a man she had known for barely a day. She
had been afraid of what Simon might think of her
once their lovemaking had ended. Lonely pick-ups
did that sort of thing. Casual women who slipped in
and out of relationships the way other women
changed dresses did that sort of thing. Casey *never*
did. Her affections weren't given so easily. What had
happened with Simon was something she couldn't explain. A heady intoxication had suffused her, nudged
at her soul and whispered, "This is the one."

Simon had looked at her after it was over, not with
the lazy, satisfied look that she had imagined would

have graced his face had he been out for a one-night stand, but with a soft and tender smile. Simon had not been in a hurry to murmur, ''Thank you, ma'am,'' and rush into his clothes, disappearing into the night once the ''thrill of the chase'' was over. He had stayed and held her in his arms, telling her that she was beautiful and making everything within her smile.

So what was she doing, standing in Steele's glass-enclosed office, reporting on her ''accidental'' meeting? She was hoping somehow to find something to clear him, that was what she was doing, hoping to find something that would clear him before other authorities got involved in the case. And she also wanted to clear him with that tiny part of herself which still had nagging doubts. But her vision was clouded over now, clouded by the petal-soft fingers of love that held her in an iron grip.

Harold Steele's tiny eyes widened as he stared at her, open mouthed. ''You met him?'' he asked, his hunched body coming to total attention. ''Where?''

She couldn't tell if he were pleased or annoyed at her revelation, and once more recalled that what she had done was highly unorthodox. ''At his hotel. There's a coin auction going on in town, and he's attending,'' she informed her boss. ''I thought it might be helpful if I observed him, and,'' she licked her lips, ''I wound up bumping into him outside the hotel coffee shop.'' She paused, watching Steele's ruddy face to see his reaction. It was growing ruddier, which, with Steele, was a sign of excitement.

''And? And?'' he prodded, lifting himself out of his seat slightly as he leaned forward.

''Um, we talked....''

"You told him you were with the postal service?" He squeaked in disbelief.

"No, no," she said hastily, but he still eyed her suspiciously. "I told him I was a coin collector. We had dinner and...he invited me down to Houston for a week," she ended, skipping over the vital parts. But her pulse didn't. Her pulse had total recall.

A smile burst out on Steele's face as he sank back into his creaky wooden chair and rocked back and forth. The creaking grew louder, and had the same effect on Casey as the high pitched squeal of chalk on a blackboard. She kept her eyes on Steele.

He ran his hands through his thinning salt-and-pepper hair. "Terrific!" he exclaimed, then stopped rocking. "Of course," he said, the smile fading into the recesses of his jowls, "if you get into trouble, you're on your own."

"It's got the smell of entrapment about it," her boss went on, making a pyramid out of his fingertips as he pressed them against one another. "Is it?"

She knew that Steele was eager for a kill. He wanted something that would ingratiate him with his superiors and get him promoted out of the glass office and into a larger office without see-through walls and with carpeting. That was the man's main ambition in life: walls and a carpet, she thought cynically. Obviously he saw this as a means to that end, and she intended to use his view of the situation to her own advantage, so she proceeded cautiously.

"No, not entrapment. I'm going along as...a friend." She hated the smirk that came over the man's face. "I thought that if I got closer to the scene of operations, I might find something,"

"It's highly irregular...." He muttered into his

chin. "Think you'll come up with anything?" he asked eagerly.

"I hope so." What she hoped was to either find out that Simon was blameless or else warn him before he got into any further trouble. No, no, she wasn't supposed to do that, she chided herself.

"Good," Steele pronounced, nodding. "Very good. Because there's more riding on this case now."

"Oh?" Casey felt a sinking sensation in the pit of her stomach. Now what?

Steele shuffled through a collection of papers. "Here," he said, pushing one toward her. "Hot off the press," he added with a smile that only added to Casey's feelings of dread. "Seems that Ashford and Ashford may now be involved in theft as well."

"What?" she cried, taking the complaint from his hands. Her eyes scanned the page, but she couldn't quite read the words that all seemed to be jumping at her at once.

"One of the coins that they've recently sold turned out to be part of a half-million-dollar collection that was stolen some months ago. Prior to this discovery, this was only a possible mail fraud case. Now it's much bigger." He smiled broadly.

Casey knew that as things had stood up to now, if the coins in question had been found unable to live up to their descriptions, the case would have become bogged down in the question of whether or not the description was simply high-flown sales copy, which was permitted, or if an actual warranty were being violated. In that case there was a chance for civil redress. Misrepresentation was a valid case for action, but if the postal service moved too fast without sufficient evidence, they could both ruin Simon's business and leave themselves open for a lawsuit. But the theft of a half-million-dollar collection was something else again.

"This might be just the beginning," Steele was saying. "If you could come up with enough evidence to bring him up on mail fraud charges and to nail him for the theft, it'd be quite a feather in my cap. I could nonchalantly hand over the information to the FBI, since the transmission of stolen goods across a state line is in their jurisdiction."

"What if he's innocent?" Casey posed.

Steele obviously didn't like that alternative. "If he's innocent," he said tersely, "and you find satisfactory proof to that effect quickly enough, you'll be saving Mr. Ashford from a visit by his friendly FBI agents. I'm sure that one of these poor dupes," he said, waving his hand over the pile of complaints, "is going to take the matter to higher authorities if we don't come up with a satisfactory solution soon."

Casey immediately thought of Dennenberg.

Steele brightened again. "But I don't think Mr. Simon Ashford is innocent," he told Casey with finality. "Yes sir, this case just might be my ticket...." he said, rubbing his plump hands together.

Casey scarcely heard him as she tried once again to make sense of the words on the paper she held. She began to walk out, numb.

"Get as much information as you can, so I can nail him," Steele called after her departing figure.

Was that what she was going to wind up doing? Casey wondered. Nailing him? No, it couldn't be true, her mind insisted as she made her way, unseeing, to her own desk. The man who had held her and loved her on Saturday couldn't possibly be a thief.

Could he?

Casey stood in her room, staring at the colorful array of dresses spread out on her bed, trying to decide which ones to take with her.

"What would Mata Hari pack?" she mumbled, pulling out a sexy evening dress and exchanging it for the sensible, tailored outfit that was propped up on her bedpost. She didn't feel like being sensible. In fact, she wasn't being sensible. Nothing in this whole situation was sensible.

The question of shoes was a far easier matter to take up. She only had five pairs to choose from. Two pairs would go in her suitcase and one she'd wear.

Casey walked over to her dresser and pulled open the bottom drawer. Nightgowns. Now there was a dilemma. What to pick. Casey chewed her lip. She really should take something practical. If she packed the aqua one, she thought as she ran her hand over the filmy material, she'd be leaving herself open to expectations that she would be willing to fulfill the promise that the article held. It was sexy and provided about as much protection from a watching eye as a cellophane cigarette wrapper. Tentatively she fingered the beige flannel nightgown that was nestled next to it. It really suited the serious purpose of her mission far better, she told herself. She half lifted it out of the drawer. Then, with a decisive flourish, she pulled out the aqua nightgown with its matching robe and tossed them on the bed before slamming her drawer shut. That was that.

"You're going crazy, Case," she said aloud, shaking her head in despair as she went out into the foyer. She opened the coat closet to get out her suitcase and was promptly attacked by her ironing board which always seemed to want to tumble out at the least opportune moments. She shoved it back and held it at bay with one hand while she pulled out one of her two pieces of luggage. It was the type that boldly professed to be able to withstand the torturous poundings of man and beast and come up smiling. Obviously, she noted as she looked at it, it didn't fare as well co-habitating with an ironing board. There was a nick on the top where the ironing board had banged into it countless times.

Casey dragged the suitcase out and went back to her bedroom to pack quickly before she changed her mind—about her choice of clothes and about going in the first place.

She wanted to go. She felt that she would probably be willing to trek off to the ends of the known world with Simon. But at the same time she was afraid. Mainly afraid, she thought, of finding out that the very thing she didn't want to be true *was* true. What if Simon were exactly what he was being accused of being? What if she were in love with a common crook?

She stopped smoothing out her undergarments in the suitcase, her hands suspended in mid-motion. In love? She turned the thought around as if it were an exquisite cut glass vase and examined it from all sides in awe. Yes, it was true. The more she thought about it, the more she realized that she was truly in love. Her eyes had fallen in love when she first saw him. The rest of her had followed at a not very discreet distance, capitulating when his lips had touched hers.

"It could all be just a ruse, you know. There's no reason in the world why he couldn't be lying to you—

about everything,'' she said into the air, voicing all her inner doubts.

She became silent once again as she held the peignoir set against her for a moment, feeling its softness and remembering the velvety feel of Simon's fingers as they had touched her. Despite her inner tug of war, a smile slipped onto her lips as Casey recalled the emotions that had overwhelmed her when Simon had asked her to come to Houston with him.

Last minute details had kept Simon from coming to pick Casey up at her apartment, and she was left to her own devices to reach Kennedy Airport. The cab driver she hailed was new and had to be guided every inch of the way, which wasn't easy. Casey wasn't much at guiding anyone *anywhere*. But they made it, to her relief, with half an hour to spare. Her heels beat out a fast staccato rhythm on the cement as she hurried into the terminal. Groups of people were milling about, coming, going or waiting, as Casey hurried up to the freshly starched women at the desk. The ticket agent promptly presented her with the ticket that Simon had reserved for her.

Ticket in one hand, overstuffed suitcase in the other, Casey tackled her way onto the escalator, fighting larger and larger crowds. Flashing her ticket at the attendant, she hurried up the inclined walkway that led to the lounge reserved for passengers. For a moment she stood rooted to the deep red carpet, looking about the circular waiting area. A jumble of faces and forms met her searching eyes as she tried to find Simon.

Finally she saw him seated near the sign for Gate 31. Their plane sat just beyond the closed doors, not yet ready for boarding. Casey forged a path toward him.

"Well, I got here," she said, just a touch breathless after the hurried pace she had set herself. She set the suitcase down.

"Yes, I see you did."

She stopped just as she was about to sit. All her senses pulled together, as if trying to find a clue. "Ethan?" she guessed.

"That's very good," he replied, a slight smile passing momentarily across his lips. "Most people can't tell us apart unless we're together."

Casey sat down. "I think it was the thrill in your voice when you saw me that gave you away," she said wryly.

Ethan flashed her an apologetic grin that was several watts below Simon's range. "Sorry."

She studied him for a second, wondering if he meant it. "You don't like me very much, do you?" she asked bluntly.

"I've got nothing against you, Tracey...."

"Casey," she corrected.

"But this is our busy season, and I do have something against anything that might distract Simon."

Was she distracting Simon? She wondered hopefully. God knew, he was distracting her. "I'll try to keep my distracting down to a minimum," she promised.

Ethan shrugged, as if indicating that perhaps her promise wasn't that necessary. "Simon usually doesn't let women distract him for long, once the chase is over."

"Oh?" she asked archly. Was he telling her the truth, or merely trying to discourage her from coming along? "Does he make a practice of stealing women's hearts and hanging them like trophies in his den?" She tried to sound glib about the subject, as if she were sophisticated and above caring—as if her heart weren't thumping madly at the prospect of being nothing more than one in a long line of women who Simon had dallied with.

Ethan looked at her for a long moment. "So he's stolen your heart, has he?" Damn, was she that transparent? She cursed her poor choice of words. "Well, it won't be the first time he's stolen something," Ethan muttered, half to himself.

Casey's racing pulse stopped in its tracks, as did everything else within her. Ethan's words descended on her like an icy cloud freezing and numbing her. Was that just a slip? What did he mean by that? She looked at Ethan's face for a clue, but he had turned away from her. Had he realized what he had just said?

For a moment the silence between them hung awkwardly, even though a continual din ebbed and flowed all around them. "Simon tells me you're coming into a sizable inheritance when you turn thirty," Ethan said eventually.

Casey could see why Simon was the one who handled people while Ethan handled paper. His comment wasn't the most tactful thing he could have said. So, she thought, Simon had mentioned her money to his brother. In what connection? That he had a rich pigeon on his hands? That their firm would soon capture some of her money? She didn't want to consider the matter, but she knew she had to.

"Where is Simon?" she asked, not answering Ethan's question. She looked around the huge area, hoping to spot him.

"Right here," said a warm voice right behind her.

Seven

Casey turned around, grateful that Simon had arrived.

"I always seem to be apologizing for being late," he said as he bent down and gave her a warm, quick kiss. "Ethan didn't pretend to be me again, did he?"

"No." She shook her head. "As a matter of fact, he was asking me about my money."

The first real frown she had ever seen cross Simon's face took hold as he looked at his twin. Was he annoyed because Ethan had made a slip, or because the question had been a rude one?

"You'll have to forgive Ethan," Simon said sharply. "The making and cultivating of money holds a lot of fascination for him and, at times, he forgets his manners."

It was a definite reprimand, and for a moment Casey thought that it would lead to hot words between the brothers. But then the annoyed look on Ethan's face subsided and he shrugged. "It comes from being initially poor, I guess. If I offended you, Tr-Casey," he amended, "I'm sorry."

The corners of Casey's mouth wrinkled in a quick smile, as if to stop any further apologies on Ethan's part. "You were poor?" Casey asked, directing the question toward Simon rather than Ethan.

"Terribly," Simon confirmed.

At that moment the PA system let out a piercing squawk followed by a melodic voice informing the passengers that Flight 15 to Houston was now boarding at Gate 31.

Before he could continue his story, Simon looked up in the direction of the announcement. "That's us," he proclaimed, putting a guiding arm around Casey's shoulders. He picked up her suitcase, along with his own. "The rest of your luggage on board?" he asked as they began walking with the swelling crowd that was filing down the passage to the plane's door.

"This is all I brought," Casey answered, raising her voice as the noise grew more intense. "I believe in traveling light," she added.

Simon grinned at her statement and looked over her head at Ethan. "Woman after my own heart," he said to his brother.

"She certainly is," Ethan replied dourly.

Casey shot him an annoyed look which was fueled by embarrassment.

The throng about them curtailed any further conversation, and it wasn't until they were all on the plane, waiting for take-off, that Casey got a chance to get Simon to continue his story.

"You've certainly come a long way from being

terribly poor,'' Casey commented, looking around. So this was first class, she thought. It certainly beat being relegated to a small space, made even smaller by suitcases that had been shoved in under seats.

"Yes, I have," Simon agreed, "and I don't ever intend to be poor again."

It was a very firm pronouncement, rather like an oath, Casey thought, noting the serious look in his eyes, despite his smile.

"That means keeping up with your work," Ethan reminded him, looking at Casey. She caught a gleam of accusation in his eyes.

"All work and no play, Ethan…" Simon said, letting his voice trail off. He strapped himself in and then leaned over to do the same for Casey. As if to give credence to his words, he purposely brushed his fingers along her lap, causing small, erotic licks of fire to spring up beneath his touch. She tried hard not to squirm in her seat. Simon grinned.

"I think you do enough playing for both of us," Ethan told his brother.

What did that mean? Casey wondered. Was Ethan just being sour? Or was Simon a playboy?

"Someone has to be serious," Ethan went on in his own defense.

Simon laughed. "And you sure handle that end of it. C'mon, Ethan, lighten up; otherwise Casey's going to think that all we ever do is squabble. Actually," Simon said, turning his blue-gray eyes to Casey, "we normally get along quite well. There's a strong bond between us," he said, affectionately, "partially because we're twins, partially because for a while there, we were all we had."

"It must have been terrible," Casey sympathized.

She always found herself growing misty-eyed at sad movies or commercials where kids called home. She was a pushover for a sad story.

"Looking back," Simon admitted, "it was. But when you're a kid, you don't fully realize things like that. All you know is the emptiness, the fact that your folks are never coming back. But we were lucky," he ended, his voice growing lighter.

"We had Uncle Jack," Ethan said, for once joining the conversation with a positive attitude, Casey thought. "And he had the tenacity to fight to keep us once he took us in."

"Is he still involved in the company?" Casey heard herself asking.

"Uncle Jack serves as our advisor," Ethan said tersely before Simon could answer. "He helps with the coin grading at times," he added.

That could mean that Uncle Jack was the one who had assigned the mint grade to the coins Dennenberg had howled were sliders. Maybe *he* was the one to blame, she thought hopefully. But Simon seemed to care a great deal about this Uncle Jack person. She could see it in his face when he mentioned the man's name. Any way she tried to solve this problem, the outcome didn't look promising.

Casey decided just to try to enjoy the flight and the fringe benefits that went with it—which were considerable. After take-off, which had an exhilarating, roller-coaster effect on her stomach, Casey was approached every few minutes by a passing stewardess who offered a variety of beverages. Casey chose to stick with ginger ale in order to keep her wits sharpened against more: Ethan, who appeared determined to cut her down verbally, or Simon, who was seducing her senses. Everything about Simon was sexy, she thought, while almost everything about Ethan put her off. It amazed her how two men who looked so much alike could be so different.

Disembarking in Houston proved to be as hectic as boarding had been in New York, except that there were a lot of Stetsons visible in the milling crowds here, Casey observed. Also, the journey down to the street level wasn't as frantic, and there were a lot more smiles evident in the sea of faces. Simon somehow managed to hold on to her hand while balancing both his suitcase and hers. Ethan brought up the rear, carrying his suitcase and an attaché case. They made it out of the building in a remarkably short time.

The bright afternoon sun shone down on them as they emerged from the building. Her flannel nightgown, Casey thought suddenly, would have been much too warm here. So might the one she packed, she added silently, stealing a look at Simon's handsome profile. Anticipation pricked momentarily throughout her body. You're here to find out the facts, not to enjoy yourself, her little voice told her.

"Here!" Simon called out over her head.

Casey turned to look where he was waving and saw a gleaming white Cadillac Seville highlighted with gold pull up in the loading zone.

"A Houston taxicab?" Casey asked glibly, aiming her comment at Ethan.

"Our car," he replied, unamused.

Casey began to doubt that he possessed a sense of humor at all. Simon seemed not to notice the exchange between them as he ushered Casey into the back seat and followed her in. "You sit up front with Maynard," he told his brother.

"Maynard," Casey took it, was the smartly dressed driver who whisked them off, nimbly weaving through the airport traffic. They sped through both city streets and country roads until they arrived before a huge ante-bellum-styled white house with blue trim and massive doric columns. Casey half expected Scarlett O'Hara to come running down the lawn, her ruffled hoop skirt held high.

"Home?" Casey asked Simon.

"Home," he replied.

At that moment the front door opened and a cherubic man with a physique like a beloved, worn teddy bear came ambling down the front steps. That had to be Uncle Jack, Casey decided, and she looked at Simon hesitantly.

"Maybe I should stay in a motel in town," she suggested, feeling suddenly uncomfortable about the situation.

Simon glanced at her quizzically for a moment before his expression softened into a reassuring one. "What would you want to do that for? Think what a long walk I'd have at night from my room to yours," he teased, squeezing her hand. "Uncle Jack doesn't bite," he told her, as if reading her mind. "He purrs. You'll love him."

It almost sounded as if Simon were intent on bringing her home to "meet the family." But Casey was sure that was merely part of his charm. His wonderful, irresistible charm. She took his hand as he helped her out of the car.

Uncle Jack stopped on the bottom step, cocking his shaggy white head as he focused on Casey. "Auctions look like they're growing more interesting," he said, looking her over intently. "Maybe I should go to the next one." The chuckle that accompanied the words was resonant and rich, coming from the deep recesses of his barrel chest.

"Uncle Jack," Simon said, ushering her forward, "this is Casey Bennett. She'll be staying with us for a few days."

Jack took her hand between his two bear-like ones and held it for a moment. She could see that he was appraising her, probably with the same finesse that he had used over the years in judging the worth of coins. She gathered by the warm smile that came to his lips that she had been put into the gem category.

"Welcome," he said, shaking her hand heartily. "Welcome." He put his arm around her shoulders, totally taking charge. He was only slightly taller than she was, Casey noted, but nearly twice as wide. He wasn't fat, just exceedingly large boned. He also appeared, even at his age, to be enormously strong. "Come up to the house and freshen up. I'll have Juanita get your room ready."

"Your room." He made it sound so homey, so permanent, as if she had been a part of this life for a long, long time. What would they say, she wondered with a strong pang of conscience, if they knew that she was there to spy on them? She glanced at Simon, but caught the expression on Ethan's face instead. Ethan, she'd wager, would say that he had known it all along. She wished that she had never gotten into this situation. The proverbial mole hill was turning into a mountain.

Quietly she allowed herself to be led into the house.

"Juanita," it turned out, was a leather-faced, ample woman who looked as old as the proverbial hills and moved with a slow, deliberate pace. She was in charge of all the housekeeping duties, which seemed to Casey to be overwhelming, considering the size of the establishment. But Juanita apparently managed everything with grudging pride. She also cooked and served dinner that evening. It was a tasty, spicy meal which tempted Casey's taste buds and took her through two helpings and three glasses of water.

Conversation at the table was light and friendly putting Casey almost totally at ease. At the same time, it made her feel miserable about her motives for being there. Even if her motives had been altruistic, she was still guilty of trying to deceive them all as to her background. If Simon turned out to be totally innocent, could he love someone who had lied to him?

And if he weren't innocent? How could she go on loving a thief? Her little voice countered.

Easily, came the reply.

After dinner Simon took her hand and proposed that they go outside for a breath of air.

"It's so...so still," Casey said, looking out from the verandah at the front lawn which was bathed in inky darkness. No glaring street lights met her gaze, no continual hum of traffic met her ear, only crickets sending messages to one another. "I'm not sure I'm going to be able to sleep tonight," she confessed. "It's almost too quiet." She leaned on the front railing, trying to get used to the silence.

"Oh?" Simon asked with a mischievous lilt to his voice. "Were you planning on sleeping?" He came up behind her and enveloped her in his strong arms. He was wearing a light blue plaid shirt rolled up at the sleeves and a pair of worn jeans, looking far more like a cowboy than a successful businessman. Casey didn't know which way she liked him best. Stark naked, probably, her little voice taunted. Her unguarded thoughts made her realize how very vulnerable she was. She tried to fight her strong feelings. The more involved she became personally, the harder all this was going to be to resolve.

She twisted in his arms, turning to face him. The action caused her to brush fully against his body. The startling hardness she felt unnerved her and made her throat dry, while rendering the rest of her far more liquid.

Casey licked her lips and managed to put her hands up against his chest to forestall the descent of his mouth to hers. "Um, Simon, maybe we'd better not...." She protested with waning conviction.

"There's nothing 'better' about 'not,'" Simon told her. "What's the matter, Casey? Are you still bothered by the fact that we haven't known each other since first grade?" he teased. "I think we got to know one another as well as any two people ever could in your apartment Saturday night." He kissed her hair lightly, with an intimate, soft gesture. Nonetheless the rest of her caught fire, and she had to struggle to keep her breathing steady.

"No, it's not that...." Her voice trailed off as she looked away. If he made love to her, she wouldn't be able to keep a clear mind and figure out her next move. The only moves she'd be occupied with would be the ones she'd be making against his body. He definitely had a way of destroying her whole thinking process.

"Then what?" Simon asked, prodding her.

She had no answer for him, and she expected him to look annoyed. After all, he had brought her all this way, and now she was acting like someone's maiden aunt, playing coy. But it wasn't coyness that was clawing at her. It was a sense of desperation at the complex situation she had managed to get herself into.

A light came into Simon's eyes. "Oh, I see," he said thoughtfully.

"See what?" Casey asked uneasily, almost afraid of the words that would follow. Somewhere in the distance a lonely coyote howled, making her jump.

Simon smiled as he leaned his back against a tall white column, crossing his arms before him. "It's what Ethan said, isn't it?"

Ethan had said so many things that she wasn't sure what Simon was driving at and tried to keep an impassive face as she nodded slightly. This could be her way out. "Well, maybe..." She wondered frantically what she was agreeing to. She could only hope that it would serve her purposes.

Simon sighed, then took hold of her hands. "Well, you shouldn't think that."

Think what? Her mind cried. Make words, Simon. Fill me in, please, she pleaded mentally.

"I'm not interested in you for your money."

Oh, thank God that was it, she thought, trying hard not to sigh with relief. She decided to play along with his belief and looked properly serious. "Well, a woman in my position can't be too careful...."

Simon gestured up to the house. "Does that look like the house of a fortune hunter?" he asked, amused.

"Money likes money," she replied evasively. And you undoubtedly have a large mortgage to pay, she added mentally.

"And it's as easy to love a rich woman as a poor one," Simon said, meeting her cliché with one of his own.

Love? Had he said "love"? Her mind sang. Steady, your eagerness is showing, she warned herself. And it still might all be a ploy.... Her ambivalent feelings were killing her, she realized, wishing she could stop thinking altogether.

Simon had slipped his arms about her again and pulled her against him. She could feel currents of electricity shooting all through her body. "I just chose to fall for a rich lady," he murmured, kissing the hollow of her throat. "You can't fault me for that."

No, but she could fault him for the feelings that were mushrooming inside her, colliding with one another. Fault him for it and love him for it at the same time. She struggled hard to keep her hands from reaching out and caressing him.

She didn't have to force her doubts to stop nagging at her. Simon was doing that for her, weaving that special magic which was his alone. The searing effect of his lips on hers reduced all her thoughts, all her doubts, to charred rubble as passion surged up within Casey and she met the force of his kiss head on.

The sound of a forced cough broke Simon's spell and Casey opened her eyes, reluctantly pushing paradise aside. They both turned to see Ethan standing at Simon's elbow.

"Sorry, I thought Simon was showing you around. Well," Ethan went on, reconsidering his remark, "I guess he is, at that."

Simon didn't lose his good humor, nor did he look as if he were about to release his hold on her, Casey noted. "If I give you a quarter, Ethan, will you go away?" he asked dryly.

"I can't be bought that easily, Simon," Ethan quipped.

"How about threatened?" Simon suggested, keeping a straight face.

Ethan held up his hands, stepping backward. "Can't stand the sight of blood, especially my own," he said, about to retreat. "I'll go in and leave you to your folly."

"I think we should all go in," Casey said, looking up at Simon. Wistfully he let her go. "It's been rather a long day, and I'm kind of tired," Casey murmured.

Simon grinned as he held the door open for her. "Remember what happened the last time you said you were tired?" he whispered against her ear.

Casey blushed, but avoided both his and Ethan's eyes as she walked quickly inside.

As they entered the house Jack called Simon into the den, and Casey took that opportunity to slip off and go up the long, winding staircase to her room. Normally she would have stopped along the way to look at the collection of faded photographs that lined the wall. She hadn't gotten a chance to look at them when Juanita had led her to her room, and old photographs always fascinated her. But right now Casey was in a hurry to retreat, to close the bedroom door behind her and lock out both her feelings and her growing desire. Not to mention Simon.

Hers was the last room on the landing, the first at the head of the back stairs. Casey had never been in a house that had both front and back stairs, she thought, closing the door behind her. Would a person who owned a house with two sets of stairs be risking everything in a series of swindles? Maybe he needed to swindle in order to maintain a house with two sets of stairs, she mused.

Oh God, Casey thought, flopping down on the white eyelet bedspread. You're going to drive yourself crazy with this. You're not cut out to be Mata Hari. She lay there for a minute, sighing and listening to herself breathe, trying to relax. She was tired, all right, but keyed up as well and the tension in her shoulders threatened to spread through her whole body.

A bubble bath. She needed a bubble bath. There was something about soaking in hot suds that was almost therapeutic for her.

"You and a sink full of dirty dishes," she mumbled. Casey knew she had as much chance of coming up with a bottle of bubble bath in a house full of men as she had of finding King Solomon's mines in downtown Houston.

Still, she realized, she needed to do something to unwind. If she went to bed feeling like this, she knew she'd never get to sleep. She settled on a hot bath, even without bubbles.

Casey filled the tub, then bound her thick copper hair high on her head. After stripping off her clothes, she slid her tense body along the rich tile of the sunken tub until all of her was submerged and turning a deep shade of pink. The hot, steamy water lapped at her as she settled in. Casey sighed, letting the water soothe her.

She needed to get away, at least mentally, she decided. This tangled web she had woven was getting to be too much for her to cope with, and who knew what tomorrow held in store? The hell with tomorrow, she told herself, moving her hand back and forth slowly in the water, creating ripples that chased languidly after one another.

"Tomorrow is another day," she said aloud, thinking of Scarlett O'Hara again. She giggled. Somehow, it was appropriate.

The hot water was doing wonders for her.

She stayed in the tub until the water grew cool. Rendered thoroughly lazy by the "healing waters," Casey grudgingly rose and, still standing in the tub, grabbed the midnight blue bath towel from the wooden rack behind her. Rather than towel herself dry quickly, she pressed the deep pile against her and allowed the towel to blot her body dry. For a moment she stood with her eyes shut, not moving, hardly breathing, savoring the temporary peace she had found.

"Beautiful."

The soft, throaty voice made her eyes fly open, instantly chasing away all the calming effects of the bath. Simon stood before her. Or was it Ethan? She thought suddenly in horror. They had both worn jeans at dinner, and their shirts had both been blue. Was Simon's the light one or the dark one? She couldn't remember. All she remembered was commenting on the similarity of their clothes, with Simon laughing about it, while Ethan had looked chagrined. Was this Ethan now, paying her back? She hugged the towel closer to her.

"Like *Venus Rising out of the Sea*," the dark figure said appreciatively, likening her to the famous Botticelli painting. He stepped forward.

Casey took a step back, the water swishing about her calves as she did so. She almost slipped and grabbed the bronze faucet to steady herself, her eyes never leaving the man's face as they searched for a clue as to his identity. If she guessed wrong this time, there was more at stake than just a practical joke.

Eight

"**H**ey, be careful," Simon/Ethan warned, putting out a hand to help her. But Casey pulled aside. He looked puzzled at her reaction. "What's the matter?"

"Wait outside, please," she said stiffly. She needed to get something more on her body than a wet towel, she thought desperately.

Her request appeared to confuse him, but he took it indulgently, saluting smartly and walking out into the next room.

"Close the door," she called after him, staying put.

"You take all the fun out of it," he informed her with mock dejection, but did as she asked.

Only when the door was firmly shut did Casey venture out of the tub. By now she was thoroughly dry. She flung off the towel and quickly put on the peignoir set she had left hanging on the back of the door.

Her reflection taunted her from the smoked-glass mirror over the sink.

"Big improvement," she muttered, wishing she had brought her flannel nightgown, or at least a decent robe, with her instead. She put her hand on the doorknob, took a deep breath and opened the door.

Simon/Ethan was sitting on her bed, waiting. From his manner, he looked like Simon. But Ethan could easily imitate his brother and pretend to be him, she thought as she regarded the man warily. Ethan clearly didn't care for her, and making love to her would be one sure way of getting rid of her. She approached the man sitting on her bed with the same cautious steps she would have used to approach a snake.

Simon/Ethan looked amused. He also looked very impressed as his eyes left her face and slowly took inventory of her form which was barely hidden behind the misty aqua veils of her peignoir. Casey crossed her arms protectively in front of her chest.

"Very nice," he told her, still not looking at her face. Casey wished she had more arms.

He sounded like Simon, but could she be sure? "What are you doing here?" she asked suspiciously.

"Room service," he told her glibly, leaning back on his elbows.

"I didn't order anything," she pointed out playing along with him for a moment and buying herself some time with which to make a further assessment.

Simon/Ethan rose and took hold of her hands. "Compliments of the house."

She looked around. He had brought nothing with him. "What sort of room service?" she asked. The warmth of his fingers was transmitting itself to her. It *felt* like Simon, her instincts told her. But her instincts could be failing her, she could just be reacting to the *image* of Simon. She had to be sure.

"I've come to help you break in your bed. New beds should always be broken in." Mischief brought out a devilish glint in his blue-gray eyes. Ethan's eyes were flat, Casey reminded herself. Simon's was unfathomable. Still, she hesitated.

"How do I know you're not Ethan?" she asked bluntly, "playing another practical joke?"

He understood everything then and threw back his head as he laughed. "Nothing very practical about going to sleep with my girl, is there?" he asked.

"I'm not a girl," she corrected, trying to withdraw her hands from his and failing. "I'm a woman."

"Indeed you are," he said, his voice low, his eyes caressing the firm, high breasts that rose and fell before him. "Still not totally convinced, are you?"

She shook her head nervously.

"Well," he said, "I told you that I didn't have any identifying marks...but you do," he told her brightly, spreading her hands wide. "You have a beautymark on your left cheek."

She stared at him, confused. "I do not," she said defensively, her hand going up to her face as if to reassure herself of the fact.

The lazy smile spread further on his lips as he cut the distance between them down to nothing. "Not your visible cheek," he clarified. "At least, not visible to the rest of the world."

It was Simon all right. Casey breathed a sigh of relief and allowed her head to sink down against his chest. She was reassured by the sound of his heart beating beneath her ear.

Simon stroked her head. "Poor Casey," he mur-

mured. "It must be confusing to you to have two of
us running around. But I give you my word, Ethan
would never try to compromise you by posing as me
and coming into your bed. Although," he went on,
lifting her chin so that he could look down into her
face, "I can see where he'd be tempted." Simon
kissed her lightly. "Sorely tempted."

Casey tried to pull herself free of the swirl of emotions that was engulfing her. Clear head, you need a
clear head, remember? "Simon, I..."

"You know," Simon began, not taking any note
of the fact that she was trying to put him off, "back
in 1916 there was a big ruckus about the Standing
Liberty Quarter that was issued."

Casey stood very still. Coins? He was going to start
talking about coins *Now?* she thought in disbelief.

"It seems," Simon went on, running one very sensuous finger along her collarbone, "that the Mint produced a quarter portraying a lady with her right breast
exposed." Simon's finger was now tracing a path
along her *right* breast. Casey tried hard not to shiver
as slivers of bright fire followed his touch. "There
was such a hue and cry that they covered the poor
lady up the next year. But me," he said, gently pulling aside both layers of her peignoir, "I like an exposed breast. There's something, very, very tantalizing about seeing just one." He breathed the words
ever so slowly, and she could feel the ripples of his
breath on her skin.

Simon's hand molded itself to her fully freed
breast, massaging it and making her quiver. He
claimed it for his own with one delicately planted
kiss. The bonds that she had used to hold her passion
in check broke.

"Remind me," Simon whispered against the hollow of her throat as he worked to free her other breast of its confining barrier, "to show you my collection of Standing Liberty Quarters. The 1916 piece has a place of honor." A fraction of an inch at a time, he moved the straps of her aqua nightgown off her shoulder until it dropped down to her waist. "Of course," Simon went on, drinking in the sight before him, "you put her to shame."

Casey stood for a moment, transfixed by the sound of his voice and the look in his eyes. Her robe lay in an airy semi-circle about her bare feet. Her nightgown rested tentatively about her hips.

Simon reached out and removed the single clip that held her hair in place, making the waves tumble down like a copper cloud about her shoulders. The unruly effect made her look like a fiery gypsy, and Casey could see the look of longing heighten in Simon's eyes.

"Come here," Simon said huskily, his voice thick with desire. His embrace was hot, and then he lifted her into his arms and placed her lovingly on her bed. He joined her before her next heartbeat was completed, raining kisses upon her face.

Every inch of Casey was being consumed by the flames that were bursting within her. She was losing herself even faster than she had the first time they had made love. The urgent lashes of desire were fanning her needs more quickly. She felt her own hands pulling his shirt out of his waistband and inching their way toward the buttons. She needed to feel the reassuring intimacy of his bare flesh against her own.

The buttons refused to give way as she tried to push them through their holes.

"What did you use, glue?" she heard her frustrated voice murmur against his ear. The words struggled out past the throbbing pulse in her throat. She felt a chuckle rumble from within Simon as he ceased kissing the outline of her cheek. Obligingly he opened the buttons for her and the material fell away. Casey slid her hands along his light-haired chest, branding it with her fingertips, absorbing the warmth that was there.

"My turn," Simon whispered, tugging at the last remaining bit of nightgown that still hung about her hips.

"No, not yet."

Simon arched an inquiring eyebrow as he propped himself up on one elbow. "Turned maidenly shy on me, have you?" he asked teasingly. "It's too late for that," he warned. "Stronger men than I have gone crazy from being refused at a moment like this."

"No, no refusal," she promised him, a smile parting her lips, a smile tinged with the rosy hues of love. "But you've got more on than I do," she pointed out. She ran a finger along the center of his chest down to his belt buckle, then down the length of the zipper on his jeans. As her fingers stroked him, Casey watched an involuntary shudder dance across Simon's shoulders. A look of intense desire sprang up in his eyes. It matched the one in her own.

"Ah, equality," he murmured. Then the teasing banter was dropped. "You do it," he urged softly.

With hands that were unused to doing something so very intimate, Casey undid his belt, then briefly struggled with the snap on his jeans before it sprang open for her. She stopped, her eyes lifting hesitantly toward his.

"Go on," he pressed, his voice hardly audible. "Go on." The words were like a hypnotic drug.

Her fingers were hot, yet her palms felt almost icy as she took the top of the zipper in her thumb and forefinger and worked it down slowly. All she could hear was the sound of their mingled breathing and the sound of the zipper as it opened. As the zipper continued on its journey, nearing its final destination she said in surprise, "You're not wearing any underwear." Very sophisticated, Casey, her little voice taunted before it disappeared entirely for the rest of the evening.

"I didn't see the need to," Simon told her as he lifted his hips and completed the job of removing his jeans. They landed in a heap at the foot of the bed. "Now?" he asked, looking down at her nightgown.

"Now," she gasped. Her desire for their mutual union was growing to overwhelming proportions as her eyes greedily devoured the total picture of masculinity that Simon formed before her. His trim, athletic body was poised, sculpted by desire and ready to take her. But though his fingers removed the last barrier between their bodies, he did not move to possess her.

"What's the matter?" It was her turn to ask.

"I'm an art lover," he told her. "I'm drinking in a beautiful sight."

"More beautiful than a 1916 Standing Liberty Quarter?" she couldn't help teasing, even while her own passion seethed within her, becoming almost unmanageable.

"More beautiful," he said, lowering his lips to hers, "than anything I've ever seen."

She clung to those words as they echoed and re-echoed in her brain for the timeless interval that followed.

His lips left hers all too soon as they pursued an uncharted path from the hollow of her throat, exploring each breast, touching her trembling belly and venturing downward. He skirted the triangular area just below, circling it with kisses that melted her and made her moan with pleasure.

She wound her fingers into his hair, pressing him against her. Peaks of excitement built upon one another in crescendos of rapture. Ragged breathing tore at the outer edges of her consciousness as Simon's tongue darted seductively back and forth, each pass fanning the flames higher and higher. Casey could keep no part of her still as she arched her back, reaching for the ultimate pleasure that would bind her soul to his.

"Come to me," she begged, the words bursting from her as if they had a life of their own.

Despite the haze of ecstasy that enveloped her Casey could see Simon's face just over hers as he balanced his weight on the palms of his hands, then lowered himself to her so slowly that she thought she would scream. The delicious imprint of his form became stronger and stronger as she moved to accept him. The expression on his face was tender and loving, and wreathed in a look almost of longing agony. An agony to match the one beating within her own breast.

And then he was hers and she his, and an explosion of power and lights went off inside of Casey, dispelling all thoughts, generating nothing but raw emotion in its wake. Casey wrapped herself in that emotion and held on for dear life, not wanting to give up any part of the feeling.

Her breathing steadied until she gave herself up to a sensation of peace and well-being. Casey opened her eyes and found herself in Simon's arms. She saw a lazy, satisfied look in his eyes, and a hint of something more hiding just beyond.

"Still need proof as to who I am?" he teased gently.

She was aware of the fact that he was still stroking her, his strong fingers gliding along the length of her unclad body, lingering on parts that held special interest for him. Despite her exhaustion, Casey felt another wave of arousal forming.

"Maybe," she answered. "A girl can't be too careful, you know."

"Woman." This time it was he who corrected her. "No mere 'girl' could have done what you just did to me."

"Oh?" she said innocently, batting her eyes for added effect. "And what is it I just did to you, kind sir?"

He took a deep breath. "Give me ten minutes and I'll show you," he promised.

Casey kissed the base of his throat, just above the dark hair on his chest.

"Maybe seven minutes," she heard him say as she continued to kiss him. She pulled him a little closer to her, so that her body wiggled in beneath his slightly.

"Three?" he murmured as she lifted her head a little and nibbled on his ear.

"Oh, the hell with it," Simon said, giving up and taking her into his arms, tumbling her back against the pillows as he found her mouth and kissed it. The kiss almost scorched her lips.

Rays of light probed her eyelids, making them flutter. Reluctantly Casey opened her eyes, first one and then the other. For a moment she had a disoriented sensation, and then the previous night filtered back to her, bringing with it the warm sensations that had filled it. She stretched slowly, then turned to her right, a smile on her lips.

But the space beside her was empty. A pang of disappointment went through her. She rose up on her elbows and looked around the room. "Simon?" she called. No answer.

Where was he? She wondered. She glanced over to her nightstand and looked at the digital clock. A quarter of seven. Quarter. He had likened her unto a Standing Liberty Quarter. If not utterly romantic, the statement, she thought with a smile, was at least highly unique. So was this feeling that coursed through her veins. She was definitely in love, she decided, getting out of bed. And she had never been in love before. Not like this, not so that every part of her felt so totally involved, so totally committed.

And so totally confused, her little voice added. It was back, she sighed, pricking at her conscience, deepening her dilemma. Disregarding her nightgown which lay on the floor, Casey padded to the bathroom and brushed her teeth. This time she ran water for a shower and was in and out in five minutes. After hurriedly toweling herself off she went back into the bedroom, keeping the towel wrapped about her securely. No telling who might knock on her door, she thought, pulling her suitcase from behind the old-fashioned writing desk where she had left it the day before. She tossed it onto the rumpled bed, then flipped the locks and stared down at the clothes that lay crammed inside. She should have unpacked yesterday, she told herself sternly, pulling out a navy knit dress and watching the wrinkles stay put as the dress unfurled in her hands.

She hoped that Simon hadn't left the house yet. She knew that Ethan was eager to get him back to the office. Was she hurrying so fast just because she wanted to catch a glimpse of him before he left, like some lovestruck little kid, or was it because she wanted to try to implement her plan?

What plan? She asked herself. Nothing had come to mind except the fact that this was one hunk of a man she wanted in her life forever. She wiggled into her matching underwear and bra, pulled on her panty hose and slipped on her knit dress, letting it glide down her body the way Simon's hands had during the night. No, that wasn't right. Simon's hands had felt amazingly silky against her skin. This just felt like soft material. Simon felt like heaven.

Clear head, eh? No, there was nothing clear about her thinking processes. She was going to have to re-sign herself to that, she decided sadly, spreading her makeup before her and rubbing a bit of blue eyeshadow onto her index finger. With short, sure strokes Casey applied the dab of color, feathering it out over her lid. She wasn't really studying her reflection closely enough and allowed the color to go further than she had intended.

"Keep that up and he's going to think he made love to a real painted woman," she told her reflection.

The image scowled back and looked a little more intent on what she was doing.

What *was* she doing? What did she intend to do? Casey sighed. If she had the answers to those questions, maybe she wouldn't feel as if a cement mixer had taken up permanent residence in her stomach. She had absolutely no idea what she was going to do or how to go about proving Simon innocent. If he *was* innocent. She began putting on her lip gloss and then stopped. What if she found proof that he was guilty? What then? Would she turn him in? This whole thing was a horrid mistake, coming to his house.

A flash of the previous night's ecstasy came back to her unexpectedly. No, coming here wasn't a mistake, she amended. Working for the postal service Consumer Protection Division was. But, she thought as she took out her mascara wand and opened her eyes wide, if she hadn't worked there, she would have never met Simon in the first place. She didn't attend coin auctions. She had been content to enlarge her collection by happenstance at first, and then through a local coin dealer. No, had it not been for her job, Casey would have never met Mr. Simon Ashford, never met her destiny at all.

A crumb of mascara fell defiantly on her cheek, and she wiped it away with her thumb, pressing hard to erase all trace of its wayward presence.

So now what? She demanded of herself. Now, she thought, rising and slipping on her shoes, then pulling a comb through her thick hair, we eat. Somehow everything would work itself out, she told herself confidently.

At least, she added, closing the door behind her, she sincerely hoped so.

The sound of voices grew louder as she came down the stairs. She used them as a guide to bring her to the dining room. Sun splashed into the large room through filmy beige curtains, bathing everything in warm tones of gold. Ethan and Simon sat on either side of Jack. It was up to Casey to figure out which was which. The man to Jack's right smiled warmly, and Casey took her cue.

"Good morning all," she said brightly. "Mind if I join you?"

"By all means, by all means," Jack said heartily, indicating a seat by Simon. "I was just asking Simon where you were."

By the looks of the plates, she had arrived just as breakfast was starting.

"Juanita," Jack called over his shoulder, his voice booming out through the open door behind him that led into the kitchen, "the lady will have her breakfast now."

Juanita appeared within a few moments, shuffling along as she carried in a place setting for Casey. Casey looked around the table, which was heavily laden with bacon, ham, eggs, hash browns and steak.

"I believe in a good meal to start you off," Jack said, as if reading her thoughts. His own plate bore testimony to his philosophy. It was piled high with food. "When I got these two boys here, they were scrawny as hell. Did a good job on them, I think. Filled out pretty well," he told her with a confidential wink. She wondered if he were referring to the fact that by now she knew exactly how well filled-out Simon was.

"Yes, they did," Casey answered, helping herself to the scrambled eggs and crossing her plate with two strips of bacon. She avoided both Jack's eyes and Simon's grin.

"We'd better hurry up," Ethan prompted.

"The office isn't going to run away," Simon told him easily. "Taking a few extra minutes to chew your food instead of bolting it isn't going to make a difference."

"We've been away from it long enough," Ethan argued. "Jack said that Palmer quit three days ago. With Lily gone, as well, that leaves everything pretty much up in the air," he insisted, wolfing down a large bite of his pancakes.

Casey marveled that he didn't choke on it. But her attention was drawn more by Ethan's statement than his eating habits. She looked to Simon for an explanation. "Trouble?" she asked, trying to sound casual.

"Not really," Simon replied as he ate.

"'Not really'?" Ethan echoed. "What do you call losing half your office staff?" he wanted to know. "There was no reason for Palmer to quit like that without giving notice," he said heatedly, looking at Jack.

Jack shrugged. Casey could see that his philosophy of life was to take everything calmly in stride. Simon seemed to take after him, even if they weren't really related. "Who knows?" Jack said. "I'm just glad you boys are back. Too much for me to handle by myself with Lily out sick."

"Did she say when she'd be back?" Simon asked.

"In between coughing her lungs out, she mentioned something about a week."

"A week!" Ethan almost yelled. "How do we get along without a secretary for a week?" he demanded angrily. The last bite of pancake disappeared behind his disgruntled lips.

"Easy," Simon told him. "We call one of those temporary agencies and hire one."

"I can type," Casey volunteered eagerly.

Three sets of eyes looked in her direction.

Nine

"**W**ell, I can," Casey insisted. "I may not be the fastest typist in the world, but I manage."

Simon shook his head. "I can't ask you to do that."

"You're not asking," Casey pointed out, trying not to sound overly enthusiastic. This could be the perfect opportunity for her to get a look at their files and perhaps find something to determine Simon's innocence...or guilt, a nervous voice added. "I'm volunteering. It'd make me feel good, helping you out. Besides, I'd love to get to know how your company operates. You were going to tell me all about that, remember?" she asked, looking at Simon.

Ethan shook his head. "No, I don't think it's a good idea."

Casey turned to look at him. He surprised her. She would have expected him to be the first one to jump at her suggestion, seeing as how it would cost them nothing. But perhaps, she thought, his eagerness was held in check by the fact that he had something to hide. She looked toward Jack and Simon, wondering if they would agree with him.

Jack shrugged his shoulders good-naturedly. "Can't see why not. I've always thought that keeping busy was a lot more interesting than watching life just drift on by while you sat on your haunches." He glanced quickly at Casey to see if he had offended her with his terminology.

Casey merely looked amused. "Well, Simon?" she asked, flagrantly disregarding the deepening scowl on Ethan's face. After all, Simon was the president of the company, not Ethan.

"I hate putting you to work when I promised you a good time...." He began, rolling her offer over in his mind. "But we are in rather a bind."

He paused, and Casey jumped in to erase his objection. "We'll still be together. You'll be getting your work done," she said, looking pointedly at Ethan and keeping a broad smile on her face, "and I'll be getting an education about coins."

"Got a great gift there, Simon," Jack said, clapping Simon on the back. "All the eager female numismatists I've ever run into could either stop a lock or pass for my grandmother. You're damn lucky, boy."

"I know it," Simon said softly, giving Casey a very private look.

He wouldn't think so if he knew the truth, she thought. She noted the look on Ethan's face and wondered if somehow he suspected her of having an ulterior motive. But how could he? She was just being paranoid.

"If you'll excuse me," Casey said, rising, "I'll go get my purse. I wouldn't want you to be late on my account."

"Aren't you going to finish your breakfast?" Jack asked.

She shook her head, and her copper tresses fairly bounced. "Can't. I'm too excited. First day on the job, you know," she said with an exaggerated wink.

She walked out, and as she went she heard Ethan grumble, "I still don't think it's a good idea to mix business and so-called friendship."

"Ethan, it's not like I've just made her a full partner," Simon said. She could detect a note of annoyance in his voice.

She heard Ethan give a rejoinder, but his voice was so low that she couldn't make out the words.

Casey headed up the stairs quickly to fetch her purse.

The offices of Ashford and Ashford were on the eighth floor of a twelve-story, modern looking building in the heart of downtown Houston. From the looks of the as-yet-unworn carpets lining the walls, Casey judged that the building was fairly new, and she said as much to Simon as they rode up the elevator together.

"Yes, it is," he replied. "We've only been here for three years. Before that," he went on as the elevator came to a halt on the eighth floor and they got out, "we were in a little rinky-dink building across town. That's where Uncle Jack started out," he told her as he pulled out his keys, beating Ethan by a fraction of a second. Ethan stepped back and let them pass in front of him. The expression he wore was no happier than the one that had descended upon his face when Casey had originally offered to come in and help. "Of course," Simon continued as they went inside, "that neighborhood was a lot nicer thirty years ago than it is now. That was the main reason we moved. A successful firm has to look successful. Otherwise we could lose the business of those clients who do stop by."

And this had all the trappings of success, Casey thought, looking about the outer office. The tastefully decorated area seemed more like the waiting room of a high-priced physician than the office of a coin dealer. Flanked by two tall, feathery-fingered palms, an overstuffed sofa covered in nubby beige fabric bespoke comfort. A coffee table formed out of one piece of curved smoked-glass held a collection of coin magazines to while away the clients' time. Over in the corner, just in front of the door to the inner offices, was a large desk. No gray metal affair this, Casey observed, thinking of her own desk, but a work of art made of richly-stained oak.

"Personally," Ethan interjected, although no one had turned the conversation toward him, "I think we were better off in the old office. Most of our business is conducted through the mails, and the postman doesn't need to be impressed with our facilities."

"Spoken like a true tightwad," Simon said affectionately.

"Well," Ethan said, unlocking the door to the inner offices, "the 'tightwad' has work to do even if you don't." With that he closed the door behind him.

Casey looked at Simon ruefully. "He's really upset that I'm here, isn't he?"

Simon tried to shrug away her statement by hugging her to him for a moment, as if the gesture would erase any negative feelings she might have about the situation. It would have—had the situation been as clear as he apparently thought it was. "Don't mind him. He has trouble warming up to new people."

"Warming up? He's ten degrees below zero," Casey said with a sigh.

Simon laughed, releasing her. "He's very protective of the firm and keeps a sharp eye on everyone who takes part in it, even for a short time. You should see what he's like at interviews. That could be," he said, as if thinking aloud, "why Palmer quit so abruptly. Ethan's a hard taskmaster until you prove yourself, even though Palmer did come with letters of recommendation from several out-of-state coin dealers. Here, this is your desk," Simon told her, pulling out the chair.

Casey let him seat her, then looked at the piles of unopened envelopes that littered the gold blotter. "How long did you say your secretary has been gone?" she wanted to know. There looked like there was a month's worth of correspondence on the desk.

"Uncle Jack said she took sick Friday. That would be the day after we left for New York. Why?"

"This is usual?" Casey asked, gesturing toward the scattered heaps of unopened letters.

"Quite usual," he assured her.

"I can see why Ethan was concerned about your being away from the office. This looks like it needs an army of secretaries to take care of it. Are all these orders?" she wanted to know.

"Mostly."

Casey ran her fingers through the collection of large, medium and small envelopes. How easy it would be, she thought, to fool just a small fraction of the people represented here. How tempting to take a chance on substituting a coin of a slightly lesser grade and cost, charging the client the price of a more valuable specimen. The price of a coin was so tied to its condition—its numerical grade, she corrected herself, feeling that she should think like a professional while she was there. A few touches here and there and an unsuspecting person could purchase a circulated coin thinking it was an uncirculated one and pay many times what it was worth.

"I need you to go through those and separate the orders from the letters that are meant for the accounting department. I'll send Ginny over to help you later."

"Ginny?" Casey asked, raising an eyebrow.

"Ginny *is* our accounting department. Works fast enough for three people," Simon told her. "Ethan likes her."

"Ethan would," Casey muttered, still looking down at the sea of mail.

"Sorry you volunteered?" he wanted to know.

"Oh, no," she said rather quickly. Perhaps too quickly, she chided herself. Mustn't look nervous. "As long as I get to go to lunch with the boss," she said, smiling up at him.

"Done," he told her, bending his head to kiss her. He captured her lips, leaving behind just enough sweetness when the kiss was done to make Casey long for more private surroundings and more time. But the feel of the envelopes beneath her fingers acted as an anchor and brought her back to earth. She had a job to do.

Casey watched Simon's retreating back and waited until the door between them was firmly shut before she started to orient herself. She opened the top drawer of the desk and found that Lily was a very orderly person. Everything was neatly lying in a specific place: pencils arranged according to size; paper clips all facing the same direction; several typing correction fluid bottles stood at attention—all unused. Lily obviously never made any typing errors, Casey thought wryly as she closed the drawer and opened the one to her left. Nothing but typing paper of different weights and various sized notebooks, also arranged by size, greeted Casey's eyes. Such neatness was almost intimidating, she thought, shoving the drawer shut. So far there was nothing to indicate that a flesh and blood person occupied the desk.

What do you expect to find? Her little voice asked. Documents held in anticipation of future blackmail? That happened in old mystery movies, not in real life. The last drawer yielded nothing either, except for a letter opener. That, at least, would be useful for the business at hand, Casey told herself as she extracted it and got to work.

For forty-five minutes she did nothing but slice open envelopes, take out their contents and sort the letters. There were either typed or handwritten notes from clients asking the firm to obtain certain types of coins for them, or invoices with checks attached to them. In forty-five minutes she had managed to amass a goodly sum of money, Casey observed, watching the second pile of letters grow. Ashford and Ashford certainly looked as if it did a thriving business. From all appearances it seemed as if the firm were on the level.

And then, as two employees walked by her desk, talking boisterously on their way to the shipping area, Casey opened a letter of complaint. The large scrawl fairly barked its anger. She skimmed down to the bottom of the page and saw that it was from Dennenberg. Casey thought it odd that he would still be writing to the firm when he had taken his complaint to her office. A glance at the postmark told Casey that the letter had been mailed more than two weeks earlier. Obviously it must have walked, she thought cynically. The post office promised delivery despite rain or sleet, but said nothing about being on time.

Casey decided to show the letter to Simon later, just to see his reaction. It might help her, she hoped. Certainly *something* had to help her on the professional level. On the personal level she knew she was beyond help. She loved Simon whether or not he were involved in something illegal, and she was resolved to stand by him—*if* he would have her once he found out about the way she had been deceiving him.

If. The word loomed twelve feet tall. Could a man's ego withstand being lied to the way she had lied to him? These were no little white lies that were involved here. These were big, glaring black ones.

And what if *he's* lying? Her little voice proposed. What if he's only after you for your money? The money that you don't have.

One thing at a time, she told herself. First the big hurdle, then the little one.

The sound of the door opening behind her made her jump. She jerked her head around to see Ethan looking at her, an unfathomable expression on his face.

"You certainly do get involved in your work, don't you?" he commented.

"I was just reading," she said almost defensively, trying to sound casual. "About the types of coins you handle," she clarified, nodding toward the invoice pile. "It certainly is impressive."

"Yes, it is, isn't it?" She could glean nothing from his tone. He'd be a wonder playing poker, she thought. "We bought up a lot of impressive pieces at the last auction as well."

"Oh?" she asked, trying very hard to sustain the conversation. After all, the more you got a person to talk, the more likely you were to learn something, and she desperately wanted to learn anything that might help clear Simon and implicate someone else—even his twin brother. "I thought Simon only bought two coins."

"That was on the second night. The night, I believe, when he met you." It sounded as if he thought the night would live forever in infamy. "We both went the first night. And the last two nights," he told her as he went to the file cabinet. He tried to open the top drawer, but it wouldn't yield. Appearing both embarrassed and annoyed, Ethan took a key from his vest pocket and unlocked the cabinet. "Simon," Ethan went on as he flipped through files, "bids for his clients, and I bid for mine."

"And between us both, we lick the platter clean," Simon said, paraphrasing the old nursery rhyme about Jack Sprat as he came out to join them. "Are you harassing our new secretary?" he asked, putting an affectionate hand on Casey's shoulder. Instinctively she reached up and touched his fingers. The pressure of his hand felt so reassuring. God, how she hated all this deception she was immersed in.

"Making her nervous, it appears. Maybe I look too much like you," Ethan said glibly.

"That's your good fortune," Simon informed him with a grin. "How's it going?" he asked Casey, looking back at her upturned face.

"There're a lot of statements to go back to accounting," Casey told him, pointing to one pile. "And these are the requests." She nodded at the less-than-neat pile of papers to her left.

"Good," Simon pronounced. "Requests are what keep us going. Have you any of your own?" he asked, his voice dropping to a seductive level.

"None that I can think of," she bantered back.

"Unusual lady," Ethan muttered into the recesses of the files as he pored over a folder, "not wanting something."

"Here, Ethan," Simon said, shoving the requests at him. Quickly Ethan spread the folder out flat in order to accept them all. "Make yourself useful. See what you can do about filling these."

Ethan left, grumbling something under his breath.

"Well, that takes care of him for a while," Simon told Casey lightly. "Now, on to you and your education."

"My what?" she asked, noticing that he was holding a slim black attaché case. It was the same one that Ethan had carried so possessively at the airport. It had spent the duration of the flight resting across his lap.

"Your education," Simon repeated with a smile.

"You said you were interested in investing in coins, remember?"

Almost dumbly, Casey nodded, wondering what Simon had in mind. Was he going to whip out a selection for her there and then, like one of the street vendors who tried to sell their wares on Fifth Avenue near Saint Patrick's Cathedral?

"I thought you might like to come along with me when I put these away in our safety deposit boxes at the bank. There are several coins I'd like to show you," he told her.

Said the spider to the fly, she ended mentally. She flashed Simon a bright smile. "That would be fine, but I haven't finished opening the mail yet."

He waved her protest aside. "That can keep until this afternoon. I'll get Ethan to call up Ginny from accounting and she'll take over the desk while you're gone." With that he stepped inside his brother's office for a moment. Casey took that opportunity to slip Dennenberg's letter inside her purse and pat her hair into place.

"All set," Simon told her, reemerging. He took her hand as they left.

The woman at the bank who led the way into the vault smiled enviously at Casey as she and Simon went through the steel doors. Simon indicated which of Ashford and Ashford's twelve large safety deposit boxes he wanted. As both the bank employee and Simon inserted their keys, the locks sprang open and Simon lifted the long, wide box out.

"This way, please," the woman said, leading the way to one of the private viewing booths. "Ring the buzzer if you need any assistance," she went on, pointing to the white button that protruded from the otherwise featureless table top. That and a chair were the only two articles of furniture within the small, well-lit cubicle. The woman closed the door and they were left entirely alone in the darkly panelled room.

Casey looked around. "I feel like I'm in a black velvet box," she muttered.

Simon gently put the safety deposit box down and set the attaché case next to it. He paused a moment before opening either.

"Makes you feel as if you're in some kind of time capsule, doesn't it?" he said, following up on her comment. "They'd probably leave us in here for as long as we wanted," he teased, coming closer to her and slipping his arms around her from behind.

"Do I have to ring for assistance?" Casey asked, nodding toward the white button.

"You don't need any assistance," Simon assured her, nibbling on her ear. "You do just fine on your own."

"Do you do this with all your secretaries?" she asked, attempting to check the hot, sizzling sensation taking hold of her.

"Only the gorgeous ones with fiery hair," he answered, as his tongue outlined the outer edge of her ear. She felt her excitement mounting.

"My education, remember?" she murmured between lips that were having an exceedingly large amount of difficulty in forming the words.

"Mmm, you're ready for a Ph.D." His progress had taken him to the rim of her chin.

"If the door springs open for some reason…we're going to be…awfully embarrassed," she breathed, almost past the point where she would even notice if someone else came in. He was like a narcotic. The more she had, the more she craved. Even as she spoke the words, he raised his hands slightly from her waist to the full thrust of her breasts.

Simon raised his mouth from its seemingly relentless journey. His mischievous eyes gleamed above her. "I'm never embarrassed about anything. But you have a point. One more moment of drinking in the luscious sweetness of your mouth and I would be compelled to use this table in a way it was never intended to be used," he told her with a wink and then released her.

Almost reluctantly Casey stepped out of the circle of his arms. She took a deep breath and then sighed audibly. "You must be a lot of fun at office Christmas parties," she quipped, trying desperately to achieve a lighter air.

Simon just smiled wickedly.

Tearing her eyes away from his, Casey looked at the attaché case. "Open it," she prodded. "I'm dying for a peek."

"So am I," he told her. The way he said it, she knew that he wasn't talking about the coins that lay within the case. "Feast your eyes on these." With that he snapped open the two locks on the case and threw back the black leather lid.

A myriad of neatly housed coins shone up at her. Casey didn't know where to cast her attention first. Simon saw her unabashed interest and launched into a narrative on his favorite subject.

"The auction that we attended in New York had an excellent selection of half dollars and quarter dollars, as well as early gold coins. The night we were there together I obtained a gold coin for a client who

I know will be interested. The 1808 Quarter Eagle is
for my own collection. When Ethan was bidding, he
was successful in getting quite a few expensive beau-
ties,'' Simon told her, taking the coins out one at a
time and putting them in pre-arranged slots inside the
safety deposit box. ''At one time most people collected a particular series of coins, as you did with
your Lincoln cents. But now that's become too expensive an undertaking for most collectors, what with
the prices of coins escalating the way they have in
the past ten years. What most people do now is type
collecting. That is to say, they put together a set of
each type and variety of a specific American coin that
was minted. For example, to get all the different major types and varieties of quarter dollars, a collector
would have to obtain twelve different pieces. The
most difficult type to collect would be the 1796
Draped Bust type. It was only minted for one year,
with a total output of only 6,146 coins.'' He paused
for a moment to see if he were boring her. The avid
look of attention on her face told him he wasn't, and
he continued, taking out another plastic-encased quarter and holding it out for her perusal. ''Look at one
of the coins Ethan got. The surfaces are prooflike,
displaying a range of natural pastel colors. There's
absolutely no sign of rubbing or abrasions.'' He
turned it over. ''The reverse side is a bit weakly
struck, though.''

''It is?'' she asked. ''How can you tell?''

''Well, here,'' he pointed. ''The eagle's head isn't
sharply defined. That's typical of this design. A well-
struck example, showing all the minute details of the
eagle, if such a coin exists, would be worth a fortune.

As it is, this coin will probably sell for about thirty thousand dollars.''

The price took her breath away for a moment. ''Is that the kind of coin you want me to invest in?'' she finally managed to ask.

''No, that's a bit too expensive to start with,'' he told her. ''I have something better in mind for you—coinwise and otherwise.'' The twinkle in his eyes danced. ''Here, let me lay out a complete type set of quarters and half dollars for you. Between what Ethan obtained at the auction and what we have in this box, we should be able to do that. There are twenty-one pieces in all.'' He took a moment, then said, ''There they are, in beautifully uncirculated condition.''

Casey looked them over carefully. ''They really are beautiful,'' she agreed.

''A complete type set of all the American coins minted, including all the gold, copper and silver coins, would total one hundred and fifteen.'' He began to put the coins back, making sure that they were returned to their proper places. ''The twentieth century coins, like the Walking Liberty Half Dollar, the Standing Liberty Quarter, the Mercury Dime and the Buffalo Nickel, are all excellent areas of investment, besides being the most beautiful group of American coins ever minted. We can talk more about that after I finish,'' he promised.

Casey watched as Simon transferred more of the plastic-encased coins from the case to neatly designated places within the safety deposit box, all the while continuing his narrative about the coins' origins. It amazed her how much he knew.

''Wait here a minute,'' he said, pressing the buzzer. When he opened the door, admitting the sights and sounds of the bank, the teller stood waiting to help him. Casey doubted that most people would have gotten such service. But then, most people didn't look like Simon.

Casey was left alone in the small room for a few minutes before Simon returned, another huge safety deposit box held tightly in his hands. The entire process was repeated five more times, and lasted almost an hour.

"How do you keep track of everything?" Casey marveled when he had finally emptied the attaché case.

"All this was extensively catalogued and photographed," he told her as he returned the last box to the large, gaping hole in the metal wall. He pocketed his key carefully before walking out of the vault.

The clang of the iron bars slamming shut behind them rang in Casey's ears as she asked, "Photographed?"

Simon nodded, guiding her past an enormous line of customers. She realized that it was noon.

"That's one of Ethan's functions," he told her, pushing open the glass door. The gold lettering proclaiming the bank's name gleamed in the noonday sun.

Casey waited to say that she was glad Ethan was good for something, but kept the biting remark to herself and listened.

"Ethan takes all the photographs of the coins, both for our files and the monthly newsletter. Lunch?" he asked as they forged their way through the sea of people on the sidewalk.

His words brought an almost immediate response from her stomach. It reminded her that she had left the table without eating very much of anything that morning.

"Don't we have to be getting back? Ethan made it sound as if we were leaving a sinking ship."

"Ethan always makes it sound that way. The ship'll hold until we get back, and what good would two half-starved sailors be, right?" he teased, leading her down the busy street.

"Right," she affirmed, her stomach seconding the motion.

Ten

Lunch had turned out to be a leisurely meal. Casey had chosen to use the time to ply Simon with questions about how the business worked and what he and Ethan actually did. She had hoped that somewhere within his answers she would be able to find something to help her bring an end to the case. She had realized that she would never know a moment's peace until it was laid to rest.

When they had stepped into a very posh, soothingly lit restaurant furnished with heavy oak tables and leather-upholstered seats, Casey had decided that it was the perfect setting in which to undertake her task.

"You said you kept a catalogue of all your coins," she had prodded, stirring the tiny pink straw in her strawberry colada.

"Couldn't operate without one. With twelve safety deposit boxes, we'd never know where anything was if it wasn't catalogued. I do the write-ups. Ethan takes the pictures.'' He took a long sip of his bourbon and water, his eyes riveted to her.

Casey looked down at her drink. ''What sort of write-ups?'' she asked.

''Describing any distinguishing marks that might be found on the coin. Whether or not it's particularly clean, the quality of the strike, whether it's brilliant or has taken on various colors.'' The ice cubes in his drink tinkled as he raised his glass and took another sip. ''That way we can tell our customers exactly what they're getting,'' he finished.

''Do you do the actual grading?'' she asked, coming to the heart of the matter. Her throat felt parched. An extra long sip of her drink didn't rectify the matter any.

''It's a combined effort. Ethan, Uncle Jack and I confer about any coins that look as if they might be open to question. Grading,'' he told her, ''is a subjective process. The decision as to whether to label a coin MS63, MS65 or even higher might vary from person to person. The hardest part for a coin dealer is seeing the difference between the AU coins and the MS coins.''

Casey knew that AU stood for Almost Uncirculated, and that MS referred to the coins that were Mint State, having come from the mint where they were formed without having seen any circulation whatsoever. She also knew that the difference in price between the two categories could be astronomical. She looked at Simon for a long moment. Did he sometimes allow the ''subjective process'' to be an excuse for mislabeling a coin, taking it out of one realm and promoting it to a higher class? She recalled the letter in her purse and frowned. How many more letters like that had come across Simon's desk without ever reaching her department?

"That sounds as if it'd keep you pretty busy," she commented, wanting to keep the conversation going.

"Not really," he replied as the waitress came over to take their order. "I've got a host of other things to keep me busy, though."

Like defrauding people? She wondered miserably. "Such as?" she prodded.

"You certainly are an inquisitive one," he laughed. Casey tried not to wince. "I'll have a steak," he told the waitress. Casey nodded when he looked toward her. "Make that two," he added, surrendering his menu.

Casey followed suit, waiting for Simon to continue and hoping that her questions were sufficiently inno-cent-sounding not to raise his suspicions.

"Where were we?" he asked after the waitress had left.

"You were telling me what keeps you busy."

"Well, there are a lot of details to follow up on. There's the newsletter to our clients, giving them the latest data from the field and updating our holdings for them. We include a list of coins in each issue, complete with pictures, so that they can get an idea of the quality of the coin and associate it with the description below it. It gives them a feel for the coin, so to speak. And one picture," he winked, "is worth a thousand words. It also attracts more customers," he added.

As she listened to Simon talk, Casey could see how Dennenberg had been lulled into believing that he was dealing with a reputable firm. On the other hand, if what Simon said were true, how could he have attempted to substitute lesser coins for the ones ordered and hoped to get away with it? It just didn't make any sense. Simon didn't strike her as a fool, perhaps a little devil-may-care, but definitely not a fool.

"All that takes a lot of reading on Ethan's part. The newsletter is his baby," Simon told her with a smile.

"And what do you do?" Casey asked. "When you're not seducing prospective coin collectors, I mean."

"Most, I've found, are not my type." He gave her an affectionate smile. He saw the waitress approach, and he indicated their empty glasses. "Another round?" he asked Casey.

Why not? It would make him more relaxed and more trusting, she told herself as she nodded affirmatively.

"Two more of the same," he told the woman. When she had gone, he went on. "I'm in charge of keeping track of the various auctions going on across the country. It's the best way I know of for keeping abreast of current coin prices. Ethan and I both attend a good many auctions, sometimes acting as representatives for some of our wealthier clients who don't have the time or inclination to attend themselves. That's one of the best parts of this business, at least as far as I'm concerned. It's like getting a paid holiday to do what I enjoy best. Well, almost best," he amended. She felt his leg pressing against hers beneath the table and forced herself not to react accordingly. "We're going to Europe soon on our annual scouting trip. Would you like to come?"

She wondered if by the time he was ready to leave

he would still *want* to take her. "Sure," she said enthusiastically. "But what do you mean by 'scouting'?"

"We look for American gold coins that have found their way overseas in bank transactions. In addition, we have various connections in the gold coin market, and this year we're thinking of expanding into European coins, as well. Lately we've acquired a growing clientele who are interested in European coins from the sixteenth through the eighteenth centuries. That's what makes this business so exciting. It's always growing. And I get to see all the coins before they're mailed out."

"You really love your job, don't you?"

"Can't think of anything else I'd rather be doing," he said as the waitress placed his drink before him. "But I think 'love' is a strong word. It should only be reserved for very special occasions."

For a moment Casey stared into his eyes, feeling herself being drawn toward him the way a piece of iron was drawn to a magnet. How could she jeopardize the promise she saw shining in his gaze? But she knew she was going to have to. She had to broach the subject of Dennenberg's letter of complaint, but her courage was failing her.

Simon seemed not to notice. His tone turned more professional as he said, "Let me tell you something about investing in coins. I think you might find this particular coin interesting. As a matter of fact, it happens to be one of my favorites—the Indian Head Nickel, more commonly known as the Buffalo Nickel."

"I remember those," she interjected.

The waitress served their steaks. Simon cut into

both his meal and his topic with equal relish. "It's the only truly American coin we have."

Casey shook her head. "I don't understand. Aren't all the coins minted here?"

"Yes, but I'm talking about the design."

"Aren't there several different coins that use the Indian head as a motif?" She knew for a fact that there were a number of coins that did.

"Yes, but this is the only one that had a real Indian model for it. Or, to be more accurate, three Indians. The other coins either had Caucasians modeling in headdresses, or bore artists' renditions of Indians. The designer of the Buffalo Nickel used the best of three actual Indians: Iron Trail, who, by the way, was at the Little Big Horn; Two Moons, a Cheyenne chief; and Chief John Big Tree, who was an Iroquois. All three became performers in Wild West shows. Big Tree even made it to the movies, attacking the likes of Tom Mix and good old Hopalong Cassidy."

"How about the buffalo? Or is he a composite too?" Casey asked laughingly as she took a bite of her own steak.

"No, as a matter of fact, he was one of your fellow New Yorkers." Casey arched an eyebrow as Simon laughed. "His name was Black Diamond, and he lived at the New York Zoological Gardens, which was just about the only safe place to be back then if you were a buffalo. Entire herds fell, slaughtered for fun by hunters out West. Unfortunately, Black Diamond didn't stay safe for long. Two years after the coin was minted, he was slaughtered for food."

"I didn't think New Yorkers were that desperate for food."

"That was 1915, and buffalo meat was a luxury

back East. Anyway, by the time the coin made its debut in 1913 it was regarded as a commemorative coin, a symbol of the fading West and the lost buffalo.''

Casey listened quietly, finding this kind of information fascinating. She had always found the history behind coins interesting. As they ate, Simon went on to talk about other areas of investment that he thought would suit her, quoting some current coin prices to her. Some of them would have given her quite a jolt had she not been intent on looking blasé when he mentioned money. She could definitely see why so many people turned to coin dealers to help them with their collections. There was just too much to know. She could also see how tempting it would be to a dealer to perpetrate fraud.

It was only after their plates were cleared away and they were lingering over their coffee that Casey found the nerve to bring up the matter of Dennenberg's letter.

''Oh, I nearly forgot to give you this,'' Casey said, thrusting the letter toward him. She had decided that an innocent, blunt approach would be the best way to handle this. She watched Simon peruse the letter. His brows furrowed, forming a continuous, angry dark line across his forehead.

''Him again,'' he muttered, folding the letter and stuffing it back into the envelope. He pocketed it and stared down into his cup of coffee for a moment without speaking.

''Do you get this kind of letter often?'' Casey asked, wondering if she sounded too inquisitive.

Simon shrugged. ''Every business has its share of problems. We've had a couple of letters of complaint from time to time. Lately, though, it seems as if we've had more than our share," he acknowledged.

"Oh?" she queried, toying with her coffee cup and avoiding his eyes entirely. She felt sure that he would see right through her. "What do you do about it?"

"Nothing, usually," he told her noncommittally. "If the customer doesn't return the coins during the grace period, it becomes their problem. We allow a full four weeks for our clients to return any coins they're dissatisfied with. But, like I said, our coins are graded by all three of us, and Uncle Jack's conducted a number of seminars dealing with numismatics in general and coin grading in particular. He's really very sharp. He taught me everything I know, and I have the utmost faith in his judgment. Almost all of our customers are satisfied. We get very few returns. I see no reason to reconsider a grade because some crank has nothing better to do than complain six months after he's bought a coin."

"What happens if some crank thinks he's been bilked out of twenty-five thousand dollars?" she asked, her fingertips feeling icy cold as she pursued the matter.

Simon stared at her intently for a moment. Did he suspect anything? Were they playing cat and mouse? "You mean this letter?" he finally asked, nodding toward his pocket.

Casey nodded.

"He hasn't been," Simon said with a finality that was meant to close the topic forever.

But it didn't. Casey knew that if she didn't come up with something soon, the entire matter would be put into the hands of the FBI, who wouldn't view this case with the same personal feelings she did. Maybe that's just the trouble, her little voice piped up. Her feelings were coloring the evidence.

What evidence? She thought as she found herself walking outside in the bright sunshine. Simon was holding her hand. Just because he had scowled when he read Dennenberg's letter, it didn't mean he was guilty. She had scowled at Dennenberg herself, and she was hardly at fault.

Casey stole a look at Simon's face. Surely he had to know that he had a lot at stake here. Was his attitude due to the fact that he knew he could stand up to a close scrutiny? Or did it come from the hope that if he disregarded the situation, it would blow over and he could go on with business as usual, whatever that might entail?

But there had been more than one letter, more than one complaint. And there was also the matter of the stolen coin which had been sold through Simon's firm. Could he have been an innocent dupe in that, as well?

Her logical little voice said no. Her inner soul prayed to find another answer.

They returned just as Ethan was walking into his office, a stack of current numismatic periodicals tucked under his arm. He gave them both a critical look, making an exaggerated show of looking at his wristwatch before closing the door behind him.

"Get this feeling that our coach has just turned back into a pumpkin?" Simon asked wryly as Casey headed for her desk.

"We *were* gone a long time," she pointed out. Ginny-from-accounting was nowhere in sight. Casey wondered if that were part of the reason for Ethan's humorless glare.

"Ah, so now you're defending him," Simon laughed. "Keep it up; you'll get on Ethan's good side yet."

Casey seriously doubted that Ethan *had* a good side, at least as far as she was concerned. For the rest of the day, each time Ethan emerged from his office, no matter where he was going, Casey couldn't escape the feeling that Ethan clearly resented having her there. For the hundredth time, Casey wondered why.

At the end of the day Casey was no closer to knowing something useful about the case than she had been that morning. She had struck up several conversations with various employees from the shipping department, and with Ginny-from-accounting, who had finally made a personal appearance, but her efforts had yielded nothing. Everyone seemed to like Simon and to have a grudging respect for Ethan, who, despite his gloomy attitude, was not a tyrant to work for. Casey had nothing to go on.

"Aren't you too tired?" Casey asked as Simon teasingly tugged at the zipper of her dress. It was past two in the morning, and she had thought that Simon would go right to sleep once they had come home. But he had followed her to her room, a very awake glint in his eye. A warm, expectant glow spread over her body, growing in magnitude as the zipper descended.

"I'll never be too tired," he murmured, letting her dress drop to the floor. He pulled her against him, his shirt already unbuttoned and his chest waiting for the delectable imprint of her breasts. "Mmmm." Just the

simple sound of satisfaction he made thrilled Casey.
"As a matter of fact," he said against her neck, his
breath tickling her, "I need something to help me
unwind."

"Oh, so now I'm a tranquilizer, am I?" she teased,
stepping back as she looked up into his face. Casey
twined her fingers into his hair, loving the silky sensation. "Shall we bottle me and make a fortune?"
she suggested mischievously. "One dose guaranteed
to put you to sleep no matter what."

"Nope," Simon said solemnly, his hands playfully
caressing her breasts, fanning the fires of her excitement. "The label should read: For Simon Ashford's
private use only. Do not touch—under pain of death."

Did that mean he truly wanted her forever? Or was
that just something to be said in the height of delicious foreplay? Casey didn't have much time to de-
bate the subject as Simon expertly freed her of her
remaining garments and availed himself of her
charms.

Once again Casey found heaven in Simon's arms
that night. His lovemaking seemed to make her shed
her outer trappings, her sense of logic, until all that
was left behind belonged to love. But while Simon
slept next to her, his soft, rhythmic breathing falling
like music on her ears, Casey remained awake with
her persistent doubts.

She reached out and touched his hair, brushing it
back from his forehead. The gesture was filled with
love. And so was she.

"What have I gotten myself into?" she murmured,
sighing and hugging her knees. "Oh, what a tangle
web we weave, when first we practice to deceive"

wasn't just a trite saying, she thought to herself sadly. It had a great deal of truth to it. She wished with all her heart that she had never met Dennenberg, never worked for the postal service, never started any of this. Why couldn't life be uncomplicated? Why hadn't she just gone to the auction like a true coin lover and bumped into Simon of her own accord?

Next to her, Simon stirred. She felt his thigh rub against her, and electricity shot quickly through her. This feeling was magnificent. She had never been so attracted to anyone before, so in love before. Why couldn't she be allowed to enjoy it?

"Damn," she muttered.

One sleepy blue eye opened in response to her comment, to be followed by the other. "No fair," he murmured, his voice still thick with sleep. "Employees are not supposed to watch the boss when he sleeps."

"I'm not an employee," she reminded him, loving the sound of his voice. "I'm a volunteer."

Simon rose slightly on his elbow as he looked at her. "Okay, volunteer something."

"Simon," Casey protested with a laugh, "we've just made love twice."

"The woman has a mind like an accountant," Simon proclaimed to the air. "Well," he said, sitting up for a moment, "I'm awake."

"Right."

"And you're awake."

"So it seems."

"Time is an awful thing to waste."

"I'm sure Ethan would agree," she said, trying hard to keep a straight face.

"Let Ethan find his own way to fill up his nights," Simon said, pulling her back down to a horizontal position. Her hair flowed like a voluminous, silken cloud, fanning out about her head.

"Most people sleep," she pointed out, giggling as he tickled her navel with the swift, darting flickers of his tongue.

"Most people don't have you lying next to them," he countered, continuing his journey, spanning the breadth of her abdomen.

Casey felt her hips moving involuntarily as she tried to hold very still and savor the delicious feeling filtering all through her. As he came closer and closer to her thighs Casey couldn't stifle the explosion of passion that made her moan and move beneath his tantalizing tongue. His breath on her skin stoked the fire that was already raging within her. She wound her fingers in his hair, pressing him against her.

When had she ever known ecstasy like this? Never, the answer came, throbbing through her.

"More." Was that her voice? It sounded so breathless. Her cry came unbidden when Simon paused for an instant in his plundering of her body. Plundering. How could she think of him as plundering, when she was offering herself to him so willingly?

Casey arched her hips, feeling as if she would never be satisfied, wanting more, needing more. It was as if she were storing up every sensation against a future time, a time when Simon would no longer be with her.

She felt his hands cease kneading her buttocks and his mouth leave the golden valley he had so completely conquered. Taking a deep breath, Casey opened her eyes to find Simon's compellingly hand-some face filling every corner of her vision.

"Still rather be sleeping?" he asked, filling his hands with her hair.

"I never said that," she corrected huskily. "I said most people sleep at night."

He nipped a rose-tipped nipple, making it harden even more, then looked back up at her, the soul of innocence. "So you want me to go to sleep?"

"Don't you dare," she ordered. She felt the glo-rious shifting of his hips as his weight came over her. The heat of his flesh branded her.

"Then what do you want?" he teased.

"Let me show you," she answered, reaching up and cupping his face in her hands. She brought his mouth down to hers and lost herself in the fiery sweet-ness of his kiss.

But when would it end? her mind demanded. When would the doors of paradise be forever shut to her? She thought of abandoning her scheme, but it was too late. She was already enmeshed. When the time came, it would be better that Simon learned about her in-volvement in the case from her own lips. Lips, she thought in despair, that he might never want to kiss again.

Her fears marred the ecstasy that should have been hers.

The next two days were like the first, except that late afternoon of the second day brought an invitation. Simon came out of his office and sat down on her desktop.

"You're squashing your order forms," Casey told him. Simon shifted his weight as she extracted the sheets from under him. "Now then, what can I do for you?" she asked, looking up.

He traced the outline of her face with his fingers. "Lots of things—all of them horribly wicked and depraved. I'll get back to you about them later," he promised with a wink. "But right now, I thought I'd pass on an invitation to you."

"You already have."

"No, not that kind, you vixen," he laughed. "This is for a party."

A party? She took mental inventory of the clothes she had brought with her. Was it going to be formal? Her only long dress was hanging in her closet back home, crushed against a jogging outfit she never wore. "I don't have anything to wear," she lamented.

"That should be interesting," Ethan commented, coming out to join them. He looked a little less hostile than he had on the first two days, and Casey wondered if he were getting used to her, or if his spirits were high for some other reason.

"Go like that," Simon said, jumping in on the comment, "and we'll never make the party."

"I feel like I'm outnumbered here," she said, looking from one to the other.

"You are, my sweet," Simon said, kissing the top of her head. "But as to your worries, this is strictly informal. Just a bunch of old numismatists and their wives getting together and comparing the killings they've made recently."

"If you think fishermen exaggerate about 'the one that got away,' you should hear coin dealers talk," Ethan told her. He glanced down at the pile of papers Casey was still holding. "What are those?"

"More order forms," Casey told him.

Ethan sighed as he put out his hand. "Give them here." Casey complied, and he turned to his brother. "Simon, did you put an ad in the newspaper for someone to replace Palmer?" he asked, leafing impatiently through the papers Casey had handed to him and already heading for his own office.

"It ran this morning, Ethan," Simon called after his brother. "If you get bogged down, Uncle Jack said he'd come by to help you out."

But Ethan had already closed the door.

"Isn't he coming?" Casey wanted to know as they walked to the outer door.

"Ethan doesn't like to leave until all the loose ends are tied for the night. Some times he stays here until all hours."

"But you don't." It wasn't a question. It was a statement.

"No, I have other things to occupy my time," he told her with a mocking leer.

"Like the party?" she asked coyly, loving the way they were able to banter so casually.

Simon reached over and pressed the elevator button, his forearm brushing against her breast. "Like you and how many times we can make love tonight." The elevator arrived and they got on, sharing the space with a severe-looking older woman. Casey gave Simon a glance that had been intended to silence him. Simon merely lowered his voice. "You're going to make a shriveled old man out of me before my time," he vowed, "but I'll die in your bed with a smile on my face."

The woman looked sharply at both of them before she turned her cold eyes around and faced forward.

Simon looked as if he were having trouble keeping his laughter to himself.

Casey made do with her cocktail dress, hoping that Simon was right about the party being casual. She didn't want to embarrass him by being underdressed. The details of her preparations occupied her mind, and she pushed her problems out of the way—or so she thought, until she nearly jabbed out her eye with the eyeshadow brush and realized that her right eyelid was several shades darker than her left one.

"Wonderful, once you leave here, you can go out and haunt houses," she told herself, taking a tissue and wiping off the excess color from her eyelid. She managed to smear some on her cheek, making her look as if she had been the loser in a fistfight. Things, she decided, were definitely not going her way. She started all over again.

Time was growing short, she knew. There she was, running off to a party when she should be looking for evidence that could clear Simon. She tried to comfort herself by pointing out that there was nothing she could do that night, since Ethan was staying late at the office. There would be no chance to find anything there.

Take heart, Mata Hari, she thought with a false note of brightness. There's always tomorrow.

But she didn't have very many tomorrows left.

Eleven

The party, she thought later that night, had been wonderful. She had gotten along far better with all of Simon's friends than she had imagined she would. There had been none of that awkwardness that usually separated the "new kid on the block" from an established group of friends. They welcomed her with unabashed heartiness. Casey would have expected people whose voices ranged from an easy drawl to a pronounced twang to look askance at someone from the East Coast. She had expected, she realized, a roomful of Ethans. But the same hospitality she had gotten from Uncle Jack was gratifyingly present amid the seven couples at the party. Casey had a good time.

She had an even better time when she and Simon returned home; though she had initially tried to prevent it. As she had realized earlier, time was running out. Her week was almost up, and she knew that unless a miracle was in the offing, Simon would very shortly be under federal investigation. Even if he were innocent, as she devoutly hoped, unfavorable attention would be drawn to his firm and financial disaster might result. Coin collectors tended to shy away from places touched with a hint of fraud, as well they might. And news of such an inquiry would spread, via the coin periodicals, to all the serious collectors. Simon could very well find himself on the brink of ruin, even if he were innocent.

And, she unhappily admitted, he might not be innocent.

All these thoughts had faded into the background during the party, while she was enjoying the company of Simon's friends. But by the time they returned to his house the calming effect of the evening slipped away. Once again she found herself besieged by her private demons. She suppressed an urge to do the only thing that was beginning to make any sense to her: tell Simon everything. But she was so afraid of the consequences that she couldn't find words with which to make her confession.

Instead she bit her lip and left Simon downstairs talking to Uncle Jack, who had waylaid them on their way in.

Casey slid her hand along the carved wooden bannister as she slowly went up the stairs, her departure seemingly unnoticed by the men who stood in the foyer, debating the validity of some point of coin grading. She tried to memorize everything about the house, knowing that soon she would be back at her desk in New York, her "holiday" over. Her dream over. And all this *was* nothing more than a dream, she told herself as she walked through the door of her room and closed it listlessly behind her. A wonderful, Cinderella-type dream. Princes didn't marry working girls. That was for fairy tales.

"Princes," she murmured aloud. "Maybe the Prince of Thieves."

She didn't care. She'd take him any way she could get him. Fat chance, she thought, staring unseeingly at her reflection in the oval mirror as she stripped off her dress and tossed it carelessly onto a nearby chair. The chair caught the underwear she hurled unhappily at it, as well. The pantyhose floated down short of their mark. You think he'll have you after he knows you were spying on him? Her mind demanded cruelly.

But he'd understand, she tried to tell herself desperately, looking into the haunted eyes that stared back at her from the mirror. Understand what? That she had lied to him? That every shred of what she had told him about herself had been a lie designed to trap him?

She drew the nightgown over her head and let it fall like an aqua cloud around her thighs as she flounced miserably down on her bed. Frustrated tears surfaced. Oh great, now she was going to cry. Well, crying isn't going to do you any good, dummy, she scolded herself. You got yourself into this, Super Sleuth. You thought you could cope with the situation. But you can't. Any way you cut it, you can't.

Casey stared down at her hands, which were kneading the nylon layers of her nightgown. She felt utterly miserable.

"Hey, don't look so sad. I'm sorry I kept you waiting."

Casey jerked her head up and saw Simon closing

the door behind him. When he turned around he was beaming at her.

"I promise to make it up to you, tired as I am." He stood in front of her for a moment, regarding her with a tender expression. "You have a way of bringing out the best in me."

Oh, Simon, if you only knew, she thought, the words bringing a throbbing ache to her throat. She almost started to tell him right then and there. But the words still refused to come. She knew that they would cut her off from paradise.

Simon lifted her chin so he could get a better look at her face. "What's this? Has the lady been crying?" he asked. He sat down on the bed next to her. His tone growing less playful. "What's wrong?"

But Casey only shook her head in response, not trusting her lips to form any words that would not betray her.

Simon drew her into his arms. The warmth she found there was so wonderful, so comforting. She tried to push him away, but when he drew her closer she gave in. If only she could be free of her tortuous thoughts...

He tilted her head back slightly with his hand, his fingers slipping along the white expanse of her throat. Simon kissed her lips so lightly, his mouth just brushing hers. The feathery movement generated an almost unbearable sweetness. Her body moved toward him, opening like a thirsty flower in his presence. She needed to get all she could of the rapture he could give her. Soon there would be no more; what she took here would have to last her for a long, long time.

She kissed him almost with a vengeance.

"Hey, what is it?" Simon repeated, holding her for

a moment at arms' length and looking into her face, as if to find a clue to her strange behavior.

Please, she thought, please don't ask any questions. "I've missed you," she said with a false laugh, lacing her fingers about his neck.

Simon furrowed his brow a little, as if he were studying her remark; then he apparently tossed it aside as he laughed. "You're a mystery, Casey Bennett. Uncle Jack warned me about ladies like you," he teased playfully, running his fingers through her long hair.

"Then you should have stayed downstairs with Uncle Jack," she said, raising her mouth to his and kissing him.

"The hell I should have," Simon murmured against her lips before he got lost in her kiss.

Casey knew that the more she let herself love Simon, the worse it would be for her when she was left without him. But she hadn't the strength or the desire to pay heed to her own warning. She was like a moth gliding toward the flame. Nothing else mattered. Disaster and heartache waited just beyond the limits of her world, but tonight...tonight she ran head-on into the flame.

Simon moved to pick her up into his arms, but Casey shook her head, even while their lips were joined. Simon opened his eyes and looked at the face that was so close to his own.

"No?" he asked, puzzled.

"Not yet," she breathed, her long, slender fingers removing his jacket for him. "We've got to get rid of these first."

"You little minx," he said, his voice throbbing with affection. "You're only after me for my body."

"Right," she quipped, undoing his tie and pulling it off smoothly. She threw it in the general direction of his jacket. Her eyes were locked with his as she began unbuttoning his salmon-colored shirt, taking her time. She felt his heart beat beneath her fingers as each button slipped out of its hole. When she reached his silver belt buckle she tugged the rest of the shirt out and then slid it off his shoulders. For a moment she pressed herself against his warm chest, loving the sensation as the hair caressed her with each breath he took. But as Simon's arms began to encircle her, Casey pulled back.

"No, not yet," she whispered, her eyes twinkling and masking the bittersweet pain she was experiencing. Her hand lingered a moment against the belt buckle, gliding wickedly along the swirling design on it and dipping a little beneath it.

"I never knew you had such a wicked side to you," Simon murmured, his words stifling a purr of pleasure.

"There are a lot of things you don't know about me," she said ruefully, circling behind him so that he couldn't see her face.

"I'm willing to spend a lifetime finding out."

The whispered words made her stop for an instant, but she forced herself to go on. She pressed her breasts against his back as she embraced him. This time she worked on his belt in earnest, opening it so that she could feel her way to the button that held his dusky gray trousers in place. She heard him give up a soft moan as she did so, and his excitement telegraph itself back to her, rushing through her veins and making her nipples harden in anticipation of what was to come.

With measured movements Casey stroked the sides of his hips, then edged her hands slowly back to the heart of his desire. Her fingers flirted with the task of undressing him completely, and her own desire increased as she sensed Simon's reaction to her tantalizing play. She felt his back grow rigid against her, as if he were trying to exercise extreme control and not move a muscle until she had finished.

Moving forward, Casey came around to face him again. She placed her hands on the sides of his hips, her palms flat against him. Slowly she slid the fabric down until the trousers descended of their own accord.

Casey felt her pulse throbbing in her throat.

Simon kicked the trousers away, never once removing his eyes from her face. Casey could see tender desire mingled with yearning shining in the blue depths.

"Just my luck," he said, his voice thick and throaty. "I've fallen for Salome, reincarnated."

"Salome did the dance of the seven veils," she corrected him, intent on ridding Simon's lean, muscular body of its last confining shred of material. "This is a little different."

"That's why I like you," Simon told her, the words melting hoarsely into her hair as he buried his face there. He shivered as Casey pulled off his briefs. "You're different."

"In a class by myself," she replied, the flippant, almost bitter words finding their way to her lips without any conscious thought.

Simon took hold of her shoulders. "In a class with me," he said just before he kissed her hard, the emotion he had been restraining breaking free at last.

His breathing grew erratic, smothering every inch of her mouth with what seemed like an infinite number of kisses that threatened never to end. Casey felt as if she were drowning, and the sense of control she had maintained while stripping away Simon's clothing vanished so totally that it seemed as if it had never existed at all. She was his entirely.

Simon's hands felt as if they were scorching her as Casey realized through her blazing fog that he was now returning the favor and removing her nightgown. His movements were maddeningly slow, just as hers had been. Now it was her turn to be impatient, desiring that ultimate moment when their two bodies would be one.

She felt her sense of urgency grow, engulfing her, making her weak. Her knees buckled as her nightgown slipped down and away from her. He held her steady, his palms flat against her ribcage, pressing her against the length of his body. His hard contours imprinted themselves on her, fanning the endless yearning that smoldered inside her. Simon pushed her back gently, and she found herself on the bed, the coolness of the bedspread against her hot body sending goose bumps dancing along her flesh.

"Let me warm you up," Simon offered, raising himself over her and leaving an entwining pattern of kisses to mark the passage of his lips.

Tongues of fire licked at her. She burned with rapturous desire. Simon rained kisses on every thirsty part of her flesh: the instep of her foot; the tender area along her thigh, where he lingered so long she thought she would scream; the flat, taut terrain of her belly; and the heavy planes of her breasts. There his tongue worked magic as he coaxed her nipples to grow harder still as she writhed, and moaned his name. The ecstasy she was enduring drove her wild.

Simon had found every erotic, sensitive point her body possessed. She would have paid him back in kind had she had the strength to do so, but all she wanted was to have him claim her ultimately the way only he could.

"You're...making...me...crazy," she rasped, clutching at his hair with trembling fingers.

"The feeling is more than mutual," he told her in a voice that was as breathless as her own.

Casey pulled his head down, bringing his lips to hers. The phrase, "I love you," was smothered by the force of their kiss, and Casey wasn't sure whether the words had come from him or from her. She did know, though, that the emotion was hers. She knew that she would love him forever, knew that she needed him *now*.

Her desire was fulfilled within moments of her thought, the union of her body and his taking place amid flames of passion and bright rays of peace. This was the one place in the entire universe, she thought, where she belonged.

And it was the one place where, soon, she would not be able to be.

That was the first thought that burst upon her as she fell back to earth. With a strength she didn't know she had left, Casey held back the damning tears.

"You're full of surprises, Casey," Simon murmured against the point of her shoulder several minutes later.

"That's me, a regular grab bag," she said sarcastically. God, how she hated this mess she was in.

Her words brought a grin to Simon's face. "Is there

another surprise in there for me?'' he asked, propping himself up in order to look down at her face.

If you only knew, she thought sadly. If you only knew.

"My friends all like you," he told her, as his kisses alighted as delicately as butterflies on the skin above her breasts.

Casey hadn't thought she had any emotion left, and yet there it was, rising up once more to meet him. She was aware of the fact that his free hand was stroking the length of her body before hovering over her lower abdomen, making her quiver.

"I like them, too," she said with an effort, trying to keep her attention away from what Simon was doing.

"Stay a little longer," Simon coaxed. "We can make a full-fledged Texan out of you in two weeks." He kissed her cheek. "Stay." The words danced seductively along her cheekbone, radiating through her whole being.

"I...don't know if I can," she managed to say.

"Anything to call you back?" he asked.

"No," she lied, after a pause.

"Then stay."

Casey licked her lips, trying to remedy their sudden dryness. Simon captured the movement, coming down on her mouth, his own tongue meeting hers.

Casey gave herself up to the all consuming flames of passion once more.

The better their lovemaking grew, the sadder she became when she was alone. A melancholy feeling held her in its grip for the next two days, growing almost intolerable the morning of the second day. She

sat at her desk, listlessly sorting the pile of mail that
had arrived that morning. Both Simon and Ethan were
out, having gone to a meeting instead of the office.
She had volunteered to go in to the office without
them, and Jack himself had driven her over.

On the trip into the heart of the city Jack had done
most of the talking. She had tried to keep up her end
of the conversation, but found that words failed her,
and that she had trouble holding onto her thoughts.

"You know, you really don't have to do this,"
Jack had said suddenly.

Casey had realized that the older man was misin-
terpreting her lapses of silence as sullenness. "Oh,
no, I don't mind. I like keeping busy," she said with
a false note of gaiety. She saw the silhouette of the
now-familiar building just ahead and was grateful that
the ride was over.

"You sure? I could turn around and take you
home," Jack offered.

Home. Her mind tried to embrace the word. But it
wasn't home. Not *her* home. It was *his* home, and
soon she wasn't going to be welcome there. Casey
shook her head, a small, sad smile lifting the corners
of her mouth.

"No, really. I like helping you out." Right, helping
him right straight to jail. Some helper she was, she
taunted herself. She realized that the car had come to
a stop and she hadn't budged from the front seat.

Jack looked at her with the kind of concern she
would have associated with a real uncle. Maybe that
was why Simon loved him so much. "Are you all
right?" he wanted to know.

"I'm fine," she said brightly, the words sticking in
her throat. "Why shouldn't I be? Well, I'd better run.

Are you sure there'll be someone to let me in?'' she asked as she got out.

The shaggy head nodded. "Ginny from accounting comes in early on Fridays. She likes to make sure the week's work is all caught up."

Good old Ginny-from-accounting, Casey thought miserably as she rode up in the elevator by herself. Sure enough, when she knocked, Ginny was there to let her in.

"Boy, you look glum today," the thin, bespectacled woman said as she closed the door. "The routine getting to you?" she asked. The words were slightly patronizing, Casey noted. The woman had used the resentful tone of someone who worked for a living talking about the idle rich. Except that Casey wasn't rich. Or idle, for that matter.

She had to do *something* today, Casey told herself, sitting down at the desk that she had come to look on as hers. Both Simon and Ethan would be gone for the morning. Perhaps if she went through their offices she'd come up with some information that would solve the whole mess. She looked up to see that Ginny was still studying her. "No, the routine hasn't gotten to me," she practically snapped back. "I've just got a lot on my mind."

"Like what shade of nail polish to put on next," Ginny mumbled cattily as she disappeared back into the accounting department.

Casey sighed. "No, like how to put the final nail in my coffin."

Maybe a quick search of the files would clear everything up. Simon had said they kept pictures of all the coins. Surely they didn't toss them away right after a sale. Perhaps if she found the pictures of the coins Dennenberg and some of the other people on her list had purchased, she could glean something from them.

The more Casey thought about the idea, the better she liked it. Besides, it was the only course of action she could think of. Looking through other files had gotten her nowhere, and no one else had said or done anything to throw any light on the dark and dismal subject.

So there she sat, waiting for an opportunity to slip into Simon's office unobserved. Mechanically she sorted the mail, mentally taking inventory of the employees who came in, passing her desk. When the seventh one had gone off to the shipping department, Casey counted to ten and began to rise. Just then the front door opened. With an impatient sigh Casey sat down again and waited for the person, a short, prune-faced man with no chin, to approach her. As it turned out, he was a prospective client who wanted to view several coins before he purchased them. Casey explained that there were no coins on the premises. Standard procedure was to call for an appointment, giving Simon or Ethan enough time to get the coins in question out of the safety deposit box and bring them back for viewing.

The man was none too happy about that, but he was finally persuaded to make an appointment and left, grumbling about being a busy man himself and not having time for this sort of prima donna nonsense.

It took all kinds, Casey thought, watching him close the outer door behind him. She waited, half expecting him to return. But he didn't. She spent the next several minutes looking around nonchalantly, waiting for someone else to come by. No one did.

Finally Casey rose. Her hands and feet felt icy as she let herself into Simon's office and closed the door silently. She leaned against it, taking a deep breath, then nearly jumped out of her skin as the phone rang. She sprang for the desk, snatching the phone out of its cradle before the second ring was complete.

"Hello?" she breathed, trying to stop her hands from trembling. "Ashford and Ashford," she said after a moment, realizing that she had failed to identify the company.

"Oh, sorry, wrong number." The phone went dead in her hand. She put it back in its cradle, her heart thumping wildly in her chest. She could feel her shoulder muscles tightening from tension.

Hurriedly she went up to the wooden file cabinet in the corner. She found to her relief that, unlike the one outside, this one wasn't locked. The first drawer she tried slid open on well-oiled runners. Hastily Casey rummaged through first one folder and then another, hoping to discover the nature of the files and the system behind them.

So what'll you do if you do find something? her little voice asked, refusing to be stilled as her heart pounded. Do you destroy it? Or destroy Simon? The dilemma threatened to drive her mad. Perhaps if she went to Simon and made a clean breast of it, then tried to convince him to make good on his deals... But what about the theft? How could he "make good" on that?

Casey swallowed hard and refused to consider the matter any more. He wasn't guilty. He wasn't, she insisted. The photographs would vindicate him, she told herself, searching through the entire drawer.

No photographs. Casey slammed the drawer shut.

They might not even be in either Simon's or Ethan's office, she thought in despair. All she could do was keep trying, though. Quickly, she went on to the next drawer.

"Looking for something?"

Casey whirled around, a guilty look painted on her features. Her normally fertile imagination went completely blank as she took in the quizzical, disapproving look on Simon's face.

"Casey?" he asked, cocking his head. "What are you doing here?"

"I...I..." Dear God, what could she tell him? No ready lies sprang to her lips; nothing formed in her mind. She hadn't prepared anything, having felt safe in the knowledge that he and Ethan would be in the meeting with their client all morning.

He strode forward and gripped her hand, which still held a file. Loose pages tumbled to the deep pile carpet like autumn leaves.

"You're hurting me," she cried.

But he didn't release her. "Tell me what you're doing here," he insisted, his voice so cold that it frightened her.

What thoughts were crossing his mind? She wondered desperately. "What does it look like I'm doing?" she heard herself asking, her voice bouncing off the panelled walls and coming back to her.

"Spying," he growled.

Well, he had half of it, she thought in despair. He had to hear the rest of it. "I'm not. I mean, it's not what you think. Simon, I work for the postal service's Consumer Protection Division." She faltered, wishing he didn't look as if he hated her.

"Go on." His voice was deadly calm.

"We've gotten a number of complaints about coins that you've shipped through the mails. And someone just reported that one of your coins came from a collection that was stolen several months ago. Oh, Simon," she cried, reaching out to take his hand. She was eager to tell him that she didn't believe he was capable of that. She wanted to swear her undying love for him no matter *what* happened.

But he pulled his arm away from her. "Stop calling me Simon. I'm Ethan," he snapped.

Ethan! Then it wasn't too late, she thought frantically. She had to persuade Ethan not to tell his brother what she had blurted out. If she could only strike a bargain with him...

"I'm Simon."

Horror stricken, Casey turned around, her hopes dashing themselves on the rocks of despair. Simon, the real Simon, was standing in the doorway. A single tissue-wrapped rose was in his hand. He had heard everything. The look he wore was even more painful to her than his brother's, because his features registered his own pain—the pain of betrayal.

"So you thought I was responsible for the theft and came running down here to find some proof." The blue-gray eyes which had adored her now cut her down angrily. "The 'accidental' meeting at the auction, that first evening in your apartment, last night, they were all planned, weren't they?" he demanded harshly.

She shook her head, a sob clawing at her throat. She pressed her lips together, refusing to cry in front of him.

"I only went to see you at the auction. I didn't 'plan' on any of this. It just happened," she insisted.

Couldn't he see that? Couldn't he see that she
loved him, that she had given him everything she had
to give? Everything, her little voice whispered, but
the truth. And she had been afraid of that, afraid to
tell him who she was in the beginning, afraid to share
her identity in the end. She had been held captive by
her own web of lies.

"Pretty snappy undercover work they have you
people doing these days," Simon said bitterly.
"Here." He shoved the rose into her hand. "Happy
anniversary." He stalked out.

She had met him a week ago that day. The realization came to her and caused more pain than the
thorn that had stuck her as she grasped the flower.

Twelve

For a moment, Casey stood rooted to the spot, frozen by the sense of devastation she felt. For that one moment everything else disappeared and all Casey saw, all she was conscious of, was that Simon had left the office and, very probably, her life. Casey felt as if she were dying inside.

Somewhere along the outer edge of her awareness, she realized that Ethan was still standing there, looking at her wordlessly. She ran past him and fled.

Casey didn't remember getting her purse or how she had gotten down to the corner of the busy avenue. It was almost as if she were standing off to one side, watching some hollow creature wave for a taxi. Her gesture was stiff and robot-like. A cab pulled up before her and Casey got in.

"Where to, ma'am?" the driver asked politely after a minute. Casey realized that she had simply gotten into the cab and sat down. Now it took several moments before she could even remember Simon's address. Her mind felt like so many scattered pieces of a mosaic. Nothing seemed to fit together.

He was gone.

The words echoed over and over in her head. She had tried to prepare herself for this, but had hoped against hope that, when she finally had to tell Simon, it would be in the proper setting. Then perhaps he would have understood. He would have realized that, initially, she had only been doing her job. Her job. Damn her job. Damn everything. All she wanted was Simon, and now she could never have him. Hot tears stung her cheeks as they slid down faster and faster, tracing their own paths and mingling with the ones that had gone before until her entire face was wet.

By the time she reached the house Casey's eyes were so swollen from crying that she could hardly see. The way she felt, she didn't think she would ever stop crying again. The tears kept coming until she was sure that there was nothing else left inside of her. They filled the void that had been created by the look in Simon's eyes before he left. Suddenly she had to find him, had to make him understand that she hadn't deceived him in the only way that really mattered— that she loved him. She loved him beyond reason.

Casey prayed that he had gone home.

He hadn't.

Casey forced herself to stop crying by sheer will. She had never fallen apart like this before. But then, she had never lost anything that had meant half as much to her as Simon did.

Jack was just about to go out when Casey came in. He took one look at her swollen eyes, her red nose and her cheeks shining with tears, and put his hands on her shoulders. "Casey, my God, what happened?"

"Is Simon here?" she asked, her throat hoarse and aching.

"Simon? No. Did you two have a lovers' spat?" he asked kindly. Somehow the archaic word sounded right coming from the older man's lips.

Casey managed to shake her head before the tears took hold again. Jack drew her into his arms and let her bury her head against his wide chest, her tears flowing into the soft lime-green weave of his sports jacket. Vaguely Casey heard footsteps behind her on the tiled foyer.

"Juanita, some tea in the den, if you don't mind," Jack instructed, leading Casey off.

He sat her down on the leather couch, offered her his handkerchief and waited until her tears had subsided before he said anything further. He prompted her with only a few words and then all that had happened came tumbling out, like the flood of evils from Pandora's box.

Casey told him everything, making a clean breast of it. The relief that would normally have followed her confession would have been wonderful—if not for the fact that, because of it all, she had lost Simon.

Jack remained silent while she talked, his face kindly, his manner encouraging. It almost made her feel worse, because she had lied to him as well. When she finished Jack's cherubic features pulled into a thoughtful expression and he rose, clasping his hands behind his wide back as he walked over to the window and looked out.

"This could ruin us," he said aloud, but it sounded as if he were talking to himself. And then he turned back around, as if suddenly remembering that she was there. "Not that I believe, for one moment, that Simon's guilty, even though he's never mentioned any of these letters of complaint to me. There has to be some other explanation."

"Ethan?" Casey ventured hesitantly.

But Jack shook his head almost violently at her statement. "Never. Ethan's in love with the business. He's practically married to it. He'd never risk it by doing something so foolish, no matter how much money was involved. I'd stake my life on it." And then he stopped, his expression softening as he came back over to her and took her hands in his. "But here I'm talking business when your heart's breaking. Why don't we—"

His sentence was interrupted by a knock on the door. He looked up as Juanita came in, carrying a tray with two steaming cups of tea. She set it down before them on the dark mahogany desk.

"Thank you, Juanita," Jack said, reaching for the cup nearest to him and offering it to Casey.

"Mr. Simon called," Juanita informed Jack as she shuffled out of the room. "He said he would be gone for a few days."

Jack looked at her sharply. "Anything else?"

"No." The woman closed the door behind her, unmindful of the pregnant silence, she had left in the wake of her simple statement.

Jack and Casey looked at one another. Had Simon run away because he was in danger of being found out? Or had he left because she was there?

Jack made no direct reference to Juanita's words. "What are you going to do now?" he asked, sitting down next to Casey.

She stared into the misty whiffs of steam rising from the golden brown liquid before her. The hot cup warmed her icy hands. "Go home," she said hollowly.

"Why don't you stay until Simon gets back?" Jack urged.

"Because he won't come back while I'm here. And how can you offer me your hospitality when I've been spying on you?" she asked incredulously.

A shrug moved Jack's wide shoulders. "You were just doing your job," he told her. "I can't fault you for that."

No, but Simon could, she thought. Simon did. "You're very kind," she told Jack.

"I've lived a long time," he said, casting her compliment aside politely. "I see things a little more clearly now than when I was young and in love."

"In love?" she echoed. "What does that have to do with it?"

"Plenty," he answered. "Simon's in love with you. Sometimes folks act a little hasty when they're in love and think they've been betrayed."

Casey rose, setting down the cup. She had to get started packing, she thought dully. "Even if he loved me before," she said heavily, "he doesn't love me now. He hates me."

"Oh, now, hate's a strong word—" Jack began, trying to stop her.

But Casey backed away, going toward the door. "You didn't see the way he looked at me when he found out the truth," she told Jack and then walked out.

She'd see those accusing eyes for the rest of her

life, Casey thought as she raced up the stairs and to her room.

Jack tried one more time to talk her out of leaving, but Casey hardly heard his words. She was touched by his kindness, but she couldn't bear to spend another night under his roof, remembering the bliss she had shared there with Simon. Besides, she wanted to get away before Ethan came home. Seeing Simon's carbon copy glaring at her would be more than she could endure.

She took the five-forty flight home.

Casey arrived in New York bone-tired. The swelling, pushing crowds at the airport jostled her as she made her way to street level, unmindful of the unintended assaults on her numbed body. She just kept moving, intent on getting home. Inside, more tears were born.

Sitting inside the taxi that brought her to her apartment, Casey drew a strange sort of solace from the darkness that swathed her. It matched the emptiness inside of her. Eight days before, she had sat in a similar cab—with Simon. Eight days. She had managed to meet, fall in love and become permanently severed from the man of her dreams in the space of eight days.

"An eight-day wonder, that's me," she said bitterly, chewing her lip to keep from crying again. She wasn't going to cry, she wasn't, she told herself sharply. She had cried all the way to the airport in Houston and for the two thousand miles during her journey to New York. Half the country was soggy with her tears. It was time to stop.

Her cheeks grew wet.

* * *

Casey spent the next two days in bed with the covers over her head. To her everlasting disappointment she didn't waste away and die. Monday morning found her with a terrible ache in her body. Probably psychosomatic, she told herself. I deserve to ache. Her stomach was also screaming. She might be intent on embracing the netherworld, but her stomach was not. With a sigh she rose and began to go through the motions of living.

Normally she would have dreaded facing Harold Steele and telling her boss that she had come up empty. This had been an unorthodox venture, and she had failed miserably for the first time in her life. She had no hard and fast evidence that could be used to convict Simon Ashford or, more importantly, to clear him. The prospect of her boss's displeasure, however, didn't scare her. Casey didn't care anymore. Her spirit, once so proud, was broken. And then there was her heart. It, she decided as she made her way to work, was beyond repair.

Harold Steele looked angry before Casey even got to him. Casey deposited her purse in the bottom drawer of her desk, wondering what had happened to make her boss look like a scowling bear before nine in the morning.

"Hi, how was your vacation?" Millie asked, coming in.

"Over," Casey replied through lips that hardly moved.

All around them other employees were busy trying to get back into the groove of work after a weekend. Casey hardly saw or heard them as she walked purposefully to Harold Steele's office. His door was open, and Casey didn't bother knocking. He had been glaring at her for the last three minutes.

"Fine job, Bennett," he said sarcastically before she had a chance to close the door behind her. She didn't particularly want this conversation overheard.

How did he know? she wondered, staring at him. Surely no one had called.

But before Casey could open her mouth to say anything, Steele went on, "That damn coin case has been solved, and we didn't get any of the credit. Not one shred. What were you doing down there, telling him everything?"

"What are you talking about?" Casey asked, finally finding her voice. "Who solved the case? What happened?" she demanded, suddenly coming to life.

"Oh, and I suppose you don't know," Steele jeered, almost shouting the words as he leaned forward.

"Know what?" Casey was fairly shouting herself in her frustration. What was he talking about? Out of the corner of her eye she could see several employees looking at them through the glass partitions. Obviously their voices were carrying despite the closed door.

"That Ashford called in the FBI and handed over the guilty party to them," Steele informed her nastily, sinking back down in his chair with a thump and knocking over his ashtray, which was already full at that early hour.

"Simon?" she said in disbelief. Her eyes grew wide.

"That's the one," Steele growled. "You were supposed to get the goods on this *before* the FBI came in."

She hardly heard his rantings. "Who did he turn in?" she wanted to know, a sense of relief flooding through her. Simon was innocent! It took a moment for the sadness to catch up to her. He had been innocent all along, and still she had lost him.

"Some guy who worked for him," Steele said, leaning forward in his chair and searching through several pages of notes on his desk, looking for the information he had jotted down. "Palmer, I think. Seems the guy's wanted for pulling the same scam at several other coin firms. What a feather in my cap that would have been!" he lamented. He squinted accusingly at Casey again. But the accusation there was nothing in comparison to the look that had been in Simon's eyes. Casey withstood her boss's anger easily.

Simon wasn't guilty, her mind echoed. She wasn't in love with a thief after all.... A lot of good that information did her now, she thought miserably. She wasn't in love with a thief, and he wasn't in love with her, period. The hollow feeling within her began to grow again.

Steele barked some other things at her, smoke punctuating his anger, but Casey didn't even hear him. She nodded once or twice to make it appear that she was listening, but her mind kept wandering away, wondering where Simon was now, and if he'd ever stop hating her. She was vaguely aware of it when Steele dismissed her, and she went off to her desk.

Casey shuffled through the papers that had accumulated in her absence, but she couldn't concentrate on anything. She glanced up to see that Millie was looking at her quizzically and realized that her phone was ringing.

"Do you want me to get that?" Millie asked.

Casey was tempted to say yes, but she knew that eventually she would have to come out of the shell she had erected around herself, and the sooner she did so, the better.

"No, thanks," she said, trying to flash Millie a quick smile. The attempt failed. Her lips just couldn't form a smile. "Hello, Consumer Protection Division."

"Is this Casey Bennett?" a strangely accented voice on the other end asked.

"Yes," she replied dully, wishing she were someone else and had been granted a second chance to win Simon's affections.

"I was told to ask for you specifically. My friend tells me you're very efficient."

Your friend's wrong, she thought sadly. I messed up the most important thing in my life. Casey didn't bother responding to the compliment.

"I've been the unwitting dupe in a mail fraud scam," the voice went on to say. Casey could tell that the voice belonged to a man, but couldn't begin to place the accent. She let the speaker continue as she tried hard to concentrate.

"I'd like to meet you somewhere and talk about it."

"Well, if you'd just come down to our office..." Listlessly, she doodled on her scratch pad. The doodles were all turning into hearts that had been cracked down the middle. If she didn't get hold of herself soon she'd be cracked down the middle, as well.

"No, no, this is a private matter," the voice insisted. "I don't want anyone else overhearing.

Please." The man sounded drenched in embarrassment.

It wasn't the first time she had encountered a red-faced victim. "Perhaps you'd like to speak to my supervisor," Casey offered. People always took comfort in going to the top.

But obviously this person didn't. "No, I have to deal with you," he said with great alacrity. "Please."

Casey sighed. It was highly irregular, but at that point she didn't care about anything, and the person did sound distressed. "Oh, all right. Where would you like to meet?" she asked. If the man suggested some out-of-the-way spot she could readily decline. But right now she needed something to take her mind off her heartache.

"There's a little coffee shop on the ground floor of your building," the voice suggested. "How about there?"

That sounded safe enough, she thought. She'd gone there many times for a quick lunch, and it was always well populated. "Okay. When?"

"As soon as you can." The voice made it sound urgent. Maybe there was something here she could use to smooth Steele's ruffled feathers—not that she cared very much about the condition of his feathers at that moment.

Casey glanced at her watch. "I have a break coming up in an hour. I can meet you then." Maybe once she met the man she could convince him to continue his story back in her office. Her break only lasted twenty minutes.

"Fine, I'll meet you there." She could tell that he was about to hang up.

"Wait, how will I find you?" Casey asked quickly.

"Don't worry," the voice assured her. "I'll find you.

She was left staring at the phone, listening to the dial tone. She shook her head, her hair bouncing against the pale pink sweater she wore. The man had probably ordered a toupee through the mail and received some shriveled little rug instead. Now he was too embarrassed to let everyone know, and too angry to let the matter pass. Casey filed the issue away for the time being and tried to turn her attention to the work in front of her.

She had still gotten nowhere when she heard the scraping of chairs and the sound of people moving about. Break time. After extracting her purse from the bottom drawer, she slammed it shut and went to meet the owner of the strange voice.

If nothing came of this, Casey thought as she walked into the coffee shop, side-stepping several people who were exiting, she'd at least get a good danish out of it. Walking slowly, so that the mysterious caller could see her, she went to the counter and sat down on a stool. She hadn't the vaguest notion how the man was going to identify her, but that was his problem. Perhaps he had had second thoughts on the matter and wasn't going to show up.

Casey felt a hand on her shoulder and turned around, half expecting to see some anemic looking little man in a nondescript suit. She opened her mouth to say hello, but her lips formed a large, stunned "oh" instead.

"Simon," she whispered in disbelief.

"How can you tell it isn't Ethan?" he asked, using the same funny accent that had met her ear an hour ago.

There was no question in her mind. She *knew* it was Simon. All her instincts told her so. "You called me?" She stared at him as if he were an apparition, and he took the seat next to her.

"I wanted to get you alone," he said, "and I couldn't wait for you to come home tonight. It took me ten minutes to get through the switchboard," he complained. A waitress hovered over them. "Two coffees, please," he ordered.

"We've been having trouble with the switchboard lately. New girl," she said, grasping at small talk until her nerves steadied. Had he come to give her another chance? Or to flaunt the situation in her face, making her pay for having suspected him? Casey couldn't wait for him to bring up the matter. "I heard you called the FBI," she said.

"It was either that or string Palmer up from the nearest tree, the way they did back in the old days." He turned to face her squarely. "You already thought I was a thief. I didn't want to be labeled a murderer, as well, although Palmer had it coming to him."

Casey winced at his words and the biting sting they carried. She put her hand on his arm. "Simon, I didn't..."

His blue-gray eyes stared at her. Ice seemed to form within her chest. Casey withdrew her hand. "Didn't you?" His face remained impassive.

Casey felt her shoulders slump beneath the burden of his accusation. "I didn't know what to think. I had a list of complaints, an irate man shouting in my face—Dennenberg came over in person—and, finally, a report about a stolen coin coming out of your office. That plus Ethan skulking sullenly about because I was coming into the office." She shrugged helplessly. "I—"

"Ethan was 'skulking' about, as you put it, because he was afraid you were a gold digger trying to wheedle your way into my affections and the business."

"What?" she cried.

The waitress looked at her quizzically as she returned with their coffees, and Casey lowered her voice. "He thought I was after your money?"

"Ethan was just getting over a bad experience. He fell hard for a woman who turned out to be more interested in what he could buy her than in the affection he could give her. She came on sweet, too," he told her.

"But I said I had an inheritance...."

"...which he didn't buy for one minute." Was she that transparent? "Women have been known to be deceitful," Simon said before taking a sip of his coffee.

She had had it coming to her, she guessed. "Tell me about Palmer," she urged, trying to sound professional. She wasn't going to show Simon how badly shaken she was. She wanted his last memory of her to be untouched by salty tears.

"One shrewd operator. He had false letters of recommendation from reputable dealers. He knew coins well and was highly efficient. He actually conducted his own business parallel with ours. He'd take some of the orders we got, fill them with lower grade coins, intercept the checks and forge our signatures. He'd stay in one place long enough to collect several good-sized checks, then go somewhere else. It turned out that he operated under several aliases and was wanted in several states. He was pretty clever. His mistake was that he grew too confident and got too greedy. His biggest mistake, though,'' Simon went on, ''was in using my firm.'' He paused for a moment as the waitress returned to ask if there would be anything else. Simon looked to Casey, but she shook her head. She was too caught up in Simon's narrative to think of food.

''I was doing some investigating of my own before you came on the scene. We had had too many complaints about coins we had no record of ever sending out. It didn't make any sense. I didn't let Uncle Jack know, because I didn't want to worry him. And then you showed up and I temporarily forgot about everything else.''

Casey stared down at the counter, unable to look Simon straight in the eye. The thought of her not believing in him must have hurt him very badly.

''After our little scene at the office I got in contact with every dealer I knew to see if any of them had had a similar problem. The ones that said yes had also had Palmer, or someone matching his description working for them at some point. I traced him to a firm in Austin. The owner there read me back the glowing words of recommendation I 'had written' about him.'' Simon said with a laugh. ''After that, it was a matter for the authorities. By the way, Palmer, or whoever he really is, had the other coins from that stolen collection you mentioned. Seems he had a partner who helped him obtain coins at a very low cost,'' he said dryly.

Simon stopped talking, and the air between them grew very still, even though all around them, people were talking.

Everything had fallen so neatly into place. All the

little clues that Casey had gathered scattered like leaves in the wind. At the airport, when she and Ethan had spoken about Simon's ability to steal hearts, Ethan had muttered that it wasn't the first time Simon had stolen something. She knew now that it had been only Ethan's feeble attempt at a joke, nothing more. And when Simon had said that Ethan was worried about the business, she should have realized that Ethan was the type to *always* worry about the business, no matter how well it was doing. She could see everything so clearly now.

Just the way she clearly saw that their relationship was over.

"Well, I guess that ends that," Casey said quietly, picking up her purse.

"Not quite," Simon said evenly. "I have a question of my own." Casey paused, waiting. "Are you really a coin collector?"

She raised her head. "Yes. I didn't lie to you about that, I really do have a collection of cents." She waited, but he didn't say anything further. "Well, I'll be seeing you," she murmured, knowing that she wouldn't be. Get out of here, fast, her little voice urged, before you start to cry again. Casey had truly come to believe that the human body was composed of 98 percent water. She had gone through her allotment already.

"Not so fast," Simon said, taking hold of her wrist. "You know, Uncle Jack's a remarkable man," he drawled slowly. "He raised me to believe in happy endings."

"Well, you're cleared," she said. Why was he keeping her there, torturing her this way. "Isn't that happy enough?"

"I would have thought so, yes. But that was before I met a woman who reminded me of a 1916 Standing Liberty Quarter."

A small ray of hope shot through Casey.

"I suspect I'd have to go through maybe half a lifetime before I met someone else who'd fit that description. By then I'd be too old to enjoy her." A mischievous glint was returning to his eyes. "You're not rich, though, are you?"

Casey felt disappointment edging out her hope. "No," she said in a small voice.

Simon got off his stool. Was he going? Was her admission enough to make him leave?

"Then I suppose I won't be selling you those coins I had set aside." She shook her head, not even able to say "no" at that point. "Guess I'll just have to keep them...and you."

Casey's head jerked up. "Keep me?"

"Obviously the only way I'm going to impress you with what an honest, upstanding guy I am is to keep you chained to my side."

"Are you asking me to marry you?" Casey asked, the words finding their way out of a mouth that felt as if it were full of cotton.

"Either that, or become my pet dog." He laughed, slipping his arm about her shoulders. "And you're a little too large for that—also too pretty."

"What's Ethan going to say?"

"Probably 'Congratulations, you lucky son-of-a-gun.'"

Neither one seemed to notice the staring crowd as they sealed their commitment with a long, lingering kiss.

"C'mon," Simon said, leading her out the door.

"I've got three nights to catch up on, and I'm going through withdrawal symptoms. I've found I can't face a day without your loving to see me through." Then he stopped, struck by a thought. "What about your job?"

"Let someone else teach them that the buyer should beware. I have some serious loving to do," Casey replied happily, resting her head against his chest as they walked out.

* * * * * *

GRAND THEFT: HEART

This book is dedicated to
Leslie Wainger,
who is truly one of a kind.

One

The crimson Corvette Stingray whizzed by, cutting through the sultry July afternoon like an arrow.

"The driver must have a death wish," Lissa muttered out loud as she flipped a switch in her car. Immediately the blue and red lights on the roof began to flash brightly as she set off in pursuit of the speeding car.

As if the driver had suddenly become aware of what was happening, the bright red car skidded to a halt, neatly avoiding a collision with an old, beat-up car that was filled to overflowing with teenagers and surfboards. With some maneuvering, the Corvette pulled up in front of a busy pottery shop and stood silently waiting. All around it activity continued as an endless stream of cars wove its way down to the Mediterranean-like setting of Laguna Beach.

As she stepped out of the car Lissa was half grate-

ful for this break in the monotony. She had given up
one of her days off to sub for a fellow officer. Her
good deed had turned into an exercise in utter boredom. Compounding the lack of excitement was the
fact that today was one of those rare hot and muggy
days that sometimes found their way onto the California weather scene. It made her feel irritable.

Her uniform chafed the back of her neck, and she
could feel perspiration running down her spine. She
hadn't realized that morning when she waved away
the mechanic's mumbled apologies about not having
had time to fix the car's air-conditioning system that
she would be roasting like this.

"No wonder Allen called in sick today," she muttered, pushing her wet bangs from her forehead.

Hot breezes mingled with the smell of the ocean
as she suddenly saw the car door open. Most motor-
ists stayed in their cars and waited for the officer to
approach. She was well aware of the fact that the most
dangerous time in an officer's life was the ten seconds
it took to approach a stopped car. Every pulled over
vehicle might well contain a dangerous criminal who
would resort to desperate measures rather than be
questioned by a police officer.

The driver of the Corvette turned out to be a
smartly dressed man who appeared to pose no immediate threat to Lissa. As a matter of fact, he provided a treat to her senses. Her eyes moved over him
in an unconscious appreciation.

The man was gorgeous. He looked, she thought, as
sleek as the highly polished car he was leaning
against. While his face was tanned, Lissa could detect
none of the telltale lines that would brand him a sun
worshiper. His smiling face was the closest thing to

perfection she had ever seen. But his easy expression was slightly deceptive, because she saw that he was intently appraising her. She knew that, in his judgment, she would undoubtedly come up lacking. The uniform, with its roomy slacks, was far from flattering and could only detract from her zestful, fresh-scrubbed California look. Her thick, blonde mane, which usually tumbled down her back, was pinned into a restraining French twist in an attempt to make her look older than her twenty-six years. As it was, she found that her looks prevented people from taking her seriously as a policewoman, and that she had to rely heavily on her serious deportment to get her point across.

She could see amusement creeping into the stranger's warm brown eyes as she pulled out her ticket book.

"I had no idea that the long arm of the law had such a pretty body attached to it" were the first words he said to her. The voice was suave, deep and polished. It suited him. Lissa guessed that he was going to try to talk her out of the ticket.

"You were doing seventy-five in a fifty-five mile an hour zone," she said crisply, ignoring his compliment.

"My fault entirely," the stranger said, raising his hands in mock surrender. "The 'Vette doesn't seem to like to do under fifty even when it's idling." He laughed.

Lissa shaded her eyes with her hand, squinting a little in an attempt to keep the sun's bright rays back. "That could get to be very expensive," she replied, trying hard not to smile. "Your license, please." She held out her hand expectantly.

In a graceful motion the tall, stranger slipped his hand inside his light gray suit jacket and extracted a soft, crushed leather wallet. He flipped it open to his license.

"Take it out, please," she instructed.

The card he handed her obligingly did not have the usual color photo on it. Instead there was a black and white shot in the corner that did not begin to do him justice. Those warm brown eyes were reduced to light gray, and the brilliance of his smile was hidden behind a serious expression. He looked rather formidable in the picture, like a man who wouldn't let anyone get in the way of his goal. Funny how an expression could change a person so much, she thought. The license number in the left-hand area was so long, it seemed to fill up the small card.

It was a New York license.

Lissa held it, glancing at the plates on the Corvette. They were not the orange plates that originated in the eastern state. These were the bright whites that came from the California Department of Motor Vehicles. He had gotten them recently, since California had only recently begun offering something besides the traditional blue plates.

"Pretty fancy car for a chauffeur," she commented.

"I beg your pardon?" he asked, confused.

"I thought only chauffeurs had licenses with their pictures on them in New York."

He shook his head. "All that means is that I'm licensed to drive something larger than a car."

He had her at a disadvantage, and she tried to cover her confusion by appearing more formal. "May I see your registration?" she prodded, glancing at the car

again. She wondered if he was just out here visiting.
Did the car belong to a friend?

"Just a sec," the man, whose name had turned out
to be Brett McKenna, said as he ducked back into the
sports car. "It's in the glove compartment somewhere." The statement was followed by the removal
of several crumpled looking maps. "Unfortunately, so
is the state of Rhode Island," he added with a laugh.

It was a nice laugh, the kind that seemed to envelop
the immediate area and make the listener feel good,
Lissa thought. She wondered what he thought of her.
Very professional, Armstrong. Here you are, about to
slap a fine on the man and you're hoping you made
a favorable impression. Bright.

"Ah, here you go," Brett said, offering the small
slip of paper to her even before he was fully out of
the car.

Lissa took it. It had his name on it, all right. But
it also had a California address. She looked at him
quizzically.

"Move around a lot?" she asked, holding on to
both items. She looked up, waiting for his answer.
God, he was tall. At five eight, she wasn't exactly
short herself, and he still towered over her.

Brett nodded. "Sometimes," he said rather evasively. "You can send the ticket to the California address. I'll get it," he assured her.

Lissa began to write. *She* started to, but her pen
didn't. A couple of shakes yielded no further cooperation.

"Here, allow me."

Lissa looked up into smiling, soft brown eyes as
Brett produced a gold-plated pen. His fingers brushed
against her as he handed it to her.

"Thank you," she muttered, pocketing her own errant instrument. His helpfulness confused her. The best she had ever gotten before when writing a ticket was abject indifference.

Write, dummy, her inner voice urged when she realized that she was still staring up into his classic, square features, her eyes held fast by his slightly crooked smile. He didn't look thirty-one, she thought, glancing back down at his license.

Hastily she wrote out the pertinent information. He was still watching her. She could feel his eyes gliding along all her hidden curves, as if he could see them despite her uniform. Part of her wished that she were wearing something else, but what would she be doing writing out a speeding ticket if she weren't in uniform?

Almost reluctantly, she handed the ticket to him. Part of her felt as if she should be apologizing. But then, the fine would scarcely put a dent into his pocket, she told herself. Not if he could keep a twenty-year-old car in that kind of condition.

"Are you revoking my license?" he asked in a teasing voice.

"Of course not," she said. Was he laughing at her? Being a policewoman was hard enough without having a Barbie doll face. She tried to stand very erect. An erect Barbie doll in a police uniform, she thought with a touch of despair.

"Then can I have it back?" he prodded, holding out his hand.

She felt a little foolish and tried not to show it. "It's rather late in my shift," she mumbled by way of an explanation.

His hand closed over the license, once more touching her fingers. If she hadn't known better, she'd have sworn that he was trying to capture her hand in his.

"Do you get off soon?" he asked casually.

Her suspicions were aroused a bit by that. Why did he want to know? "A police officer is always on duty," she said evasively.

"I feel safer already," he told her, a slight teasing edge in his voice.

"You'll be safer," she informed him soberly, "if you drive within the speed limit." She had a sudden feeling that she wasn't referring only to the rules of the road.

"Yes, ma'am," he said, his sensuous lips curving into a smile, and saluted her.

Lissa turned on her heel and marched back to her car. Hotshot, she thought crisply, trying to dismiss the man from her mind. She got into her car, switched off the flashing lights and sat for a moment.

Normally the recipients of traffic citations couldn't wait to pull away from the scene, but Brett was still there, watching her. She almost felt as if their roles were reversed and she had been the one who had done something wrong.

Lissa tucked the ticket book away and started her car. Where had he been going in such a hurry? She wondered. Was it some important business meeting that he was rushing to, or perhaps to the arms of a beautiful woman?

You're on duty, Armstrong. You're supposed to think with your badge, not any other part, she reminded herself wryly.

The teasing half-smile of the speeding stranger did not fade away at her stern injunction, however.

It stayed with her on her way back to the precinct,

refusing to be blotted out by either the beautiful, colorful scenery on either side of the road, or the uncustomary heat that was licking at the black and white car. The only thing that managed to nudge the image aside slightly was the burning steering wheel. Gingerly Lissa tried to direct the car by holding on to the wheel with her fingertips.

"My kingdom for an air-conditioned car," she sighed. Even her eyelashes felt hot.

Dazzling waves of bright purple, blue and pink ice plants blended together into a velvet carpet lining the road to her right. To her left was the beach, almost hidden by several small rustic houses. Then the houses disappeared behind her as Lissa's view of the ocean became virtually unobstructed, the beach fenced off by a chainlink barrier and a sign that declared the area to be the private property of some exclusive club.

The land may be, but not the view, Lissa thought, looking to her left. She didn't really have to look. The ocean, the sky, the lapping waves, they were all etched solidly into her brain. She had grown up here, spent entire summer vacations on the beach, tasted her first kiss, mingled with salt water, here. All this was home to her, home the way no other place could ever be.

And now she was patrolling it, she thought, thinking of those few friends of hers who still had time to spend on the boardwalk, allowing the idyllic days to flow into one another without concern for the future.

Lissa, on the other hand, had her future mapped out in her mind. At least, part of her future. She wanted to work her way up to the rank of detective. To this end, she had already picked a field of expertise: security systems. Her father had been a locksmith before retiring, and even as a child, Lissa had had a natural curiosity about barriers. She could pick a lock, much to her mother's dismay, by the time she was ten. Now she hoped to use her more legitimately accumulated findings to help further her chosen career. Despite the fact that her parents thought of her as their rebellious daughter, Lissa had everything well thought out. By the time she was thirty, she was determined to have all the comforts that a good career could provide.

She already had a home of her own. That had been left to her by her mother's mother. Admittedly, right now it didn't look like very much. But it sat two blocks from the beach, gathering its army of succulent plants about its borders, and Lissa loved it. She spent every spare moment she had renovating the small, weathered, two bedroom house, painting it, replacing cracked windows with stained glass creations constructed out of countless bits of colored glass arranged to form breathtaking scenes. In due time, a brilliant phoenix would rise out of the ashes of the old house.

The time she spent on her house and her career left little time for dating, and somehow Lissa had found herself sliding into a pattern of peaceful solitude. It was a striking change from the whirlwind socializing that had been so important to her during her high school years and into her early twenties. But it suited her at the moment. She didn't want to get serious about a man right now. She was content to be laying the foundations of her career.

As if to scoff at her thoughts, the face of the handsome stranger materialized in her mind as she turned up the familiar driveway to the police station. Ordi-

narily Lissa had a good eye for detail, but this time
she had outdone herself. Every feature of Brett's rugged, flawless face came back to her as clearly as if it
were being shown on videotape. She saw the sensuous, easy smile; the sexy, half-closed brown eyes
framed by long, luxurious lashes; the perfect, straight
nose. The lush, dark blond hair that covered the tops
of his ears and feathered down along the back of his
collar, which she had barely brushed against as he
had ducked into his car in search of his registration,
seemed so vivid to her that she felt as if she could
touch it.

Lissa parked the car in its prescribed place. She sat
with the keys dangling in her hand, thinking. Who
was he? Was he married and running off to snatch an
afternoon's pleasure with his mistress? The address
on the registration had been in an exclusive area in
Beverly Hills. He was a long way from home, and he
certainly hadn't been dressed as if he planned on
spending an afternoon in the sun.

Lissa became aware of the beads of perspiration
collecting on her brow, curling bangs into unruly
waves. Get out of the car, dummy, she told herself.

He hadn't perspired, she recalled. He had looked
cool and calm and dry, while she felt wet and rumpled. Maybe he wasn't real. He certainly hadn't
looked real, even for this area of stylish people. No,
he had looked as if he belonged to the cosmopolitan
world of places like New York, Paris, London. Rich.
A whole different world, Lissa thought.

"Some lousy weather, eh, Lissa?"

The raspy voice lifted her out of her thoughts and
placed her squarely back in the parking lot in front
of the precinct. She looked toward the owner of the

voice, one of the older policemen she had become friendly with.

Lissa nodded, her bangs springing loose. "I hate humidity, Leopold," she admitted, falling in step with the tall, heavyset man as they walked into the modern-looking one story building. "That's supposed to be the best part about living out here—next to no humidity."

The policeman waved a dismissing hand as he laughed. "This isn't humidity. This is a little discomfort," he drawled. Lissa could clearly hear his Louisiana accent clinging to every word. "You haven't seen humidity until your shower curtain turns a living green," he told her with a chuckle.

"No, thank you, this is enough for me," she assured him as they parted company in the long, antiseptic-looking corridor. She turned left and pushed open the door that led to the women's locker room. Hailing a few friends, she headed toward her locker. Normally the area was abuzz with various conversations splintering into one another. Today, perhaps in deference to the weather, the conversation was next to nil, as if talking were too much of an effort in this heat. Everyone seemed to move at a slower pace.

Not Lissa. She was in a hurry to get out of her uniform and home. She had been promising herself a long, cool shower and a lazy, peaceful evening all day.

She slipped out of the blue uniform and rolled up her shirt. After taking the belt out of the trousers, she rolled them up as well, then shoved the entire uniform into a gray canvas bag. She was going to wash and iron them before she came back on duty Tuesday. She

took out a bright red sundress from her locker. Red.
Like the Corvette.

Again the image of the man and his fast car crashed
into her thoughts. But not for long. She determinedly
pushed it aside as she tied a white belt about her small
waist. The whiteness accented the white polka dots
on her dress and the white piping that ran along the
edge of the light frock. The wide skirt draped saucily
about her trim hips and flirtatiously brushed against
the tops of her knees as she reached down to slip into
a pair of white high-heeled sandals.

Deftly Lissa pulled out the pins that anchored her
hair in place, allowing the heavy tresses to spill down
like a golden river as she quickly brushed them. Without bothering with a mirror, Lissa fashioned a single
long braid and let it fall down her back.

"Big date tonight?" Linda Ramirez asked, donning
her own civilian clothing.

Lissa shook her head at the large, square-faced
woman. "Just a nice, quiet evening at home," she
said, grabbing her purse and canvas bag. "Anything
interesting today?" she asked as she pushed her
locker closed.

"No, same old dull stuff. This sure isn't where the
action is," the other woman observed. "Not even an
interesting family ruckus. This isn't a thing like my
days in Venice Beach," she said sadly, referring to
an area that was known for its unorthodox, bohemian
populace. "How about you?"

Lissa shrugged. "Nothing out of the ordinary."
Her thoughts flittered back to the crimson Corvette.
Yes, he was out of the ordinary, but not the way
Linda had meant.

Her answer puzzled Linda. "No?" the other

woman asked. "Funny, you weren't that far away from the break-in," she commented.

"What break-in?" Lissa asked, forgetting her shower in the face of this carelessly tossed tidbit.

"Our elusive burglar has struck again," Linda told her. "I heard Brom talking about it. Happened just about an hour or so ago."

"Another private collection?" Lissa guessed. For the past two months Lissa had avidly followed the investigation of a series of robberies, all involving the homes of wealthy people who collected rare expensive items, such as guns and swords.

"You guessed it," Linda said, her dark hair falling into her face as she leaned over to tighten the laces of her faded blue sneakers. "But this time we've got something to go on," she said a bit mysteriously.

Lissa knew that Linda loved to draw out a story. "What?" she prodded eagerly.

A grin split the wide face. "Our thief doesn't sound all that bright to me. Someone in the neighborhood thought they saw 'the suspect' driving off in a red sports car. Seems to me that if you're going to pull off a robbery, you don't drive off in a flashy red car. Well, see you."

With a swish of her ample hips, Linda was gone, leaving Lissa standing openmouthed in the locker room.

No, it couldn't be.

She repeated the phrase aloud as she left the police station and walked out to claim her weather-beaten Mustang, a car her father had presented her with on the night of her high school graduation. It had been secondhand even then. She loved the old car, treating it with the same affection and care she gave to her toy poodle. But cars were the furthest thing from her mind right now. At least, *her* car was the furthest thing from her mind.

He didn't look like a burglar.

C'mon, Armstrong, the first thing they teach you is that suspects don't look like suspects. The shifty-eyed hood on the corner is trying to look tough, and the polished executive is embezzling millions. You can't tell the good guys from the bad guys without a score card. Just because Brett McKenna looked as if he came out of *Gentlemen's Quarterly* doesn't mean he's as pure as the driven snow....

But what would a man with two residences want with old swords? Collectors' items, she reminded herself, driving home. She picked out the route unconsciously. He had looked so cool, so relaxed when she had pulled him over. He had looked like he didn't have a care in the world.... Well, if he was the guilty party, that would have been the smartest way to play it, and Brett McKenna had looked like one smart, cool operator.

Innocent until proven guilty, she reminded herself. Still, she promised herself to get the details of the newest robbery from Brom as soon as she got back on duty. The robbery had occurred in her area, and she did have Brett's address...at least, one of them.

You're just looking for an excuse to see him again, she told herself. She had no proof, nothing to go on except a gut feeling that had less to do with the robbery than with the color of Brett's eyes and the warm quality of his lazy smile.

Think about it later, Armstrong. Your shower awaits. The thought filled her with happy anticipation as she turned her car down a side street until she came to her wood-framed, cheery-looking house.

Two

Lissa parked her car in the driveway and walked toward her house, bypassing the path between rustic-looking railroad ties, choosing instead to travel over the grass. It needed mowing, she thought as she fished her key from the depths of her purse. Always something. She'd rather be working on the stained glass pieces she was making for the back window. The house had required an awful lot of work when Lissa had moved in a year ago. By and large, it had been a labor of love. But at times, she thought, glancing at the grass, it was just labor.

Oh, well, she was off tomorrow. Maybe she could do both—as long as she got to the mowing first. If the stained glass claimed her, as it was apt to do, the grass could grow another foot before she remembered it.

Lissa grinned as she unlocked her door, hearing a

welcoming yip from her toy poodle. She had a tendency to become utterly involved in the task at hand and forget everything else. Unfortunately, that did not put her at the head of the list as the best housekeeper in the world, she thought ruefully as she entered the house and looked about at the small, less than immaculate living room.

"Hi, Agatha," Lissa said affectionately, stooping down to pet the eager dog. Within a moment, Lissa was almost on the floor, her face covered with a multitude of licks. "That's right, play hard to get," Lissa laughed, stroking the black fur. "Well, I'd love to continue this, Agatha, but right now I'd sell my soul for a shower," she told the dog as she rose again, leaving her purse where it had fallen. She tended to be as disorganized in her personal life as she was organized in her professional one. The only thing Lissa methodically did was put her service revolver away.

She picked up her canvas bag and walked to the kitchen, which was only a few steps beyond the cluttered living room, then rested her bag on the table. After pulling out her shirt and flinging it on the chair, she came to her gun. Her actions ceased being haphazard as she drew it out of the bag and walked over to her linen closet, where she carefully placed the gun on the uppermost shelf and covered it with a peach hand towel. She left the door open.

"Have a good day, Aggie?" she asked the poodle, who followed her every movement with her shoe-button eyes. The dog thumped her tail on the hardwood floor. "That good, huh? Well, your day was better than mine. Dull with a capital D. Except..." Lissa paused for a moment as Brett's smile seemed to float right before her eyes. "Well, there was this one guy who was speeding..." Her voice trailed off as she kicked off first one shoe and then the other.

Lissa glanced down to see that the dog was looking at her, as if waiting for her to go on. "Nothing much to tell, girl," Lissa said, her voice becoming brisk and breezy again. "I left him with a ticket—best-looking man I've ever seen," she confided, talking to the dog as if she were her best friend. "Maybe I should have arrested him and then paroled him into my custody, eh, girl?" She laughed, unzipping her sundress as she went to her bedroom.

The cool hardwood floor felt good under her bare feet as she padded toward her newly installed shower. When she had moved in, Lissa had found only an old corroded-looking tub in the bathroom. Had it been an antique, with old-fashioned legs, she would have kept it. But it wasn't. The only thing you could truthfully say about it was that it was ugly. So her first order of business had been to have her bathroom remodeled. Now pink shiny tiles gleamed at her, and the bathroom looked perfect, like something from a women's magazine. Eventually Lissa hoped to upgrade the rest of the house to match the quality of the bathroom.

"And then," Lissa told herself, "you're going to have to do something about the way you keep house—or don't keep house," she amended. She caught herself dropping her dress on the floor as she spoke. Shaking her head, she stooped down and picked it up, then stuffed the dress into the hamper. Agatha pranced out of her way. "'Can't teach an old dog new tricks,' they say. No, not you," Lissa said in answer to the look on the dog's face. "Me." After flinging her panties in after the dress, Lissa turned the antique brass faucet on, searching for just the right temperature. Finally the spray was to her liking and she withdrew her hand to replace it with her body.

She spent over twenty minutes there, enjoying the luscious feeling of the cool water caressing her body. It sapped all the tension from her, making her relax and feel like a new person. A contented laziness filtered through her.

"Well, all good things must come to an end," she sighed under her breath, opening the shower door and reaching for a towel. She came up empty-handed, suddenly remembering that she had thrown the towels into the hamper. "The only piece of housework I did this morning," she muttered, "and I didn't get it right."

Leaving a trail of puddles, Lissa quickly made her way to the linen closet. Just as she stretched up to get to the shelf with the bath towels, the doorbell rang. Immediately Agatha started her high-pitched barking.

"Oh, no," Lissa moaned. "Now what?" She looked around for something to throw over herself and spied her police shirt hanging half off the kitchen chair. Hastily she flung it on, buttoning the three bottom buttons as the doorbell pealed more and more insistently. The shirttails flopped against the tops of her thighs as she hurried to the front door.

Peering through the peephole, Lissa drew in her breath sharply. There was the owner of the Corvette, standing on her doorstep. A flood of bewilderment filled her.

"You can get a better look if you open the door," she heard him say. He seemed to be staring directly at her.

What was he doing there? She wondered. "Just a minute," she called, hurrying back to the linen closet and taking out her gun. Carefully she wrapped it in the hand towel that had been hiding it just a minute before. Trying to carry it nonchalantly, she unlocked the door and stepped back.

Brett appeared to have something to say, but the words died unspoken as Lissa saw his eyes rake over her, a sparkling gleam mingling with his look of surprise. His lazy smile broadened appreciatively.

"Haven't you forgotten something?" he asked smoothly. "Where's your hat?"

Lissa suddenly realized the way she was dressed—or undressed, as the case was. A deep blush formed beneath her tan, spreading all through her body, hand in hand with a strange, tingly sensation.

"I was taking a shower," she replied tersely, feeling uncomfortable as the heat of his gaze penetrated her.

Once more his eyes slowly took inventory, and Lissa realized that the dark blue shirt was clinging to her, clearly defining her body. Despite herself, she suddenly felt her nipples harden, plainly showing, she was sure, against the fabric.

"Do you always shower in uniform?" he asked.

"I believe in being prepared," she said wryly. The smile on his lips was beguiling, but Lissa remembered what Linda had told her in the locker room. This could very well be their odd burglar with the expensive tastes. What was he doing on her doorstep? And how did he know where she lived?

"What are you doing here?" she asked, her voice gaining a professional air of authority.

"Mind if I come in?" he asked, then did so before she answered.

Lissa stood with her hand on the doorknob, looking at him curiously. Linda's words came back to her. Was this the suspect someone had seen fleeing the area? If so, why on earth was he coming to see her?

Agatha yipped at his heels once or twice, then rose eagerly on her hind legs, her tail waving madly. "Some watchdog," Lissa muttered disparagingly under her breath, looking at the animal accusingly.

In response to Lissa's voice, all Agatha did was lie down on her back, turning her belly up toward Brett, who obligingly bent down and petted her. "Don't be too hard on her," he told Lissa. "I seem to have this effect on females." His eyes returned to her own slender form.

"Go out with a lot of dogs, do you?" Lissa asked dryly.

"Not a one," he replied, his voice low and sexy.

For some inexplicable reason, goose bumps suddenly popped out on her arms. "What are you doing here?" she demanded again, cradling the towel and its contents against her midsection.

"Looking for you," he said, rising. She got that overwhelmed feeling again as he towered over her.

Lissa took a step back, as if to calm her senses. "Why?" she asked suspiciously.

"You took my pen," he said simply.

"Your pen?" she echoed.

He nodded. "That thing I lent you so you could write out my ticket," he elaborated, his warm eyes teasing her. She made herself look at the rest of his face instead. It did nothing to alter the strange heady feeling she was experiencing. Maybe that was because his was the kind of face that women dreamed about and every adolescent male wished he had. It was, Lissa thought, damn near perfect. It had a slightly chiseled, rugged look, but there was an underlying tenderness to it. Had he been born a hundred years ago, with a family crest, the word "perfect" would undoubtedly have been stamped on it, she decided.

His deep resonant voice floated back into her consciousness. "Ordinarily I wouldn't bother about anything so insignificant as a pen, but this one has special sentimental value," he told her.

"A graduation gift?" Lissa guessed.

"Something like that," he answered. "It was the last thing my father gave me."

As Lissa searched for something appropriate to say in response, she was surprised to see him reach out to her.

"May I?" he asked, his eyes aflame with mischief as his fingers brushed against her shirt pocket, lifting the pen from its place and briefly touching her breast at the same time.

Her tongue felt like cotton in her mouth. A strange warm feeling flirted through her veins before fading away. The smile on Brett's face grew fuller, as if he sensed what she was feeling.

"How did you know where I lived?" she asked, forcing her mind to focus on questions rather than the feelings that were floating through her.

"Your name's on the ticket," Brett pointed out. "And in the phonebook." Before she had a chance to comment on his detective work, Brett looked around. "You have a party here last night?" he asked, gesturing at the living room's state of disarray.

Actually the living room looked a little better than it normally did. At least, there were no pantyhose strewn about, just cups, dishes and newspapers. That was what she got for rarely eating in the kitchen, Lissa thought. She preferred eating in front of the warm glow of the television set, letting it fill her in on the doings of the world beyond Laguna Beach.

"No, no party," Lissa answered, picking up the nearest dish, which stood balanced on the arm of a brown and beige chair that had seen better days. But she would be hard pressed to find a more comfortable place to sit, Lissa thought each time she was tempted to replace it.

"Too bad," Brett said. "Want to have one tonight?" His meaning was quite clear.

"Have you always been this shy?" she asked, putting the cup down on the kitchen table.

"Shy never got me anywhere," he told her.

"Neither will crass," she informed him coolly. She looked at the pen he was still holding. "Well, now that you have what you came for..." She let her voice trail off as she led the way back to her door.

To her surprise Brett sat down in the armchair. "Oh, I wouldn't say that," he said. Agatha sat down at his feet, totally irritating and confounding Lissa.

Her mixed feelings added to her consternation. Ordinarily she would have expelled a man for acting the way Brett was, giving him no more thought than a rude stranger deserved. But there was something about Brett that held her spellbound. She could feel something between them, some sort of intangible force compelling her to permit this man to stay in her home. The force made her feel warm and responsive all over, as if a pleasant, teasing wine were spilling all through her veins. It also worried her. Was she reacting this way to a thief?

"Just what are you after?" she asked point-blank, wishing that she were wearing something more. It was rather hard to sound forceful and authoritative when all you had on was a blue shirt that just about covered everything worth covering. She could tell that Brett was amused by the whole scene.

His smile unnerved her. So did his answer. "You."

"I beg your pardon." Did that sound stuffy, she thought. But she said it in self-defense. Her knees were turning to water.

"I've never gone out with a policewoman before," he told her easily.

Lissa blinked. "Is it your ambition to date a woman in every walk of life?" she asked.

"If they all look like you, yes."

"Smooth," she commented.

"True," he responded.

Lissa stood for a moment, contemplating the situation. She really did want to go out with him. How often did a man like Brett McKenna walk into a woman's life? Besides, if he did have an ulterior motive, Lissa was intrigued enough to follow this thing through to the end and see what it was. Who knew? Maybe this charming man was the elusive burglar they were all looking for. Think what a fantastic collar that would be, Armstrong, she told herself.

Fantastic collar. The word "fantastic" seemed very apt when applied to Brett, she thought.

"Are you busy tonight?" he asked.

"No," she finally admitted after a moment's hesitation.

"Would you like to be?" His eyes seemed to peer

into her very soul, as if he knew what her answer would be before she ever said anything.

"All right," she agreed. "Just give me a moment to change."

He caught hold of her hand as she went by. "Do you have to?" he teased. "I kind of like that outfit."

Lissa pressed her lips together, feeling suddenly very vulnerable beneath the flimsy layer of polyester. "This isn't exactly what they call 'full dress.'"

"The police department should always leave themselves open to suggestions," Brett said, his eyes burning away the shirt.

Lissa sucked in her breath for a moment as she saw Brett take in the firm, full swell of her breasts.

"They do, but the police department also grants itself the right not to take those suggestions," she said flippantly and turned on her heel. She expected Agatha to follow. The little dog looked at her, then stayed where she was.

"Agatha," Lissa called.

A mournful yip came in reply.

"Why 'Agatha'?" Brett asked.

"After Agatha Christie," Lissa told him. "I love a good mystery."

"I'll try to remember that," he said thoughtfully.

Lissa had no idea what to make of that comment. Or of anything else, for that matter. She went into her bedroom and silently locked the door, feeling better that she had her service revolver with her—and yet feeling strangely foolish at the same time.

Who was Brett McKenna? Why was he there, charming her dog to pieces and saying sexy things that made her feel unsettled, as if she were anticipating something? You'll get no answers talking to your mirror, she told herself. Get ready!

She threw open her closet door and rummaged around, searching for something suitable to wear. Suitable? What would be suitable around someone like Brett? Probably something that made her look like a mysterious spy would be in order. Since she didn't have anything answering that description, Lissa pulled out a light blue dotted swiss dress that was comfortable, and casual enough that she hoped he wouldn't think she was making too much of this "date." She threw the dress on quickly, then opened the door a crack to see if Brett were wandering around ransacking her home. Anything is possible, she thought. Agatha certainly wasn't about to stop him, even if he wanted to make off with the entire house.

No, there he was, playing with a very contented-looking Agatha. Why was she picking on Agatha? Wasn't she herself going out with a possible thief? The whole thing had a quality of unreality about it. But she loved it.

Lissa shut the door again, then searched the floor of her closet to find two shoes that matched each other and, just possibly, the dress as well. "Serves you right for tossing in your shoes at night," she muttered. Of course, it didn't help matters any that Agatha liked to take naps in her closet, nestling happily amid all the shoes.

Finally she was rewarded for her effort. Two matching, light blue high-heeled sandals emerged from the disorganized rubble. After getting back to her feet, Lissa quickly rid her hair of its remaining pins and pulled her brush through the tangled blonde mane. A light gold curtain flowed down to her shoul-

ders in shimmering waves, catching the afternoon sun
that shone through her window. She looked decidedly
different from the policewoman who had stopped
Brett only a few hours earlier.

Lissa came out of the bedroom quietly, hoping to
catch Brett in an unguarded moment. The only unguarded thing about him was the warm look that came
into his eyes when he sensed her presence and looked
up.

"Wow."

It wasn't a remark one would particularly associate
with a sophisticated-looking man of the world, but it
made Lissa happy. He probably instinctively knew
that, she thought. Nonetheless, she couldn't keep the
smile from her face.

"Thank you," she murmured.

"Thank *you*."

"For what?" Lissa asked, puzzled.

Brett rose and came toward her. "For the feast for
my eyes," he told her simply.

It almost sounded as if he meant it, Lissa thought.
But of course he couldn't. A man who looked like
Brett McKenna was probably used to having beautiful, worldly women on his arm. And while Lissa
knew that she was attractive, she didn't think of herself as that exceptional. Certainly not exceptional
enough to merit being singled out in this fashion.

"If you lay it on any thicker," Lissa said briskly,
"I might get sugar poisoning."

"Wouldn't want that," Brett replied, taking her remark in stride. "Ready?" he asked.

Lissa pressed her lips together. "That all depends,"
she said.

"On what?"

"On what you have in mind."

Brett laughed softly. It was a laugh that curled her toes and did delicious things to her body. "You still don't seem to trust me." He shook his head. "What is it about me that bothers you? My speeding ticket? My Corvette? The lecherous look that comes into my eyes at the sight of you?"

Lissa stared at him, flabbergasted. He certainly was honest. Or was he?

When she didn't answer, Brett went on. "I assure you, all I'm after is a pleasant evening with a very beautiful woman. I am entirely trustworthy; I even come with references," he said with a sly sink.

From a myriad of women, no doubt, Lissa thought dryly, but she still didn't speak.

"May I remind you, constable, that if there is any shifty character in this room, it might very well be you."

"What?"

"After all, it was you who purloined my pen, not vice versa. And if you had done that in any government office, you could have gotten a five-hundred dollar fine, a jail term, or both," he said, reciting the words that were posted above the chained pens hanging in post offices and the like. "I, on the other hand, am exacting no restitution whatsoever, except for a quiet dinner and a drink."

Lissa finally opened her mouth to say something, but Brett wouldn't let her get a word in.

"I realize that's hardly in the same league as a five-hundred dollar fine, but I'm in a magnanimous mood, and I think you've learned your lesson. I'm quite willing simply to have you paroled into my custody."

"You're crazy, do you know that?" Lissa asked,

picking up her purse as Brett began to walk her to the door. An inconspicuous squeeze assured Lissa that her gun was inside. She was never supposed to be without it, even on a date. Tonight she could see the wisdom in that.

"I'm not crazy," he informed her with a touch of amusement. "Merely eccentric."

The red Corvette was waiting for them in the driveway. Lissa let Brett open the door for her, then slid inside. "So, what's an eccentric man like you doing here?" she asked, watching him carefully.

"Funny thing happened to me on the way to Beverly Hills. This gorgeous policewoman had to fill her Sunday quota—"

"You were flying," she interrupted.

"—and she ticketed my heart as well as my car."

This time Lissa made no protest. She merely laughed and decided to enjoy herself. True, he might not be all he claimed to be, but she was too sharp, she felt, to be taken advantage of. If he did turn out to be the overconfident thief, she could very well be on to something. And if he were just an eccentric, she might as well enjoy her evening out.

Brett gunned his engine, and Lissa raised her left eyebrow warningly.

"Sorry," he muttered sheepishly. "Habit. Besides, can you give a man a ticket if you're off duty—and on a date with him?" he challenged.

"I can give a ticket any time, any place," she told him, a smile fighting its way to her lips.

"Does that include the bedroom?" he asked innocently.

Without blinking an eye Lissa answered, "If you're moving too fast."

"I'll try to remember to go slowly," he said, his voice low and sexy as he pulled onto Pacific Coast Highway, following the winding road toward the nearby city of Newport Beach.

He was the most outrageous, cocky, vibrant man she had ever encountered—and he was utterly irresistible, she thought, trying vainly to stay detached.

"Very sure of yourself, aren't you?" she asked, trying to stay aloof from his banter.

They came to a red light, and he turned to look at her for a moment. "I just get feelings about things," he told her. "And I'm hardly ever wrong."

"Brace yourself," she said wryly.

His smile deepened as his eyes touched her face. "We'll see," he whispered with a promise of things to come.

Lissa felt annoyed at his manner, and yet very uneasy that he just might be right. Logically, she had to view him as a potential suspect. But her mind was obviously at odds with her body, which found itself responding to this stranger the way she had never responded to any other man. So this was what was meant by instant attraction, she thought, settling into a silence as Brett drove her toward their unknown destination.

Something told her to be careful, that she was headed for trouble. Something else told her that no matter where she was headed, she was going to enjoy it.

Three

For a few minutes she heard nothing but the low-toned purr of the Corvette's engine. On the left she saw the ocean; its waves lapping along the coastline. On the right was hilly terrain blanketed with grass. In the daytime cows and horses grazed the area. Right now they were absent, put away for the night, as, it appeared, was the moon, which had chosen to stay hidden, tucked away in the amorous arms of an encircling cloud.

Amorous arms? Steady, Armstrong, this man's having a dangerous effect on your brain, Lissa told herself. And it was true. Even in silence, there was something overpowering about Brett McKenna. Something sensuous. Lissa found herself wondering what it would be like to be held and kissed by him.

Undoubtedly wonderful.

Undoubtedly dangerous, if he turned out to be who

she thought he was—and he probably would. Why else would he have made such an effort to seek her out? She was attractive, yes, but men didn't exactly collect at her door every night, taking a ticket and waiting to pay her court. She was going to have to keep these unbidden romantic feelings in check if she knew what was good for her.

"Where are we going?" she finally asked. She wanted to end the silence before it became uncomfortable. Anyway, she needed more input than her own thoughts.

"There's this little supper club on Balboa Island that I think will be to your liking," Brett told her.

"How would you know what's to my liking?" she asked. "You don't know anything about me."

"I wouldn't quite say that," he told her quietly.

Just what *did* he know about her? She wondered, her suspicions once more coming to the fore. "What do you mean by that?" she demanded. A smattering of specialty shops lined both sides of the road as they passed the last of the undeveloped beach front property and entered the city limits, but Lissa was more interested in Brett's answer than in the town. She turned to him, waiting expectantly.

"A man doesn't get to my position in life without being able to intuitively size people up quickly," he assured her.

"And just what *is* your position in life?" she asked.

"Is this an interrogation?" he asked amiably. "Don't you think you should read me my rights first?" he teased.

"You have the right to take me back home," she began.

"Pass."

"Then you have the right to tell me just who it is who's whisking me off to parts unknown."

"Balboa Island isn't exactly thought of as 'parts unknown' these days," he assured her. Brett took a sharp left onto a road that snaked its way to the bridge leading to the island. Clusters of old, expensive homes framed each narrow street like mute sentinels.

"You're very good at wordplay," Lissa told him.

"When I have to be," he admitted lightly.

Lissa sighed. This was going to be difficult. A tall streetlamp illuminated the interior of the Corvette for a moment, casting a warm glow over Brett. It made him look even more attractive, highlighting his dark blond hair. She caught herself wanting to run her fingers through it. It looked inviting. All of him looked inviting. Part of his fatal charm, no doubt.

She became aware of his grin. It wasn't a smile. It was a definite grin, as if he were peeking into her mind and could read all her thoughts. "You still haven't told me what you do for a living," she said coolly, trying to erase her unguarded moment.

"Live," he said glibly.

Lissa scowled.

"I'm an architect," he said after a slight pause. He pulled the car into a parking lot the size of a postage stamp. They had arrived.

"And you have two residences," she scoffed as he opened the door to her. "Business is that good?"

"Business is that good," he said simply, taking her hand and putting it through the crook of his arm. He led her to an inviting little building that was bathed in blue and white lights. Two tall palm trees, their heads tilted toward each other some twenty feet above the roof, stood guard at the entrance.

"I thought we were in the middle of a recession," Lissa prodded, trying to catch him in a lie.

Brett opened the door for her, and she stepped across the wooden doorsill. The door creaked a little as it slowly closed behind them. The atmosphere was the embodiment of tranquillity, she thought as she stepped into a semidarkness that took a moment to get used to. The interior was done entirely in dark oak.

A maître d' appeared, smiled and wordlessly led them to a cozy table for two. Lissa looked around. They were all cozy little tables for two. Romantic, dreamy music filtered through the area, adding to the relaxed aura that pervaded the room.

Brett waited until they were seated to continue their conversation. "For the rich, there is no recession," he said philosophically.

"You build houses for the rich?" Lissa asked.

"Build them or renovate them," he told her. "The rich like to change their houses around the way most people like to change their clothes."

"Nice work if you can get it," Lissa commented as a waiter came with their menus.

"I can," he assured her. "I'm very good," he said blatantly.

"Are you now?"

He smiled. "Yes. You'll have to let me show you sometime."

Step into my parlor, said the spider to the fly, Lissa thought. She hid her face behind the menu, squinting slightly as she tried to read the small black lettering. The dim lighting made it difficult. Her stomach felt

strangely unsettled. She really wasn't in the mood for
a meal. She scanned the menu for something simple
and light. She decided on a salad.

As she placed the menu down, she became aware
of the fact that their knees were touching. She tried
to shift over a little, but wound up with his knees
practically in between hers. Lissa looked accusingly
at Brett.

"I didn't make the tables," he said innocently,
reading the look on her face.

"You chose the place," she reminded him.

"Yes, I did, didn't I!" The look in his eyes was
pure mischief.

Lissa tried to tear her gaze away from his. "I'll
have a Caesar salad," she said to the waiter who had
quietly appeared at her elbow, his pencil poised.

"Anything to drink?" the waiter asked.

No, her mind said. He's intoxicating enough as it
is. But aloud Lissa responded, "A strawberry daiquiri, please."

Brett ordered a Scotch on the rocks and a broiled
scallop concoction that the menu promised was equal
to a little piece of heaven on earth. Within a moment
the waiter had gone and they were alone again. Alone
in a restaurant full of people, Lissa thought dryly.

"Care to share a dance?" Brett asked. The song
that filtered through the air had something to do with
strangers meeting in the night. Lissa thought it a very
appropriate song for the two of them.

"Fine," she agreed, rising. A ripple of excitement
washed over her at the prospect of being held by this
man. He took one hand in his and embraced her body
with his other arm, pulling her close to him as he
swayed to the beat of the sultry music. Lissa felt an

uncontrollable hot surge pulse through her. Instantly she was aware of every contour of his body as it touched hers. Somehow the familiarity was almost natural, as if it were supposed to be this way.

Lissa found herself struggling to control the delicious sensations that were beginning to overpower her. The situation is getting out of hand, she told herself. Some detective she'd make, letting the potential suspect disarm her like this. She was supposed to be trying to observe him, not falling under his spell.

"Hey, what's the matter?" Brett asked.

"What do you mean?" she asked back, a bit self-consciously.

"All of a sudden you feel like you're coming to attention. Relax," he said, his voice low and captivating. "Dancing with me is painless, I promise you. I've never lost a partner on the floor yet," he told her, smiling into her eyes.

"How have you lost them?" she asked wryly.

"A mutual parting of the ways, usually," he answered.

Lissa had her doubts about that. Judging from outward appearances, the man would be a fantastic catch for any woman, and if there had been any parting done, she was sure he had been the one to do it.

She rested her head against the soft fabric of his gray, stylishly cut jacket. The warmth of his body came up to caress her cheek as the scent of his cologne became more apparent. It was a strong, masculine fragrance. It aroused her.... As if she needed arousing, she thought, then reminded herself that she wanted to find out more about him. So far, what she knew could be inscribed on the head of a pin.

His hand pressed against the small of her back, his

fingertips slightly spread apart, just brushing against the top of her dress and touching her bare skin. Each time he touched her a network of enchantment sprang up, making it difficult for her to think about anything except Brett.

She was aware of everything: the way his hips fit against her as they swayed to the melody; the way her breasts felt, pressed against his hard chest. She might not be finding out very much about him, but she was certainly learning things about herself, she realized. She was fast becoming a victim of a phenomenon she had always dismissed as so much rubbish: physical attraction.

The music drifted into silence, and Brett escorted her back to their table. Their drinks stood waiting for them as Lissa slipped back into her seat.

"To chance," Brett said, cavalierly lifting his glass as he eyed her closely.

"To chance," Lissa echoed, following suit. She watched him over the rim of her goblet as she sipped a little of the fruity liquid. The sweet taste wound its way through her system, adding to the warmth that his presence generated.

Had it *all* been purely chance? She wondered. Or had it been something more that had brought him to her? And if so, what? Like it or not, things did point toward the likelihood that he was the suspect the department was after. But the greater her attraction grew, the more reluctant Lissa was to commit herself exclusively to this line of thinking. Could she be this attracted to a common thief?

She turned these thoughts over in her mind as she drew her eyes away from his and looked toward the inky harbor that lay just beyond the windows. One

entire wall of the restaurant was made of glass, allowing the diners a clear view of the bay. A string of
strategically positioned lights helped illuminate a variety of sailboats housed for the night at the nearby
dock and enabled Lissa to see a large gathering of
pigeons on the beam just below her. But her mind
wasn't on sailboats or pigeons. It was on the man who
sat opposite her now, studying her face so carefully.

She sensed his eyes on her and looked up into
them, smiling brightly.

"Been a policewoman long?" Brett asked her as
the waiter appeared with their dinner.

Lissa pulled back her gold-colored napkin, placing
it on her lap as the young waiter served her dinner
first. "Two years," she answered.

"What made you want to become one?"

Lissa arched her brow, wondering if he was going
to be like all the rest. Without realizing it, she took
on a formal tone. "I became a policewoman because
I wanted to." She waited for him to say something
disparaging.

He didn't. Instead he merely nodded. "Good reason as any." He began to eat, then continued. "You
sound a bit defensive. Are you?"

He asked the question so easily that she found herself explaining before she realized what she was doing. "I guess I am, in a way. I've had to try to justify
my choice to everyone who ever mattered."

Inadvertently, her mind went back to Tim, her former boyfriend. The relationship hadn't been anything
serious, really, but it had hurt when he left. He had
picked his time well, she remembered, leaving just as
she entered the academy. He had left in the heat of

an argument, shouting something about not wanting *his* girl to be playing cops and robbers.

"Parents didn't approve?" Brett guessed.

"Approve?" She laughed. "They talked about locking me away in a tower and cutting off my hair to ensure against escape." The laugh died in her throat as her tone became more serious. "You see, I have two sisters, Megan and Brenda. Both of them fulfilled all my parents' expectations: got straight A's in high school, went on to college, got married, had the prescribed number of children...." She sighed as she paused for a moment. "And then there's me."

"The black sheep?" Brett offered, amused.

"The nonconforming sheep," she corrected with a smile.

"How nonconforming?"

"I didn't go to college...."

"For shame," he teased, his eyes sparkling. Lissa felt herself liking him more and more.

"Well, actually, I did go," she clarified. "I just didn't stay. Learning about life from textbooks and stuffy professors made me feel very restless," she admitted. "All the excitement was missing."

Brett laughed. "That sounds like the way I feel about marriage," he admitted freely.

"Oh?" Lissa asked. "I take it you have something against the great institution." For some reason she was curious about his answer, despite her own feelings that marriage for her was far in the future.

"Perfect word for it. Institution, as in prison. Institutionalized, as in having your wings clipped. Not for me." He finished his drink. "Want another?" he asked, looking at her near-empty glass.

"Please."

She watched him signal for the waiter. Well, so far she had learned that he wasn't the marrying kind. That wasn't exactly the kind of information she was after—or was it? A tiny voice whispered. She dismissed it.

"So, what it is you've been working on lately?" Lissa asked as soon as Brett ordered two more cocktails and the waiter had disappeared into the recesses of the restaurant. She saw the grin come over Brett's face. "By way of buildings, I mean," she corrected.

He didn't answer right away, as if he were searching for the right words to use. Finally he said, "I've just put the finishing touches on a New York penthouse for the Viscountess Rothenberry," he said, rolling the noble woman's name off his tongue as if he were talking about his next-door neighbor instead of a fabulously wealthy member of the world's elite.

"I thought you just built and renovated houses," she said, purposely acting confused. "Wouldn't this be more in the way of decorating?"

For a moment she thought she had caught him off guard, but then he said, "I handle all facets." His manner was smooth, flawless. "We did go as far as knocking down a wall or two. The decorating scheme called for it," he told her. "But I'm involved in all areas. I oversee the decorating once the blueprints are done. I even put the owners in touch with someone to install their security systems, although at the moment I'm looking for someone around here who's better qualified than my usual man. I hear that there have been a number of local robberies lately involving the theft of priceless antiques."

That was a nice touch, Lissa thought. She wondered if he had put that in for her benefit, or if it was really true. To all intents and purposes, he was who he appeared to be, yet Lissa couldn't shake the feeling that there was something she was missing about the man.

"Strange you should mention that," Lissa said, fingering the stem of her glass. "I'm involved in the investigation. Security systems are my field of expertise." She cocked her head, waiting to see what he would say in response.

He took in the information and seemed to digest it for a moment. "I guess it was just a matter of fate that we met." He laughed. "Now I have a reason for calling on you—you can tell me how everything's going. One of my clients had a priceless sword stolen, and he's been beside himself ever since the robbery. Have any leads?" he asked with what Lissa considered a great deal of interest.

"One possible one," she said evasively, thinking of what Linda had said about a witness seeing a red sports car leaving the area. She wondered if he had seen the driver, or if he now recalled the license number or make of the car.

"Can't elaborate, eh?" he guessed. Was it her imagination, or was he prodding her?

"Not yet."

They eyed one another for a moment, and Lissa got the strangest feeling that they were playing a game, a game each secretly knew about.

"Caught any desperate criminals lately?" Brett finally asked, breaking the mood.

"Only some flashy architect flying by in a crimson Corvette," she said coyly, playing with the remaining ice chips in her goblet. She pushed them around with her straw and sipped the last bit of liquid.

"Flashy, eh?"

"Well, in comparison to the usual traffic, cutoff jeans, surfboards, sunstreaked blond hair—yes, you looked flashy."

"Looked?" he repeated. "And how do I look now?" His voice was mellow, beguiling, pulling her into a special world that he created. A world where only they existed.

"Nice," she had to admit, rolling the word over in her mouth. "Very...nice." Lissa didn't trust herself to say anything more. She glanced down at her watch.

"Do you have to be home by a certain time?" he asked, picking up the hint.

"No, it's just that I've put in a long day—"

"Would you care to put in a long night?" he asked enticingly.

"—and Agatha worries about me when I'm out late," Lissa ended, ignoring his invitation and her own reaction to it.

"Well, we wouldn't want to upset Agatha," Brett agreed, turning to call for the check. "Although I think I did manage to pass her inspection."

"Pass it?" she echoed. "I think she's in love with you." Lissa laughed, picking up her purse. She reached for the light lacy shawl she had brought with her, but Brett was there ahead of her, slipping the delicate fabric about her shoulders. He ran his hands over her arms at the same time. Lissa suddenly shivered as a warm ache filled her.

"Score one for my side," Brett murmured under his breath, and Lissa didn't know if he was referring to the reaction he had just generated or commenting on her statement about Agatha's obvious adoration.

The torrid air had abated somewhat by the time

Lissa and Brett walked back to his car. The cool ocean breeze helped clear her head a little, and she took in several deep whiffs, as if to protect herself against the sexy feeling struggling to take hold of her every time Brett touched her. She sidestepped a couple deep in conversation, and as she did so Brett slipped his arm around her shoulders, melding her against his side. She seemed to fit there so well, she couldn't help thinking.

"You don't waste any time, do you?" she asked, amused. Keep it light, Armstrong, she cautioned herself.

"Time is a very precious commodity, never to be wasted, always to be enjoyed. I see what I want," he told her, stopping at his car, "and I go for it."

Good motto for a thief, Lissa told herself as she struggled to escape the magic he was creating. For a moment their eyes met and held. She tried to see what lay beyond those beguiling soft brown eyes, but although they seemed bottomless, they gave her not a clue. The man behind them was a mystery.

"Meaning me?" she asked, phrasing the question bluntly.

"Meaning you." His voice was low, almost a purr. She felt a little uneasy. This route was definitely not leading toward an impartial investigation.

She swallowed, trying to dispel the sudden dryness in her mouth. "Well, forewarned is forearmed," she murmured lightly, opening her door and sitting down in the passenger seat.

Brett shut her door and didn't say anything until he got in behind the wheel. "I'm not planning for this to be a duel to the death," he said, turning the key. The soft hum of the well-tuned engine came in answer to his light touch. At the same time the radio went on. Seductive, silky music filled the interior of the car.

"You make it sound like you collect women as well as antiques," Lissa said archly, forgetting for a moment what she had told herself was her main purpose for going out with Brett.

"I don't collect antiques," he corrected her, "though I do specialize in obtaining them for my clients. I'm not a brave enough soul to collect women, either," he told her. "By and large, women are temperamental creatures who get upset if you spend too much time and attention on your work. I need my space." He paused for a moment, and Lissa wondered if he was waiting for her to take that as a challenge. Some women, she knew, would. It was tantamount to his saying that he would never be cornered by a woman. Well, she had no desire to corner him, only to find out if he was the burglar in question. At least, she told herself, she had no designs on cornering him.

"I know what you mean," she said. "Having your own space is a very important thing. I find that some of my happiest moments are spent alone, working on my stained glass projects."

He turned to her, a quizzical look in his eyes. "Stained glass?" he repeated. "You don't look like the type."

"Why?" she wanted to know.

"Because things like that take time and patience, and I can't picture you working on something little. You look like a woman who's used to things that are larger than life."

Meaning you, she thought. Out loud she said glibly, "That's what makes me interesting."

"Definitely worthy of close scrutiny," he agreed.

For a moment there was nothing but the quiet hum of an old song coming from the radio. Lissa stared straight ahead, trying to make out shapes along the road in the darkness. Only an occasional passing car helped break up the shadows along the lonely highway back to her house.

Brett McKenna was an utter enigma to her. On the one hand, she felt quite at ease with him; she had told him things that she usually didn't share with anyone, much less someone she had only known for a few hours. On the other hand, there was something about him that made her feel nervous. But it wasn't the kind of unsettled feeling that came from confronting the dangerous aspects of her work. No, this was the flustered feeling that had to do with being a woman who was out with a handsome, charming man who appeared to be bent on her ultimate seduction. Never having come in contact with a man who was so open about his intentions before, Lissa didn't know what to make of the situation. She decided to let the whole thing ride and try to concentrate on him as a possible suspect. That path, she hoped, was safer.

She saw her house appear to the right as Brett brought the car to a halt in her driveway. Lissa barely had time to put her hand on the handle before Brett was on her side of the car, opening the door for her.

"Ah, chivalry is not dead," she joked, swinging her long legs out. Her dress had climbed up a little, and her thighs showed. She caught Brett staring down unabashedly at the sight.

"It has its little rewards," he said just before she tugged her skirt down. "Like now."

Before she knew what was happening, or had time

to brace herself, Brett took her into his arms and kissed her. The taste of Scotch mixed with the flavor of her strawberry daiquiri, creating an almost lethal combination. Lissa felt her head reel as she tried to get hold of her senses.

His arms tightened about her as the kiss grew in intensity, moving beyond the pleasurable sensation it had originally created and forging on. It wasn't a kiss any longer; it was an entire experience. A huge wave of excitement surged through Lissa.

When the kiss ended Lissa felt desolation wash over her.

"Can I come in?" Brett asked softly, still holding her, his touch sending little tongues of fire licking up and down her arms.

It took her a moment to find her breath. To let him come in when she was so uncertain as to his role in the robberies would be folly, she told herself. She was playing with fire, as the old saying went. Leaving herself open to falling for someone who might thrive on living on the other side of the law could be disastrous. "I don't think so," she said with an effort. Her words didn't sound very forceful to her.

"Just to say good night to Agatha," Brett pressed innocently.

"I'll make your apologies to Agatha. She'll understand."

"She might not," he warned. "Females are funny about being snubbed."

"I'll give her a bone," Lissa murmured, totally mesmerized by the man in front of her.

Brett drew her closer as he bent his head to kiss her again, and somewhere in the back of her mind the "Hallelujah" chorus mixed with *Taps*.

Four

It wasn't the sun streaming into her eyes that finally woke Lissa up the next morning. If it had been the sun, she would have done what she usually did: simply rolled over, muttering "Five more minutes" to herself until sunrise gradually unfolded into early morning. But it wasn't easy shutting out having your face licked.

Lissa bolted upright. "Agatha!" she cried, then sank back down against her pillow, relieved. "I thought you were him," she said to the animal dancing beside her on the bed.

She stroked Agatha under the chin while her thoughts drifted back to last night. "If I hadn't stood so firmly on my principles," she murmured, half to the dog, half to herself, "it wouldn't be a dog I'd be stroking right now." She grinned a little, congratulating herself on outmaneuvering Brett.

Still, victory was a little hollow, she thought as she got up, leaving a crumpled ruin in her wake, and padded sleepily off to the bathroom. Now that she was semiawake, she was conscious of the dull ache in her body. An ache that was definitely not the result of too many hours on the volleyball court, or too much time spent bent over her latest stained glass project. It was the kind of ache that came from longing. Or so she surmised. Nothing like this had ever happened to her before.

"He certainly wasn't easy to resist," she told Agatha while she brushed her teeth with a multicolored toothpaste. "I'm not even sure how I did it," Lissa concluded. She stood holding her toothbrush under the stream of water for some time, her mind elsewhere. Suddenly she realized that she had been standing there for a good five minutes or more. If I keep this up, I'll wash away the bristles as well, she thought. She shut off the water, but not her thoughts. He had been charmingly forceful, but not pushy. Just when he could have pressed his advantage—when a man with a typically large ego would have thought he had the advantage—he hadn't.

As she haphazardly stuck the toothbrush back into the medicine cabinet she remembered the mixture of relief and surprise that had fought for equal shares within her when Brett had backed away.

"Be sure to tell Agatha it wasn't my fault," he had said, a mischievous expression on his face. "That it was her owner's doing that the evening ended this way."

"I'll tell her," Lissa had replied, a strange thumping in her ears. It was her heart. What a weird place to feel your heartbeat, she had thought, and what a

weird heartbeat. The man, she had told herself, was
an operator. A smooth, shrewd operator. And that was
exactly what she was afraid of.

She had thought he was going to kiss her again. At
that point, if he had, she would probably have let him
in, unable to stem the tide of emotions coursing
through her veins. She was only so strong, only so
resilient. But all he did was kiss the tip of her forefinger and run it lightly along her lower lip. Lissa
shook her head as she realized that she was trying to
relive that moment and recapture the wild sensation
that had burst through her veins. It had been such an
inconsequential moment in her life, she tried to tell
herself. Why was she trying to remember every detail? And what if he *was* the thief? Then what?

Her thoughts shifted away from that avenue, holding the idea at bay temporarily.

He hadn't even said "I'll call you." Nothing. Disappointment claimed her.

"Well, if he's the guilty party, we'll be seeing him
again, right, girl?" Lissa said to the dog sitting at her
bare feet. Agatha seemed to be following the conversation intently, obviously hungry for attention.

Lissa tried not to think about Brett as she took a
quick shower and then slipped on her worn jeans and
baggy sweatshirt. But she found that it wasn't easy
not thinking about Brett. Aside from being handsome,
he had a presence that she couldn't forget. His image
filled her mind as she ate her breakfast.

He was still with her as she went into the spare
bedroom where all her stained glass equipment was
laid out, patiently waiting for her artistic hand to form
a pattern out of the bits of lead and glass.

"If this keeps up," she muttered under her breath,

"I'm going to wind up making a stained glass image of his face. Wouldn't that be great?" she asked the dog sarcastically. "Whoever used my guest room would wake up having those brown eyes staring at them."

Somehow she could think of worse fates than waking up to have those eyes looking at her. They had been soft, shimmering and utterly mesmerizing.

"Good stock-in-trade for a con man if he's going to be dealing with women," she said, carelessly tossing the remark toward Agatha as she seated herself before the huge mosaic that was spread across her large art table. "But not a burglar. A burglar should be sleek, skinny and sneaky." She laughed. "And if I keep on thinking like that, they'll demote me to crossing guard at the local elementary school."

She tried very hard to occupy her thoughts with her work. She told herself that she had only a limited amount of time each week to devote to the project, and that she had better get to it if she ever expected to see her handiwork finally mounted. The collection of tiny red roses would look beautiful catching the morning sun. She had already envisioned it countless times in her mind's eye. But now all her mind's eye seemed to see was Brett's sensuous smile unfurling. It made his features even more handsome than they already were, and took hold of something inside her. He possessed, she decided, what the writers of dictionaries undoubtedly had in mind when they set down the word "charisma."

Just as she had finally evicted his image from her mind and gotten down to serious work, the phone rang. She tried to ignore it, but the jangling persisted, accompanied by Agatha's insistent yipping.

"I hear it, I hear it," she told the dog, putting down her tools. Maybe it's him, she thought suddenly, her steps unconsciously quickening as she made her way to the kitchen, picking up the receiver just as the eighth ring shattered the otherwise-peaceful air. Agatha had ceased her barking on command.

"Hello?"

"It's about time you answered."

Disappointment took hold of her as she recognized the chief's voice. "I was busy working in the next room," she explained. "I didn't hear the phone."

Police Chief Hanson didn't bother commenting on her excuse. She could hear the impatience in his voice as he spoke. "Brom came down with ptomaine poisoning," he barked out in a staccato voice.

Brom was the detective assigned to the burglary case. Why was the chief telling her this? He wasn't in the habit of phoning people with news bulletins, especially not her. Since the day she had joined the force, she had had an uncomfortable feeling that Hanson didn't care for her. Not because of anything she had done, but merely because she was a woman. Hanson didn't believe that women had any place on the police force beyond operating the switchboard.

A tiny spark of hope began to nibble at her mind, held in check by her common sense. Don't get excited yet, she told herself.

"What happened?" she asked.

"I dunno. He had some kind of takeout food from this new restaurant. Got sick within an hour." His voice was totally devoid of any sympathy. "Serves him right for not brownbagging it."

Lissa knew that Hanson firmly believed in not wasting money and looked down his nose at people who didn't cleave to his theories. She also knew he was stalling, despite the impatience in his voice. He sounded as if he were about to do something he didn't want to do, but was being forced to because of circumstances. Her hopes grew a little larger. She wanted to say, "You didn't call me up to tell me he should have packed his own lunch," but she didn't. There wasn't much of anything she *could* say, she thought uncomfortably, waiting for his next comment.

"Yes, chief?" she prodded.

"You don't have to sound so damn eager," he snapped. "It's only temporary, and only because I'm shorthanded."

"What's only temporary?" she asked, trying very hard not to sound as eager as she felt.

There was a long pause, as if Hanson were having trouble forming the words. Grudgingly he continued. "I'm putting you on the burglary case," he told her. She could hear the glaring reservations in his voice. "But only until Brom gets well, or one of the other detectives wraps up his case." There were only two other detectives on the force, and she knew that they more than had their hands full. "I wouldn't be doing it at all, but you are studying to take the exam and..." His voice trailed off, irritation punctuating his sigh.

"Thank you, sir," Lissa said, her mind racing. A chance. She was being given a chance. If she solved this thing...

"I need you down here right away," Hanson growled. She knew he hated every word he was uttering, and she didn't care.

"Right away, sir," she promised enthusiastically. She was on her way practically before she hung up.

Her enthusiasm waned a little as the day pro-

gressed. In all fairness, the day wasn't any different
from the day before, but then she had only been
watching for speeding cars. Today her attention was
directed to patrolling the residential neighborhood
that the burglar had made his own. She was looking
for anything that looked remotely suspicious. She
would have liked to be out interviewing victims, but
all the victims were accounted for, having already
been thoroughly questioned by Brom. The information was all there in the reports, reports that were
lengthy and wordy and that she had had no time to
leaf through at the station. So she had requested per-
mission to take the files home with her in order to
become familiarized with every shred of evidence,
every detail of the case.

She was determined to crack it. If she did, she
knew that the chief would have to acknowledge her
ability and see his way more clearly toward giving
her the promotion she sorely craved. She had come
close once before, a year ago, only to be thwarted. It
wasn't going to happen again.

"Detective Armstrong," she murmured to herself
as she slowly cruised the quiet, tree-lined streets.
"Has a nice ring to it." She smiled. A very nice ring.

If only something would *happen*.

But it was Monday. It was broad daylight. And it
was too much to hope for. The last robbery had occurred just yesterday. The thief was thorough, but he
wasn't reckless. From the little fill-in information she
had gotten from the chief and what she had read on
her own in the newspaper, Lissa knew that he, or she,
never pulled off a robbery two days in a row.

Perhaps he'd get overconfident, she thought. After
all, he had pulled five robberies and he was still out

there, practicing. But with just a little bit of luck on her part the thief wouldn't be out there for long.

Maybe a lot of luck, Lissa amended several hours later as she continued cruising. Nothing more sneaky than an overfluffed Angora cat stalking a bird in a tree had crossed her path all day. She was getting irritable and longed to move on to the reports. Perhaps there was something there that would help her. Once she had familiarized herself with the background information in the reports, she would have an excuse to talk to the victims firsthand. The idea heartened her as she rounded a corner and drove the unmarked car down a long winding street.

All her thoughts skidded to an abrupt halt as she spied a red Corvette. Every nerve ending within her came to sudden attention.

Brett!

The car was some distance in front of her. She tried to tell herself that, while Brett's car was distinct, it wasn't exactly a dinosaur. There were other red Stingrays in the world. She picked up speed and tried to draw close enough to read the license plate. At this range she could barely make out the first two letters. But that was enough to make her heartbeat increase. The numbers that she *could* see matched Brett's plates. Squinting to catch a glimpse of the driver, she thought she could make out a man with light hair. For a man who lived in Beverly Hills, he certainly liked traveling a long way from home, she thought, then reminded herself that she wasn't even sure it was *him*.

There were a thousand reasons why he could be out there, she told herself. He could be consulting with a client. Meeting a friend for a late lunch. Taking out a woman.... Or casing the area for another break-in.

She was thinking like a cop. Well, was that bad? She demanded of herself. She was *supposed* to be thinking like a cop. You've got the badge and everything, she told herself wryly. The trouble was that her badge was competing with unfamiliar emotions that went far deeper than any she had known before.

"You're a policewoman," she said aloud. The "police" comes first, then the "woman." And that was justification enough to try to catch up with Brett....

But wasn't she also trying to catch up with him because he hadn't said anything last night about seeing her again? Wasn't she just the least bit...um... anxious, perhaps, to cross his line of vision again in hopes that he would make some sort of advance? Even make another date?

Terrific, a date with a thief. What was coming over her?

This was getting very confusing. Also frustrating, she noted.

While she was having her interior dialogue, Brett—or whoever it was—turned another corner, and by the time she reached it, the red car was gone.

Damn!

As she stepped up her patrol of the streets, traveling up and down the area, she didn't catch sight again of the sleek crimson automobile. Or its driver. It was as if he and his car had disappeared into thin air.

Like a thief in the night.

The incident haunted her for the rest of her shift. The next two hours were studies in boredom, and restless frustration began building up within Lissa. What she really wanted to do was go tearing up to Beverly Hills and wait for Brett to come home. But, being basically logical, she didn't feel she had enough evidence to justify doing so. At least, not during her shift. After her shift was another story.

The moment her shift was over, Lissa zipped back to the station and exchanged the midsize, roomy Ford LTD for her scrappy little Mustang and took off. She had to fight the urge not to exceed the speed limit.

You just want to see him again, she argued with herself. Well, she'd be lying if she said that it would all be one and the same to her if she never laid eyes on him again. But that was beside the point right now. Granted, it was all purely circumstantial, and she wasn't even sure that it had been Brett she had seen in the red car, but she had this gut feeling that Brett was involved in the case somehow.

Gut feeling, she thought with a touch of self-deprecating amusement, trying her best not to take herself too seriously. That sounded like a line out of a detective novel. Of course, if she called it women's intuition, it sounded just as stereotyped. Whatever it was called, though, she had this overwhelming feeling that Mr. Brett McKenna wasn't exactly what he seemed to be. There was definitely more to the man than met the eye.

And there was a lot that *did* meet the eye, she thought, allowing a dreamy smile to slip over her lips for a moment. Steady, Armstrong. It's work first, remember? She suddenly found herself hoping that Brett wasn't the suspect they were looking for, promotion or no promotion.

Detective work wasn't turning out to be as easy as she had thought. Other people got suspects who looked as if their noses had been broken several times over and had faces that could chill a mother's heart. Why did the person she was tailing have to look like the model for the Prince in Cinderella? It definitely made it harder for her to concentrate on her work—and to remain dedicated to it. Here she was, a Laguna Beach policewoman, rooting for a possible thief. Lissa sighed.

The traffic was a bear. As she inched her way up the San Diego Freeway, competing for space with a trailer truck that was belching dark clouds of gasoline fumes in her direction, Lissa had a lot of time to re-examine her motives. The longer she spent at it, the worse the situation became, until she gave up entirely, telling herself that she was following the only possible lead she had come up with all day. She wished she could read the reports that were next to her. Traffic was moving, or not moving, at such a pace that she was strongly tempted to do just that. Instead she switched on her radio and tried to pay attention to that. She discovered that her dial was set to a station that played only soft music. It had a dreamy effect on her.

That would never do. Dreamy was one thing she didn't want to be around Brett, even if she was off duty. She wanted to be super alert, super sharp. If he did turn out to be the thief in question, she'd need every weapon at her disposal not to let his charm and looks seduce her away from her main intent. Her *only* intent, she amended, then realized as she switched to a blaring oldies station that she had used the word "seduce."

Call a spade a spade, Armstrong, she thought. He could, in all likelihood, seduce any woman he set his sights on. The more resistance he met with, the better, probably. He looked like a man who thrived on challenge.

She was still psyching herself up as she exited the freeway and merged with the flow of traffic crawling along Wilshire Boulevard. Lissa fell into definite agreement with those who complained about the profusion of cars in Los Angeles.

The traffic had thinned out by the time she entered the Beverly Hills city limits. There was almost a hush to the place as she drove down the streets, searching for the house number that would match the address in her ticket book. It was like entering another world, she thought. Would someone living in an atmosphere like this risk everything by turning to a life of crime? Who knew what went through people's minds? She thought. Maybe he needed the money to hang on to the old homestead.

There! That was it! She zeroed in on a house whose street number was partially obscured by an overgrowth of ivy. It had all but engulfed the tall column that bore a brass plaque with the address. Lissa stopped her car before the towering black gates. Now what? If he wasn't home, she'd be stuck out here in her Mustang, feeling like an eyesore in a land of Rolls-Royces, Mercedes and Ferraris.

As she stepped out of the car she hunted around for a way to reach the large house that she could barely see at the end of the curved stone driveway. The ivy, she noticed, was also swallowing up a buzzer. Lissa pressed the button and waited to see what would happen.

"Yes?"

It was a surly, demanding "yes." It was a "yes"

uttered by someone who didn't like being bothered. It was a "yes" with a cold.

This is it, kid. Make your big play. "Officer Armstrong to see Mr. McKenna, please. Official business." The words had never sounded quite as stilted to her before. She half-expected the person on the other end to laugh uncontrollably and fade off into the recesses of the house, leaving her standing there with her finger on the buzzer.

Instead, to her relief, the heavy gate began to open. Quickly Lissa jumped into her car and made it inside just as the gates appeared to have a change of heart and started to close again. Whoever belonged to that nasal voice certainly didn't give you much time to get in. If she had had a big car it would have gotten severely dented, she decided. But then, would an "Officer Armstrong" come up driving a long car? She was sure the owner of the voice instinctively knew that the answer to that question was No.

Well, our possible burglar doesn't live alone, Lissa told herself. He probably had to steal to pay for the butler as well as the house. Salaries run high these days. The thought brought back part of their conversation from the previous night. He had said that business was good, but... Stop it, she commanded herself. You're working against yourself. Get this thing cleared up once and for all.

With that intention uppermost in her mind, Lissa brought her little blue car to a halt in the spacious driveway right in front of a seven-car garage. Marble steps led her up to enormous front doors that begged to have an appreciative hand reach out and touch their intricate carvings. The artist in her stood for a moment, lost in admiration for the person who had spent so many hours sculpting the complex pattern of linking flowers and leaves.

She was till standing there, delighting in the work, when the door swung open, startling her.

Brett grinned at her, thrusting out his hands, his wrists held close together. "Here," he said. "Take me away. I'm guilty."

Lissa's eyes grew wide. Was he making a confession? But that was ridiculous. He didn't even know why she was there—did he? The grin told her that a guilty conscience had nothing to do with his words. "What?" she asked uncomprehendingly.

"I'm guilty," he repeated. "I haven't called you all day."

He was making fun of her, she thought, trying to look annoyed. The feeling died before it could register on her face. "I wouldn't know," she said in a detached manner. "I've been working all day."

"But that doesn't mean you've been out of my thoughts," he was saying, appearing not to have even heard her reply. "You've been right there in the center all day," he assured her charmingly. "Won't you come in?" he asked, taking her arm and ushering her inside without waiting for an answer. The man was obviously used to having his own way with everything and everyone. Get set for a rude awakening, McKenna, she thought as she stepped inside.

"Inside" was breathtaking, and for a fraction of a moment Lissa's attention was diverted from Brett to the interior of the house. "Mansion" would have been a better description, she decided. The place definitely befitted an architect. It was spacious and airy, with a ceiling that began high and slanted upward until it reached the stairway, where it broke, contin-

uing up to the second floor. The floor beneath her feet
was done completely in expensive tile and shone bril-
liantly. It was gleaming white. Everything was white
with blue accents. It made Lissa feel that she should
take her shoes off and walk around in hushed reverence. The effect of the house was not unlike the effect
Brett had on her.

White carpeting led up the winding stairway. A
white openwork banister guarded each step of the
way. White wallpaper with tiny free-flying blue birds
covered the two-story wall along the other side.

"Like it?" Brett asked in a careless tone. Only
someone with plenty of money could assume that
careless tone, Lissa thought. If you had money, you
didn't think about the cost of anything, only whether
or not you liked it.

"'Like' seems a pretty tame word for…all this,"
Lissa commented, turning around to face him once
again and making a sweeping gesture that took in the
entire room.

"Does that include me?"

Very clever, she thought. Suspect uses words
against officer. Officer must remember to tread lightly
here—and with purpose foremost in mind.

"You," she said, keeping her voice matter-of-fact,
"would never be classified as part of anything. I think
you know that you deserve center stage wherever you
go."

Amusement was evident on his face as he tried to
lead her farther into the house. This time she held her
ground. The foyer would do quite nicely for what she
had in mind. "This sounds interesting," he said.
"Tell me more."

"I intend to," she said, crisp and businesslike. So

what if his head looked like a bust of Apollo? The call to thievery did not strike only ugly people, she reminded herself. "Mr. McKenna—" she began after a fortifying deep breath.

"Brett," he corrected, driving the breath she had just taken from her lungs.

"Mr. McKenna," she repeated doggedly, "I have some questions to ask you."

He nodded. "Only fair. I have some questions for you." His words threw her off just long enough to get his question in first. "Are you on duty?"

Was there a sly look in his eyes, or was that her imagination? It certainly wasn't due to poor lighting. There was enough light in the foyer from the massive crystal chandelier overhead to illuminate Angel Stadium during a night game, she thought. "No," she had to admit, "but—"

"Good. Then you can have a drink," he said, turning away for a moment as if to look for someone.

"No, I can't," she informed him firmly, refusing to be shaken from her purpose. "I—"

"All right, we'll skip the drink and go right onto the tour," he told her, gripping her arm and guiding her to his side. But the pressure he exerted was still gentle, despite the fact that Lissa felt it would take more than a tug to loosen his hold on her.

"What tour?" she asked, surprised.

"Why, of the house, of course. I saw the look in your eyes when you came inside. I'm not immodest enough to think that all that awe and wonder was meant for me alone."

Half a dozen sputtered sentences started and died on her lips as he very calmly led her up the stairs.

Five

"I like to start with the bedrooms first," he told her. "Most people end their tours there, but I prefer to begin upstairs and work my way down."

Was it just her, or were those words pregnant with meaning? She was about to protest that she had absolutely no interest in seeing any of his bedrooms, that all she wanted to do was ask him a few questions and be done with it. But somehow she never managed to say the words.

Brett was being too smooth, too compellingly charming, as he ushered her from one elegantly furnished room to another. It was, she thought, like wandering through the pages of *House Beautiful*—or was that *Mansion Beautiful?* Whatever it was, it was a feast for the eyes. Lissa had had no idea that there could be so many different varieties of blue and white wallpaper. Outside of a few model homes she had visited, where an interior decorator had scrupulously matched every piece of furniture in each room, Lissa had never been in a house where everything was so color coordinated. It was magnificent. It also looked as if no one lived there. Covertly she stole a glance at the man at her side. This was too cold a place to reflect Brett. She couldn't picture him living here. Yet here he was.

And she couldn't picture him as a burglar, either, when she came right down to it, yet there were a lot of things that pointed in that direction. Time to stop speculating, she told herself, and get down to work.

Initially it had been her intent just to ask him a few basic questions. But as he led her around from room to sprawling room like some society tourist, Lissa decided that perhaps it would be better if she took him down to the station for questioning. The stark soberness of being inside a precinct station might just take the smooth edge off Brett and give her an opportunity to find out if any of her suspicions were warranted.

"This is all very nice, but I'm afraid you're still going to have to come down for questioning," she told him patiently as they reached the master bedroom.

"Questioning?" Brett echoed, turning away from the flagstone fireplace. "Just how big a ticket did I rack up yesterday?" he asked, looking a bit confused.

"It's not about the ticket," she said as he moved closer to her. Once again his cologne seduced her senses. Yes, the precinct was definitely the best place to go with this. She felt just a wee bit vulnerable standing in this room. Unlike the rest of the house, this room seemed to fit Brett. For one thing, it was done in warm shades of brown, with blue touches.

There wasn't a shred of antiseptic white anywhere at all. Warm shades of brown, she thought again, like his eyes.

"Then what *is* this all about?" he asked, puzzled.

"Would you mind if we went back downstairs?" Lissa asked, then led the way out, not waiting for him to answer. She had felt at a definite disadvantage in that sumptuous bedroom. It had made her feel unprofessional. Face it, Armstrong, it makes your mind take a direction that has nothing to do with the investigation, she reprimanded herself. For all she knew he might even have set it up that way. She gave him a lot of credit for being astute.

"Wait," he said, taking her arm as she started for the stairs. "What is it you can't tell me until we're standing in the foyer?" There was amusement in his voice, but beneath it, Lissa could detect a very serious tone. Did she have him worried?

"I'd like you to come down to the precinct for a few routine questions concerning a series of burglaries we've had in the area you've been... frequenting," she finally said, for lack of a better word.

She watched as the muscles along his jawline tightened slightly and an incredulous look came over his face. It was the only outward indication of a whole myriad of emotions that were running through Brett.

And then he laughed. Well, she could hardly have expected him to do anything else, under the circumstances. Laughter did get rid of tension. She saw his face relax.

"So you think I'm involved in the burglaries?" he asked, obviously tickled by the accusation.

Cool. Very cool. She noted, though, that he wasn't

denying the connection. She had been right all along. A sense of professional pride and satisfaction flitted briefly through her. It was pushed out of the way by a very real wave of depression. She had been right all along, she thought again, but sadly this time. He was a thief.

"Are you arresting me?" he asked. She thought he was going to laugh out loud.

He certainly wasn't short on bravado, she'd give him that. "No, this is just for some informal questioning—if you don't mind." She leveled her gaze at him, daring him to object.

"Are you sure you want to go through with this?" Brett asked her.

"I'm sure."

"But you're not charging me with anything?" he asked as they walked down the stairs.

"No," she answered. Not yet, she added silently.

"Can't think of a thing I'd rather do than accompany you somewhere," he said with an air of gallantry.

Smooth to the very end, Lissa thought as they reached the entrance hall.

A rather emaciated man dressed in dark livery approached them just then. From his rather labored breathing, Lissa concluded that this was the owner of the wheezing voice she had heard over the intercom at the gate.

"Will you be going out again, Mr. McKenna?" the wizened man asked.

"Yes, it would seem so. I'm not sure just when I'll be back, Edgar. Tell Ethel not to bother with dinner. I'll throw something together when I get back."

"Ethel?" Lissa couldn't help asking. Was there a Mrs. McKenna in the shadows after all?

"The cook," Brett answered. From his tone, she could tell that he knew exactly what she was thinking. She was growing increasingly annoyed with herself. A good detective could keep a poker face at all times. This was supposed to include a "poker voice" as well. Nobody ever knew what was on Joe Friday's mind even when he *wasn't* around a suspect. But that, Lissa reminded herself, was television, not real life. And Brett was certainly real life, all right.

"Just how old *is* he?" Lissa asked in a whisper as they began to leave.

"Eighty-three!" crackled the hoarse voice. "And still able to hear quite well, thank you."

Lissa couldn't bring herself to turn around to look at the butler as they left the mansion. Brett had the good graces not to laugh as they went down the steps.

"He's cantankerous and takes some getting used to, but he seems to do his job pretty well," Brett told her.

"Seems?" she echoed, turning to look at him. It struck her as an odd thing to say.

Brett cleared his throat, as if he had just caught himself in a slipup. It caught Lissa's attention. Why did he look so uncertain? The look quickly faded. Had it been her imagination?

"Well, from all appearances, Edgar seems to be doing a good job. I'm not around very much," he explained.

"Your architecting?" she guessed drolly. Or your secret life as a burglar? She thought. She was becoming surer and surer that her gut feeling was right, but it didn't make her any happier.

"Right," he answered.

"Any clients in the Laguna area?" she asked casually.

"No," he replied, a bit too quickly for her liking. She was definitely glad he was coming in for questioning.

"My car's this way," she needlessly pointed out. Maybe she'd get a new paint job for it, she thought as Brett wordlessly moved to the passenger side.

She didn't know why, but for one moment she was tempted to give it all up. To tell him that she had made a mistake and just go home. There was something about Brett that made her want to shield him. Shield. She had taken an oath when she had put on her police shield, she reminded herself, and she hadn't just been mouthing words at the time. Nothing had changed about her feelings regarding law and order. Nothing except that Brett McKenna had entered her life. She forced herself to look at the case clinically, and she wondered if the man who had seen the red sports car pulling away from the scene of the burglary was available. Would he be any help in identifying the driver?

She realized that Brett was still standing outside the car. Was he afraid? She wondered. "Do you want to get in touch with your lawyer?" she asked kindly. After all, the man did deserve a fighting chance, she argued with herself.

"I don't think one will be necessary."

God, he was sure of himself. Lissa's compassionate feelings abated. She was doing the right thing. He had been spotted in the vicinity of one burglary, and she had seen him in the area the next day as well. If he had no clients there, why was he so far away from home, and in that particular neighborhood? It needed to be explored.

She watched him hesitate for a moment, as if he were going to say something further. And then she saw him look into the interior of the car. His eyes narrowed as he read the heading on the cover of the reports. Quickly she scooped the folder up and deposited it on the backseat.

Without any further discussion, Brett got in.

The chief was still there when she arrived with Brett in tow. The man's brows formed a long dark line across his forehead in direct contrast with his bald head. "What's this?" he asked. "Giving your boyfriend a tour of the precinct?" His tone was less than friendly.

Lissa couldn't wait to put Hanson in his place. When she solved the case... But she was getting ahead of herself. Her day would come soon enough. "No," she said. "This is the red sports car," she explained.

"What are you talking about, Armstrong?" he snapped. "I don't have time for riddles."

Lissa caught the sympathetic look that Brett gave her. Wonderful, now the burglar was siding with her against the chief.

"The burglary case," Lissa stressed. She could feel Brett smiling even though her back was to him. At that moment she didn't know who was irritating her more, Brett, with his smug manner, or the chief, with his high-handed attitude.

The chief now looked a little befuddled, as well as annoyed. He tapped the newspaper under his arm. "I'm going home, Armstrong. This is yesterday's paper. I still haven't had a chance to catch up on what happened in the world twenty-four hours ago. If you want to talk in riddles—''

To his surprise, Lissa took hold of his arm, stopping him in his tracks. "This is only going to take a few minutes," she promised, her voice firm. She wasn't about to be put off. "I believe I have a suspect here."

"Oh?" She could tell that she had finally snared the chief's interest. He turned his attention to her fully. "Have you read him his rights?" he asked as if he were speaking to a novice.

Lissa overlooked that in light of what she had to say. "This isn't exactly a formal charge," she told him. She was taking this one step at a time. Had the chief not been so quick to frown at everything she did, Lissa thought, he would have realized that.

"Then what is it?" Hanson wanted to now.

Brett stepped in neatly at that moment, rescuing her. "I volunteered to come in," he said. Hanson's puzzled expression deepened. "To clear a few things up," Brett added.

Why was he being so nice? Lissa wondered.

"What things?" Hanson asked, turning to Lissa.

Lissa took hold of the chief's arm again and maneuvered him aside. "He's the driver of that red sports car the witness saw. It was a Corvette," she said, lowering her voice. She looked over her shoulder at Brett. "I'm positive of it."

Hanson had his doubts. Women aren't good at these kinds of investigations, he thought. Especially not when there's a good-looking man involved. He sighed, knowing he couldn't very well turn his back on the matter now. "Take him into the other room,"

Hanson instructed, pointing behind her with the rolled-up newspaper. "I'll be along in a minute."

"Isn't he cooperating?" Brett asked as Lissa joined him.

"Never mind about him," she said tersely, pushing open the door to the room Hanson had indicated. "I don't care if he cooperates, just as long as you do."

"I intend to be the soul of cooperation," he told her solemnly. "I'm at your disposal."

A game. He thought it was all a big game. Well, he'd soon find out just how serious all this was. His charm might stand him in good stead in some places, but it wasn't going to cut it here.

She motioned for him to be seated on the other side of the table that, along with several chairs, was the only furniture in the room.

"Is this when you bring in your spotlight and blackjack?" he teased.

"We don't use blackjacks," she said. "You're awfully cool for a man who's involved in a serious crime," she observed.

He looked at her for a long moment. "I find that a cool head serves me much better than flying off the handle."

He was too cool, she thought, beginning to have doubts again. She would hate to be wrong in front of Hanson. It would give him something to hold over her—as if his natural prejudice wasn't enough. No, she decided, Brett was just playing the smooth operator to the end. Another pang shot through her. Why did he have to be a burglar? She thought in a moment of unguarded despair. She fought to keep her feelings from registering on her face.

The door behind her opened, and Hanson walked in. "Okay, Armstrong, let's get to it."

Before her eyes Brett's expression turned serious and he held up his hand. "Wait, before this thing gets out of hand, I think I had better tell you who I am," he said to the chief. "Officer Armstrong," he said, nodding at her as he got up, "hasn't really let me get in a word edgewise."

Lissa opened her mouth to protest, but Hanson acted as if she weren't even in the room. "All right, just exactly who are you?" Hanson asked, crossing his arms in front of his broad chest.

Brett began to take out his wallet, then looked questioningly at Hanson. "May I?"

Hanson gave him a curt nod. Brett pulled out his wallet and showed him his license. His *other* license. One Lissa had never seen.

"A private investigator?" Hanson hooted.

Lissa could have been knocked over with a feather. A private investigator?

"If you need any further proof," Brett said, taking his card back and putting it into his wallet, "why don't you call in Mr. Howard Simeone?" he suggested, naming one of the local residents who had been robbed. "Or Mr. Abernathy? They're the ones who initially hired me." He pocketed his wallet and gave Lissa a smile that she correctly construed as contrite. Well, he could save his smiles. She was furious. He had made her look like a fool. Why hadn't he revealed his identity to her right from the start? Why had he lied to her?

"Hired you to do what?" Hanson was asking, glaring in Lissa's direction. Lissa held her head high. If he was expecting her to flinch, he had another think coming. She wasn't responsible for the fact that Brett had deceived her.

"Well," Brett said slowly, "client confidentiality precludes my going into any great detail," he told the police chief. "But the crux of the matter is that I'm supposed to catch the man responsible for the burglaries and recover the stolen goods."

Lissa knew that the unspoken part of his statement included the fact that the people were losing their confidence in the police and were taking matters into their own hands. That didn't sit too well with Hanson, but she didn't have time to care about that. She had made a major mistake and had come up red-faced in front of the chief. The man didn't need reasons to look down on her. She had been trying to do something to raise her stock in his eyes and get the promotion she had been dreaming of. Now she was standing in front of him with egg on her face.

It was all Brett's fault. Why hadn't he told her who he was once she had voiced her suspicions that he was involved in the case? Why had he gone on with the charade?

"As for my presence in the area yesterday," Brett said, turning his attention to Lissa, "I was just questioning the latest victims. I was just hired yesterday morning. Mr. Abernathy's number is—" Brett began, digging into his pocket.

But Hanson waved him away.

"Forget it. We can check your story out at any time—not that I believe it needs checking out. Armstrong here's a little overzealous. Women in these positions usually are. Thinks maybe she can be a detective," he said disparagingly to no one in particular as he began to leave the room. "Might do you some good to work with the man,'' he said to Lissa. ''We need a little public goodwill. Besides, you might learn something. Now, if you'll excuse me, I have some overcooked pot roast waiting for me at home.'' He glared accusingly at Lissa.

Brett began to head toward the door as well, but Lissa stood in his way. ''Wait a minute; we're not finished yet,'' she said, her voice cold.

''I was hoping we weren't,'' Brett said, looking into her eyes.

''You can put a hold on that for the time being.'' For the time being? What had made her say a thing like that? She thought in exasperation.

''I'd much rather put a hold on you for the time being,'' he said. ''Do you know that all I could think of all day was how sweet you felt against me last night? I kept imagining what would have happened if I had forced my way back into your house and...'' His voice was low, melodious.

But Lissa was having none of it. ''You would probably have woken up in the intensive care unit of the nearest hospital,'' she said coldly. ''What is all this about being a private investigator?'' she demanded. ''You do that in between decorating houses?'' she asked sarcastically.

''No,'' he said quietly. ''I do that full-time.'' He produced his license for her. ''You're free to check it out.''

''Thank you,'' she said coldly. ''I will.''

''Let's go get a cup of coffee, and I'll explain it all to you,'' he offered, taking her arm.

But Lissa shrugged him off. ''I'll hear the story now, thank you, without benefit of any props, soft lights, or caffeine. That's an awfully ritzy house for a private investigator," she said.

"That's because it belongs to my cousin, Richard. *He's* the architect," he explained. "Richard's in Europe right now, working on some marchesa's summer château. I'm just housesitting for him for six months."

"Then why did you say...?"

"It made a good cover," he said with a shrug. He sat down on the tabletop right before her and took hold of her hands. "In my experience, most police officers aren't too crazy about private investigators."

"With good reason," she said coldly.

Right now she was in no mood to be charitable. He had made a fool of her in front of Hanson. For all she knew, he might be flirting with her now with some ulterior motive—perhaps something to do with the fact that she was working on the case. By his own admission, he had just started working on it yesterday. There were a lot of facts he didn't know yet, a lot of facts that were in the reports on her backseat. The reports he had eyed just before he had gotten into her car, she suddenly realized.

That was it, she decided. He wanted to save himself some time and pick the brain of the officer assigned to the case. What better subject than a would-be detective who was working on the case and had shown herself all-too-susceptible to his charms? Lissa's eyes narrowed as she looked at Brett. Oh, no, I'm not falling for any of your ploys, no matter how smooth you are, she thought.

"And besides," he was saying, "you said you liked a good mystery, remember? I thought maybe I'd intrigue you a little by being mysterious."

Lissa pulled her hands free of his. "Well, you thought wrong," she informed him. "Now, if you'll forgive me, I have work to do," she said icily, turning from him and heading toward the door.

But he reached it in two strides, putting his hand against it and preventing her from opening it. "I thought you said you were off duty."

She looked at him sharply. "Thanks to you, I'm going to have to work three times as hard to prove myself in that narrow-minded man's eyes."

Brett leaned his back against the door, folding his arms in front of him. "Might I remind you that the chief said you were to work with me?"

"The chief says a lot of things that don't make any sense. And I work alone," she said firmly.

To her dismay, she couldn't seem to daunt him. "Just give me a chance."

"I *am* giving you a chance," she told him. "I'm giving you a chance to get out of here before I have you arrested for harassment, or obstructing a police officer, or anything else I can think of? Now, let me out of this room!" she warned, her eyes blazing.

He stepped aside, giving her a clear path. "Hold it," he said as she began to walk down the corridor.

"Now what?" she demanded, whirling around.

"You drove me here," he reminded her, catching up to her.

"Yes, I already know that," she said impatiently.

"That means you have to take me back."

He pushed the glass door open for her. Outside, the first touches of dusk were coming in, gingerly prodding at the blue skyline. It was going to be a lovely night. But Lissa hardly noticed as she marched to her car and opened the door.

She sighed, reining in her temper. He was right, of course. No matter what she felt personally at the moment it was her duty to take him back. Getting into her car and staring straight ahead, she practically growled, "Get in."

Six

The entire trip back to Beverly Hills had been spent in relative silence. Brett had made a few attempts at conversation and been rewarded with monosyllabic answers from Lissa. She had left him on his doorstep with a curt "good night." There was no absolution forthcoming for him that night.

Or the day after. He called her at six, claiming to have been thinking about her while he was out jogging. She hung up on him. He called her at seven as she was pounding the last shriveled raisin out of the cereal box. She hung up on him. At eight, as she was leaving the house, the phone rang. Agatha went into a frenzy of barking.

"I hear it, I hear it," Lissa said, continuing toward the front door. "If you're that concerned about him, *you* talk to him," she told the animal. And then a smile inched its way across her lips as a nascent thought quickly materialized. "Yes," Lissa said, doubling back. "You talk to him." With that she picked up the receiver and laid it down on the floor, where Agatha could clearly express her views on the matter.

The last thing Lissa heard as she walked out the door was a muffled voice coming out of the phone, calling her name. Agatha, she thought, was undoubtedly trying to tell him that her mistress had left.

Lissa smiled all the way to work.

Nothing eventful happened during the day. Having stayed up all night with the reports, Lissa was cognizant of every minute detail of the case. But it did her no good. There wasn't very much to go on except that the thief seemed exceptionally clever. He always broke in when the people were away from the house, always seemed to know just where the rare collections were kept, and always managed to bypass the security systems, much to the chagrin of the companies that had installed them.

Lissa paid each of the three companies a visit. She sighed as she came to the last name on her list. The owner was an owl-eyed man with a shallow chest and an almost scholarly way about him. He professed to have gone over and over the actual electronic hookup, searching for some sort of proof that his system had failed in its job. He told Lissa proudly, although with some confusion, that his systems were working a hundred percent.

"Except that they didn't register the intruder when he came in," Lissa said, asking to see the plans for the system herself. Later she spent a good three hours with all the various plans she had collected, going over every detail.

Empty. The day was frustratingly empty. Whoever

she was up against was very shrewd. And he had expensive taste. He never touched anything else in the house, just the collections. One victim, according to the report, marveled over the fact that the burglar hadn't touched his wife's diamond necklace, which had been lying next to the collection of antique swords that were stolen.

"Must be nice to be so rich that you can just toss your jewelry any old place," Lissa had commented when she read the report.

In two instances she discovered that the victim had been approached by phone and given a chance to ransom his collection. The thief, it appeared, was smart enough to take items that were both valuable and had considerable emotional value for the owner as well. That way he had several options available to him, two of which were fencing the items, or selling them back to the owner.

This was no ordinary thief, Lissa thought as she continued cruising the area.

And Brett McKenna was no ordinary man.

The thought crept up on her by surprise. Why was she still thinking about him? She demanded of herself. For that matter, why was she continually craning her neck every time a red car came into view? Was she hoping to run into him again? She taunted herself. And give him another chance to make a fool out of her?

No, he wasn't going to get a second chance at that, she told herself calmly, finally turning the car toward the station. Her shift was over. Time to get home and do some more mental work on the case, she decided. An achy feeling in her back reminded her that she hadn't exactly gotten much sleep last night, having dozed off in her armchair, clutching the report of the last robbery.

When she let herself into the house, the first thing she saw was the phone on the kitchen floor. As she picked it up, fending off Agatha's affectionate attentions, Lissa thought she discerned strange noises coming from the phone. She realized that Brett's line was still open and had been tied up this way all day. No clients had been able to get through.

Serves him right, she thought, letting the receiver fall back into its cradle.

She had just begun to rummage through the refrigerator, wondering what she could do with half a jar of mayonnaise, a head of lettuce and a container of peanut butter that boasted of having no preservatives and was as hard as a rock, when her doorbell rang.

"Who is it?" she called out, closing the refrigerator halfheartedly. Maybe she could send out for a pizza.

"Telephone company," a low voice declared. "We've had some reports that your phone's out of order."

"Just a minute," Lissa called out, getting her service revolver—just in case. Holding it behind her, she opened the door. "It's all a mistake, you see—" Her words died in her throat.

Brett. She might have known.

He was standing on her doorstep, holding a large bag of groceries. "Whatever you're selling," she said, looking annoyed, "I'm not buying." She began to close the door, but Brett stuck his foot in, stopping her.

"All I'm peddling," he said, wedging his shoulder against the door and juggling the groceries, "are apologies. And actually, I'm not selling them, I'm giving them away for free."

"Good, find someone who's interested," she told him, still trying to close the door. But she was beginning to slowly relent.

"Is that any way to treat a man bearing you a peace-offering dinner?" he wanted to know.

Lissa softened letting the door go, and Brett walked in. Agatha came up to greet him, excitedly jumping up on her hind legs.

"Well, at least someone's happy to see me," Brett said, heading straight for the kitchen.

"Agatha doesn't know any better," Lissa told him dismissively. She watched as he seemed to make himself right at home. He set the bag on the table and, instead of the frozen food she had expected him to pull out, began taking out things like sour cream and mushrooms. She stared at him, mystified. Nonetheless, she told him, "You're wasting your time with all this. I don't want to have dinner with you, or spend any more time in your company. We have nothing in common."

Brett took off his jacket and rolled up his sleeves. "I've brought flour, but I'm going to need a little paprika," he said, totally ignoring her words. "You do have that somewhere in the rubble of your pantry, don't you?"

She shot him a murderous look in response to his apt description of the state of affairs in her pantry. It took her several minutes to come up with the paprika.

"Thank you," he said, taking it from her. "Now I'll trouble you for a pot. Preferably a large one." As she hunted one up from the depths of her cabinet, Brett set about searching through the various drawers under the kitchen counter until he came up with a knife. As he did so, he finally turned his attention to her previous comment.

"As for having nothing in common, there's always that adage about opposites attracting."

"That's fine—" Lissa said, shoving the pot against his midriff. He took it graciously, considering the circumstances. "—if you're dating a magnet. I've always thought that being male and female was opposite enough."

"All right," Brett told her, picking up the knife and beginning to expertly dice the rather juicy sirloin he had pulled out of the shopping bag. "Then I'll concentrate on what we do have in common. I'm a detective and you, I gather, would like to be one. Seems like common ground to me." For a moment he stopped what he was doing, turned and just looked at Lissa. She felt as if he were looking directly into her soul.

But, she wasn't about to melt, much as that might satisfy him, she told herself. He might not be a burglar, but he *was* a con artist, and she wasn't about to be taken in. She planted her hands firmly on the kitchen counter next to him and his dicing knife and leaned forward as if to make her words perfectly clear. "The only reason you want to see me is to pick my brain." There, deal with honesty for a change, she thought triumphantly.

"Actually," Brett said, turning his attention back to dicing the meat, "your brain was the furthest thing from my mind." For a moment his voice drifted off, hanging sensuously between them. She was about to inform him rather tersely that her body wasn't available for "picking," either, when he added, "It's your company I'm after. How about it?'' he asked, bending down and giving Agatha a rather juicy scrap of meat and thereby assuring himself of her undying loyalty for life. "Truce?" Brett asked, looking back up at Lissa.

He had the eyes of a soulful puppy when he did that, she thought. She felt herself weakening. Still, she tried to keep up the appearance of indifference. "I can't be bought that easily," she said, nodding toward Agatha, who was staring up at Brett, waiting for more.

"I know," Brett said, rising. "That's why I brought a whole dinner. Salad, blue cheese dressing— made from scratch," he added, impishly raising and lowering his brows, "beef Stroganoff. And French pastries. The pastries, unfortunately, are from the bakery. Although I can testify to their fine reputation."

"Too bad they can't reciprocate," Lissa muttered wryly, watching him as he went on with his preparations. Except for the paprika, Brett seemed to have brought everything with him, right down to the butter he used to sauté the meat. "I'm surprised you decided not to make the pastries from scratch, too," she said with a touch of sarcasm. She still wasn't at ease with what was going on there.

"If I did," he told her, a meaningful look creeping into his eyes, "I'd have to stay here all night. In order to prepare them, I'd need a good deal of time. All good things take time," he said significantly.

His words got under her skin in record time, teasing her, tantalizing her, and making her think of things that did not come out of a grocery bag. She took a deep breath. On to another topic—quick!

"How did you learn all this?" she asked, gesturing

at the pot and the items he was dropping in so methodically. To the men she knew, making dinner meant calling up a fast-food place for a delivery.

Brett grinned, his eyes crinkling slightly at the corners. Something within her responded to his smile despite all her efforts to the contrary. He had succeeded in stripping her of her anger. She felt almost naked without her emotional shield. He was definitely up to something, she tried to tell herself. She'd stake her badge on it.

"I have five sisters," he told her. "All older. When we were growing up they were determined to pull me into the fold so that I wouldn't feel left out. I know all about cooking, am pretty handy with a needle and know just how to kiss a hurt to make it all better." His eyes were twinkling as he told her the last part.

She had no doubt that he could perform the last item in his repertoire quite well, or that he was referring to things that went deeper than a scraped knee or a cut finger. "That just about qualifies you for the doctor of the year award, doesn't it?" she asked, looking past him and watching as he stirred the simmering meat, mushrooms and seasonings in a broth of consommé. The aroma was wafting up to her, reminding her stomach that she was very, very hungry. It smelled delicious.

And so did he.

Lissa stepped back self-consciously.

"My, my. Dr. Kildare and Julia Child all rolled into one," she said, trying to cover herself. Brett had given her a probing look when she had backed away. Somehow, her remark hadn't sounded as flippant as she had intended. "You're an extraordinary man."

"That," Brett said, putting down the large spoon

he was stirring with, "is what I've been trying to tell you."

He was going to reach for her; she just knew it. Her pulse suddenly took off, accelerating wildly as she backed up against the countertop. Not the smartest maneuver, was it? Her mind taunted.

But when Brett did reach, it was for the knife that was behind her. Somehow, though, Lissa thought he came unusually close to her. After all, he did have long arms. There was no need for him to practically press up against her in order to pick up the knife. With a studied note of carelessness, Brett turned his attention to the head of lettuce.

As if he didn't know the effect he had on her, Lissa thought accusingly. Yet at the same time she was relieved that he hadn't pressed his advantage. Her vulnerability was growing by leaps and bounds, even though she was still highly suspicious of his motives for being there.

She realized that she was getting highly agitated. Idiot, that's just what he wants, she snapped at herself. He's playing a game with you, trying to break down your defenses. Well, he was getting there, she was forced to admit. She had to stop him somehow. Logic demanded it. The rest of her, however, was beginning to demand something entirely different. She was becoming more and more reluctant to send him on his way. Maybe after dinner... After all, it wouldn't be polite to send him away before it was ready. And she had no idea how long everything was going to take to cook....

"You really don't have to go to all this trouble," she said for lack of anything else to say. The silence made her feel uncomfortable. No, the word was nervous. It was as if she were anticipating impending doom. She reached toward the radio nestled in the corner of the counter and switched it on.

"No trouble," Brett assured her. "I have to eat, too. Besides, I like to cook." A song from the sixties provided healthy background noise. "Ah, an oldies fan," he commented with an approving nod as he mixed mayonnaise with several drops of vinegar, beginning to prepare the dressing he had promised. "Another thing we have in common."

Lissa had no doubt that, had she switched on *The Barber of Seville,* Brett would have claimed to be an enthusiastic opera fan. But she left the remark alone.

Instead, convinced that he was really there for the purpose of pumping her for information, she decided to turn the tables on him. "How's the case coming along?" she asked.

He gave her a long, serious look. "I don't know," he said, setting the dressing aside and beginning to work on the salad. Cherry tomatoes were mixing with lettuce leaves and green pepper slices in amiable cohabitation as he considered her question. "I'm not sure if the lady forgives me yet or not."

Starved, Lissa was reaching into the bowl for a cherry tomato when his words stopped her. He was always in there pitching. She gave him points for perseverance. "I meant the burglary."

"Right now, I'm more interested in the lady," he said.

She sincerely doubted it, even though a little thrill skated through her at the idea. The thrill came back for an encore as he kept his eyes leveled on her face and asked, "How about it? Does the lady forgive me?"

With a voice like that, and at a look like the one that was in his eyes, Lissa felt sure that a legion of women would have forgiven him anything. But all this was for show, she reminded herself. Instant attraction was a lovely thing for movies that had only ninety minutes or so to resolve themselves, but it rarely happened in real life. At least, not in her life. She earnestly doubted that Brett was bent on currying her favor for the sheer thrill of her company. There had to be more to it than that. And there was. A fee for catching the burglar. Well, the collar was going to be hers, not his, and if it was information he was after, by hook, crook or beef Stroganoff, he wasn't going to get it, no matter what Hanson said. She had shared information on a case once before and seen the other party get all the credit, much to her stunned amazement. No one was beating her out of this one.

"That all depends," she finally murmured, trying her best to sound demure. Let the oaf think she was falling for this.

"On what?" he asked, the last lettuce leaf suspended in midair above the bowl.

"On how good your Stroganoff is," she said blithely, moving away and getting out her dishes in order to set the table.

"My Stroganoff," Brett promised her, "is always excellent. Guaranteed to melt the stoniest of hearts," he added, coming up behind her as she pulled out two salad dishes and stacked them on top of the dinner plates she was already holding. He took them from her, somehow managing to brush his hands ever so slightly along her bustline.

At his touch a one-alarm alert immediately went

off in her mind. Lissa made a mental note to keep him at arm's length for the remainder of the evening.

"You don't have to grab the dishes," she informed him, trying to sound impassive. Inside her, there was a good deal of turmoil going on, which she tried very hard to quell with cold logic. Logic, though, was heating up rather quickly, she noted with dismay.

"Didn't want to break anything," he explained innocently. He looked at her cluttered kitchen table. "Is there a flat surface around her we can use?"

Blushing, Lissa made no answer as she quickly scooped up the newspaper and cereal box that had been left over from breakfast.

"Architect, private investigator, chef, comedian," she recited bitingly. "Is there no end to your talents?"

Her sarcasm died rather quickly when Brett answered. "Try me and see," he suggested invitingly.

"I'll sample the dinner when it's ready," Lissa answered with careful emphasis.

No matter what she said, he seemed to go right on as if she were being the epitome of cooperation. "I'm completely at your disposal.... Speaking of which," he said, turning back to her sink, "what's wrong with yours?"

He had neatly turned the conversation around from the intimate to the mundane, something she hadn't been able to do no matter how hard she had tried. The man was a worthy opponent. Perhaps too worthy.

Lissa joined him at the sink, where he threw the switch that would normally have resulted in a hearty grinding noise, indicating that all was well within the pipes. But all was not well, and a whimpering whine came back in response.

Lissa shrugged self-consciously, turning the switch to "Off." "Why don't you bother yourself with something else?" she suggested. "Your—"

But he wouldn't be put off. "Did you drop something down there you shouldn't have?" he interrupted, gingerly pushing back the black rubber covering with a knife.

Why was he always making her feel so inadequate? Was this part of a campaign to unnerve her, seduce her and then get all the information he could out of her? Of course it was. Lissa squared her shoulders, answering his question crisply. "As a matter of fact, yes."

"Okay, what?" he asked, still probing around. It was too dark inside the pipes for him to make anything out.

"My belt," she said, not looking at him.

Since she wasn't looking at him, she couldn't tell if it was a laugh or an incredulous gasp that she heard. "Your belt?" he echoed.

"It was a cloth belt,' she explained, as if that fact made the situation better. "I was rinsing off my dress, and I guess the belt slipped out of the loops. Anyway, when I was finished, the belt was gone. I didn't realize what had happened to it until after I threw lemon peels down the disposal and turned it on. That's the result," she said, gesturing at the disposal, which was once more whimpering as Brett played with the switch.

He made no comment on her story. "I'll come by and fix that for you sometime."

Oh no, he wasn't going to use that as an excuse to come back. This visit was about all she could handle.

"Don't bother. I'll call a plumber when I get around to it."

"No bother," he told her. "My dad taught me always to cooperate with the law. This is just a fringe benefit."

She couldn't help wondering what else his father had taught him to do as she followed Brett back to the microwave. The little bell went off. End of round one. So far, he was racking up all the points. But the evening, she promised herself, would be hers, not his. She was determined to usher him out right after dinner.

Determination had a way of flagging on a full stomach, she discovered. Her normal energy seemed to be gone. As she sat, watching her fork sink into the swirling mound of whipped cream that decorated her pastry, a warm, almost sensuous feeling seemed to be running through her. This was undoubtedly part of his plan, she told herself, but she couldn't seem to muster any helpful indignation. Well, she thought, she was a mature adult; she could easily fend him off. She might be full, but she wasn't stupid. She wasn't about to give him what he was after—on any level.

"Did you enjoy dinner?" he asked.

She took a deep breath before answering. "Very much."

"Good," he said, rising. "You go ahead with your dessert. I'll take care of the dishes."

"You're overdoing it," she said as he turned on the water.

"What?" he asked casually, not bothering to turn around.

"Dinner was enough," she told him. "You don't have to do the dishes." She got up and turned the water off. "Hadn't you better be going somewhere?" she prodded.

But he covered her hand with his own and turned the water right back on again. "I never eat and run. It's the height of rudeness. My sisters taught me never to be rude to a woman."

"Your father taught you. Your sisters taught you. Didn't you ever learn anything on your own?" she asked, feeling a little like walls were closing in on her. Too late she realized the opening her words had provided.

Brett's smile lit up the entire room. "I hope to show you that, too, in time."

Lissa pressed her lips together and marched back to the table. She was losing ground rapidly, she thought, jabbing at her pastry.

"That deserves to be savored, not attacked," Brett said, turning to look in her direction. "Savoring," he added, "is the best part. Everything good has to be savored slowly, or you lose the flavor."

His eyes were laughing at her. She just knew it. Despite his advice, she finished the pastry in three forkfuls, secretly marveling at how she managed to finish it at all. "If you must do them, I'll help," she said grudgingly, picking up a dish towel.

"Feel free to jump in whenever you get the urge," he told her.

Somehow, she felt that he wasn't talking about just the dishes. She kept her eyes on her work.

"Uncle," she finally said.

This time it was her turn to catch him off guard. "What?"

She looked at him. "I said, 'Uncle.' I give up. Or, more aptly, I forgive you. You are hereby absolved

of your part in making me look like an idiot in front
of Chief Hanson. For what it's worth, I'm sure you
endeared yourself to him for that. The man can't stand
me," she said with resignation as she reached up into
the cupboard to put away the dish she had been drying
for the past three minutes.

"The man obviously has no taste—and not a brain
in his head," Brett said charitably. She wondered if
he was saying that to butter her up, or if he actually
meant it. Brett handed her another dish and she began
to wipe it mechanically, mulling over her thoughts.
He pulled the stopper out of the sink, and the water
gurgled away. "Why were you so eager to rush down
to the precinct?" he asked, looking at her. "More
importantly, why were you trying to get me into a
crowd scene?" His voice was soft again, not lofty,
not teasing, just soft.

Lissa turned away, sliding the dish into place on
top of the first one. "I don't know what you're talking
about," she said breezily.

To her startled surprise, instead of replying, he took
the towel in both his hands, lifted it over her head
and wrapped it around her waist, then used it to pull
her against him. She managed to turn around within
the circle before it tightened and then began to doubt
the wisdom of that maneuver. She was now held securely against him. There wasn't enough room for so
much as a fifty cent piece between them.

"Are you afraid of being alone with me?" he
asked.

"Absolutely not," she lied.

"Good," he said just before he lowered his lips to
hers. "I love a woman with spirit."

Subsequently that spirit was engulfed by a kiss that,

had it been a flame, would easily have started a raging forest fire within a few seconds. As his lips moved teasingly over hers, Lissa fought desperately to keep her wits about her. She could feel him outlining the inner part of her mouth with his tongue. Brett Mc-Kenna, Lissa thought, trying vainly to keep from succumbing, might know how to cook a superb dinner, but he was even better at kissing. And therein, she knew, lay her problem and, just possibly, her ultimate undoing.

So why wasn't she struggling?

Seven

"It's wet," Lisa managed to mumble against his mouth.

"What?" Of all the things he might have expected her to say, that was not one of them. Drawing back just a fraction of an inch, he looked at her with uncertainty.

"The towel," she elaborated. "It's wet."

"Oh." Brett dropped it to the ground, holding her against him with his hands instead. They fit comfortably about the curve of her waist. "Better?"

"Drier," she conceded.

"We'll work on better," he promised as he leaned down to give her another kiss.

"We'll work on nothing," she informed him, moving her head in order to avoid his lips.

Brett got a mouthful of blonde hair. He also found the outline of her ear and began to run his tongue over it lightly. A hot shiver darted up and down Lissa's spine.

She glanced up at him quickly, hoping he had missed her reaction, but knowing that he would have had to be made out of stone to be oblivious of the way she was melting. And he was definitely *not* made out of stone, Lissa thought as the hardened contours of his body awakened an awareness of her own. Sudden anticipation seized her, intense and demanding. Giving the lie to her own words, Lissa stood up on her tiptoe and wrapped her arms around his neck, the silky texture of his dark blond hair registering itself in the back of her mind. The rest of her mind was busy, taken up with wondrous sensations that the gently demanding pressure of his mouth was creating inside her. The more he kissed her, the less able she was to pull away. Kissing him created an instant addiction She wanted more, more of his lips, more of him.

She was acting totally out of character, she tried to tell herself.

She didn't care.

All through dinner Lissa had attempted to ignore the intense attraction he held for her. Telling herself that he was just trying to charm information out of her didn't seem to change the fact that deep down, beneath her bravado, Lissa found something about Brett utterly endearing. It went beyond the mesmerizing softness of his brown eyes and the eternal twinkle within them. It had something to do with the essence of the man.

If he felt that victory was at hand, he was still taking his time, she realized, as his hands swept along her back, pressing her against him. His mouth contin-

ued to draw out her very life, draining her of her
sweetness and filling her with his in turn. Lissa felt
almost drugged. Never had she known this kind of a
reaction to a man. This was the kind of response she
had thought you were supposed to have in the arms
of someone you had known for a long time, someone
you had loved and yearned for for a long time. Not
for a man who cooked dinner for you after embarrassing you in front of your boss.

She stopped trying to analyze the situation. Her
sense of logic was already floating away, allowing her
to simply feel and enjoy what was happening to her.
And what was happening was awe-inspiring.

"Is this part of your cleanup philosophy?" she
asked with extreme effort, catching a glimpse of the
discarded dish towel out of the corner of her eye.

She felt him smile against the curve of her shoulder. It tickled her. It also aroused her. Everything
about him aroused her. "Not until now," he answered. "But I might add it to the list. Make sure all
the dishes are properly taken care of," he teased, darting his tongue along the point of her shoulder. He
came to where the string holding up her halter dress
was fastened. After liberally spreading a blanket of
small kisses around the area, he moved his head back,
replacing it with his fingers. Very slowly Brett began
to pull at the bow, his eyes holding hers.

A knot was forming in her throat, making it difficult for her to get words out. But she tried. "Is that
what I am? A...dish?"

"Only in that you're delectable," he assured her
with another kiss. Another bolt of excitement flashed
through her, splintering into a thousand pieces as it
found its way into every corner of her being.

Without her realizing just when it had happened, the ribbon lay undone, dipping down along her breast, tempting him to pull it down further. With movements that were maddeningly slow, he tugged at it. Lissa was sure that she was going to lose her mind before he was finished as he stopped to cup the half-covered treasure. Desire blazed its way further into her body as Brett gently massaged her flesh, tender reverence in every stroke. With each pass of his hand the material moved lower and lower, teasing her, tormenting her and drawing her further into a state of mindless passion.

Lissa caught her breath as the sundress slipped down, finally leaving her breast exposed.

"I've always favored an off-the-shoulder look," he told her just before his searching mouth covered her nipple. Arrows of fire shot through her as she moaned and arched herself toward him, unabashedly eager to gain more pleasure. Her breathing became progressively louder, until it was almost all she heard.

"Don't you...think...this should...be done... somewhere...else...?" she asked.

"What part of you would you like me to kiss?" he asked, his voice tantalizing.

She shook her head, a half-formed laugh echoing in her throat. "I meant not in the...kitchen...."

He raised his head so that his eyes were level with hers. "Why not? The table's been cleared." His voice was mischievous, but there was no missing the desire that was there. She felt another thrill assaulting her senses.

Again she shook her head. He didn't understand. The kitchen just wasn't romantic enough for what was happening between them. But before she had a chance to explain, he was speaking again.

"The bedroom?" he asked tenderly, picking her up in his arms, her exposed breast pressing against his chest. She felt the heat of his body transmitting itself to hers, and it overpowered any last-minute objections that might be struggling to make themselves known.

The smile she gave him was warm. Suddenly all her doubts faded.

"Then the bedroom it shall be," he said, kissing the top of her hair. "Where is it?"

Oh, God, she wanted him so badly. She pointed, wishing her heart weren't beating so fast. "Beyond that door."

"I guess I can hold out," he murmured as he started walking. They were light, teasing words, spoken with a mellow smile on his face. But Lissa thought she saw something beyond that. Was she trying to read something more into this? *This?* Exactly what *was* this? She squirmed as he pushed the bedroom door open with his foot.

"Put me down," she said, momentarily regaining a little of her common sense.

She had thought he would put her upright on the floor. Instead he laid her on the bed. Horizontal was not exactly the best position from which to be fighting for her cause. She tried to get up, but that course of action was abruptly aborted when Brett lay down next to her. She reached frantically to refasten her drooping sundress, but he put his fingers between the material and her flesh.

"Don't," he whispered.

She waved.

"Please?"

Lissa felt as if she were completely undone. One little word uttered in a half-whisper had the power to do that when it came from Brett.

"Please," he repeated, reaching for the other ribbon and tugging at it. It followed its mate, dangling precariously along the hardened outline of her nipple.

Brett proceeded with care, looking at Lissa as if she were a breathtaking sunset, a sight to be captured and savored before it faded out of existence.

"Beautiful," he said, gazing at her face.

The man had an incredible technique, she thought vaguely, and then she was past caring. The parts of her that had balked against Brett had been cerebral, mental. And the resolve they had counseled had all been undone along with the ribbons of her dress. All she was doing now was feeling. The momentary respite she had experienced when he carried her into the bedroom vanished, taking her thoughts with it.

"You must have been a maddening child," she said, not even sure where the words were coming from.

"Hmm?" A concentric pattern of kisses was being bestowed along the outline of her halter top, stoking the fire that burned beneath.

"At Christmas," she clarified, her head beginning to spin. "Did you take this much time unwrapping your..." She faltered. What word could she use? Presents? That would sound as if she were giving herself to him. Well, wasn't she? Hadn't she somehow felt that this was going to happen ever since he had walked into her living room, claiming to be pursuing his pen?

"My gifts?" Brett asked, ending the sentence for her as he eased the dress from her other breast. Lissa tried hard not to move. "Only if I knew there was something special waiting for me. Then going slowly only heightened the ultimate thrill."

Had she been in possession of her mental faculties, she would have told herself that what he said was a wonderful line, nothing more. But she wasn't in possession of anything but an insatiable hunger that was consuming her as she gloried in every movement he made.

Lissa realized that he had stopped talking and had taken the rosy tip of one breast captive, teasing it mercilessly with his tongue as he slipped his hand beneath the hem of her flared dress. As they inched their way up, his marauding fingers claimed every fraction of her thigh, gaining access to a higher plane.

"Thank God you don't wear pantyhose," he sighed against her breast. His light touch was now up to the rim of her underwear, working its way underneath.

"I…thought…you liked…prolonging…the unveiling…."

"There is a difference," he said, kissing her mouth, "between savoring" —another kiss flitted along her mouth— "and masochism." The next kiss was more intense as his fingers conquered the region they sought to plunder. "I, unfortunately, do not have those kinds of hang-ups." His lips left a mark on each closed eyelid. The fluttering sensations within her grew.

Hooking his finger along the center of her underwear, Brett gave a little tug. Lissa felt her panties giving way, sliding down her hips. Brett's smile grew as he kept his gaze on her face. Another tug, and the underwear was gone. His next target was her dress.

Slipping his hand behind her, Brett parted the zipper. The dress disappeared as well.

Lissa's hands slipped beneath Brett's shirt, seeking to touch his chest. Her fingers grazed the light labyrinth of hair as they followed the muscular ridges of his pectorals. Everything about him excited her. She knew it showed in her face but she didn't care. Ambition, turf and prized information could be jealously guarded tomorrow. Right now they were all a thousand miles away from her. All that mattered was the music Brett was creating within her with every subtle movement of his splendid, athletic body. All that counted was the tender look in his eyes. Though it might well be make-believe, she was still a true believer. At least for now.

"Here," he said, unbuttoning his shirt for her, then shifting her slightly so that his chest pressed against hers. "Better?"

"Getting there," she acknowledged.

"—is half the fun," he ended. "Except that this time, 'getting there' will ultimately be eclipsed by 'there,'" he promised.

Lissa meant to lower her head and kiss him first, but suddenly his lips were on hers. She could feel his control slipping away as her own hunger grew to almost savage proportions. She felt his heart pounding against her breast, and she splayed her fingers across his chest, pushing his shirt off his shoulders as she pressed her body against his. He slipped his hands out of the sleeves as he continued his explorations. With a sudden movement he rolled Lissa onto her back and pulled himself up on his knees, gazing down at her.

His smile told it all.

Lissa watched in poorly concealed anticipation as

he unbuckled his slacks and slid them down his well-developed legs. And then, wanting to be something more than a passive spectator, she raised herself up on one elbow and shyly slipped one finger beneath the waistband of his briefs.

"Let me," she whispered. Her reward was the look on his face. She saw her own passion mirrored there.

A devilish, inviting grin met her words. "By all means," he said, arching toward her slightly.

She could hardly contain herself as she slid the cotton material down his hips, her fingers luxuriating in the feel of his hard, sculptured body. Curving her fingers she swept them along the crest of his buttocks, removing the briefs entirely.

Brett embraced her, pressing her to him and igniting an even greater fire within her. As their bodies met, she had no way of knowing where her senses ended and his began. It was all one and the same to her as they tumbled back onto her bed.

Over and over again, he stroked the long delicate lines of her body, his fingers trailing from the slope of her shoulder down along her hip until they reached the sensitive area of her inner thighs. He explored, he plundered, he took, all with gentle, loving patience. Though she wanted to send him tumbling into the same valley of mindless passion, Lissa seemed able only to receive the erotic messages his body was sending out.

And then she was experiencing that delicious shifting of his body onto hers, the restrained pressure of his thigh against hers. She moved the way both his body and hers dictated. The initial explosion of pleasure as he sealed their intimate pact nearly made her cry out loud. But she pressed her lips together, trying to hold back just a little.

It was too late. The king had taken the queen. The game was over.

But not the victory celebration. The thrust of his warm, supple tongue into her mouth was echoed by an even more forceful thrust that threatened to unravel her entirely.

Clutching him with every ounce of her swiftly ebbing strength, Lissa hung on as the whirling passage to paradise accelerated, leaving earth and reason behind. Make it last forever, her mind cried out just before her sanity faded away, lost in the miracle of lovemaking, in the matching of two kindred souls.

It seemed an eternity later that she opened her eyes to find that she hadn't been swept away; she was still in her bedroom. But this time she wasn't sleeping—only dreaming. Dreaming of wonderland. She tried desperately to hold on to the incredible sweetness and contentment she felt inside.

She was cradled in the space created by the circle of his arm, and he was stroking her ever so lightly. Even in her exhaustion, Lissa could feel her nerve endings beginning to tingle again.

"And that," he said softly, kissing the top of her head, "is a sample of what I learned myself," he said, returning to their earlier discussion.

"Just goes to show you," she said, her voice still thick with emotion. "People learn best when left on their own." She stretched her hand out, following her own exploratory path along his body. A crackle of electricity seemed to snap through her veins.

"No, I think this wouldn't have been quite the

same if I had been alone," Brett told her, his eyes intent on her face.

She could see that he was waiting to see what she was going to do next. She took his expression as an unspoken challenge and moved accordingly. Her hand slipped lower. She saw his eyes widen just a touch as he drew in his breath. Emboldened, Lissa went further, her strokes shortening as they intimately possessed him. For a moment he allowed his eyelids to slip closed as he cherished what was happening. Delight was etched into his rugged features. And then his eyes sprang open, sparkling once again. "Yes," he announced, "it would definitely have been different if I had been alone."

A resurgence of energy eventually brought them to a second paradise, made that much richer as it built upon the first.

As she began her morning routine two days later, Lissa tried desperately not to allow what had transpired between them to color her views about Brett and his motives. He was a private investigator who was on a case and naturally determined to solve it, even though the police were in on it, too. To accomplish that, he knew he had to stay one step ahead of the police. What better way to do that than to make someone on the force his informant, knowing or otherwise? She thought as she scanned her notes again, trying for the hundredth time to find something that she might have missed before.

But she came up empty-handed, both in her search and in her efforts to disentangle her emotions from the situation. She and Brett had made love, and like it or not, the situation had changed for her. She knew herself well enough to know that the other night had not been strictly a matter of being won over by the mood and the beef Stroganoff. It had been the man who had won her, not any of the trimmings. And it hadn't been a matter of spontaneous combustion, either, even though it had felt that way at the time. There was something about Brett that drew her to him. That same something, no doubt, that he was counting on to make her help him with the case.

Well, think again, McKenna. This case, if I can solve it, is mine.

Meticulously, she filed her notes away in the top drawer of the gateleg table that nestled beneath a smoked mirror right by the front door. She locked the drawer and pocketed the key.

"Time for work," she announced to Agatha. Just as she left she glanced at the phone, but it was silent. She hadn't heard from him since he had left her house after breakfast the day before.

What was he up to?

"Trying to make me miss him, no doubt," she said aloud as she went to her car.

He was succeeding.

But thoughts of Brett had to be pushed aside when she entered the precinct. The burglar had struck again. The victims had been away, staying overnight at a friend's house. They had returned home to find that they themselves had had a very unwelcome guest. The wife had placed the call, sounding, the desk sergeant informed Lissa, very shaken.

She still looked rather upset when she opened the door to Lissa half an hour later. Holding the door slightly ajar, she looked at Lissa suspiciously. "Yes?"

Lissa took out her badge. "Officer Armstrong, ma'am. I'm here about the burglary."

The woman's face softened immediately, flooded with relief. "Oh, come in," she urged, throwing the door wide open. "I'm so sorry, but with the robbery—well, you understand," she said, taking Lissa by the elbow and leading her to the family room. Lissa could hear the low murmur of voices growing louder as they approached.

Lissa nodded in response. "That's quite all right. It must have been an awful experience for you," she said sympathetically. The woman looked as old as her grandmother had been, and Lissa couldn't help equating the two. Her determination to capture the burglar intensified another notch.

"Harold, the police are here," the woman announced cheerfully.

"I don't care! Send them away!" a gruff voice snapped.

By this time they had reached the family room, and Lissa got a good look at Harold, who appeared to be as crotchey as his wife was chipper. All things considered, he had every right to be crotchety. The coins that had been stolen were quite valuable. What she couldn't understand was why he had kept them in his house. A collection like that was best left under lock and key in a bank vault.

"Mr. Andrews, I know how you must feel—" Lissa began, but got no further as a hard eye turned to scrutinize her.

"Do you?" he demanded, his voice creaking slightly. "Do you know how it feels to have something you cherish snatched away from you? I thought you people were supposed to beef up your patrols."

His shaggy white brows drew together as he stepped closer to her. He was a little taller than she was, but he somehow gave the impression of a towering ogre at that moment. An ogre in a shapeless brown sweater. "Adding on skinny girls who should be home with their kids is not my idea of 'beefing' it up."

There were a number of things she would have liked to have told him if she weren't a policewoman—and if she hadn't noticed, for the first time, who it was that he'd been talking to just before she entered the room. The other party had been hidden from her view because he was seated in a huge overstuffed wing chair facing away from her.

Brett McKenna.

"Mr. Andrews, if you give Officer Armstrong a chance, I'm sure you'll see that she's really trying to do her job," he said, getting up to join her. The amusement in his voice cut her to the bone. Why was he always turning up this way?

Mr. Andrews waved a dismissing hand at Lissa. "Trying isn't good enough," he aroused, turning his back on Lissa.

"Harold, please," his wife pleaded, obviously distressed at his rudeness.

For a moment Lissa let her impatience get the better of her. "I can't succeed if you don't give me the facts," she said tartly, hoping to make the man come around. She could feel Brett watching her, and that just added to her frustration.

"I've already given all the facts," Mr. Andrews retorted, turning to glare at her. "To him." He pointed his cane at Brett, steadying himself by bracing his hand on the armchair that Brett had vacated.

"Harold, it isn't nice to talk to the police that way," his wife chided.

"It isn't nice for the police to let a robber break into our house and make off with our coin collection, either," he snapped back.

"It isn't as if we had a choice, Mr. Andrews," Lissa told him, wishing that Brett weren't hearing every word of this. His face was expressionless, but she could just bet that he was feeling smug inside. "If you tell me what happened—" she coaxed, taking out her notepad.

"I was robbed," the man barked. "See, she's not even paying attention," he complained to Brett.

"I'm sure she's paying attention, Mr. Andrews," Brett said soothingly. "Why don't you just sit down and tell her exactly what happened?" he prodded, sitting down on a love seat and urging the old man to follow suit. "My father always said you should do your best to cooperate with the police. You wouldn't want to get on their bad side, would you?"

"Can't be any worse than their good side," the wispy-haired old man grumbled. But he sat down nonetheless. "Listened to your father a lot, did you?" he asked Brett, still frustrating Lissa.

"All the time. Best way to learn things is to have a good teacher," Brett said.

Lissa thought that her breakfast was going to come up. But Brett had managed to placate the victim for her, allowing her a chance to ask her questions. She owed him one—and she hated it.

"Okay," Mr. Andrews mumbled grudgingly. "But get your questions over with fast," he warned. "Amelia and I have a bridge game to go to. Haven't missed a session in fifteen years," he said rather proudly.

Half an hour later Lissa walked out of the house with several pages worth of notes that contained detailed descriptions of the stolen coins and absolutely nothing else. She had nothing to go on. The thief had once more managed to bypass the security system, forcing his way in through the French doors that led into the family room. Nothing had been disturbed except for the coin collection. He had even opened the glass display case where the coins had been housed rather than break it. He certainly was a neat burglar, she thought.

"Want to grab a cup of coffee?"

Lissa turned to find that Brett was directly behind her. She was still smarting from the treatment she had received from Mr. Andrews, and in no mood to sit down and socialize with the enemy. "No, I have work to do," she said, trying to sound impersonal. But how did you sound impersonal with a man who has seen you nude and eager for his touch? It wasn't working.

"I wore him down for you," Brett reminded her. "You owe me one."

"He would have had to file a report with the police eventually," she replied, reaching out to open her car door.

Brett put his hand on hers. "But wouldn't it have been embarrassing to have to tell Chief Hanson that the victim didn't want to talk to you?"

Lissa sighed and stared down at the gravel driveway. "You've got a point," she conceded.

Brett raised her head with the crook of his forefinger. "Hey, something happen since last night?"

"That was two nights ago," she corrected.

The light seemed to dawn. "Oh, and you're mad because I didn't call," he said, folding his arms across his chest.

She became indignant. "I am *not* mad because you didn't call." She didn't want him thinking that she had stayed near the phone all evening—even if she had. She knew that he meant trouble for her, that his efforts would probably reflect negatively on her own, and she had enough of a handicap with the way that Hanson felt about her. She didn't need Brett getting the jump on her. She wasn't all that sure that Mr. Andrews hadn't kept something back just to be perverse. After all, he was paying Brett to solve the case, and it was easy to see where his confidence lay.

"One cup of coffee," Brett cajoled. "I'll keep my hands on the table at all times," he promised. "Besides," he added in a more serious tone, "we need to talk."

About what? She wondered silently, though a small hope had been born within her, desire and passion its unwitting parents.

Eight

"**O**kay, so what is it you want to talk about?" Lissa asked. She had followed Brett to a picturesque café overlooking the ocean. A bed of velvet ice plants undulated up the steep slope from the sandy beach to the manicured lawn surrounding the café.

"Don't be in such a rush to get this over with," Brett said, opening the menu that the hostess had handed him. "Aren't you going to open the menu?"

"You don't need a menu for coffee," she said crisply.

"Coffee always goes better with something," he said as he scanned the long columns.

"How about aggravation?" she posed.

He looked curiously at her. "What are you so aggravated about?"

"You," she said before she could stop herself.

"I was hoping the word you'd use in connection

with me would be 'excited.' Or maybe 'enthused,' or 'aroused.' 'Aggravated' definitely doesn't have the right ring to it.'' He took her hand in his before she had a chance to pull it away.

"Don't get cute with me," she warned. "I'm not some brainless little beach bunny you picked up. I'm a career-oriented woman with definite goals in mind. I'd appreciate it if you'd treat me with a little respect," she told him as she removed her hand from his grasp.

"All right," he allowed. "Point well taken. So what's on your mind? Why am I aggravating you?" he asked seriously.

"Because this is all a game to you," she accused.

Brett shook his head. The waitress thought the gesture was meant for her and turned away before she reached their table. "I think you lost me somewhere along the line."

"You're trying to weave your way into my confidence."

"Among other things."

"You're doing it again," she accused, pressing her lips together. "You're making up to me solely to pick my brain."

He sighed. "Again with the brain-picking. Woman, I've been an investigator for five years, and a pretty damn good one at that. This might come as a shock to you, but I don't need your brain to help me." When he saw the exasperated look that came over her face, his smile melted away into a semiserious expression. "Look, I was just trying to be nice. I was about to suggest that we go along with what Hanson said to you and work together on this—''

"Ah ha!" she declared triumphantly.

"Ah ha?" he echoed, confused again.

"I knew that was what you were after. Well, forget it. I work alone—"

He lowered his voice, taking on the dramatic tones of an old-time TV announcer. "—said she, handing out a silver bullet and riding off into the sunset. Her faithful Indian companion stared into the horizon, wondering if it was something he had said...."

Lissa found it very hard to maintain a straight face, even though she knew that the joke was being made at her expense. She took a deep cleansing breath, trying to clear her mind. She needed to regroup. "I'm not going to share my information with you," she said flatly.

He didn't even look mildly interested. It was as if he thought she wasn't hiding anything worthwhile. For some reason that irritated her even more. "Have it your way," he said with a shrug.

Just like that? The battle was over? She didn't believe him. Or trust him. Her guard remained up. "You're not going to try to make me change my mind?" she asked.

He looked surprised that she should even suggest such a thing. "Who can argue with a woman of iron?" he asked. "Your mind's made up."

She wasn't buying it. Any of it. But she felt that it was best to leave the matter alone. He had a way of drawing her out and making her say things that she'd had no intention of saying. "That's right, it is. So, if there's nothing further you want to discuss..." she said, rising.

But once again he placed his hand over hers. "There's still coffee—if we can ever get the waitress to look our way again."

"Sorry," Lissa said, taking her other hand and lifting his off hers. "I've got to be getting back. I've got a report to write about the robbery at the Andrews residence."

For the first time since she had joined the force Lissa was actually grateful that there were such things as reports to write.

Of course, by the time she got to the station her gratitude had dwindled somewhat. This was the part of police work that she hated. Putting words on paper had never been her forte. She sat at the typewriter, trying to shut out the multitude of conversations on finding the right words to use. Also the right keys. Her typing, she thought as she bit her lower lip, had never gone beyond the hunt and peck stage, nor had she ever had any desire to improve it. She wanted to be out protecting people and solving crimes, not caressing typewriter keys.

Caressing... The word, thought in annoyance, made her attention momentarily drift away from Mr. Andrews and his frown to Brett, with his warm, sensuous smile. When she had left the café, she had sounded angry at him. Actually she was really disappointed with herself. Why couldn't she keep her personal feelings out of this case? She was definitely not living up to the image she had of herself. Detached. Cool. Competent in every situation. *That* was what she wanted to be. That was what she normally was—until Brett had come into her life. That was grounds enough to be annoyed with him, she tried to tell herself. *He* had shaken up the orderliness she had achieved, and besides, he only wanted to use her. She was sure of it. She had been through the routine once before, trusting a fellow officer who had lent an eager, attentive ear to every step of her investigation, only to whisk in at the last minute and steal the glory—and the promotion. Lissa knew all the signs.

But how could you be annoyed with someone who melted your very soul with a well-placed look from his brown eyes or a casual touch of his hand? Their evening of lovemaking came back to her, the details running erotically through her brain.

"Having trouble, Armstrong?"

Lissa's head jerked up. The gravelly voice had startled her, bringing her back from her mental wanderings. "Um, no. I—"

"Kind of jumpy today, aren't you?" Hanson observed. There was more than a touch of condescension in his voice. Why was he always catching her at her worst moments? She was a much better officer than he thought she was. She just had to show him. Which brought her back to her case and her determination to solve it before Brett did. And before Brom got back.

"I was just thinking about the case," she said in an offhand manner. "There's been another robbery."

"Yes, I know," he said sarcastically.

Lissa pretended not to notice. "How is Brom doing?" she asked casually, hoping that she didn't sound too interested. Most cases of food poisoning didn't last very long. If she was very, very lucky, Brom would be out a couple of days more, at best. If she was even luckier, she tacked on, she'd solve the case before then.

"Better," Hanson growled. "I called him today. He said he might be back on his feet day after tomorrow. Dunno what's taking him so long. All you young people are pampered," he grumbled.

Lissa pretended to be looking over her report, though there wasn't very much to look over. "Must have really been potent stuff he ingested," she commented.

"Some strange thing he picked up at one of those exotic new restaurants that are springing up. Me, I never eat anything I can't spell," he said haughtily as he headed toward his office.

That would mean he ate nothing but steak, she thought, hunting for the next key. She knew better than to voice her sentiments out loud.

A couple of days. Maybe. She had a couple of days to solve this thing. That meant working on it after hours as well. Two days wasn't much time in which to prove yourself. She hunted harder for the keys.

When she got home, Lissa fixed herself a quick hamburger and got down to work. She had been tempted to pick up a hamburger at a fast-food place, but she was definitely not taking a chance on landing flat on her back the way Brom had. It was bad enough landing flat on her back because of Brett.... Now why had that come into her head? She had to stop thinking about Brett if she was going to get any work done, she told herself. In this case, with the clock running on her, business had to come before pleasure.

But what if, once the case was solved, she asked herself as she cleared off her kitchen table, Brett disappeared from her life, too? What did she mean, what if? His only interest in her *was* the case, and she wasn't at liberty to prolong it, not even for a moment. There were too many factors working against her.

"Enough of this mental bickering," she said to the

refrigerator as she closed the door, a diet cola in her hand. "Detective Armstrong has work to do."

Agatha looked at her dubiously.

"Okay," Lissa conceded, "so it's a little premature, but I'll get there. Swimming upstream through a river of paperwork, maybe, but I *will* get there," she vowed. She sat down at the table, spreading out all her notes and wishing that an inspiration of some sort would come. But nothing spoke to her. The reports said just what they had the night before and the night before that. No, wait a minute. The night before that, the reports hadn't said anything. That had been *his* night.

Lissa closed her eyes and leaned her head against the palm of her hand. Why couldn't she get rid of his image? Why did it keep haunting her mind at the least opportune times? Was this part of his plan, too? To keep her so mesmerized with thoughts of him that she couldn't concentrate on anything else? That would give him a clear shot at solving the crime ahead of her.

She popped the top off her diet soda and poured it, then watched the fizz make a little cloud over her glass. This constant vacillation had to stop. Her career was going to be around a lot longer than Brett was, and it was up to her to make the most of the opportunity that fate had tossed her way.

She tried again.

This time she was interrupted by Agatha, who began to yip excitedly. Lissa looked at the dog, who pranced around her feet, sliding slightly on the slick tile floor in her enthusiasm.

"I'm sorry, Aggie. I know I've been neglecting you lately," she began soothingly, only to stop herself as Agatha took hold of her pants leg. "What *is* it?" Lissa asked impatiently. Agatha ran off toward the back of the house, then came tearing back toward Lissa. "Someone there?" she asked the dog, lowering her voice.

The yipping grew more pronounced. Lissa rose from her seat and took her service revolver out of the linen closet. Beach communities had their share of weird people, she thought. Better safe than sorry.

"Shh," she warned Agatha, then moved to stand next to the long drape that covered her sliding glass door. Simultaneously she threw the light switch that flooded her backyard with light and pulled back the curtain. She was ready for anything. Or so she thought.

She lowered her revolver and put the safety catch back on before she unlatched the sliding glass door.

"Just what do you think you're doing, lurking in my backyard?" she wanted to know.

Agatha was almost beside herself with joy as Brett bent down, allowing the furry black animal to lick his hand and leap up toward his face.

"Now that's what I call a real greeting," he commented. Holding the dog's head still between his hands, he pretended to address her seriously. "Do you train mistresses?"

"Very funny," Lissa said, leading the way back to her kitchen. "That still doesn't explain what you're doing here." Her eyes fell on her scattered notes and, with a large sweeping motion, she gathered them hurriedly and returned them to the drawer. After locking it, she slipped the key into her pocket.

"I was hoping to find you," Brett said, coming up behind her and slipping his hands into her front pock-

ets. Just the presence of his hands made her feel warm
all over, even while she strove to fight the sensation.
Anticipation began to nip at her senses.

"Is that why you were trying to sneak in the back
way?" she asked.

"I thought maybe if I surprised you, you wouldn't
have time to get your guard up."

A likely story, she scoffed silently, turning around.
As she did so Brett withdrew his hands from her
pockets, lightly brushing the area beneath her navel.
A sensitive shiver ricocheted all through her.

"Like now," Brett said, watching her face. "I've
missed you."

"You saw me this morning," she pointed out, not
believing his line for a moment. But somehow his
words were weaving their way beneath the uppermost
layer of her disbelief. He had a way of bypassing all
that and reaching her inner core. The core that had
no career goals, no desire other than to be held and
loved by him.

"Looking at you and wanting you while some poor
disgruntled old man bemoans the theft of his beloved
collection can hardly be called seeing you," Brett
said, trying to take her into his arms.

Lissa stepped back into the kitchen. Another
smooth line, she told herself. But the smooth line was
chipping away at her hastily thrown-up veneer. And,
like true veneer, the protective shell did not go very
deep.

"So," she said, searching for words that would not
give away her true feelings, "I take it you're not getting anywhere on the case eith—" Too late she realized her slip. Her eyes darted to his face, but there
wasn't a trace of a smug look. Only amusement.

Which still bothered her. Let's face it, Armstrong, she told herself, the man himself bothers you.

"No, not yet. But I've got a few leads, and I'm working on it," he told her matter-of-factly.

Immediately her interest was piqued. But had he said that just to throw her off guard? To make her warm up to him? The last thought made her smile. As if he really needed something to make her warm up to him. She felt as if her body temperature registered two-hundred centigrade every time he came near her.

"You have informants?" she asked, turning the tables on him. Maybe if she got him to slip up...

Brett shrugged nonchalantly. "Oh, a well-placed dollar here, a dollar there. It gets results."

"And are you?" Lissa prodded, her excitement building despite all her warnings to herself. "Getting results?" she added when he didn't answer her question.

He ran his hand over the outline of her face, touching her cheekbone and skirting the border of her hairline, making wild things happen. "I don't know," he said softly. "You tell me." He was tilting her head back just a little, his lips maddeningly poised over hers. It took everything she had not to stretch up and kiss him first.

Agatha came to her rescue for once, her insistent barking breaking the spell.

"I have to take her out for her walk," Lissa said a bit too quickly, springing away from him in order to fetch the dog's leash.

"Fine," Brett said. "I'll go with you."

There was no getting rid of him, she thought. And a tiny part of her rejoiced at the way things were turning out. He was using her against herself, she thought with a sigh as she attached the leash to Agatha's collar.

As she walked Agatha along the grassy area that bounded the beach, Brett took her hand. Holding hands in the moonlight. She hadn't done that in years. Warm memories of her high school days came back to her. But none of the faces of her past boyfriends were clear. Brett had blotted them all out.

"Pretty moon," Lissa commented, looking at the bright globe above them.

"Prettier woman," Brett said, looking only at her.

She tried not to pay attention to the effect his words had on her. She looked out to the deserted beach.

"How about a walk along the beach?" Brett suggested.

"Can't. Dogs aren't allowed on the beach," she said, nodding at Agatha. And right now, Agatha is my only protection against you, she thought.

"We can pretend she's a police dog. Surely exceptions can be made for police dogs," he teased, whispering the words against her temple. They vibrated along her skin. She felt powerless to refuse his suggestion. And she didn't.

Agatha kept her part of the bargain she seemed to have struck up with Brett. Not a single joyous yip pierced the air as she raced off across the sand, setting off grainy little showers in her wake. She scurried in front of them, seeming to play her own game. It was as if she sensed that there was another game, one with higher stakes, in progress just behind her.

Smart dog, Lissa thought absently. It was practically the only thought she gave the dog as Brett led her to the glistening shoreline. The water lapped at

the wet sand, white waves gleaming in the moonlight.
The ocean was warm. Brett held her hand as she
pulled off her sandals, then braced himself on her slim
shoulder as he followed suit. And then they strolled
along the beach, lost in each other.

"Where do you live?" Lissa asked suddenly, looking for something with which to fight the romantic
feeling that was seizing her.

He didn't understand what she was driving at.
"You were there," he reminded her.

But she shook her head. "No, I mean when you're
not staying at your cousin's house. Where's home to
you?"

"New York," he told her.

It was just what she told herself she wanted to hear,
and yet a terrible sting came with his words. Idiot.
What's the matter with you? She asked herself impatiently.

"I live in a quaint little brownstone with ceilings
just as high as those in Richard's house. To tell the
truth, I think I got hooked on it because it reminded
me of the designs Richard was so fond of. I guess I
was trying to emulate him."

She couldn't see him trying to emulate anyone.
This revelation added another dimension to Brett,
making him more real to her. "Are you and he very
close, then?" she asked.

"We used to be very close. Time," Brett said with
a touch of sadness, "has a way of changing things,
though. He's caught up in maintaining his career, his
reputation. And I had my cases to keep me busy. That
was why I was surprised when he gave me a call last
year and asked me to come out to help him with
something."

Lissa waited for him to elaborate, but Brett was silent as his thoughts drifted back to the past. She saw him rouse himself before her eyes, abandoning his mental journey.

"Anyway, we grew up together," he continued. "Practically lived in each other's pockets. Richard's older by a couple of years, and I guess I had a serious case of hero-worship. He had a way with everyone," he said fondly. "Still does."

"Seems to be a family trait," she murmured.

"What?" Brett cocked his head to one side, trying to hear her better.

"Nothing," she said. She didn't want to let him see how much he had gotten to her in such a short time. "If you wanted to be just like him, why did you become a detective? If you'd studied architecture, maybe the two of you could have opened up shop together."

In answer, Brett began to laugh. It was a deep, hearty laugh that brought a smile to her own lips even though she had no idea why he was laughing. It was infectious. *He* was infectious. "I can't draw a straight line with a ruler, and I have absolutely no imagination when it comes to inanimate objects." He pulled her closer as they walked, his hand resting on her shoulder. She tried not to react to his warmth, but it was hard not to shiver with excitement. *Light, you've got to keep it light. It's your only hope.*

"People," he said, "are another story entirely."

She could testify to that, she thought cryptically.

"I thrive on mysteries; love fitting the pieces of a puzzle together. I love knowing I make a difference in people's lives. And it's great using my mind."

And your hands, she added silently. *Lord, can you*

ever use your hands. She tried to clear her mind of her wayward thoughts, knowing that she was at cross-purposes with herself. He was unraveling her, she thought, digging her toes into the wet sand as she walked.

"I guess it all started when I was fourteen. That summer I took a spill off Richard's motorcycle and broke everything worth breaking. Spent the entire summer in a body cast. My father brought me arm-loads of Mickey Spillane books and I got hooked. So while my friends were out there learning all about the true meaning of puberty and male-female relation-ships, I was getting my education from Mike Ham-mer."

He had stopped walking and was staring off toward the horizon. She stood next to him, touched by his stories, drawn to the boy who still existed within the man. "You must not have been paying very strict attention," she said, trying to sound casual. A lump was growing in her throat. "As I recall, Mike Ham-mer didn't treat women very admirably."

Brett looked down into her face, framing it with his hands. "Maybe that's because he never met any-one like you."

With that, he kissed her.

The surf began to beat harder against the shore, and her heartbeat increased to match it. All her carefully planned defenses, all the words she was going to use to keep him in place, dried up and blew away in the cool evening breeze. All that was left was an over-whelming desire to have him hold her. And holding led to other desires, desires she suddenly didn't want to keep in check any longer.

She felt her heart overflowing with a host of emotions that took her breath away, mainly because, at the center of the whirling hurricane, was love. She wanted this man in her life. She knew she was flirting with disaster, but she couldn't help herself. Nor did she really want to. All she wanted was Brett.

He seemed to sense her need from the intense response that his gentle kiss evoked. He swept her into his arms, kissing her now with more than tenderness. He could feel that her desires were mounting as fast as his.

"Where can a guy go to have a little privacy with his woman?" he murmured against her fevered lips.

His woman. If she believed that, she was a fool, and yet she let herself cling to the words with a tenacity that was frightening.

"We can't do anything on the beach," she said slowly, wishing there were a little cove or a nice cave somewhere in the vicinity.

"FUTURE DETECTIVE FOUND RADIANT AND NUDE IN ARMS OF LUCKY LOVER," he teased. "No, that wouldn't make a very good headline," he agreed. "But neither would PROMISING P.I. FOUND SHRIVELED UP ON BEACH, VICTIM OF ALL-CONSUMING DESIRE."

She laughed. "Aren't you ever serious?" she asked.

To her surprise, the look on his face turned just that. "Yes," he said, his voice low. "Sometimes I'm very, very serious."

Meaning with her. He's a New York sharpie, she reminded herself. He knows all the right words to use, all the right buttons to press. If you buy that line, Lissa Armstrong, you're a fool.

She was a fool.

She kissed him, kissed him so hard that she felt her knees giving way, and suddenly they were lying on the beach, the moist sand cradling them as their souls met. The kiss went on forever, growing in magnitude and demand as it progressed. She thought that she'd never get enough. Desperately she raked her hands over him, pulling his body to hers, reveling in the hot imprint he left on her. Her needs were growing at an alarming rate; she couldn't release him. The most important thing in her life was the kiss they were sharing. It said more to her than any amount of spoken words.

Her ragged breathing seemed to fill the air as his lips left hers so he could bestow the blessings of his mouth along the upper planes of her breasts. She could feel the tingle increasing as his lips encircled the rounded tips that pressed urgently against her yellow T-shirt.

More, her mind cried as she shuddered with his kiss. More.

He stroked the tempting silhouette of her body, his touch seeming to burn away the jeans that stood in his path. She felt only him, and yet was frustrated in her desires to feel him. She slid her hands beneath his shirt, searching for the comforting feel of his strong chest. The beat of his heart seemed to echo her own.

She couldn't get enough of him. She was going insane, she told herself. There was no hope for her. Only he had the power to do anything, to save her.

She felt him pull away, and when she opened her eyes, she found him looking down into her face, a strange expression playing over his. For a moment he seemed to be struggling with himself.

Why?

Brett looked at the way her gleaming hair was fanned out beneath her on the sand. She looked like a fairy sprite, not like a determined policewoman out to get ahead. The image made him smile. "About those headlines..." he reminded her.

Thank God he had more self-control than she did, she thought ruefully, although she would never have admitted the fact to him. She took a deep breath and grabbed his outstretched hand, pulling herself into a sitting position. Sand rained down on her.

"This is going to require a bit of shampooing," Brett told her, raking his fingers through her tangled hair. More sand spilled down, as if in response to his words.

And how do I get rid of these unsettling feelings inside? She wondered. Would shampooing do it? With industrial strength cleaner? Lissa knew that no cleansing process could ever restore her to her former self.

Nine

Agatha led the way home, acting remarkably subdued. It's as if she knows what I'm going through, Lissa thought. She knows that I should send him away at my door. She also knows I won't, even though there's no future in this.

She had begun to entertain the smallest spark of hope that maybe, just maybe, he was there because of her and not for any other reason. But even if that turned out to be true, what would that leave them? A pleasant interlude. All right, a passionate interlude, but an interlude nonetheless, she told herself. She had seen the light in his eyes when he talked about "home." Home to him was New York, with towering dark buildings and crowds of people. That was where his excitement lay. Hers was out in the open, with sunshine on Christmas morning and a beach that was almost always tempting. The two didn't mesh. But he hadn't mentioned anything about future meshings. Only present ones.

When had life gotten so complicated?

But the emotions that flooded through her when he pushed her front door closed behind them and took her into his arms were the simplest, most basic ones. In the heat of the moment, no complications existed, only raw, vibrant feelings that demanded responses.

Responses that he was quick to give.

"Well," he murmured against her cheek, "you've ruled out the beach. Where would you like to fulfill all my dreams?" Although there was a smile in his voice, there was nothing teasing in his manner. If appearances were all she had to go by, he wanted her as much as she wanted him.

Was there a logical answer to a question like that? How could he expect her to make sense when her insides were vibrating like an overzealous tuning fork? Maybe he wasn't as perceptive as she thought, this private eye of hers. Hers? For the moment. Until the whims of fate, or destiny, or whatever, took him away from her. No, Virginia, there's no Santa Claus, she thought sadly, but for now, we can sure pretend.

"Anywhere," she breathed.

"If that was the case, I should have taken you on the beach just like in *From Here to Eternity*," he told her as he started to undo her jeans.

"I don't like salty kisses," she said, images of the old movie coming back to her as she stood still while he helped her out of her clothes. She kept her eyes on his face, watching the glow in his eyes increase as the amount of clothing she wore decreased.

"What kind of kisses *do* you like?" he asked.

"Yours," she answered without a moment's hesitation. She felt incredibly warm despite the fact that all she had on was her underwear. Her air-conditioning unit let out a whoosh and began to hum as it shot out drafts of cold air. But that didn't matter. She was hot. Hot all over. And only he could quench the fire.

But first he stoked it.

He took her hand and walked over to the couch. Sitting down, he pulled her onto his lap, facing away from him. He kissed the back of her neck as he gently massaged her breasts through her bra. Then, very carefully, he undid her bra and slid the straps off her shoulders. It amazed her how such gentle, tender strokes could arouse such a fury of emotions within her. The lighter the touch, the more urgent the passion that rose to meet it. Ever so slowly he ran his hands all over her exposed body, from her thighs to her stomach to her breasts, all the while kissing her shoulders and neck.

Needing to touch him, she twisted around on his lap until she faced him. Then, taking his face in her hands, she kissed him ardently. Her passion felt so great that it almost hurt. Dropping her hands from his face, she began to unbutton his shirt.

Still kissing him, she stood up, leading him. As he stood to join her, his lips on hers, Lissa unfastened his trousers and eased them off.

"Now we're even," she told him, happy that she didn't sound as breathless as she felt.

"Where do we go from here?" he teased.

"Your deal," she whispered as his hands went around her delicate shoulders, caressing the sculpted lines.

After working his hands around to the front of her,

Brett rubbed the tips of her breasts with his palms, smiling into her eyes. "I'd say I had a wining hand," he said softly.

She smiled ruefully. She didn't consider herself very well endowed. Tantalizing cleavage was something she had never quite achieved, and there were times when she had felt cheated. She looked at Brett, all her past feelings of inadequacy returning. "Not exactly a full house," she said.

His touch did wondrous things to her as he whispered, "It is to me," against her neck just before he claimed the area with a pattern of burning kisses. "Besides, what could I possibly do with more than a handful?" he asked her, assaulting the other side of her neck, zeroing in on all her erogenous zones as if they were completely mapped out for him.

She would have answered him if she could, would have made some sort of light, witty comment perhaps. But for that she would have needed the use of her mind, and it was now out of her control, holding on to images, rather than complete thoughts.

Their eyes holding, Lissa and Brett simultaneously slid their hands along each other's hips, slipping beneath the cloth barriers that represented the last frontier to be conquered before achieving mutual ecstasy.

He slid her underwear down a fraction of an inch. She followed suit. And so it went, microscopic gains being made as they excited each other to overwhelming proportions.

Finally, their underwear no longer an obstacle, the game was forgotten. All that remained was the mingling of their bodies and their souls. As he placed her gently on the floor, arranging himself over her, Brett's eyes sparkled with a radiance that whispered to her very being.

"Adam and Eve had the right idea," he said, his warm hands once more sweeping over the supple warm mounds and valleys of her body before he finally took one breast in his mouth. His tongue teased her so erotically that she could hardly answer.

"Oh?" The single word took an almost immeasurable amount of effort to utter.

"Fig leaves are much easier to get out of. So much less time lost."

A chuckle tried to find its way out of her throat. "You don't exactly seem to be dragging your feet here."

"Would you expect a starving man to fast when he's standing before a feast?" he asked, turning his attention to her other breast. As his tongue touched the rosy peak Lissa began to shudder, her impatience growing, though she tried to control it, to relish every tiny experience.

She loved the things he was saying. Perhaps she would have laughed them away if she were sober. But her senses had long since become inebriated, and all with him. "'Eat, drink and be merry,'" she told him, wrapping her arms around his neck and pulling his mouth to hers.

"'For tomorrow we die,'" he completed the adage for her just before he covered her waiting lips.

Tomorrow. Oh, yes, tomorrow. Tomorrow would hold more doubts, some regrets, and a whole collection of confusing thoughts. But right now was different. Right now she was holding the unsettling realities of tomorrow at bay. She didn't want to think, only to feel. What was happening right now was the most wonderful occurrence of her life. She felt almost reborn in his lovemaking. Exhilaration raced through her veins, making her feel as if she had never been alive until he had touched her, that she had only existed on the sidelines of life until he had opened the door for her.

Lissa loved him.

But even at the instant when they became one, at the moment when thoughts and realities had no place, she felt a touch of sorrow. All this would be over soon. One way or another, it would be over. She threw herself into their lovemaking with such a fierce abandonment that she startled Brett.

"Oh, baby, baby," he murmured, his voice harsh with his own breathless state. "What's the matter?"

But she refused to acknowledge his question, clutching him tightly as their bodies spiraled upward to the ultimate plateau of mutual fulfillment and pleasure. It was all she wanted. All she needed. In the end, it was all she knew. She arched her back as the final starburst occurred, then fell back against the blue carpet, a low moan escaping her lips. Her hair was a golden halo around her head. All she had strength for was a small contented smile.

Brett nestled her against his body, his warmth surrounding her. She wished she could get lost in it forever. But even now the diaphanous ties of ecstasy were slipping away, leaving a sadness in their wake. She closed her eyes tightly, as if that could keep reality away. She fell asleep.

When she awoke the next morning, Lissa was in her own bed. Alone. She looked down at her body and found that she was still nude. Nude and alone.

"Fine state of affairs," she muttered, getting up

and rifling through her closet for her robe. When she came up empty-handed after one impatient pass through the clustered hangers, she pulled down a long football jersey. She had forgotten she had it. She just barely remembered who gave it to her. Brett had routed all her memories of other men from her mind.

She slipped the jersey on, and the hem settled about her knees. So dressed, Lissa went in search of her quarry. She had as much luck finding him as she had her robe.

"Brett?" she called as she walked out into the living room. But he wasn't there, nor in the kitchen. Agatha ceased lapping her bowl of water in the corner of the room and looked at her with soulful eyes.

"So now my dog's taken to pitying me, eh?" she said to the animal, giving her an affectionate scratch behind the ears. As she got down on her knees Lissa noted that the bowl was full. "Well, at least he's kind to animals," she muttered. "Is he here, girl?"

But Agatha went back to drinking. Lissa rose to her feet. The clock on the wall told her that she had exactly half an hour to get ready for work. Maybe it was just as well that Brett wasn't there, she thought. If he were, she'd never make it in time. She walked to the front door and peered outside. The Stingray was gone.

Why had he left like that? She wondered, closing the door behind her. Last night had been perfect.... A piece of paper on the table next to the door caught her eye.

Darling,
Have to run. Got an early appointment. You were wonderful. Be careful. I'll call you.

                                        Brett

She held it for a moment, staring at the paper, her mind drifting. She'd seen more passionate notes to the milkman, she thought cryptically. Well, what did she expect? Poetry? No, she expected to find him next to her in the morning, not running off like some thief in the night. She felt strangely cheated. She felt... Thief in the night. The phrase stuck. Suddenly she looked at the drawer in the table. One tug on the handle opened it. She was sure she had locked it last night. Yes, just before they went on their walk. Adrenaline running madly through her, Lissa pulled out her notes. He had read them. That's what last night had been all about. Her notes.

"Damn!" she cried, hurling the papers to the floor. She didn't even stop to pick them up as she went into her bedroom. Angry tears burned her throat as she headed for the shower, where she let the scaldingly hot water assault her skin.

There was nothing in the notes to help him. At least, not as far as she could see. But the very fact that he had looked for them—and through them—told her that while he had been seducing her senses, whipping them into a frenzy, he had had an ulterior motive. Well, hadn't she told herself that all along? She demanded a little while later, forgoing breakfast and heading straight for her car, her hair still damp after her shower.

The realization that she had been right didn't help matters one bit.

But it did make her more determined than ever to solve the case.

* * *

"Leopold," Lissa said, coming up to the florid-faced policeman. She knew that he always paused to get himself a cup of coffee and a candy bar from the vending machine after the morning briefing. She managed to corner him just before he went out to his squad car.

Leopold leaned his nonregulation-size bulk against the machine and looked at her questioningly, his small eyes peering out above crinkled round cheeks.

"What's on your mind, Lissa?" he drawled.

She waited until several other policemen had passed them on their way to the parking lot. Leopold took the opportunity to devour his candy bar.

"Don't make them like they used to. They were a lot bigger when I was a kid," he said with a nostalgic sigh, sloshing the chocolate down with a large gulp of lukewarm coffee. The cardboard taste didn't seem to bother him, Lissa marveled.

"You were a lot smaller when you were a kid," she pointed out affectionately to the man she half regarded as her mentor. If Hanson seemed to be after her proverbial hide, Leopold was always ready to go out of his way to help her. In the scheme of things, she guessed, that balanced things out.

"Too true," Leopold agreed, feigning remorse. But then he laughed and patted his round stomach. "Good thing I have seniority. But you didn't come here to discuss my breakfast," he said, encouraging her to talk.

"I need information," Lissa said, her light tone turning serious. "That case Hanson temporarily assigned me to—it's just not jelling for me. There aren't any leads," she moaned softly.

They had begun to walk toward the rear of the building. "I hear there's a P.I. involved, too," Leopold said.

Lissa's expression hardened. "Yes," she said, her voice stony.

"Talk is he's pretty good-looking. One of the ladies saw him when you brought him in for questioning." Leopold always referred to the policewomen as "ladies," but she had not time for his southern gallantry right now. Her feelings of betrayal were too raw.

"He's pretty sneaky, is what he is," she corrected Leopold with a toss of her head. "He's out to crack this case any way he can."

"And you want to do it first," Leopold finished for her, crushing his cup as he held the glass door open for her.

"Yes," she said vehemently.

"For the glory of the force," he added with a twinkle in his eye.

She realized how pompous she must have sounded. "And for a feather in my cap," she added with a touch of humor. "Any suggestions? I've been through the notes on the case until my eyes can't see straight."

"Hit the pawnshops," he suggested as they reached his squad car.

"From what I gather, this guy likes to keep what he gets. He's only called a couple of victims to offer to ransom back the loot," she said, feeling a bit defeated. She leaned on the car door, hoping that Leopold would have another suggestion.

"Well, I'd question those victims myself if I were you. And I wouldn't rule out the possibility of pawnshops. Hit the higher class ones first with a list of items. You never know when you might come up lucky. In the meantime, I'll ask around," he promised her, getting in and shifting his heavy frame in order to get comfortable behind the wheel. "I'll see what I can come up with. Good luck," he said as he started up the engine.

Lissa waved at him just before she turned to her own car. Luck. She felt as if she had exhausted all claim to that. Being lucky meant having fortune smile down on you. She figured that fortune had done enough smiling by letting her experience the ultimate in lovemaking. There was no place to go from here but down—to the gutter, where she'd find Brett, the rat.

Her renewed feelings of hostility made her slam her car door as she got inside. She'd show him! And she wouldn't do it by being sneaky.

She headed for the first robbery victim on her list.

"Not very much I can tell you," the bony, angular man said to Lissa after welcoming her in and plying her with seven kinds of cookies. "Never know when company's coming by," he had said when she had looked at the huge box in surprise. The cookies were stale. Company must not come by very often, she thought as she gamely ate a hardened wafer.

They sat in the man's parlor. The warm morning sun felt good. Warm. Like the touch of Brett's hand. Stop it, she snapped at herself. This poor old man is talking to you and you're off mooning about a rat. She put on her brightest, most encouraging smile. But she could tell that this was one avenue that was going to prove fruitless.

"Then you didn't see the thief when you went to reclaim the stolen goods?" she asked, disappointed.

The gaunt head moved from side to side. "No. He told me to leave the money on the bench in that little alcove overlooking the beach. Then I was supposed to wait half an hour at that little café—"

Lissa nodded. The café Brett had taken her to for coffee. The coffee she had never drunk. How much better for her if the coffee hadn't been the only thing left unsampled. "I'm familiar with it," she said somewhat abruptly. Well, at least she stopped the flow of any more useless description.

"And he said the collection would be waiting for me when I got back."

Wonderful. She not only had a burglar who broke in to take things, he liked to break in to return them as well. Whoever it was must have been getting a thrill from all this. This was no common criminal, she thought again.

Okay, no description. "What did he sound like?" she asked. Perhaps he had a telltale lilt to his voice, or an accent.

But the man once more shook his head. "It was a low, raspy voice. He did laugh kind of nastily," he offered hopefully.

Terrific. Peter Lorre had come back from the dead and was making phone calls. Lissa rose. "Thank you very much for your time," she said, hoping that he wouldn't press any more cookies on her.

"That's quite all right," he said, mercifully forgetting about the box. "I like company," he told her needlessly. "And today I've been lucky twice."

There was no reason for his remark to stop her departure, but it did. After all, the man could be referring to one of his friends. But somehow she knew he wasn't.

"Oh, did someone else come to see you?" she asked innocently.

"Yes, that nice young man who's working on the case. Unfortunately," he said, his shoulders slumping forward a little more, "I couldn't tell him any more than I could tell you."

She hated following in Brett's shadow, she thought, annoyed. She hoped he wasn't thinking of hitting the pawnshops as well. More than that, she hoped that she would find something helpful when she did. Lissa tried to keep her inner turmoil from showing on her face.

"Nonsense, Mr. Whittaker, you've been most helpful. Cases are solved by pulling a whole network of details together. You never know where you might find the most helpful clue."

She left him beaming on the front steps.

She, in turn, was fuming. Damn Brett, anyway. This was her case. He knew it was important to her, and yet he had used her against herself, taking his pleasure while he was at it.

Hey, now, let's not color this all black here, she told herself, coming to an abrupt stop as the light turned red at the corner. He wasn't exactly ravaging you against your will. As I recall, you weren't what could be termed passive in what transpired last night.

No, she hadn't been passive. That made the situation bother her all the more. She had opened herself up to him, had allowed herself to fall for him, and all the time, all he had been after were clues.

The line "Hell hath no fury..." floated through her mind, but she refused to finish it. She'd show him fury, all right. Don't get mad; get even. And getting even would mean solving the case.

She made her way to the address of the second name on her list. When she left him she was no more enlightened than she had been at the start.

Two o'clock found Lissa stopping in front of her fifth pawnshop, thoroughly tired of her venture. This was all getting to be pointless. But what else did she have to go on? She asked herself, getting out of the car.

As she pushed the shop's door open, a bell heralded her entrance. Quaint, she thought, looking at the strange paraphernalia that filled every available space in the tiny store. She doubted that her burglar would come here. But it was the last one in the area, and she was determined to be thorough.

On closer scrutiny, the items being offered to the customer were not the run-of-the-mill articles that had seen better days. These appeared to be high quality possessions whose owners had seen better days instead. She leaned against the glass counter, waiting for someone to come out in answer to the bell. A gleaming diamond bracelet caught her eye, a testimony of the hard times that had befallen someone. Maybe there was some hope after all: *if* the burglar had decided that he had no use for some of the valuable items he had stolen and had no desire to offer them back to the original owner. A lot of ifs here, she thought with another sigh. But once more she reminded herself that she had nothing else to go on.

The owner of the store came out. He looked more like a nine-to-five executive than a pawnshop proprietor, she thought, taking in his charcoal gray suit and dapper manner. He looked at her critically from behind a pair of pince-nez. She had always wondered how someone could manage to keep those things perched on the bridge of his nose with no visible means of support. But this was no time for trivia. She was still facing frustration, and for more reasons than one, her mind whispered. She ignored it.

"How may I help you?" the man asked in very precise tones. "What is it you have to sell?"

Why didn't he think she was out to buy something instead? Did she look down on her luck? She tried to repair the image she felt she must be presenting, realizing that her four other failures were probably showing on her face.

"Nothing. But I do have some questions I'd like to ask you."

The shoulders squared beneath their shoulder pads. "My dear young woman—" the owner began in a brittle tone.

Lissa didn't say a word. She just took out her identification and watched the man's brows rise a little.

"I see," he said, handing the ID back to her. "Always happy to cooperate with the local *gendarmes,*" he muttered. "Although I am getting a little tired of answering questions," he said.

"Oh?" Please, please don't tell me he's been here, she thought. He hadn't shown up at any of the other dead ends. She had thought that she had the jump on him, at least for the time being. "Whose questions have you been answering?" she asked.

The curtain behind the well-dressed man parted. "Mine," Brett told her.

Ten

"**I**'d be happy to spare you the inconvenience of having to recite the details all over again," Brett told the shopowner as he himself moved around the counter to join Lissa. He flipped open his notebook. "I have all my notes here." He waved the pages in front of Lissa.

She stared past him as if he weren't there at all. "If you don't mind, Mr....?"

"Aquarius," the man said formally, extending a very impersonal hand in her direction. As she took it, Lissa couldn't help thinking that she had touched fish that were warmer.

"Mr. Aquarius," she echoed, not believing for one minute that that was his real name. "I'd like to have any information you might have firsthand. Things sometimes get muddled the second time around."

"No second time around," Brett said, interrupting.

"Look you can read them yourself," he offered, trying to hand her his notebook.

The look she gave him could have frozen the ocean that beat out its steady rhythm a scant quarter mile away. "Unlike some people, I don't read other people's notes."

"Are you two having a fight?" Aquarius asked, looking alive for the first time. His eyes passed from Lissa's face to Brett's then back again.

"No," Lissa retorted, realizing that she had let her emotions slip through again.

"Yes," Brett contradicted her.

Lissa looked at him sharply.

Aquarius cleared his throat. "Well, it's none of my business, really," he said. From his tone, it was obvious that he thought the world at large *was* his business. "But I think things would go more smoothly if the local police learned to work hand in hand with the people."

Lissa tried to keep her annoyance from surfacing on her face.

"Want to go work hand-in-hand?" Brett proposed, amused.

Lissa shouldered him aside. "Mr. Aquarius, I'd like to get out of your way as soon as possible." She thrust the list of stolen objects in front of him. "To your knowledge, has anyone brought any of these items to your shop?"

Rather than study the list, all Aquarius did was give it a cursory glance. "You two sure you're not working together?" he asked. "This list is identical to the one he just showed me," he said, jerking a thumb at Brett.

"I'm sure it is," Lissa said, pressing her lips together. "But I assure you, we are *not* working together."

Her answer left Aquarius somewhat confused, but he shook his head dismissively. He had no time to ponder their problems. The bell behind Lissa tinkled again, signaling the entrance of a patron. Aquarius became impatient. "As I said to Mr. McKenna, someone did come in with that item there." A long finger pointed to the last item on her list.

The coin collection. Lissa couldn't help wondering why the burglar had pawned it. Surely the owner would have paid more than twice as much as the pawnshop owner could. This didn't fit with the overall picture she was getting of the thief. Maybe this burglary had been committed by someone else. But then, the basic MO still held. Easy entry when the victims were not at home. Right back to where she started from—except...

Her eyes lit up. "Did he give you a name, an address?" she prodded.

"Right here," Brett said, pointing out the information in his notebook.

Despite herself, Lissa glanced at the name and address. Undoubtedly both were fictitious. Still, it had to be checked out.

"What did the man look like?" she asked, giving Brett no indication that she had even read the name.

"Medium height, rather on the thin side. Older gentleman. Very refined-looking. Mustache. Can I go now?" Aquarius asked, looking at the woman behind Lissa.

"Yes," Lissa said, folding her list and tucking it into her purse. "But I'm afraid you'll have to give up the coins. Someone from the station will be along to pick them up. Evidence," she added, noting the surprised and annoyed look on the man's face.

Aquarius didn't even bother to nod as he turned his attention to the well-dressed older woman who was taking out her checkbook.

"Well, shall we check this out separately, or do you want to ride with me?" Brett asked as he held open the door for Lissa.

She marched through it, her head held high. "I don't want to have anything to do with you," she informed him coldly.

But he grabbed hold of her arm as she unlocked the door to her car.

"How would you like to be arrested for harassing an officer?" she threatened, giving him a murderous look.

"I'll risk it if you give me a chance to explain," he said seriously.

She didn't want to listen. She wanted to take her wounded pride, her hurt ego, and just drive off. But somehow she stayed there, against her better judgment. "What's to explain? You invested a little time and got what you wanted."

"Yes, I did," he conceded.

She fought back the urge to strike him.

"But," he said, turning her so that she squarely faced him, "I think we're defining what I want differently. I want you."

The sentence was uttered in direct contrast to his other statements. There was nothing quick or snappy about his words. Just firm. And she would have given anything to believe them.

It's just a ploy, she thought. But her body remembered last night. She felt herself weakening.

"You went through my papers," she upbraided him.

He didn't even bother to lie. "Yes, I did."

"Why?" Her tone was accusing, even though his ready admission had surprised her.

"Because you wouldn't let me see them on your own."

Well, that was direct enough. "I want to solve this case," she said. "It means a lot to me."

"You're inexperienced," Brett pointed out.

"Well, I'm not going to get experienced if I don't get out there and do something," she insisted.

"Okay," he said, sounding game. "We'll work on it together."

She shook her head. "And have Hanson say I rode in on your coattails? Oh, no, I have to do this alone. It's the only way I'm going to prove myself. And I wish you'd stop getting in the way."

Her last remark made him smile. "Oh? Am I getting in the way?" he asked.

Why did he have the knack of melting her anger away? She couldn't concentrate on her work if she kept thinking about him. "Yes, you're getting in the way."

"Nice to know," he told her. "C'mon. I'll drive us over," he offered.

But she turned him down. "No, thanks. I'll use my own car. Besides, I'm still on duty." So take the hint and go away, she begged silently.

But though she was dropping hints, he wasn't picking them up. "How much longer?"

She could tell by the velvet tone of his voice exactly what was on his mind. Something she couldn't

give in to if she were going to try to put the pieces
of this thing together. "Until five," she said.

"Thirty-five minutes to go," he said cheerfully.
"Okay, I'll follow you."

She had no doubt that he would, whether or not
she agreed to it. But the idea of having him around
no longer annoyed her the way it had earlier. He was
getting to her again, and she was just being foolish,
she told herself. He was just trying to keep tabs on
her, since he could see how determined she was to
solve the case. Stick-to-itiveness was at least part of
the battle. One would have thought, she mused as she
drove down Pacific Coast Highway, that he was the
Californian and she the New Yorker. He was completely laid-back, not at all the way she would have
expected someone from New York to be. So much
for stereotyping, she thought with a hint of amusement.

The address she had memorized from Brett's notebook led to a dead end, just as she had feared it
would. She parked her car in a lot across the street
and got out. The address belonged to a run-down theater. Somehow she sorely doubted that the suspect
was the projectionist and slept in the back. Now
what?

"Want to catch it?" Brett asked as he brought his
Stingray to a halt right next to her car.

"What?"

He pointed a thumb at the marquee. "The movie,"
he clarified. "Bogie's one of my favorites."

"No, I don't think so." How could he be thinking
about going to the movies? Their burglar was still at
large. Their burglar? Since when had he become com-

munity property? More of Brett's subtle encroachment on her life, she thought in despair.

"It's *The Maltese Falcon*," he told her needlessly. She was about to retort that she could read, thank you, but he went on. "It's about a detective. C'mon, you'll love it," he urged, already taking her hand and pulling her away from the parking lot and toward the very sleepy-looking woman in the ticket booth.

"I've got five more minutes left on my shift," she protested, trying to pull free.

Brett let her hand drop as he glanced down at his watch. "Okay, I'm not unreasonable."

"Oh, yes, you are," she said. "Besides, I have better things to do than waste my time watching old movies."

Brett shook his head. "You've got to loosen up, Constable. Learn how to have a little fun."

He was making her sound as if she were a strait-laced old-maid librarian. That certainly wasn't who he had made love to last night—or whose papers he had gone through.

"It'll do you good," he coaxed.

"I—"

"Three more minutes," he said, looking at his watch again.

"Wonderful," she muttered, looking around and feeling cornered. "Laguna always needed a town crier."

"I'll cry harder unless you agree to come in with me."

She gave up. She didn't quite know why. All she needed to do was walk away. Or, more correctly, get in her car and drive away. But something made her stay. Something that was trying, despite everything, to stay with Brett McKenna as long as possible.

"All right. I'll give Bogie a chance," she conceded.

"How about me?" he asked. "Gonna give me a chance, too?"

"You I'll have to think about," she said, not wanting him to think she had let him off the hook so quickly. He was overconfident as it was.

And whose fault was that? A little voice nagged.

"Time's up," Brett declared, lowering his arm. "You're a free woman."

No, she wasn't, she thought. Not anymore. The long tangling threads of love might be as translucent as a spider's web, but they were as strong as steel. She was hooked but good. She wondered if the man was a part-time magician in addition to being a detective.

"I've still got to call in, or else the chief will think I ran off with the car. Already he doesn't think too highly of me."

"I hadn't noticed," Brett said, sticking his hands in his pockets and rocking slightly on the balls of his feet. The personification of innocence, she thought disparagingly.

She made her call to the precinct, telling the policewoman who operated the switchboard that she was working late on something and that she'd bring the car around after she followed this latest lead to its conclusion.

"Nicely worded," Brett commented as she hung up.

"Don't smirk at me that way," she chided. "I *am* following a lead. If you're so intent on keeping tabs on me in case I come up with something, then, mister, it's a two-way street and I intend to do the same thing.''

"Terrific," Brett enthused. "After the movie, let's go over to your place and...um...'watch' each other.''

"Are you sure you're a New Yorker?" Lissa asked as Brett held up two fingers for the cashier's benefit.

"Positive," he answered.

There were very few people in the tiny theater. "No balcony," he said with a touch of disappointment.

"What do you need a balcony for?" The man was a constant puzzle.

"What does every red-blooded American male need a balcony for?" he asked, looking at her wickedly.

She tried not to laugh. "What is it you miss most about New York?" she asked, not answering his question. Don't forget, she told herself, he'll be going back soon. He made it sound as if he were definitely just passing through—house-sitting for his cousin for six months. Six months wasn't a long time for anything unless you were a fruit fly.

"The basics," he informed her, escorting Lissa with his favor, but before she had a chance to sit Brett bent down and checked her seat out for her. "No gum," he said triumphantly. "Your throne awaits, madam,"

"What basics?" she prodded, taking her seat. What do you care? He's going to be leaving. Three-thousand miles is a long way for affection to reach—not to mention lips.

"A good pizza. Ice cream sodas. Soft ice cream."

She stared at him, disregarding the movie that had just begun. "These are your basics?" she asked incredulously.

"Some of them. Shh. Watch the picture. We were just in time."

"That," she muttered, "is a matter of opinion."

"Of course," Brett said some minutes later, catching her by surprise, "California does have things to offer that New York lacks."

"Such as?" She felt her heart beat just a tiny bit harder.

"You people make a hell of a good hamburger."

Why did his words deflate her so much? She had nothing against hamburgers.... You're acting like one now, she chastised herself. He's got your brain turned into so much ground beef. You should be home, working on the case, trying to find a clue you've missed, not sitting here watching a movie. "Hamburgers, huh?" she muttered despite herself.

"And you seem to have the cutest cops I've ever seen."

Cute. Well, there was her compliment, yet she found herself taking offense, feeling that if she didn't assert herself, she would always be relegated to the category of "cute." Her back became rigid. "I'll have you know—"

"Shh," he whispered against her ear, his breath warming the inner shell. "I didn't mean to get you all stirred up—at least, not that way," he amended.

Lissa didn't have to see the twinkle in his eyes— she could hear it in his voice. "Watch your movie," she whispered, keeping her face front.

"Somehow Bogie doesn't seem to hold the same fascination for me that he has in the past," Brett said, gently running his hand along her leg from her knee to her thigh and back again.

His movements awakened a myriad of electrical impulses within her. She wished she had better self-control. She wanted to be immune to Brett. She wanted to enjoy him on her own level, to be in control for once. Instead she found herself continually reminded of his overwhelming magnetism.

"That's strange," she said, still keeping her eyes on the screen. "I'm just discovering that he's even better than I thought he was." She was trying to direct Brett's attention back to the movie, but her attempts were only halfhearted. His roaming hand was creating havoc within her. So much so that when he suggested forgoing the rest of the movie, she readily agreed.

"And that's entertainment, huh?" she asked, shaking her head. She shielded her eyes as they left the theater. Dusk was still more than half an hour away.

"For some people," Brett said, slipping his arm around her shoulders. "Me, I'm beginning to realize that I like my entertainment firsthand, not vicariously."

"Is that why you're a private investigator?" she asked, attempting to alter the direction that the conversation was taking.

"Yes," he answered, knowing full well what she was doing.

Stalemate. My move, she thought. She glanced around and saw an ice cream shop that belonged to a local chain. "Miss ice-cream sodas, do you?" she asked suddenly, remembering what he had said earlier.

"Yes, but—"

"Well then, come on," she urged, taking his hand.

Deftly avoiding traffic and one determined skate-
boarder who nearly mowed them down in the cross-
walk, Lissa dragged Brett across the street to the ice-
cream parlor.

"What's your favorite flavor?" she asked once
they were seated.

"You," he answered, leaning across the table as
the waitress approached.

"He'll have a strawberry ice-cream soda," she told
the waitress, who looked enviously at Lissa. "Make
it two."

"Well?" Lissa asked once the tall foamy sodas had
arrived and Brett had had a chance to sample his.
"Live up to your high standards?"

Brett didn't answer at first. He was too busy drinking the soda. She had to work hard at stifling her
bubbling laughter. Never, ever would she have ever
pegged him for an ice-cream aficionado.

"I have to admit," he finally said, holding his
straw over a nearly empty glass, "it's as good as any
I've ever had in New York. You wouldn't happen to
know of a good pizza parlor, would you?" he prodded.

"You bet I do," she said gleefully. "Your problem, hotshot, is that you just need someone to show
you the proper places."

"Some of them," he said, looking up at her as he
bent over the soda again, "I've managed to find myself."

It made her smile. "Drink up," she instructed.
"Pizza next."

The pizza parlor, crowded with patrons and filled
with the tempting aroma of zesty toppings, was ten
miles away from the ice-cream parlor.

"Back in New York," Brett said as they sat at a rickety round wooden table, "everything's just a couple of blocks apart."

"This way you can anticipate and savor while you travel from one place to another," she replied, undaunted. "You were the one who did all that talking about savoring, weren't you?"

"I was," he admitted, highly amused.

She didn't think she was being that amusing, but she let it pass. Tonight she found that she was having too much fun to worry about the future. She had made up her mind, somewhere along the line in the darkened run-down theater, that tonight was going to be totally devoted to fun. Tomorrow she was going to throw herself back into the case with a vengeance. But for now she wanted to be as carefree as Brett appeared to be. One last hurrah? She asked herself. Once the case was over and his cousin was back, there would be no reason for Brett to stay. She knew that. Like the busy ant, she was storing up for the long dreaded winter ahead. The winter with no sunshine. The winter with no Brett.

"There. The crust is thin. The mozzarella is thick and stringy. The sauce is perfection itself. What more could you possibly want?" Lissa enthused a little while later.

His eyes met hers over the sloppy fare. "I can think of one thing," he said. The words weren't particularly romantic, considering the situation, but they gripped her nonetheless.

"You've already got that," she said quietly. The words weren't lost in the surrounding din as she had half-hoped they would be. She could see by the look in his eyes that he had heard her.

"Waitress!" he called out above the noise. The harried blonde came shuffling through the sawdust that covered the floor. "We'll take the rest of this to go, please."

The waitress gave him a pained look and turned around.

"Let's go home," Brett said as the grumbling woman went off in search of a box for the pizza.

Home. As if her house belonged to him, too. You're letting yourself get carried away, she warned, feeling familiar sensations beginning to awaken again, filling her with an anxious anticipation.

Eat, drink, and be merry. That was exactly what she had intended to do, right? And what Brett was silently proposing with his gaze came under the heading of making merry, she told herself lightly.

But there was nothing light about the way she was feeling. Excitement pulsed through her veins as he took her hand and led her outside, the pizza box balanced precariously on his other hand. "Do you want to hold on to the pizza, or shall I?" he asked as he walked her to her car.

"You're the one with the appetite," she said. "Besides, I don't want to run the risk of having to clean pizza stains off the upholstery. I'll meet you at the house," she told him.

"Count on it," he assured her, returning to his car.

This was crazy, she told herself over and over again as she drove back down Pacific Coast Highway. She needed a clear head. Brom had already been out for an inordinate amount of time. How much longer did she think her luck was going to hold out? And she was no further along than she had been to start with. Nothing was leading to anything....

No, she couldn't quite say that. Things were leading to other things...but they had nothing to do with the burglaries. Just with him. Well, if that's the case, don't fight it, she told herself, pulling up in her driveway. But that didn't quite work, either. Her instinct for self-preservation kept getting in the way. Neither fish nor fowl, she thought dismally.

Just hopelessly in love, a little voice said as she watched Brett pull up behind her and step out of the car, bearing the pizza before him.

That was the word for it, all right. Hopeless.

Eleven

Eleven

Brett stayed the night and everything else was put on hold.

Lissa felt like one of those ancient navigators who feared that if he sailed out too far in a straight line, both he and his ship would fall off the edge of the world, never to be seen again. That was her, she thought as Brett held her in his arms in the wee hours of the morning, his nude body curling against hers. She was the navigator, skimming the ocean in a ship of paper, heading toward the edge of the world and certain disaster.

Why couldn't she exercise any common sense, any control? He had turned her world topsy-turvy. She knew it. He knew it. Why was she still letting it happen?

Because it was the best thing that had ever happened to her, no matter what the problems, no matter what the outcome. The relationship, such as it was, with Brett was the most wondrous, the most exciting, thing she had ever inexperienced or hoped to experience.

Brett propped himself up on his elbow. "I can hear you thinking," he told her, pushing aside a strand of golden hair that had fallen into her eyes. "What is it?"

"I'm contemplating falling off the edge of the world," she muttered, staring at the ceiling. If she looked into his eyes, he'd see all her tortured thoughts, and she didn't want that. Besides, if she looked at him, her mind would sink away into the quicksand formed by her overheated emotions. It was bad enough being aware of the very warm, very real outline of his body against hers. Bad enough? What's so bad about feeling good? Grab your happiness when you can, she silently counseled herself. Don't analyze it, or demand a signed contract promising endless tomorrows. Today was all that was supposed to count. Wasn't she part of the now generation? She wanted Brett now.

But she also wanted him tomorrow.

"I think you lost me," Brett said, lazily beginning to trace whorls along the soft contours of her body. Teasingly his fingers circled her breasts, closing in on her nipples. Yearning filled her once again. What of the yearning when he was no longer there?

"You're not getting much use out of Richard's house," she said evasively. "Isn't he supposed to be coming back soon?"

"In a week or so. But getting use out of Richard's house isn't exactly the most important thing in my life," he told her, cupping a breast.

More fireworks, she thought, beginning to stir against his touch. It was almost as if her body had a mind of its own. Her senses were already swimming in a deep sultry pool created by his very presence. "What *is* the most important thing in your life?" It was a question she shouldn't be asking, yet she was. She couldn't help herself.

But rather than answer her, Brett closed his mouth over hers and sealed the fate of any further discussion.

All it meant to Lissa was that she was still right. The case was the most important thing to him. He was too honest to lie about it, so he said nothing at all. Along with the fire that claimed her soul that night, there was a deep bittersweet feeling of sadness.

The empty page in the typewriter mocked her. Records had to be kept on every step of the fruitless investigation—and she hated it. Lissa could see writing a report once the case was neatly solved. She could understand addressing yourself to the highlights of the matter. But the drudgery of cataloguing details that seemed to mean nothing at all, that led nowhere, was, as far as she was concerned, a colossal waste of time.

She was oblivious of the conversations going on all around her. She was oblivious of everything except the fact that time was running out for her in more ways than one.

To add to her frustration, the burglar appeared to be lying low. He hadn't struck since he had taken Mr. Andrews's coin collection and perversely pawned it the next day. Had he lost his taste for theft after his disappointment—if that was what had prompted him to sell the stolen goods in the first place? This was terrible. Here she was, an officer of the law, dedicated to keeping the peace, and she was hoping for the thief to strike again so that perhaps this time she could apprehend him.

Well, she thought, trying to justify her feelings, she didn't want him to get away with it. She wanted him to leave some kind of telltale clue in his wake.

"Dream on," she muttered. Barring anything else coming her way in the next few minutes, she had only one course of action open to her. A course of action, she thought with a sigh, that probably wouldn't yield anything and would most certainly generate another mountain of paperwork.

Lissa shut off the unnerving hum of the electric typewriter, leaving the unsightly naked page where it sat. She went out to interview the victims again.

She came up empty.

Most of the people were retired and in their late sixties. One, however, was in his forties. He was Mr. Keller, a warm, genial man who lived alone in a rather modest house. He was the one, Lissa realized after checking her list, who had had his gun collection stolen. He had been the robber's second victim. As he welcomed her into his house, Lissa heard a familiar sound. The TV was on, apparently playing to the empty living room. Mr. Keller gave it only the most cursory attention, glancing over his shoulder from time to time to keep tabs on the action.

"Bogart," he apologized. "It's *Casablanca*. My favorite."

There were a lot of those people running around, she thought wryly. For God's sake, don't think about Brett now!

"I have a fondness for him myself," she told the

wiry man with a smile. Or, more correctly, she thought, she had a fondness for Bogart enthusiasts.

"Oh, then would you like to join me?" Keller offered, picking up a newspaper from his floral couch.

He was a bit messy, she noted, feeling an immediate kinship with the man. "No, I'm afraid I'm on duty."

But despite his friendliness, he could tell her nothing new about the case. As she walked out she noticed three framed certificates hanging on the wall. The windowless foyer received no daylight and was poorly illuminated, but with a bit of effort she managed to read the inscriptions. They all proclaimed him to be the bridge champion of some club. The certificates were dated consecutively, stopping abruptly at the previous year.

"So, you like to play bridge," she said just as he was showing her out.

He gave a nod. "Not much else to do when you're retired." It seemed rather odd for a man in his late forties to be retired, but then she recalled from the reports that he had received a substantial sum from Workmen's Compensation because of an accident he had had five years ago. Something to do with a back injury. "Besides, it keeps my mind sharp." And then he frowned. "I lost the championship this year."

She sensed that that was as important to him as losing the Super Bowl was to a football team.

His mouth was grim. "He was an absolute idiot. Dumb luck was all—" And then Keller stopped himself abruptly, his smile returning. "I guess you can see I get a little carried away." The sound of gunfire behind them brought Keller's attention back toward the TV.

"Well, I'll let you get back to your movie," Lissa said, reaching for the doorknob.

She still didn't have anything to go on. All afternoon she searched for something, anything, not knowing what it was that she was looking for, just feeling that once she came across it, she'd know. Very scientific, she chided herself.

Back at the precinct she chipped in with several other officers and sent out for pizza. As she sat wrestling with both her mind and the mozzarella, Lissa couldn't help thinking of Brett and the previous night. No matter what kind of a barrier she put up in her mind, no matter how serious or involved her thoughts were, his image seemed to seep into the center of things, reducing her thought processes to just so much confetti. With a frantic stab at mental orderliness, Lissa began to make a list of facts about the case, setting her pizza down where it could do the least amount of damage.

Okay, what did she know? Precious little, she thought glumly, fighting an urge to doodle. The thief was meticulous, thorough and always went in when the people were out. He only took certain things. Collections of various sorts. It bespoke someone who knew exactly what he was doing and who knew his victims. The victims all lived within a five-mile radius. What did they have in common except age? No, age wasn't it, either, she corrected herself. Keller was younger than the rest. But in the same situation. Retired. So? What did that point to?

Nothing, she sighed. Nothing at all. She doubted very much that there was some burglar out there methodically robbing retirees who had collections of

valuable objects. But there had to be something. What
was she missing?

A fly buzzed in her ear, then swooped down, hovering over her half-eaten pizza slice. She shooed it
away, but it returned several times. Something was
nagging at her. What? She closed her eyes, thinking
hard. Something was in the back of her mind, and she
just couldn't draw it out.

When her shift was over, Lissa turned in her car
and got behind the wheel of her Mustang. It coughed
as she switched the ignition on. Not exactly the most
reliable vehicle in which to conduct surveillance, but
it would have to do, she thought. She was going to
patrol the area in hopes that something would eventually hit her.

Be honest, she told herself. You're hoping that the
burglar strikes again. She knew she was fighting tremendous odds, but periodically people did break the
bank at the casino. Maybe she'd come up lucky.

All she was coming up was tired, she thought as
she drove around. Her gas tank needle was beginning
to court the E. She knew that she'd have to leave the
residential area soon and get some gas. If he strikes
at all tonight, it'll probably be when I'm filling up
my tank, she thought glumly.

Goodness, her back felt stiff. Unbidden, the memory of Brett caressing her bare shoulders came to
mind.

She sighed. Why was she constantly bridging momentary gaps in her thinking process with thoughts
of Brett?

Bridge.

That was it! That was what had been nagging at
her all afternoon. Mr. Andrews had told her to hurry

up because he didn't want to be late for his bridge
game. Mr. Keller had been the club champion. Maybe
they all played bridge. Maybe they all belonged to
the same club! Excitedly Lissa told herself that it was
definitely worth checking out.

But so what? So they belonged to the same club.
What did that mean? One step at a time, Constable;
this'll fall into place yet. Constable. She had referred
to herself by the same name Brett used. Yes, he was
most definitely getting to her. She almost wished he
were there with her now. Almost? She had been wishing she was with him all day. But being with him
wouldn't help her solve this case. She reminded herself that she needed to make this collar all on her own.
Solo. Just the way she'd be once he left for New
York.

Damn that place. Maybe it would fall into the
ocean. No, that fate was supposed to be California's,
right after the next quake. See, she smiled grimly,
there's no way out.

She was just about to turn her car toward a gas
station when something caught her attention. Someone was running. Whoever it was was dressed all in
black. Had it not been for the fact that she was straining to see along the semidark streets, she would have
missed him. Making a sharp turn, Lissa drove straight
for him. At the sound of the approaching car the figure in black began to run faster and climbed over a
chain link fence, temporarily making good his escape.
After bringing the car to a screeching halt, Lissa
leaped out and cried, "Stop! Police!"

Her identity did not impress her suspect. He ran all
the harder. For a tall man, he certainly could move,
Lissa thought, clambering over the fence. The man

was running down toward the docks where a small
fleet of yachts of varying sizes bobbed gently in the
bay.

The sound of her own breathing and the thump of
the wooden slats meeting her feet were all Lissa heard
as she sprinted after the thief. He had a good head
start on her, but she was leaner. Suddenly he turned
back for a moment. A shot rang out, accompanied by
a burst of light. He had a gun!

As she darted behind the hull of one of the yachts
that lined the dock, Lissa took a moment to collect
herself. She had never been fired at before. Ever so
slowly, she peered out, her gun raised and ready.
Nothing. Well, she couldn't just hide behind a yacht
all night, she told herself, creeping out inch by inch.

Nothing.

With her heart beating a wild tattoo, Lissa left the
cover of the yacht. At the same time she heard footsteps behind her. He had an accomplice!

As the thought hit her, another round of gunfire
exploded just in front of her. Someone dove at her
feet, pushing her out of range—and right into the bay.

She gasped as she fell, taking in a mouthful of water. The cold dark bay momentarily swallowed her,
swirling all around her. Lissa fought to pull her senses
back into focus. Water. Drowning. Swim! Commands
flashed through her head as she came back up to the
surface. Treading water, she turned around toward the
dock. But just as she did so she heard a second splash.
Someone was diving in to join her. Frantically she
looked around, trying to spot her assailant before he
reached her. Her best course was to swim out and
then attempt to get back to the dock indirectly.

As she started to do just that, Lissa was startled to

have someone bob up right in front of her. She was all set to fight for her life when the man's face was illuminated by a narrow beam of moonlight.

"Brett!" she cried, numbed. "What are you doing?" she asked as he gripped her with one strong arm and swam for the dock.

"What does it look like I'm doing?" he asked. "I'm rescuing you."

"I don't need rescuing!" she sputtered as a wave splashed her in the face.

He ignored her protests. With one hand he grabbed the dock, and then he thrust her onto it ahead of him. "I've always wanted to do that," he said, pulling himself up next to her. "Wait here," he ordered, springing rather soggily to his feet.

She knew what he was up to in an instant. "Oh, no, you don't," she cried, running after him. He wasn't about to catch her suspects without her.

But it seemed that no one was going to catch anyone that night. There was no one on the dock. As they reached a bench at the end of the pier, Lissa collapsed onto it. Brett joined her.

They looked like two drowned rats, she thought. "Did you get a look at them?" she asked, pushing her dripping hair out of her face.

"Them?" Brett echoed. "There was only one guy," he said, getting up and extending a wet hand toward her.

"No, there wasn't," she insisted. "I was chasing one guy, and then someone tackled me from behind."

"That was me," Brett said a bit sheepishly.

"That was you?" Lissa asked, drawing her brows together and looking at him suspiciously.

"I tackled you."

She couldn't believe it. "You threw me into the bay?" she asked incredulously. "Why did you 'rescue' me, then? Can't you make up your mind if you want to drown me or not?" she asked sarcastically. He had ruined it for her. She could have captured the thief, and he had gotten in the way!

"I've already made up my mind about what I want to do with you," he informed her. That was a rather ambiguous statement, Lissa thought. "As for throwing you into the bay, that was an accident. I was just trying to get you out of firing range. You were a sitting duck."

"I have a gun," she informed him coldly. Just how incompetent did he think she was?

"All right," he amended. "A sitting duck with a gun. Nevertheless—"

Lissa didn't let him get any further. "My gun!" she wailed, looking back into the waters beyond the dock. "Oh, this is terrific, just terrific. Hanson's going to love this. He'll have me holding up stop signs for kids going to school." She shot Brett a murderous look. "It's all your fault," she accused.

He held up his hands. "All right, guilty as charged," he told her, surrendering without a fight, a fact that made her all the more suspicious. Just what was he up to? "But I was worried about you...."

Ordinarily this profession of concern would have warmed her. Right now, though, nothing was warming her because a cool night breeze was going right through her. She rubbed her nose. "That's very nice of you, but I was a policewoman before you arrived on the scene, and I survived very nicely, thank you."

"Right now I think we'd better see about getting

you out of those wet clothes," he said, motioning her back toward the path that eventually led to her car.

"Is that all you ever think of?" she asked.

"Sometimes," he said, "yes, that's all I can think of. I'd like to undress you, layer after layer, a fraction at a time, until both of us are so wild we can't stand it. I think about that a lot."

He stopped, pulling her into his arms and kissing her soundly, their two wet bodies pressing against each other. The heat he ignited within her would go a long way toward drying her clothes, she thought.

The kiss was abruptly broken off when she gave a very unromantic sneeze.

"Bless you," Brett said gallantly, fishing out a handkerchief and handing it to her.

She wrung it out before using it. "C'mon, let's throw both of us into the dryer," she proposed.

He put his soggy arm around her shoulders. "Why not? You've already got me on the spin cycle."

"That's on a washer," she corrected.

"When you're dizzy, you're not sure," he quipped.

But she doubted very much if anything got Brett so dizzy that he didn't know exactly what he was doing at all times. He might be laid back, but there was a tremendously sharp mind behind all those smiles, and it was working. Constantly.

"What were you doing out there?" she asked, unlocking her door. Agatha attacked them before they had taken two steps inside. She gave Lissa a quick yip, then turned her attention toward Brett. "See who feeds you tomorrow," Lissa warned, walking into the kitchen to put on a kettle of hot water. She needed a cup of hot tea in the worst way.

"Patrolling the area," he told her, scratching Agatha behind the ears. "Same as you."

"Seems odd that we were in the same place at the same time," Lissa observed, waiting curiously for his answer. She turned off the water and put the kettle on the back burner.

"Not so odd," Brett answered, joining her. "I spotted your classic little relic and followed you."

"Why?" she demanded.

"Because I didn't want anything to happen to you."

Or you didn't want me getting the jump on anything, she amended silently. "Touching," she murmured, reaching into the cupboard for two cups.

Suddenly he was behind her, reaching around her to unfasten her skirt. Then he stopped to run his hand along the outer curve of her hip.

"What are you doing?" she asked, nearly dropping the cups.

"Touching," he said innocently. "Just like you told me to."

Lissa turned around to face him. "You didn't understand—" she began, although she was beginning to feel that she was the one who didn't understand. She didn't seem to understand anything anymore. Clues were hiding out there, but they were all lost whenever Brett came into range.

"Oh, I understand touching very well," Brett persisted, sliding down the zipper of her skirt. With a little coaxing the skirt dropped to her feet like a wet mop. Not very pretty imagery, Lissa thought. But then, neither was she, as she stood there looking like a wet rat.

"You do it here," Brett was saying, parting her

blouse, his fingers stroking the detailed stitching on her bra. Her breasts were already straining against it, yearning to be touched, to be possessed.

"And here." Bending his head, he brushed his lips along the silken line of her throat. "Good thing I like salt," she heard him whisper.

She would have laughed if she were able. But she wasn't. All she could do was wait for the next wave, the next sensuous assault that would take her further out to sea, separating her from everything but her feelings. And him.

"Touching takes on especially great proportions when exercised here," he said, slipping both hands down about her hips. She realized then that somehow or other he had taken off all her clothes. She quivered slightly as his fingers skimmed along her intimately. Heaven. The man created heaven with a mere pass of his hand.

"Taking notes?" he asked. There was only a trace of devilishness in his eyes.

"What?"

"Let's see what you've learned," he coaxed, guiding her fingers toward him. "Show me."

She tried to look amused and wondered how well she had succeeded. "All right, class," she said for his benefit, "touching is done here." She unbuttoned his shirt, bathing his chest in wet salty kisses as she stripped the shirt away. She teased the hairs on his chest with her tongue. When he swayed slightly, she felt a burst of excitement go off within her. "And here," she said, her voice lower, matching the descent of her hands as she undid his slacks. But rather than first removing them and then his underwear, Lissa took a teasing shortcut, hooking her thumbs into both layers of clothing. Rhythmically she brought them down on one side and then the other. The slow, syncopated movement was engineered to arouse him, to make him as passionate as she was.

From the response she was getting, she knew she was succeeding. Bending down just a little, she dropped his wet garments on the floor. Strong fingers gripped her shoulders and pulled her back up to him. The impact of their bodies sliding against each other made her want to cry out loud. She loved it, loved the feel of his hard body pressed tightly against hers. Every detail delighted her and brought her closer to a state of ecstasy. Best of all was the feel of his lips on hers. She had never tasted anything sweeter, more compelling, more exciting. It opened up her senses to their full scope. She was firmly hooked on his lips, she thought almost giddily.

The kettle screamed for attention, sending up a violent stream of hot air.

"You'd better get that," Brett murmured against her mouth. Without withdrawing her lips from his, Lissa reached behind her and groped around until she found the right knob and shut the burner off. Brett bent slightly and lifted her into his arms.

"Where to?" he asked whimsically.

"Anywhere your lips can take me," she said, and then she sneezed.

"Shall I bless you again?" he asked, carrying her to the bedroom. "The first time didn't seem to work."

But she already felt blessed. At least for the evening. Very, very blessed.

Twelve

She felt like hell warmed over.

"Are you sure you want to go in to work today?" Brett asked, looking at her questioningly. He sat on the edge of the bed, listening to Lissa cough and then sneeze.

"I'll live," she told him, trying to sound cheerful. "I may not want to, but I'll live. Besides, I don't know why Brom is taking so long to get back on his feet, but I've got to take advantage of the situation for as long as it lasts," she said, sliding over to the edge of the bed and swinging her feet onto the floor.

"You sound like you shouldn't be on your feet."

"Now, don't start that again," she warned. Because I might not be able to stop you, she added silently, and I've never been late for work yet.

"No, I meant you should be taking care of yourself,'' Brett clarified as he followed her into the kitchen.

"I wouldn't have to be trying to take care of myself if someone hadn't pushed me into the bay,'' she said accusingly as she began to look through her refrigerator, trying to find the egg carton. Why was it that everything she wanted always seemed to be hiding somewhere in the back? "Do you think that was our man last night?'' she asked, shoving things around in the refrigerator.

"Here, let me,'' Brett said, taking a firm grip on her shoulders and moving her out of the way. "No,'' he answered, "I don't think aggressive action is our burglar's style. You just foiled another robbery in progress.'' He smiled at her. "Eggs?'' he asked.

"Yes,'' she answered, sinking onto the kitchen chair, too achy to protest. She raked her hand through her hair. The roots hurt, and her eyelashes felt as if they were on fire.

"And, might I point out again, I wasn't trying to push you into the water, just out of the way. In case you hadn't noticed, those were real bullets he was firing. Scrambled?''

"Yes, please,'' she nodded. "I'm a policewoman. Don't you think I know the sound of real bullets when I hear them?'' she asked, trying to muster some indignation. It was hard to muster anything when your left ear was ringing, she thought miserably.

"I don't know,'' Brett said after studying her for a moment. "I'm not too sure of anything when it comes to you.''

Then we're even, she thought, tracing her forefinger over the daisy imprint of her tablecloth. This is no time to sit around and be mopey, she told herself. Get up and get dressed.

She sat where she was.

"Where do you keep your vitamins?" he asked, opening her pantry and shifting several items around.

"Back there." She pointed to a cupboard in the corner. "I think. Why?"

"You think?" Brett echoed. "I thought all you healthy Californians thrived on vitamins."

She closed her eyes, wishing her headache would go away. "I haven't been keeping up with my California manual of proper behavior lately," she said drolly, getting up. "All I want is about ten aspirin—and my gun." Oh, no. She was going to have to file a report with Hanson about her gun first thing. Her headache became worse.

"Here, take this," Brett instructed, shoving a glass of water into one hand and about five vitamin C capsules into the other.

She stared down at the speckled pills. "There are enough capsules here for me to start my own orange grove," she protested.

"Take them. They can't hurt."

"They can if they get stuck in my throat. I hate pills," she grumbled.

"So do I, so don't be one. Just be good and do as you're told," he coaxed, pressing the pills on her.

"You sound like my father," she muttered, grudgingly taking one pill into her mouth and swallowing it.

"I don't feel like your father," he said, running his fingers along the opening of her robe. As it parted slightly he could see her naked body beneath the blue cotton.

She knew where this would lead—and it wouldn't be the office. "Yes, I know. My father," she said, taking another pill, "would never throw me into the bay."

"No wise remarks, just take your vitamins."

"I don't believe in vitamins," she protested. Nevertheless she swallowed another one. "Those," she waved toward the closet, "are from a well-meaning friend," she said, denying all claim to them.

"You don't have to believe in them, just take then. They're not sensitive. They work whether you like them or not," he guaranteed.

"What will work," she informed him, finally downing the last two tablets, "is tea." She emphasized her statement by picking up the kettle. Seeing the amused look on his face, Lissa glanced down at the kettle. It was scorched. She groaned. It was going to be a bad morning.

She was late, just as she had feared. What was worse, Hanson seemed rather happy about it. She hadn't planned on checking in with him. She had gone directly to her typewriter to type out the explanation of why, where and when she and her service revolver had parted company. She was into her third agonizing sentence when Hanson came out of his office and saw her struggling.

"Oh, Armstrong," he barked.

She didn't like the sound of that, but tried to attribute it to the fact that everything seemed to have an echo to it this morning.

"Yes, sir?" she asked, looking up from her work.

"You're off the case," he said gruffly. That was all. No explanation. Nothing.

Lissa scrambled away from her desk. Had someone told him about her gun before she had a chance to? But that was impossible. The only person who knew was Leopold. She had passed him on the way in and had needed a tiny shred of sympathy before she attempted to beard the lion in his den. Dragon, she amended. The man was a definite dragon.

"Why am I off the case?" she asked, following him into his office. She knew that he hated to be challenged, but she had a right to know. Brom wasn't back. Leopold would have told her. Leopold always seemed to know everything that went on at the precinct.

"Because I said so," Hanson said, his fair complexion turning a shade of light pink.

"Is Brom back?" she pressed.

She saw the look of anger crease his brow. It seemed rather overdone in the face of her inquiry. Something else had to be up. "No, Brom is not back. Brom won't be coming back. Seems that he used his 'sick' leave to find another line of employment. He's tired of stakeouts and—"

Although the news took her by surprise, she had no time to dwell on Brom. "Then, why are you taking me off the case? I can be—"

"Jessop's finished with his last assignment, and he can take this on," Hanson informed her coldly. "It's time the case had a real detective working on it. Well? What are you waiting for? Go and put your uniform on. You're back in your blues again."

"But I think I'm getting close to something!" Lissa protested.

"Give it to Jessop," he ordered.

Lissa bit her lip, fighting back the urge to tell him

what she thought of him. Instead she turned on her heel and walked out.

For two cents she'd quit, she thought angrily, marching into the corridor. But that would mean throwing her career away, and she wouldn't let Hanson goad her into doing that.

The trip back to the locker room seemed endless.

For the rest of the day she made sure she was unavailable to Jessop. She was going to solve this case even if she wasn't officially on it. Hanson couldn't stop her—not if he didn't know. She intended to look into the bridge club connection on her own time.

Unable to wait until her shift was over, Lissa drove toward the Andrews's house. She tried to still her conscience by arguing that, after all, their house was within the confines of her beat.

Mr. Andrews wasn't home, but Mrs. Andrews was more than happy to give Lissa the name of their bridge club and the club's location. *That* turned out to be just outside her assigned beat, but Lissa drove there anyway.

It took some prodding, but Lissa prevailed, and the woman who ran things at the tiny recreational facility provided her with a membership list. If she questioned all the members one by one, maybe she'd come up with something.

But as she drove back to the precinct she felt her energy dissipating. She had all these wonderful intentions, but absolutely no oomph to carry them out. A few aspirin and a nice hot cup of tea and she'd feel better, she promised herself, not even bothering to change at the station. She just checked in and parked the squad car in the lot, taking her own in exchange.

She bet Brett didn't feel this way. When he had

left her house that morning, *he* hadn't been sneezing or coughing. "But that's because he's perfect," she muttered as she drove home. "He cooks, rescues and romances. People like that don't catch colds. They only get their hair mussed once in a while. And only on cue."

You're getting delirious, she thought to herself, pulling up in front of her house.

Lissa didn't even remember walking in. She just got her aspirin bottle, headed straight for her bed and collapsed.

It was the tapping sound that woke her. It had made its way into her subconscious, nudging at her. She tried to ignore it, thinking that it was part of her headache. When she felt the bed move a little, she thought it was Agatha. But there was no yipping, no thumping tail whacking against her comforter. And the bed dipped lower than it normally did to accommodate Agatha's puny fifteen pounds.

Lissa opened her eyes. Everything looked blurry. But there was someone sitting on her bed. She pulled herself upright as the features of the man's face took their proper form.

"Brett," she breathed, dropping her head back onto the pillow. "What is it, a slow night? Can't find anyone to push into the water?" she mumbled. As she talked she became aware that her body no longer felt as if it had been in an altercation with a truck and lost. Some of her achiness was gone. Absently she wondered if it was due to the Miracle of the Vitamins.

"You're going to need a search warrant," Brett told her.

"Goodness, what a romantic thing to say," she

mumbled, still half-asleep. "I thought I was already familiar with the terrain." She giggled, then realized what she had just said. Maybe she wasn't as well as she thought she was. Focusing her eyes, she saw the open bottle of aspirin on the nightstand. She must have come to and taken some, although she didn't remember doing so. For some reason, aspirin always made her feel light-headed. She looked at Brett, wondering what he must think.

There was a tolerant smile on his face. If she had had enough energy, she might have resented it. But then, she knew she deserved it. God, she felt confused, she thought, putting her hand to her forehead.

"For that you'll never need a warrant. I'm willing to subject myself to any kind of body search you might have in mind. But right now I'm talking about the case," Brett told her.

She tried to prop herself up on her elbow. Brett drew her into his arms and leaned her head against his chest. Much better, she thought. "What about the case?"

"I think I have our man," he said. "As a matter of fact, I'm sure of it," he admitted. "The goods are all in his house."

"How do you know that?" she asked, her deathbed condition a thing of the past in light of this information. She turned and clutched at his arm, as if the action would make him explain the matter that much more quickly.

"Off the record?" he asked, cocking his head.

"Off the whole stereo!" she cried eagerly. "Tell me!"

"I broke into his house. He has everything in his den."

"You broke in?" she echoed, her eyebrows rising.

"I don't subscribe to the theory that a burglar is immune to being burglarized himself. Are you going to play the perfect policewoman—or are you interested?"

"I'm interested. I'm interested," Lissa assured him, her adrenaline beginning to pump, clearing out all the cobwebs that had been lining her brain.

"I had a hunch," Brett told her. "And I checked it out this afternoon. By the way, how are you?" he asked, purposely dragging the story out.

Lissa punched his arm. "I'm fine. I'll get even finer if you'll tell me all about this."

For one moment he touched her cheek and a look of tenderness filled his eyes. "Somehow I don't think that's possible." And then the look faded, mystifying her completely. "It's Keller," he said simply.

Lissa rocked back on her heels. "Keller? But he's disabled," she protested.

"No," he corrected, warming up to his story. "He's collecting money for being disabled. After the first three years or so, Workmen's Comp got a little sloppy about investigating him. A back injury isn't always a permanent condition, but recovery is often almost impossible to prove. When Keller recovered, he kept it to himself. Why work when you don't have to? Unlike the other 'victims,' he's not well off."

"But why did he do it?" she pressed.

Brett shrugged, getting comfortable on the bed. "Boredom. Challenge. A little revenge, so to speak. Andrews beat him out of the championship at the bridge club this year. It seemed to set him off. I got the date of the tournament. The first robbery was the next day. I think he may have been practicing before he hit Andrews, and also stalling, so no one would make the connection.''

Lissa sat very quietly, contemplating Brett's story. ''He does match the pawnbroker's description,'' she said, mulling the thought over. ''Except for the mustache. He doesn't have one.''

''Just his attempt at a disguise,'' Brett told her.

''But why would he risk exposure by pawning the items so close to home?'' The pieces didn't fit.

''For the same reason he was so incensed over losing the tournament to Andrews. Overconfidence. He thought he could outsmart everyone. He didn't really do it for the money, just for the thrill of getting away with it—and the joy of owning valuable objects.''

''Then why did he pawn—''

''He doesn't like Andrews. He didn't mind letting some of the others get their stuff back. But he has a real grudge against Andrews for winning the tournament.''

''Okay,'' she said. ''But how did he do it? Those security systems were all bypassed.''

''I did a little research. Guess what Mr. Keller used to do for a living?'' His brown eyes teased her.

Lissa closed her eyes and sighed. It all seemed so obvious now that he was saying it. ''Installed security systems.''

''Smart lady,'' Brett said fondly. ''He got all the information he needed just by keeping his ears open at the club. People do a lot of talking and boasting while they're waiting for a card game to progress.''

That made sense, she thought. ''My, you've had a busy day,'' she said with a touch of envy.

Brett rose, taking her hand and pulling her to her feet as well. ''So, are you going to get that warrant?''

"Absolutely!" And then a thought struck her. "Why did you come to me with all this?" she asked. "Why didn't you just bring Keller in and let the police find the evidence in his house?" The light began to dawn on her, slowed down somewhat by the surprise she felt. "You're handing the case to me, aren't you?"

"Sure looks that way."

"Why?"

"How else am I going to convince you?" he asked with a shrug.

"How else are you going to convince me of what?" she asked.

He took her into his arms. Without her shoes on, she had to crane her neck to look up at him. "I thought that if I gave you the collar and let you crack the case the way you wanted to, that would clear the road for us. Maybe then I could finally make you believe that I cared about you for yourself, not for any miscellaneous bit of information you could give me. Every time we made love I could feel your doubts. I could feel you holding back just a little. I don't want our relationship to be marred by doubts."

It took her a moment to take in his words. "Our relationship?" she repeated quietly. "Does that mean we're going to go on having one?"

Brett shook his head, feigning unabashed admiration. "God, you're quick."

"None of your wit, McKenna. I want some straight answers," she said seriously.

"The straightest," he promised, raising his right hand before returning it to its proper place around her waist.

"I thought Richard was coming back," she said.

"He is. Want to meet him?"

"That's not the point," she said, wishing he would let her get this all out. She was suddenly finding it very difficult to put her thoughts into words.

"Then what *is* the point?" he teased, sensuously touching her lower lip.

The movement teased her, making her ache in a different way. Making her want to kiss him. But she kept at it. "The point is, I thought you were going to New York once the case was solved and Richard was back."

"Why? Do you want to get rid of me?"

"No!" she said a bit too strongly. "No," she repeated, her voice lowered to a longing whisper. "I don't. But I thought—"

"Look," he said, mercifully cutting in as he pulled her back down to sit on the bed, "much to my surprise, California does have good pizza and terrific ice-cream sodas. And I found something that California has that New York doesn't."

"What?" Would it be enough to make him stay? She wondered hopefully.

"You," he replied softly, kissing her temple. "And I get the distinct impression that if I uprooted the California lady and transplanted her to New York, she wouldn't be all that happy."

Could he read her so well? Well, hadn't she once read that people in love were on the same wavelength? She had always believed that it was only so much bunk. Now she began to think otherwise.

"What about your business?" she asked.

"In case you hadn't noticed, my 'business' is rather portable. It's me that counts. And I need to be happy in order to function well. I wouldn't be very happy with three-thousand miles between us. Besides, there's a certain amount of attraction in spending Christmas Eve kissing under the boardwalk and not freezing my assets off." His eyes danced merrily.

"So you're staying?" she asked, hardly able to believe what she was hearing.

"For as long as you want me. You do want me, don't you?"

"If you have to ask that, you're not as good a P.I. as you claim to be."

"Oh, but I am, I am," he said, pushing her down on the bed and lying down next to her. "Especially the 'private' part." He kissed the hollow of her throat, then stopped. "Lissa?"

"Hmm?" She was already beginning to fall into the delicious abyss that his kisses always created for her.

"Would you mind terribly if you weren't a policewoman?"

His words brought her back with a jolt. "What?" He was going to ask her to resign. To enjoy her moment of glory and then fade into the woodwork. Something within her began to rebel, while the rest of her listened in hushed misery.

"I thought that maybe you could quit the force," he said. "You know, leave in a blaze of glory—and come to work with me."

"As what?" she heard herself asking. "Your secretary?"

He began to laugh. "I've seen the way you type. No thanks. I meant as a partner."

"Are you serious?" she cried. She could hardly keep the excitement out of her voice.

"Why shouldn't I be serious?" he asked. "You

have a natural flair. It's a little bumbling at the moment—"

"Bumbling?" she cried indignantly.

"—but nothing that can't be worked out. Besides," he told her with a deep sensuous smile, "I'd like to have my wife around where I can keep an eye on her."

"What wife?" He was going too fast for her, she thought, her head beginning to whirl again, but not from the aspirin this time.

Brett's forefinger slid down to the middle button of her shirt, touching the area just above her breast. "This wife. You're only allowed to have one in this country, you know."

"I know, I know, but—"

"And I've picked you for mine. How about it, Constable? Do we have a deal, or do I bring Keller in myself?"

She pretended to frown. "This is blackmail."

"You bet it is," he said with a laugh as he pulled her into a kiss. The laugh faded as the kiss became longer and more pronounced.

"Lucky for you," she whispered, passion beginning to claim her, "that I have a policy of always giving in to blackmailers after dusk."

"Good policy," he murmured, kissing her again.

* * * * *

A WOMAN OF INTEGRITY

This book is dedicated to
Jessica.
May she grow up to be
a woman of integrity.
(But not a stuntwoman.
My heart couldn't take it.)

One

_____

"**T**hey tell me you're trouble," Matt Harrigan said with an edge to his deep voice.

"That depends," Chyna O'Brien responded tersely, looking up and meeting his gaze head on.

"On what?"

"On your definition of trouble."

The two stood scrutinizing one another the way the Indians and Columbus might have at their first fateful meeting in the New World. Each was filled with curiosity and apprehension. Neither knew what to expect.

Chyna waited for the producer's next words. For a moment she forgot how uncomfortable she was, broiling beneath the intense Philippine sun that was beating down on her and the other people involved in setting up the location shots for Bounty Studios' latest film. Her china blue eyes stared up unwaveringly at the stern, uncompromising face of the producer. She hadn't expected to be accosted so soon. She had only been in Manila three hours.

"My definition of trouble, Miss O'Brien—"

"*Mrs.* O'Brien," she corrected. Neil might be gone, but she had still been his wife, she thought.

"My definition of trouble, *Mrs.* O'Brien," Matt said, beginning again, "is someone who disrupts production, who makes waves in a calm sea." There was no mistaking the warning in his voice.

"If the sea is calm," Chyna said, a slight smile on her lips, "there'll be no waves." She could see the skepticism in his eyes. "I promise."

His dark brows knitted in a scowl. "I'm surprised the stunt coordinator hired you," he told her flatly, eyeing her diminutive, well-proportioned figure with no visible reaction. He was the type, Chyna decided, who let nothing get in the way of business.

"I'm not," she replied, jutting out her delicately shaped chin. She reminded him of a bantam rooster.

"Oh?" he challenged. For a moment she thought she detected just a hint of interest in his green eyes.

"I'm the best there is," she informed him. It wasn't a matter of boasting. It was a matter of record.

"Are you, now?" he asked. She thought she heard the faintest touch of amusement in his voice.

"Yes," she answered firmly. "I was trained by the best—until some director's overzealous desire to cut corners cost him his life."

She could tell by the look on his face that Matt didn't like the turn the conversation was taking. All around them, people were passing by, occupied with their own separate personal tasks. Neither Chyna nor Matt took any notice of the crowd as they eyed one another, two boxers coming out of their corners to touch gloves before the first bell sounded. The tension hung heavily in the humid air.

Just then someone called Matt's name and he turned his dark blond head away from her. The bright sun accented his profile as Chyna took in the rugged planes of his tanned face, her eyes skimming along the almost perfect cheekbones. He was the image of a proud man. His nose, she caught herself thinking, might have been a little smaller. It marred the otherwise classical lines of his face. But it did add a dimension of reality.

After nodding toward the man who stood beckoning to him, Matt momentarily turned his attention back to Chyna. "No waves," he warned her, his eyes clouding just a little.

"It's a large ocean—the waves go in both directions," Chyna pointed out as Matt began to walk away. She could tell by the set of his shoulders that he didn't like her answer.

Despite her outer bravado, Chyna was as surprised as Matt was that she had been hired. It had been less than a year since she had raised her voice against the studio's flagrant disregard for life and limb. After Neil's death she had been instrumental in organizing the Committee for Safety Precautions, and had tried in vain to get the heads of the larger studios to lend a sympathetic ear—or any ear at all—to the problems the stunt crew faced.

Sighing, Chyna picked up her canvas bag and slung it over her shoulder. On the flight over here, ever the optimist, she had hoped for a fresh start. All she had wanted to do was concentrate on getting her timing right for the dangerous stunts that lay ahead of her.

But that was before she had learned that Matt Harrigan was the producer of *The Adventurer*, and that he would be coming along to oversee the entire production.

Chyna pressed her lips together. Harrigan had been the producer on Neil's last film. In the beginning she had held him partially responsible for Neil's death, even though he hadn't even been on the set. Word had it that the director had been rushing in order to satisfy a front office edict form Harrigan. She had never met him, but she had spent several months damning his soul. A year had given her a long time to think. She had ceased blaming the man logically. But emotionally was another story.

Now he was here.

And instead of telling him about the feelings she had harbored, she was going to have to bite her lip and behave. It was either that or get out of the business. This was her first real assignment since Neil's death. If she was thrown off this picture, her career was over. What a rotten predicament, she thought miserably, slapping away a hungry mosquito. This was definitely going to be an endurance test.

"Hey, Chyna, over here!"

Chyna turned quickly. Her chestnut hair, heavy with the weight of absorbed humidity, didn't respond to the motion and blocked her view. She sighed. It was going to be a long two months. But at least she was working again, she reminded herself.

"Hi, Pepper," Chyna said, smiling as she tucked a strand of wayward hair behind her ear.

The long-legged stuntwoman strode toward Chyna eagerly. Her dutchboy haircut, also a victim of the humidity, hung about her face. Her white shorts and tube top were already stained with perspiration. "What are you doing here?" she asked excitedly.

"Rolf twisted some arms and landed a few gags for me," Chyna answered modestly. She remembered the first time Neil had used the term and she had corrected him, thinking he had meant to say "gig." That had been before he had drawn her so completely into the world of stuntwork.

"So they actually hired you!" Pepper said, surprised.

"They better have," Chyna answered with a laugh. "I don't fall out of planes for free."

"Saw you talking to that hunk. How did you get to first base with him so fast?"

"That 'hunk' is the producer," Chyna informed her. "And I wasn't on first base. I was in the dugout, being given a warning about messing up the game plan." She looked over the taller woman's shoulder in the general direction that Matt had taken. He was busy talking to several grips who were moving sound equipment.

Was it just her imagination, or was he looking her way? What was he afraid she was going to do, organize everyone into a strike five minutes after she got here? Was she going to be looking over her shoulder the entire time she was here? The thought brought a frown to her face.

"What's the matter?" Pepper asked.

Chyna shook her head. "Nothing. Look, let's move. I think I'm getting deep fried."

Pepper followed her to the dubious shade cast by the long, wispy leaves of an exotic tree in the throes of shedding its bark.

"I'm still surprised to see you," Pepper said. "I

thought that after Neil died and they gave you such a rough deal, you'd kind of, you know, disappear from the movie scene.''

Chyna smiled at the notion. No, she wasn't the disappearing type. She was a survivor, a hanger-on no matter what. Her marriage to Neil had just reinforced that. Neil. Gentle, soft-spoken, competent Neil, who had been so good at his work, so careful. If he hadn't allowed that director to hurry him that day, if he had only checked the airbag himself instead of taking the stunt coordinator's word for it... ''What?'' Chyna suddenly realized that Pepper had asked her a question and was waiting for an answer.

''Where are you staying?'' the woman repeated.

''Same place you are, I guess,'' Chyna answered, thinking of the wooden two-by-four shacks she had seen lining the road a quarter of a mile back. From all appearances, they'd need considerable upgrading just to be called cabins. The studio didn't go to any trouble for the lesser people involved in making a movie. Only the stars and the brass rated accommodations that ran the range from tolerable to terrific, depending on how much pull each person exerted. Chyna had no doubts that Matt's personal trailer was the last word in comfort.

Pepper screwed up her mobile face as she slung her unwieldy suitcase over her shoulder. ''Think there'll be bugs?'' she asked.

''I'm only hoping the bugs leave a little space for us,'' Chyna replied philosophically. ''They might resent us invading their territory.'' Together they began to head back in the direction of the shacks.

''I can't see why they couldn't film this thing in

Hawaii. They've got palm trees there, too," Pepper complained.

"Would be nice, wouldn't it?" Chyna slapped away still another large mosquito that threatened to deplete her blood supply. "But I think they need more in the way of scenery than just the palm trees. The movie is supposed to take place somewhere in the Philippines in the 1930s—so what better place to film it than here? This certainly fits the bill," Chyna said, gesturing with her free hand at the lush area.

"Not my bill," Pepper muttered.

Chyna laughed in agreement as they approached their living quarters.

The sunbleached shack they decided on was plopped down between two lanky palm trees which stood like two drunken centurian guards with choppy, unkempt haircuts. It was a tiny shack. Tiny, Chyna thought, as in "crammed," not as in "cute."

Pepper hung back, as if expecting Chyna to do battle with any stray tropical insects or rodents that had staked out the shack first. Chyna couldn't understand how anyone who didn't mind risking her life daily could be afraid of a mouse.

As she pushed the creaky door closed behind them, Chyna felt the prick of a splinter entering her palm. She glanced down at the sliver. Was this an omen of things to come? she wondered dryly. Wasn't having to work on one of Matt Harrigan's pictures enough?

The light that made its way through the dirty, cracked windowpane was just bright enough to highlight the primitiveness of the living facilities.

"Ugh," Pepper moaned, for once justified in her complaint, Chyna thought.

"Look," Chyna announced brightly, "indoor

plumbing." After sweeping away a sticky, grayish web that appeared to have been part of the rusty pump handle since time immemorial, Chyna began working the handle gingerly, afraid that it might come off in her hand. To her surprise the first thing to emerge from the antiquated faucet was an unwilling, multi-legged hairy creature.

Finally, through her diligent efforts, Chyna produced a slow drip. She tried to convert it into something resembling running water, but she might as well have been trying to turn water into wine. Several additional minutes of hard pumping yielded nothing but a cramp in her upper forearm.

"We'll work on it," she promised Pepper, who looked far from optimistic.

The only furniture in the room consisted of two old, rickety cots.

"Well, at least we won't have to sleep on the floor," Chyna commented.

"How long did they say we're going to be here?" Pepper asked.

"Two months," Chyna said.

The atmosphere in the shack felt oppressive. The air hung there, thick and sticky. Chyna pushed aside a curtain which had worn so thin that it came apart in her hand. Sighing, she tossed it on the wooden floor as she tried to pry open the window. It wouldn't budge, and she gave up.

"Two months," Pepper echoed unhappily, sinking down on her cot. It groaned as it accepted her weight.

Chyna knew how she felt. But stuntpeople couldn't afford to be choosy. You never knew when the next job was coming, and if you turned one down, there were more than enough people out there willing to

take your place, even if they were ill prepared to do
so. That's when accidents happened. Then, and when
you had thoughtless people in charge. Chyna's mind
went back to Matt. Rolf hadn't told her that Harrigan
would ultimately be in charge of the picture.

A faint smile came to her lips. He had probably
thought she wouldn't take the job if she had known.
And she probably wouldn't have. But she was here
now, and she would have to make the best of it. She
tried to bury the angry feelings simmering just below
the surface of her mind.

"Hey," Pepper said, breaking into Chyna's moody
thoughts, "I'm starved. When's our next meal? I
haven't eaten since I landed."

"Whenever they set up the cafeteria, I guess."

"Well, let's go see," the other woman urged.

Chyna looked at her unpacked bag and decided that
it would keep. After pushing the bag under her bed,
she followed Pepper out the door, not bothering to try
to lock it on her way out. She was sure that neither
the lock nor the door would be strong enough to keep
anyone out.

Other people must have been of the same mind as
Pepper, Chyna decided, because parts of the kitchen
were already set up. A handful of the production staff
were there ahead of them, filling their trays. Most of
them were just getting something to drink, she noticed. Overhead the sun hung like a big ball of fire,
letting no one below forget its hard, merciless presence for a moment. Chyna picked up a tall glass of
lukewarm iced tea, bypassing a ham and cheese on
rye that looked as if it too yearned for cooler tem-
peratures.

She and Pepper sat down beneath a tree, trying to

keep out of the way of the cables being strung from monstrous-looking generators. The clanging of hammers was just beginning to be heard. The crew were setting up the facades necessary for some of the outdoor scenes. Chyna didn't envy them their task. It felt too hot to talk, much less work. She leaned against the tree, watching the scene that was haphazardly unfolding all around her.

She loved this life, loved being a part of the seamless world of make-believe that was somehow pieced together from a thousand miscellaneous loose ends. She knew that when she became immersed in her part of all this, all her thoughts, all her other problems, would slip somewhere far away—almost as if they had never existed at all.

Several stuntmen drifted by to exchange a few pleasantries. Everyone was surprised to see Chyna in their midst again.

"Wonderful to see you!" one stuntman enthused. "I didn't think you'd be back working so soon."

Soon?

To other people soon meant that their own lives had gone on as planned; they never noticed that time had been passing unfruitfully by for someone else. "Soon" had been a year for Chyna, a long, endless, creeping year that had been full of gnawing emptiness. It had started with an emotional earthquake: Neil's death. It had limped on its way as she helped form the committee that tried to have rules passed and adhered to by the boards of all the studios. And it had ground to a halt as both she and her rules were rejected. Oh, there had been a token investigation into Neil's death, and everyone, including Matt, had been absolved of blame. The director had received a wrist-slapping and a five hundred dollar fine. Five hundred dollars in exchange for Neil's life. No charges. He had died for nothing.

And the work offers for Chyna had ceased. There had been little or nothing she could do except wait and hope things would change. In the meantime, she took odd jobs. Rolf, a friend and fellow stuntman, came through, giving her a job with his stunt workshop more out of kindness than out of any necessity for extra help. Eventually, using his influence and her reputation as one of the best stuntwomen in the field, Rolf had talked Alex, the head stunt coordinator, into giving her a chance on this film.

But why did it have to be on *his* picture? Thinking of Matt, Chyna found herself looking for him. It was hard to miss the man. Although he wasn't overly tall, close to six feet at most, he managed to stand out, a center of calm within the storm of moving bodies. The first day on the set was always marked by spurts of furious energy alternated with long periods of inactivity. No one was sure what they were doing most of the time, and everyone looked to someone else for instructions. When that someone turned up, issuing orders, a frenzied pace would ensue for a while and then subside once again.

It was unusual to have the producer on the set, Chyna thought, especially when the film was being made on location. Normally, when producers came at all, they came for a short visit. Harrigan appeared to be settling in for the duration. Chyna had heard that Harrigan, always a stickler for detail, had become even more personally involved in his projects after Neil's accident. She wondered if he was doing it out of guilt.

She watched him now. He appeared to be a portrait of subdued control, his manner a definite contrast to the director's. The latter kept gesticulating, pointing to people and things as if, in his mind, they were all lumped together. He was shorter than Matt and wore a gaily knotted neckerchief which for some reason wasn't wilting, and he looked like a caricature of a high-ranking enemy general from an old war movie. His bald head added to the demonic picture that he seemed to delight in casting.

But it wasn't the director who held Chyna's attention. Her eyes kept drifting over to Matt, even as different people vied for her attention with their greetings.

Annoyed. That was the word for it, she decided. Underneath his control there was an underlying layer of annoyance. Was she the cause of it? she wondered. She had seen firsthand his displeasure when he had discovered that the stunt coordinator had hired her.

Well, no matter, she thought as his powerful, athletic figure cut across her line of vision once again. She had other things to think about.

She rose, dusting off her faded jeans. They were adhering to her legs and making her decidedly uncomfortable. She was going to go and change into shorts. When she raised her eyes she noticed that her movements had caught Matt's attention. He was watching her again. She was used to people watching her. That was her job, to do things that made them sit up and take notice. But this was different. There was something about the way Matt watched her that made her uneasy. He was probably trying to psych her out, she told herself, and get her to quit the picture. Her presence was too much of a reminder of the fact that his schedule had cost a man his life. Well, if he thought he was going to get rid of her that easily, he was mistaken. She was here for the duration, and nothing and no one was going to make her leave.

"C'mon," she said to Pepper, who was talking to a member of the crew. "Let's go and find Alex and let him know we're here," she urged.

"He was watching you," Pepper said in a loud whisper.

"I know," Chyna muttered, instinctively knowing who Pepper was talking about. She left and quickly snaked her way through the construction crew. The more distance she put between herself and Matt Harrigan, the better.

"Hey, where are you rushing to?" Pepper wanted to know as soon as she caught up.

Chyna stopped dead in her tracks. Why *was* she rushing? she asked herself. The stunt coordinator wasn't going anywhere. None of them were. Was she subconsciously trying to avoid being around Matt? She had nothing to hide, nothing to be ashamed of.

"Are you looking for someone?" Matt asked her over the din of the crowd.

Chyna stood perfectly still as he made his way over to her, adrenaline rushing double-time through her veins.

"Hi, I'm Pepper," the blond woman said cheerfully when he reached them.

Matt nodded politely, but it was obvious that he wasn't taking any particular notice of the other woman. His smoky green eyes burned into Chyna's skin, causing more of a reaction than the hot sun. A warm nervousness was creeping over her, and the back of her neck prickled. Either she was in the beginning stages of malaria, or Matt Harrigan was having a definite effect on her. What did that tanned face look like when it was smiling?

Chyna suddenly realized that he had asked her a question and was now waiting for an answer.

"I'm looking for Alex, the stunt coordinator," she said, her throat dry.

"Good," he said solemnly. Chyna could feel herself growing indignant. What did he mean, "good"? Did he think she needed a keeper? "Alex is over there," he said, pointing out a dark-haired man in a sweat-soaked shirt.

Chyna looked in the direction he indicated, and when she turned back to Matt, she found that he was gone.

TWO

After spending the night on her cot, Chyna began to eye the floor more favorably. At least, she thought as she stretched, trying to reach the sore spot in the center of her back, the floor didn't sink down in the middle.

"Boy," she muttered, feeling more dead than alive, "my neck feels like it's made out of wood."

She received a "mfph" in reply from the almost circular heap in the next cot.

"She could probably sleep through the Apocalypse," Chyna said to the scurrying spider that ambled across her bare foot as she tried to come around.

A shower would be heavenly. But she knew that, as of last night, the shower facilities hadn't been set up yet. Yesterday's sweat felt as if it had settled into a permanent gritty layer on her body.

Oh, well, things wouldn't get any better if she complained, she thought, taking off her pajamas. Quickly she put on a pair of dark blue shorts and a powder blue halter top. At least she felt a little cooler now, she tried to console herself.

It took her five minutes to get enough water into the basin she had purloined from the prop man to wash her face. She had just finished brushing her teeth when an unidentifiable green bug decided to commit suicide in her water.

"So long, fella," Chyna muttered, dumping the sudsy water into the sink.

Looking over her shoulder, Chyna could see that Pepper had changed position on the cot; two limbs now dangled over the side.

"Want to get a little exercise?" Chyna asked the lump brightly.

"Zoomifh," came the muffled answer.

"I take it," Chyna said wryly, putting a clip in her hair as she raised it off her neck, "that means no."

In response Pepper waved an arm at her, putting off any further conversation. Chyna slipped on her size five running shoes and went out.

She had to blink twice to acclimate her eyes to the brighter light. She hadn't realized how gloomy everything looked inside the shack. Out here there was life, in living color, she mused, taking in the lush foliage.

At this hour of the morning it was too early for most people to be out, so for the moment it felt like a secluded paradise—even if it had to be shared with mosquitoes that were outfitted with bayonets instead of stingers, she thought as she ducked one.

She looked up at the clouds that were moving languidly above her, wisps of cotton across the sky, and a feeling of peacefulness came over her.

Where to run? she pondered—and not get lost. She didn't quite trust her homing instincts just yet, so she decided that the best place to jog would be along the shoreline of the nearby beach. At least there she wouldn't run the risk of tripping over half-hidden roots. With that settled, she trudged out across the sand.

Just me and the waves, she told herself, listening to the rhythmic slapping of the water against the endless beach. Knowing that running on the wet sand would be good for her leg muscles, Chyna took off her jogging shoes and stuffed her socks into the toes, leaving them on the beach. Warm sand squished between her toes as she paced herself. Soon she fell into a comfortable breathing pattern. She felt as if she could run along the golden beach all day.

Effortlessly she ran along the shoreline, then turned around and started to run back to where she had left her shoes. She began to feel the emotional surge that came from jogging, that inner glow of health and satisfaction with one's own efforts. Time melted away as she relished the euphoric feeling. It wasn't until she was practically on top of him that she realized she was no longer alone. A man in light clothes sat on the beach not far from her shoes.

Matt Harrigan.

She felt her breath growing shorter. As she drew closer Chyna saw that Matt did not appear to be taking any notice of her presence. He sat facing the ocean, looking utterly lost in thought.

Chyna took a deep breath. If she ignored him, she would be being purposely rude, and it would serve no purpose. After all, he *was* the producer. "Hi," she ventured, coming to a halt beside him.

"Shh." He waved a dismissing hand at her.

She could feel her temper rising. She was a person, not a mosquito. "What?"

"I'm thinking," he growled.

"About what?" she said, bending down to retrieve her shoes. "How to cut corners and save time?" she asked. The words had just tumbled out. She couldn't help herself.

He turned his brilliant green eyes on her. "As a matter of fact, yes," he said coolly. "Times are tight. You save wherever and whatever you can."

"Does that include lives?" she asked archly. The words were out of her mouth before she even knew she had thought them.

Matt raised one dark brow—incredibly dark for someone with such fair hair, she thought. "That includes everything," he said firmly.

"I'm glad to hear that," she said evenly. She turned to go, her shoes dangling from her fingertips.

Matt grabbed her wrist, making her drop her shoes. "Are you implying something?" he asked testily.

"If the shoe fits..." she said, glancing down at the sand. Why was she harping on this? She knew she didn't really blame Matt anymore. And yet, there were all those deep-seated feelings that she had tried to conquer, those feelings that had kept her awake at night, wondering why Neil had had to die. She had to get them out in the open.

"The shoe doesn't fit," he told her. He drew a deep breath. "I'm sorry about what happened to your husband. I thought my note explained my position."

She looked at him sharply. "What note?"

His expression became slightly puzzled. "The one

I sent after the accident. The one you never answered.''

"I never answered it because I never got one.'' Was he telling the truth? His silence at the time had convinced Chyna of Matt's guilt in the matter. Was he now just making up a convenient lie to smooth things out for the duration of the movie?

For a moment they stared at one another, at an impasse. And then Matt picked up her shoes and handed them to her. When he raised his head, his eyes were level with her breasts. It seemed to Chyna that he was taking his time in straightening up.

"Here.''

"Thank you,'' she said crisply, hiding her embarrassment at his intent stare. "Fine pastime for a grown man,'' she mumbled. "Staring down the front of women's shirts.''

"There are worse ways to spend one's time,'' Matt replied. "Like prejudging people,'' he added.

Chyna bristled visibly. "I wouldn't be throwing any stones if I were you. You were the one who hauled me aside to give me that thinly veiled warning. What are you afraid I'm going to do, call a strike?'' she demanded.

"You seem to be capable of a lot of stupid things—''

"Stupid!'' Chyna's voice went up an indignant octave.

He looked unruffled by her tone. "Bringing suit against the studio and trying to get it shut down was a stupid thing to do,'' he said honestly.

"So is wasting lives,'' she retorted. "My husband was one of the best in the field. He worked hard and did everything that was expected of him—and then some. He wound up taking a two-hundred-foot dive into an airbag that burst because the director was in too damn much of a hurry to let him check his own equipment. He had a schedule to meet.'' Chyna's voice dropped slightly. ''All Neil's cooperation earned him was a short paragraph on page thirty-nine of the local paper. He was a good, decent kind man, and he ended up as filler in a tabloid.'' There was no hiding the bitterness in her voice. Neil had deserved better, much better. More than that, Neil had deserved to live a long, full life and wind up like Rolf, teaching other stuntpeople how to practice their craft safely. Chyna bit her lip. She was showing him more emotion than she had intended. But the pain had been locked in her heart for too long.

''Well, you certainly weren't filler,'' Matt commented. ''You were page one material.''

Chyna shrugged, looking off at the sky that was turning a deeper shade of blue. ''I wasn't looking for page one. I was looking for something meaningful to come out of his death. I was trying to keep something like that from happening again. Too many stuntpeople's lives are cut short by speed,'' she told him firmly.

Matt looked puzzled. ''Drugs?''

''No,'' she said evenly. ''Careless directors hurrying to meet unrealistic production schedules.''

Matt studied her for a moment, the slight vein in his temple more prominent than it had been a moment ago. ''Shutting down a studio deprives a lot of people of their livelihoods.''

Chyna's face was solemn as she met his steady gaze. ''At least they would still come home at night.''

"Nobody forces stuntmen into that line of work," he pointed out.

She felt her temper growing short and tried vainly to hold on to it. You weren't supposed to shout at your producer. Not if you wanted to go on earning a living in the film business. "That's the kind of argument they used a hundred years ago to justify putting little boys to work in the mines. Nobody forced *them* to go, either."

"This is a little different."

"Is it?" she persisted.

They stood eyeing one another. And then Chyna thought she detected the makings of a smile edge its way onto his rugged face. It was like the sun coming out after a cloudy day. Despite the subject of their discussion, she found herself responding to him before she knew what was happening.

It had been far easier to hold Matt Harrigan responsible when she didn't know what he looked like, when he was just a name in the newspaper. Standing toe to toe with the man was something else again. It wasn't that she was intimidated. She was... She didn't quite know what she was.

Looking at him covertly, Chyna was too aware of the taut, hard muscular frame beneath his form-fitting pullover. His shoulders and arms were well developed without a muscle-bound appearance. Since he was wearing shorts, Chyna could see that his muscular development didn't begin and end above the waist. His every movement was filled with sensual grace. He looked more like the star of one of his movies than the producer.

"A fine pastime for a grown woman," she heard him say and realized that she was staring at his Vneckline, taking in the fine layer of evenly distributed hair on his chest.

A red stain worked its way up from her damp neck until it settled on her cheeks. Chyna felt every painful inch of its travels.

"Tit for tat," she retorted without thinking. The red stain turned crimson as Matt threw back his sandy head and laughed out loud. It was a deep, rich, wonderful laugh that she would have enjoyed under different circumstances.

In desperation Chyna looked at her watch. "I've got to get back."

To her utter surprise, rather than nodding dismissively at her, Matt took her arm. Even in her frustrated embarrassment, she felt a definite wave of electricity telegraph itself all through her nervous system.

"I'll walk you back," he offered.

"No, I can find my own way, thank you," she told him. "Besides, I don't want to intrude any more on your precious time." She punctuated her statement with an unreadable smile.

As she forged straight into the forest without so much as a backward glance, Chyna was nonetheless quite aware of the fact that Matt was watching her. She could *feel* it. Her stomach made a noise that was a cross between a rumble and a gurgle, informing her that she had other things to think about besides a pensive, enigmatic producer.

But she couldn't seem to erase Matt's face from her mind. A fine way for you to act, she told herself sternly. What would Neil think about your reactions? *All* your reactions.

Neil would undoubtedly have said forgive and forget. He had been the most mild-mannered man she had ever known. Very different from the way Matt appeared to be. There was a smoldering intensity about Matt that was intriguing.

Intriguing, huh?

"No, no, no! How have you reached your age without learning the proper way to hold a woman in your arms?"

The words—and their angry tone—cut through Chyna's thoughts as she walked into a clearing and saw the director gesticulating madly. Even from where she was standing, Chyna could see the leading man frowning down at the director's gleaming bald head.

"This way!" Phillip Dussault insisted, taking the leading lady, Sally Kittridge, into his arms and holding her as if she were a vessel of precious wine. "With reverence, not like she's a hamburger from one of those fast food places!" he declared, still not letting go of Sally. "We're shooting a picture about an aristocratic woman, not some flophouse floozie who can be had for a drink!"

"Nobody ever complained about the way I held her before," Evan Beaumont growled.

"That," Dussault said imperiously, "is because you've probably only held flophouse floozies in your arms and worked with tasteless directors. I am an artist!" Abruptly he released Sally. "Now let's go, people! Time is money; time is money!" He clapped his hands together impatiently. "Cameras!" he commanded.

Chyna shook her head and kept walking, her stomach leading the way to the cafeteria. There were going to be a lot of arguments and battered egos in the days ahead. She had been on enough sets to know the signs. Well, none of that concerned her. All she wanted was to do her job, collect her pay and go home none the worse for wear.

She got in line behind an actor dressed as a fighter pilot. He wore a natty-looking leather jacket and an old-fashioned cap with earflaps dangling about his thin face. Probably a starstruck extra, she judged. Why else would he be wearing his full costume in the rising heat? she thought, amused.

The food on the steamtable looked less than appetizing. It could use a touch-up from the makeup department she told herself as her mind drifted to her job. The stunt coordinator had wound up giving her the lion's share of the female stunts, partially because of her close resemblance to Sally, but mainly because of her expertise. When she had finally gotten to see him yesterday, Alex had told her and Pepper that there wasn't enough time to train Pepper to do the more dangerous gags.

Speed. Always speed. She had worked with Alex before, when he was just another stuntman, and had hoped that as their coordinator he was going to be more concerned with safety than with speed. But the way he had talked about his method of awarding the gags had made it clear to Chyna that he was very concerned about remaining on the director's good side. She had been given her assignment with a veiled warning. So much for old friendships.

Chyna remembered that after Neil's accident she had received a lot of kind condolences and offers of help from Neil's friends. But when she had approached them to join her in bringing suit against the studio, as well as the director and Matt, for their gross negligence, suddenly the camaraderie had melted

away and she had been left standing alone. Everyone
had been afraid, concerned that they might not be able
to get any more work. Stuntworkers depended on
staying in the good graces of directors and studios for
their livelihoods.

She slid onto the end of a wooden bench that had
been set up under a sagging canopy that was meant
to fend off the blistering sun. It failed.

Several people smiled and greeted her as she joined
them. They all began discussing the picture and
Chyna's thoughts of the past faded away.

The man next to her, the one dressed as a pilot,
was beginning to have second thoughts about his
dashing image and was shedding parts of his costume.
Chyna hid her smile and jabbed at the overfried eggs
on her chipped plate. She had time to take only a
forkful before Pepper hailed her.

Chyna looked up and saw the blonde walking toward her, flanked by two very able-bodied men. It
didn't take Pepper long to find playmates, Chyna
thought wryly.

After a quick introduction Pepper casually turned
down Chyna's offer to join her for practice and went
off with her new friends, Pete and Rick, to explore
the island.

Chyna looked after them, shaking her head. She
had seen Pepper wavering when she had made her
suggestion, but Rick had convinced her that there was
no need to practice something she had done so many
times before. Chyna had seen his type before: the so-
called professional who had a god-complex and
thought that he didn't need to go over a stunt. He
gave the rest of them a bad name.

Suddenly breakfast was very unappealing. She

rose, taking the dull gray tray with her, and went looking for a trash can. She found one and dumped the contents of her tray with a heavy thud.

"It's that bad, eh?"

She turned around to find Matt standing behind her.

"I was just about to get some breakfast. I think you talked me out of it," he said, nodding toward the trash can.

She smiled wryly. "I had no idea I was that persuasive."

Matt looked at her for a long moment, his eyes sparkling. "You strike me as a woman who can be very persuasive when she wants to be."

Now what did he mean by that? Was he referring to the committee she had organized? Or was there another meaning to his words?

"Don't let me dissuade you," she said lightly. "I just seem to have lost my appetite."

"The heat'll do that," Matt commented.

The silence hung clumsily between them, as if each was waiting for the other to say something.

Finally Chyna made an effort, although for the life of her, she didn't know why. "There's always a silver lining to everything. Now I don't have to wait so long before I can go and practice my stunts."

"You're doubling for Sally, aren't you?" he asked, and she nodded. "She goes through some pretty harrowing things in the script," he commented. "That is, you do," he amended.

Chyna grinned. "Thank goodness for that, or else they wouldn't need a stuntwoman and I still wouldn't have a job."

"'Still'?"

She was surprised at the note of interest in his

voice. She would have thought a producer had more important things to do than associate with a stunt-worker—especially one who had tried to take him to court.

"I thought you knew everything about me," she said with a soft laugh. "You made it sound as if you thought you had my number yesterday."

"How long have you been out of work?" he asked.

"Ever since I tried to bring the studio to court," she said evenly.

"That long, eh?"

"That long."

He considered the matter for a moment. "Well, did you learn anything from the experience?"

Learn anything? What did he think she was, a trick dog? "Yes," she said with a toss of her head, slamming the tray down on top of the open trash can. "I learned not to trust the studio brass. Now, if you'll excuse me, I have some heavy practicing to do."

With that she marched off into the surrounding greenery, fervently hoping that she wouldn't get lost.

Three

Chyna felt achy.

The humidity had seeped into her joints, making them feel stiff and puffy. Her cheeks felt as if she had a permanent blush embossed on them, and even her eyelashes felt heavy with moisture. The strict concentration she needed to do her stunts was frequently broken by visions of snow-filled scenes dancing before her mind's eye.

It got to the point where she felt she couldn't go on if she didn't have a tall, cold glass of *something*. Calling it a day, Chyna made her way over to the cafeteria. But the people in charge of providing the meals were having their own problems with the weather. The refrigeration system was out, and the coldest thing available was a collection of several large lettuce leaves.

Chyna thought of the beach and her spirits rose

again. With renewed enthusiasm she hurried off to get her bathing suit.

When she got inside her stifling shack she pulled out a gleaming white bikini from her suitcase. Quickly Chyna stripped off her perspiration-soaked clothes and threw them in a small heap on her cot, then slipped on the bikini. It complemented her bronzed tan rather nicely, she thought, looking down at the network of lacing and very little cloth.

She was fully aware of all the looks and apprecia-tive stares she garnered as she walked through the camp to the beach. But then, she reminded herself, there weren't that many things to look at out here in the middle of nowhere.

"Where are you going, darling?"

The voice was familiar. She had heard it piercing the din over and over again all afternoon, uttering cutting, cryptic words. She turned around to look at the puffy, round face of the director and saw the wide, semi-leering smile on his lips fade away into his jowls.

"Oh, it's you," he said, his tone both disappointed and dismissive. "I thought you were Sally." He walked off abruptly, annoyed at his mistake.

"Hello to you, too," Chyna said under her breath. She shook her head and went on.

When she arrived on the beach she found the as-sistant director and his crew wrapping up a shooting session. On both sides of Chyna miniarmies of extras, all dressed in multicolored native garb that recalled the 1930s, ambled by. Many gave her the once-over and grinned beneath their heavy cocoa-colored make-up.

Water. All she could think of was cool water.

Lovely, wet water cascading all over her hot, parched body. Chyna ran into the surf and found that the cold water she had longed for was warm. But at least it wasn't hot, the way everything else was. Reveling in the delicious sensation the water produced, Chyna began to swim further out, willing herself to think of nothing and no one. With her back to the shore she didn't see the one lone figure approaching the beach just as all the others were retreating from it.

The peaceful early morning waters had changed; they were now churning restlessly under the afternoon sun, taking Chyna's breath away and making her exert herself as she tried to maintain control over the direction she was taking. After a few minutes she decided not to swim out too much further. All her practicing had made her tired, and she didn't want to risk being in a position where she might have to struggle against the current to get back.

Just as the thought occurred to her, a large wave washed over her head, sending her underwater and snatching away her breath entirely. Worse than that, it snatched away something else as well.

"Oh, no!" she gasped, bobbing up, one hand running over her naked breasts in horror. Her bikini top! She looked frantically around in all directions, but it wasn't anywhere to be seen. It had disappeared, a casualty of the last wave.

"Anything wrong?"

Matt's voice reached her over the noise of the waves. He was standing at the edge of the water, and she could make out a look of concern on his face— or was he scowling again? Who cared? She had something more important to worry about right now.

"Yes!" she called back.

Then, to her horror, Matt began to wade in toward her. He must have thought she was having trouble swimming, she realized.

"No, stay back!" she cried, swimming a little closer toward shore to keep out of the rougher waters. By now she was thoroughly miserable. What was she going to do? She couldn't just parade back into camp. What an idiot she was for not bringing something with her. A towel, a robe. Anything!

As Chyna bobbed up and down in the water she realized that Matt, who had stopped momentarily to look at her quizzically, was now coming toward her again. Water was steadily lapping up the sides of his jeans, turning them a darker shade of blue. An orphaned thought that this should be filmed by someone came flashing through Chyna's brain. He looked like a masterful warlord stalking a feudal peasant girl who had been promised to him by some penniless, spineless farmer instead of this year's tithe.

"Stop!" she pleaded again as the water came up to his thighs.

"You sound like you're in trouble," he called back to her, but he did as she asked.

Chyna breathed a sigh of relief, then realized that there was nothing to be relieved about. Her predicament hadn't changed.

"I am in trouble," she shouted unhappily.

"Then get out of there!" he ordered.

"I can't!"

"Okay," he said decisively, annoyed with the situation, "then I'm coming in to get you." The waters slapped hungrily at his waist, making him look like an artist's rendition of a young Neptune.

"You can't!"

"Why not?" he demanded impatiently, totally confused by her lack of cooperation.

"Because I'm not dressed!" she retorted in exasperation.

He cocked his head. "Come again?"

The sun danced on his sandy blond head as he waited for an explanation. She could see a smile forming on his lips. He had guessed her problem...or could he see her now?

She moved back a little, but the unruly waters made progress difficult. "The water ripped off my top," she finally called out.

"Oh." The single word was loaded with a good many things Chyna didn't want to explore at the moment. "What do you propose we do about it?" he asked, his tone changing to one of amusement.

"Your shirt!" Chyna cried suddenly. "Can I have your shirt?"

He laughed. "First she wants to take me to court, now she wants the shirt off my back." He shook his head. "Some people have a lot of gall." For a moment she was sure he was going to go on tormenting her, but instead she was relieved to see him strip off his shirt. The sun gleamed down on his tanned shoulders, making Chyna's heart quicken of its own accord.

"Wait, go back," she ordered as he began to approach her again.

"Then how are you going to get this shirt?" he wanted to know.

"Turn your back and hold it out. I'll take care of the rest," she told him, watching him carefully.

He did as she asked, and Chyna swam over rapidly,

afraid that he would turn around at the last minute, but he didn't.

After taking the pullover from him, she quickly slipped it over her own shoulders and let it fall about her hips. The water lapped at the ends and inched its way up the fabric. Another wave came, throwing her against Matt.

"Hey, steady now," he cautioned, grabbing her firmly by the shoulders. The momentary touch of their bodies, even with the water between them, had generated a burst of fire through Chyna, and she looked up at him, stunned.

She became conscious of the fact that he was staring at her, and looked down to see just what he was looking at. She might have guessed! His blue pullover was clinging seductively to her breasts.

"We'd…um…better get you out of here before the waves decide to rip that off you, too…not that I'd blame them."

The last part was said in a muttered aside, as if he were talking to himself and not even conscious of having said the words aloud.

Chyna felt embarrassed, and she chided herself for being childish. After all, they were both adults, and this was an accident. It wasn't as if she had planned all this on purpose, or… She looked up at his face as he took a firm hold of her elbow and practically marched her out of the water. Just what *was* he thinking?

"I haven't thanked you," she mumbled.

"I'm the one who should thank you," Matt said.

"And just what does that mean?" she asked, as they stepped back onto the sand.

"My shirt's never looked so good," he said, a boyish twinkle coming into his eyes as they once more left her face and skimmed the terrain below her neck.

Chyna crossed her arms over her breasts. "I just might retract my thanks," she said, her voice strained.

"I just might retract my shirt," he countered, reaching for her collar.

"Oh, no, don't do that!" she cried as she felt his fingers brush against her throat. Heat danced across her skin and her nipples tautened.

For a moment there was a potent silence between them. The cry of a faraway sea gull threatened to break the spell, but Matt bent his head toward her, as if moved by some unseen force. Chyna stood rooted to the spot, watching him, yet wondering if any of this was really happening. He slipped his hand along the outline of her jaw and cupped her cheek, touching her throat and neck ever so lightly as he did so. Then he drew her mouth up to his and kissed her, appearing almost as surprised by his action as she was.

Chyna had thought she had sampled all the joys that one could glean from romance. But never in all her experience had she felt anything close to what was bursting upon her senses at that moment. A second before his lips found hers, her heart started pounding wildly. She had the same queasy feeling in her stomach that she felt just before jumping out of a plane without a chute. The exhilarating feeling sped throughout her body with an intensity so great that she dreaded it and yet desired it at the same time. She scarcely knew herself as a tidal wave of desire broke free within her; she was drawn to the surging force of his mouth as if her very life hung in the balance.

Her mind felt clouded, yet she was aware of everything: the feel of his hard chest as it pressed against her heaving breasts; the outline of his urgent body as it moved against hers; and the strangely comforting touch of his hand as it roamed along her back and shoulders, pulling her closer to him until she didn't know where she ended and he began.

Breathing. She wasn't breathing! The thought registered itself suddenly. His kiss had stolen away her breath and played havoc with her senses at the same time. She filled her lungs with air, but the action just added to the heady feeling as she heard the rasping sound of her own ragged breath.

Hardly conscious of what she was doing, Chyna wrapped her arms around Matt's neck, kissing him back as demandingly as she was being kissed. One high wave crashed against them, dragging back some of the sand beneath Chyna's feet and finally breaking the spell that held them in its grip. She blinked several times as Matt let her go. The moment was gone for him as well.

He looked at her solemnly now, his face no longer teasing, his eyes no longer pulling her toward him like powerful magnets. He seemed to be disturbed by what had happened between them.

"I'm sorry," he said.

The words both stung and surprised her. It had been a wonderfully exciting, mystical moment—and he was sorry? Hadn't he felt something happening? Or was it just she? Maybe it was, she thought. Maybe it was just the heat.

Although they didn't look anything alike, there was something in Matt's competent, reserved manner that reminded Chyna painfully of Neil. But there was something more about Matt. Just being near him

made her tingle and the tiny hairs on her body stand
erect. That had never happened between her and Neil.

But Matt had said he was sorry. Her brain echoed
with the word. Why? What had caused him to turn
away? It was as if a curtain had fallen over his face.
Was it that he thought, just as she did, that any sort
of a relationship between them was just asking for
trouble? Or was there something else?

"Why are you sorry? Was it so bad?" she heard
herself asking. Embarrassed, she turned her flushed
face away and looked straight ahead in the direction
she was walking.

Quietly, Matt fell into step beside her, shortening
his stride in order to keep pace with her. "No, it
wasn't," he answered in a low voice. "But I took
advantage of the moment."

"Advantage?" she echoed, stunned. She had never
expected to hear that from any man, and especially
not him. Most men were out to take every advantage
they could. Matt sounded as if he came from the Vic-
torian Age. "'Advantage' would have been if you'd
dragged me by my hair into a cave and"—she laid
the back of her hand across her forehead dramati-
cally—"had your way with me."

Her words succeeded in bringing a small, sensual
smile to his lips. The inner thrill returned. At the same
time, part of her was wondering what on earth she
was doing trying to make Matthew Harrigan feel better. Had she lost her mind?

Matt stopped walking for a moment, standing just
on the outskirts of the camp. For a second she thought
he was going to kiss her again. But he didn't.

The look in his eyes changed, clouded over by
some inner thought. "I've got rushes to see to," he

told her. "Don't go swimming by yourself anymore," he ordered. And then he added with a grin, "Or at least wear a stronger bathing suit."

Chyna stared after him as he left, feeling tremendously let down. Telling herself that her reaction was totally illogical didn't help matters any. Neither did the sudden realization that she was attracting quite a few stares, standing there in Matt's clinging shirt.

Get back to your shack, dummy, and stop thinking about him, she told herself, hurrying through the camp.

She reached her shack in record time.

Four

Matt's shirt lay on the newly cleaned sink counter where Chyna had tossed it the day before. Each time she passed it, the shirt caught her eye, drawing her attention as if it were a magnet.

"You keep looking at that shirt as if the guy were still in it," Pepper commented as she stretched lazily on her cot, conquered by the late morning sun and a strenuous workout.

Chyna kept rummaging through her clothes, looking for something that hadn't been destroyed by the humidity. "No more high jumps for you," she declared carelessly. "The thin air is scrambling your brain. You're beginning to hallucinate."

Giving up her half-hearted quest, she decided to remain in the shorts and halter top she was wearing, and to return Matt's shirt right away. She slung it over her bare shoulder and headed for the door. "I'd better see about returning this," she said.

Pepper propped herself up on her elbow. "Or filling it," she teased, leaning over.

Chyna tugged at the other woman's arm, pulling it out from under her, and Pepper fell face down on her cot, laughing as if she had uncovered a secret.

"Definitely scrambled," Chyna announced, walking out.

But she grinned as she began walking toward Matt's trailer on the far side of the set. What would he say if she held up his shirt, batted her eyes prettily and murmured, "I'd like a refill, please."

He'd probably say, "Ah, ha, I've won. I've dazzled her. She won't be any more trouble to me," Chyna thought, rolling the scene over in her head. Well, Mr. Harrigan, I don't intend to be any trouble—just as long as you intend to run a safe production. And I also don't intend to be dazzled by you, no matter how cute your cleft chin is....

Chyna stopped abruptly. He had a cleft chin? When had she noticed that? *Why?* had she noticed that? Maybe a little dazzle was slipping in, despite her efforts not to let it. The shirt began to feel heavier on her shoulder. The sooner she rid herself of anything belonging to Matt Harrigan, the better, she decided.

Ribbons of color were fanning out across the sky, stretching until they merged with the light haze of blue and disappeared. The idyllic scene above was in direct contrast to what was transpiring below. The air was blue there, too, but for another reason. As Chyna approached the area where the film crew had been working for several hours, setting up for a shot that would last less than six seconds on the screen, she heard the director's voice thundering above the din.

"Damn it, are we going to fall behind schedule already?" he demanded of the world at large. The world wasn't answering him. But his glare finally prodded an unwilling reply from Alex.

"He just needs a little more time to practice," the stunt coordinator explained, nodding toward the man under discussion.

"What's to practice?" Dussault demanded, waving his arms around. In his furor he also managed to save himself from a low-flying mosquito that had been about to use his bald head as a landing strip, Chyna noticed, coming closer. "He's either got it down or he doesn't," Dussault groused. "The pads'll absorb most of the wear anyway. Now, does he do it, or do we get someone else?" He crossed his arms in front of him, glaring over the bridge of his hawklike nose.

Chyna saw the muscles around the stuntman's mouth twitch slightly. She knew what was at stake here. The man didn't want to be labeled a troublemaker. Directors, she thought wryly, don't hire troublemakers. They avoid them. And being avoided makes it tough to eat. Especially if you only know one trade. There isn't much call for people who only know how to crash cars.

Chyna leaned against a tree, watching, knowing that she had other things to do, knowing that she had promised herself not to pay attention to anyone's work but her own. But she couldn't help herself.

"I'll be ready in a minute," the stuntman said quietly.

A triumphant look came over the director's face. "That's more like it," he said, a satisfied smile spreading over his wide mouth. He turned to see Chyna watching him. "What the hell are you doing here?" he demanded.

"Watching," she answered lightly.

"You're not in this scene," Dussault snapped dismissively.

"I know that," she said, not moving. "I thought I might pick up some pointers."

Her answer and her tone irritated Dussault. "I thought you said she was the best," he growled at Alex.

Alex opened his mouth to offer an excuse when Chyna cut in for him. "That's how you stay the best," she said, keeping her voice light. "By watching and concentrating. It's what keeps you alive."

The expression on her face was the embodiment of sweetness, but it didn't fool Dussault. It wasn't meant to. He spun on his heel and stormed off, not saying a word, leaving a gaping crowd behind him. Chyna moved away from the tree she had been leaning against. "I guess you've got time to practice now," she said to the stuntman before she walked away.

"Chyna," Alex called after her.

She stopped, but didn't turn around. She knew what was coming. Absently she hooked her finger into the collar of Matt's shirt and played with it, waiting for Alex to catch up to her.

"I told you that I didn't want any trouble out of you," he warned.

Chyna bit her tongue. She wasn't used to being spoken to this way. What she wanted to say was that it was Alex's obligation to stand up for his people, not let them be browbeaten into doing gags they weren't ready for. But she kept her words to herself, chewing on the inside of her mouth.

"No trouble," she said finally. "I'm the soul of cooperation." She offered him a big smile. And then the smile turned serious. "Why didn't you say something to Dussault instead of siding with him?" she asked bluntly. Someday, Chyna, you're going to get the gift of eloquence—or else someone is going to wind up feeding you your teeth, she thought. But she didn't retract her question.

"Chyna, stay out of what you don't know. It was up to Rick to be ready. Dussault is only working according to the schedule."

He left, muttering something inaudible under his breath, and Chyna let out a big sigh. Maybe Alex was right. She had noticed that Rick had a penchant for not practicing. Hadn't he lured Pepper away that first day? When was she going to learn to keep quiet? Well, no damage had been done, she told herself. And maybe Rick had learned his lesson about the need to practice.

Forget it, Chyna. They don't need a den mother and nobody likes a person who butts in all the time. She decided to put the incident out of her mind. She had a shirt to return.

"That broad's got to go," Dussault railed at Matt, bringing his fist down on Matt's desk and causing a minor earthquake that caused several piles of paper to collapse.

He couldn't bring himself to regard her as "that broad," but Matt had known immediately who Dussault was referring to when the director had stormed into the trailer and made his demand. An image of Chyna, his wet shirt clinging to her supple body, came back to him. "Take it easy, Phil," he said soothingly.

"Phillip," the director corrected haughtily. "I can't work with her looking over my shoulder, making notes every time I tell some sniveling stuntman to earn his oversized paycheck."

"She was taking notes?" Matt asked, his voice more serious. Was she out to start trouble already?

"Well, not exactly, but I could see by the way she was looking that she's making notes," Dussault said evasively, although his outrage didn't abate any.

"Oh," Matt said, relief lacing his tone. "Mental notes."

"Yeah, 'mental notes.' Mental notes, shmental notes, what's the difference? She's trouble. Look at all the problems she caused you last year."

But Matt put his hand up, stopping the other man from going on. Why he felt compelled to defend her was a mystery to him, but he didn't like Dussault's tone. "That was over her husband—" he began.

"So, she could've worn black like any other widow and kept her mouth shut. I warn you, Matt, she's gonna be nothing but trouble for us." The director's voice echoed in the enclosed area like an omen of doom.

"She comes highly recommended and we need her," Matt reminded the shorter man, trying to hold on to his patience.

Dussault took umbrage with Matt's laid-back attitude. He pulled back his shapeless shoulders, sticking out a barrel chest that had long since sunk down to his pants line. "Just keep her away from me," he ordered.

"Don't worry," Matt promised, rising. He put his hand reassuringly on Dussault's shoulder. "I'll take care of her."

Oh, no, you won't, Chyna thought as his words floated out to her through the trailer door she had just opened. She had arrived on the scene just in time to overhear the last bit of conversation. It confirmed her gnawing suspicions of Matt's genial attitude toward her. He was hoping, no doubt, to keep her quiet by taking advantage of the tropical setting and romancing her. After all, a woman with love on her mind wouldn't have time for anything else, right? she thought with a cryptic smile. Well, Mr. Producer, sir, you are in for one hell of an awakening, she promised him as she sidestepped Dussault. I'm not about to fall in love with you.

The director looked surprised to see her. He also looks as if he wishes he were driving a tank, Chyna thought, amused. She nodded toward him, then turned to walk into the trailer.

For a moment the air-conditioning was a shock to her whole system. It felt as if she had just stepped through the looking glass into another world. It took her a moment to get acclimated to it. And then it took her another moment to get acclimated to Matt. Why did he have to be so breathtakingly good-looking? she thought. But then, if he wasn't, he probably wouldn't think he had much of a chance of distracting her from any transgressions that might be going on during the filming.

Just a man, Chyna. Ninety-eight percent of that is all water. Water never looked so good, she decided.

He looked surprised to see her. He also looked pleased. Come into my parlor, said the spider to the fly, Chyna thought. Except this time the fly had come willingly—bearing a shirt. She suddenly recalled the object of her mission and reached for it.

"I've brought back your shirt," she said, holding it out to him.

He took it, using the opportunity to take hold of her hand as well. "Thank you," he said softly. The words, though simple, still managed to curl their way into the pit of her stomach, making it queasy. "Why don't you sit down?" he suggested, nodding toward the beige sofa under the window.

"No, I—" She began to make a million excuses. Being in a small area with Matt wasn't wise. She wasn't a fool. She knew when she was in trouble. But the idea of staying was so appealing.....

"You look like you're ready to take flight," he commented.

Chyna lifted her chin. That had decided her, and she settled down on the sofa. He wasn't slow in joining her, and he chose the same side as she did.

"Don't you think you need a little more room?" she asked, meeting the challenge in his eyes.

"This is fine," he told her, smiling. It was a perfect smile. The kind, she thought, that was bought from some beaming orthodontist. Still, in this case the end justified the means. His smile *was* beautiful, no matter what its origin. Think about something else, she ordered herself. She looked down at his shoes. Scuffed. He was human.

"Have you eaten?" he asked, suddenly breaking her concentration.

She shook her head, her scalp tingling as her hair

began to dry in the cool atmosphere. At least she assumed the tingling sensation was from the air conditioning. "The line's too long," she explained, looking for a safe topic. "I figured I'd fry before it was my turn to order a dead tuna on rye."

"Then share this with me," he suggested, taking her hand and rising.

Just what was it that he wanted her to share? she wondered warily, ready for anything. But all he did was lead her to a small table with two chairs. Beams of sunlight streamed through the window, dancing along the long silver tray that stood in the center of the table, still covered.

"You believe in living well, don't you?" she couldn't help commenting.

"Whenever I can," he answered. "I've earned it." His tone was utterly straightforward.

"I'm really not up to eating," she protested, trying to pull her hand free. For some strange reason the touch of his hand made her feel very vulnerable. "This heat has killed my appetite. It's a wonder all the people on the island aren't forty-pound weaklings."

He didn't seem to be listening to her as he used his free hand to uncover the tray. A tempting array of crabmeat, shrimp and scallops reminded her that there was some life left to her appetite after all.

"This, I take it, didn't come from the lunch trucks," Chyna said.

Matt laughed. It was a delicious, compelling laugh that made her feel good. "No, I had it brought in from the city," he confessed.

Chyna deposited herself in one of the chairs. "I don't blame you," she said. "The food on the trucks is pretty awful. But it's either that or starve," she said philosophically. "And it's kind of a long way to brown-bag it." He was still holding her hand. She raised her brows as she looked at him. "Do I ever get to use this again?" she asked, glancing down at her captive hand. His skin felt warm against hers, despite the air conditioning. Despite a lot of things. "I need it for my knife," she added.

"Which I trust will be applied only to your lunch," he said, finally releasing her hand.

"Meaning?" she asked, beginning to eat. She wasn't going to make this easy for him if he was planning on a lecture. As far as she was concerned, she had done less than nothing. And definitely not enough to merit Dussault's fury.

"Meaning that Dussault says you're driving him crazy."

She speared a shrimp and dipped it in cocktail sauce before she answered. "It's not a drive," she said casually, taking a bite. "It's a short putt."

She noticed that Matt had to struggle to keep back a grin. "Dussault's an excellent director," Matt told her. "His methods may be a little hard to put up with at times, but he gets results—and," he added, leaning forward, "his bark is a lot worse than his bite. I've worked with him before. He knows what he's doing."

She nodded her head absently. There was no point in debating the subject. And maybe Matt was right. Maybe she was just being overly sensitive. Time would tell.

"But of course, I'm not a fanatic on the subject. If you have any complaints about the way Dussault is handling the stunts, come to me, okay? I don't relish having him unduly upset, or seeing my set become the scene of screaming matches. Fair enough?''

"*I* don't scream," she said quietly, but she smiled. "Fair enough," she echoed. At least, it *sounded* fair enough, she added silently.

He sat down and regarded her thoughtfully for a moment. She looked over at his empty plate. "Has the food been tampered with?" she asked lightly. "Is that how you get rid of potential problems?" she posed. "You feed them a last meal that's been laced with cyanide?" She pretended to sniff the rest of the food on her plate. "Funny, I don't smell any almonds." She looked up at him, her eyes twinkling. "That's what cyanide's supposed to smell like, isn't it? Almonds? Or did you use something else?"

"Nothing else," he assured her. "The food's fine. See?" To prove his point he took a golden scallop and consumed it in one bite. "I wouldn't use anything as crude as poison on you. You're too valuable."

So you're going to sweep me off my feet and off my guard, she thought with a smile. Well, put your broom away, Matt Harrigan. I don't fool that easily. She retired her fork. Time for the game to end before he decided that she was going to be dessert. She needed this job and didn't want to be put in the position of having to say no to any propositions. She glanced toward the door.

"In a hurry?" he asked.

She nodded. "As a matter of fact, yes. I promised Pepper I'd—"

"Pepper," he echoed. "Chyna. Don't you people have real names?" he marveled.

"Chyna *is* my real name," she said, taking exception to his supercilious tone. "My father was a history professor at Cal State, Fullerton. He loved the Orient.''

''He must have been thrilled when you told him you'd decided to risk your neck for a living,'' he commented. He thought of his own daughter and how he would react if she told him she wanted to be a stuntwoman. Of course, at five, that was some distance in the future...

He realized that Chyna was withdrawing from him slightly. The expression on her face told him that she thought he was laughing at her. ''As a matter of fact, he raised me to be a free thinker,'' she said with just a hint of resentment. ''To try my hand at anything that moved me.''

Something drove him on to comment, ''So you decided to try legalized suicide.''

Chyna pushed her plate away. ''Where would you be without us legalized suicidees?'' she asked, wondering why he was baiting her this way. He's trying to confuse you, she warned herself. He was succeeding admirably.

''Probably making movies that were relegated to second-rate theaters for limited runs that no one would attend,'' he admitted. He wasn't sure just what had made him say what he had about stunt work. But he had found himself going over the script earlier that morning, picking out the dangerous stunts Chyna was slated to perform. She would be facing death no fewer than eight times. For the first time the idea bothered him. He wondered if having Chyna around had brought back the specter of last year's accident. ''Don't get me wrong, you perform a very necessary service,'' he told her. ''I just always thought of stuntmen as, well, men.''

"The proper term," she informed him, amused, "is stuntworker or stuntperson. Use the word 'stuntman' again and I'll report you to the nearest women's lib chapter," she threatened, hardly bothering to check the smile blossoming on her lips.

"I'd rather you looked into the matter personally," he said, leaning toward her over the table.

Too close for comfort. Time to retreat, she told herself, pushing back her chair. To her dismay, he rose with her. "Thanks for lunch," she said cheerfully, although the words sounded strained.

"You hardly touched it."

"I ate more than you did," she pointed out.

He stopped her at the door, one arm barricading her into the trailer. "I had other things on my mind."

No doubt, she thought. As she looked up into his eyes, she saw exactly what those other things were. Her pulse went up a notch, just the way it did before she hurled herself off a cliff. Same difference, she thought, except in this case there was no springboard waiting to break her fall, no air mattress to cradle her. A woman could break her neck like this—or something else.

Searching for a way to avoid the inevitable, she looked down at the desk. Her eyes fell on a framed photograph.

"Who's that?" she asked suddenly.

Matt pulled his head back. Saved! Chyna thought in relief. "That's my daughter," he said. There was no mistaking the fondness in his voice.

"Is she home, with your wife?" Chyna asked, emphasizing the last word. She knew next to nothing about this man and naturally assumed that he came

equipped with a family neatly tucked away somewhere out of sight.

"No," Matt answered. "With the housekeeper. I
don't know who's home with my wife. My ex-wife,"
he corrected. "Actually, she's probably not home at
all. That was part of the problem," he said, sounding
so coldly indifferent that Chyna wondered if he had
ever cared for the woman.

"Refused to stay home like a good little wife, did
she?" Chyna asked, thinking back to his comment
about stuntmen. He was probably a card-carrying
chauvinist of the first degree. With looks like that,
why not? she thought. Women probably threw themselves all over him, hoping that he could further their
careers and make their dreams come true. Why should
he have any respect for women at all?

She stopped herself, wondering whose side she was
arguing, his or hers.

"No, as a matter of fact, Laura wanted a career
more than she wanted me or Meredith," he said flatly,
his face showing no expression whatsoever.

So that was it, she thought. That was what was
responsible for the bitterness that she saw in him from
time to time. She wondered how much he had loved
his wife and how hurt he had been when she turned
her back on him. "I'm sorry," she said quietly.
"Sometimes I'm a little too flip for my own good.
I..." I'm tripping over my tongue again, she thought
desperately.

Mercifully, he accepted her apology quickly
enough. His eyes swept over her warmly. "I'm not
used to women who'll admit it when they're wrong,"
he said, touching her hair. His fingers buried themselves in the silkiness he found there, gently touching

her scalp. The tingling sensation was back, she noted with alarm.

"I'm not afraid of admitting that I'm wrong," Chyna said, trying to meet him on equal footing. "When I am."

"No?" he asked, studying her face. The blueness of her eyes captivated him.

"No," she said. It sounded like a pulsating whisper.

"What *are* you afraid of, Chyna O'Brien?" he asked, his voice like velvet. He cupped the back of her head in his hand, tilting it just a little.

You, she wanted to say, the thought springing to her mind. You represent something that frightens me, something that has nothing to do with faulty equipment or gags that go sour.

"Not much," she lied, wondering if he noticed that the pulse in her throat was throbbing wildly.

He lowered his mouth until it was just a breath away from hers, teasing her. "I'm glad," he said, his words gliding along the outline of her lips.

She wanted to say that she was in a hurry. She wanted to say that Pepper was waiting for her. She wanted to say that she had to go practice her gags. She wanted to say a lot of things that didn't get said just then.

It's hard to say anything when your mouth is otherwise occupied.

Five

As his mouth moved over hers, evoking a thousand pleasures, Chyna felt as if a Pandora's box of emotions had opened within her. Vainly she tried to shut the lid. She didn't want to feel anything. Not for him. All he was trying to do was distract her. There was nothing else behind this kiss but business.

Why did business have to feel this good?

She had to stop this, she told herself. But all she did was sink deeper into the pleasure of Matt's kiss. A moment longer, just a moment longer, something within her pleaded, something that was enjoying this immensely.

You're kissing him back, her brain telegraphed to her. You're giving him the wrong idea. You're making him think you like it.

It was hard not to like having every fiber of your

body tingle with electrifying excitement, she thought as her sanity faded away.

Slowly Matt massaged the contours of her slim back, delicately exploring the slope of her shoulder blades and rimming the lower edge of her halter top. Involuntarily Chyna shivered.

The air-conditioning. The air-conditioning was making her shiver. She would make sure he understood that—if only she could regain control of her lips. But they were still being laid siege to. And still hungrily giving back as good as they got. It was as if she had no say in the matter.

Chyna's arms wound around Matt's neck, making her body stretch against him. As he pressed her to him, Chyna felt the outline of his hard muscles. This was no soft executive given to relishing the comforts of life. He honed his body in the same manner he honed his production—with an eye out for every minute detail.

But details were beginning to fade into oblivion, forced urgently away by the wild, churning sensations he awoke in her. It had been a long time since anyone had loved her.

No!

The last thought brought her back to her senses before she allowed the roller coaster to take her to the crest of her desire. And before it went down the long valley, flying out of control.

She struggled to regain her breath. Slowly, breathe in slowly, she instructed herself. Don't look like a panting puppy in front of him. He told that troll of a director that he would take care of you. Don't let him think he did it with one silly kiss.

But it hadn't been a silly kiss, her racing pulse

insisted. It had been a poem. A poem? It had been an entire epic. And she had loved it. There was definite danger here, she thought. The man's mouth was lethal.

She tried to summon a blasé look. It didn't quite match her flushed cheeks. "Taking advantage again?" she asked, hoping that she sounded amused instead of breathless.

"No," Matt said, smiling into her eyes. It was as if he saw right through her, damn him. "Not this time."

He was stroking her. His hands were at his sides, yet he was stroking her, she thought incredulously. His eyes were like liquid magic. She had to get out of there before she did something that one of them was going to regret a lot. Namely her.

"Sure you won't stay?" he coaxed, this time reaching up and sliding a finger along the ridge of her jaw.

Was this how Napoleon felt when he arrived at Waterloo? she wondered. Well, at least she was going to be able to retreat. And she fully intended to. She groped behind her, searching for the doorknob. Eureka.

"I'm sure," she said, her voice sounding incredibly calm, despite the turmoil that was going on inside her, "I have to get—"

He reached around behind her, placing his hand over hers, snatching freedom away once again. His warmth penetrated not only her hand, but her senses, telling her that no matter how she fought it, she liked being touched by this man.

Primitive approach, primitive reactions, she tried to tell herself. But something in her wasn't buying it. She knew herself too well.

"Chyna."

It was the first time he had called her by name, and it gave her a thrill. For an unguarded moment she wondered what it would sound like, coming from his lips, uttered with the thickness of deep desire. Get hold of yourself, Chyna! You're letting the romance of the movie affect you. Serves you right for staying up last night and reading the entire script.

"What?" she asked. She tried to make the word sound like a challenge. I'm not going to make this easy for you, she thought with ebbing determination. I'm not. No one's seducing me just to keep me quiet.

His voice was low, melodic. Thrilling. "Why don't we just go along being exceptionally wary and cautious with one another...and see what develops?" he suggested.

It was a line that would have fit right into the movie, she thought. And it was just a line. So why did she feel like a pat of butter on a hot skillet?

Calling on all her powers of concentration, Chyna managed to block out some of her feelings. "Nothing is going to develop," she said with firm control, "except, I hope, a good movie that's utterly trouble free." Good. Strike a blow for your side, she told herself, feeling just the tiniest bit smug.

She watched him, expecting to see constrained annoyance in his eyes because she wasn't taking his cue and falling into his arms. Instead he looked amused. She didn't know whether to take exception to that or not. The man plays a hell of a confusing game, she thought with a touch of admiration. She just wished it wasn't at her expense.

"That, too," he said, laughing softly. "But I

wasn't quite thinking of the movie just at this moment.''

She wished he'd let her out of this tiny space. He was so close that he was making it difficult for her to compete in this verbal tennis match. ''Oh, weren't you?'' she asked a bit sarcastically. ''I thought I heard that the movie is always uppermost in your mind.'' She hoped she sounded flippant enough. Anything but eager.

''I'd be lying if I said it wasn't important,'' he told her, and she gave him an A for sounding sincere. He must have picked up a few acting tips along the way, she reasoned. ''But I'd be a robot if that was all that occupied my mind a hundred percent of the time.'' He took her hand and placed it on his chest. ''Do I feel like a robot to you?''

The look in his eyes was teasing, yet she could have sworn that there was something somber there, too. Was she just imagining it? Or wishing for it? Wishing? Oh, no, that had a lot more connotations to it than she cared to delve into at the moment—at any moment.

She tried to pull back her hand, not wanting any further physical contact with him. But he held it fast against his chest. She felt the excitement flowing through her. Just as she was sure he wanted her to. This whole thing was going to take an awful lot of willpower on her part.

''I don't know,'' she said lightly. ''I'm not sure what a robot is supposed to feel like. I've heard that they've come up with some pretty realistic-looking ones—with all the right working parts,'' she added humorously.

"I assure you, I'm not a robot." His voice surrounded her like silk.

She pushed him back, although not as hard as she would have liked. After all, he *was* the producer, and she did want to maintain a working relationship with him, she told herself. "I'll take your word for it," she said, this time managing to swing the door open behind her and escape.

There wasn't any other word for it. She escaped, escaped before his seductive manner broke through her hastily constructed barriers. He certainly wasn't acting the way she had initially expected him to. When she had found out that he was going to be the producer of *The Adventurer,* she had prepared herself for a gruff, blustering man who barked out orders and assumed the attitude that he was ruling by divine right. She could have handled that. This was a good deal more unnerving. But his goal was the same, she told herself. He wanted to render her docile, incapable of doing any harm to his picture no matter what went on during the filming. Well, no matter what his ploy, the man was in for a big surprise, she promised herself as she wove her way through a gaggle of extras who were still lined up waiting to play Russian Roulette with the food that was being offered.

What she couldn't seem to weave her way through was the wall of intolerable heat. It was all around her, sticky and oppressive, making it hard for her to breathe. There was a lot of that going around lately, she thought wryly.

Everyone around her looked as if they were wilting. It was hard to work up any enthusiasm for doing something strenuous when you were surrounded by lethargic-looking people who appeared to have glue in their veins. Chyna searched the area for Pepper. She finally found the other woman sitting cross-legged on the ground, away from everybody else.

"Where've you been?" Pepper asked as Chyna sank down next to her. "I waited as long as I could."

"I got held up," Chyna said evasively. She looked at her friend's fast-disappearing hamburger. "I take it you're in no mood to practice now."

Pepper shook her head, polishing off the last bit, then denuding her fingers of any extra ketchup. "Not now. If I move, I'm going to throw up," she moaned.

"Lovely imagery," Chyna commented dryly. She got up, brushing away several insects that had decided to get to know her better. "Well, we can at least plot out your gag. A little mental rehearsal won't hurt you."

Pepper looked a little uncertain about moving anything at that moment. "I dunno, Chyna," she muttered.

But Chyna wanted someone around to help get her mind off other things, things that flourished in air-conditioned trailers. "C'mon, it'll do you good," she urged, extending her hand to the other woman.

Reluctantly Pepper took her hand and got up.

For the next few days Chyna tried to do nothing but concentrate on her upcoming stunts. She spent hours getting herself in condition, and made it a point to examine all her equipment daily for signs of wear. She could only approximate some of the conditions that would be involved in the actual stunts. Some things would not come into play until the cameras were actually rolling. The exploding gasoline tanks, for instance. There was no way to physically practice for them. It was to be a one-shot take. If she missed, there'd be no second chance. Not unless she suddenly sprouted wings.

Pepper sat watching Chyna work out on the trampoline. Tired, she had opted for a break, but Chyna had doggedly gone on. Behind them loomed the mountain that Chyna was to use in her leap. As far as mountains went, it wasn't all that tall. It would never make the inside of *National Geographic,* Chyna had thought when she had first seen it. But an unprepared fall from any height could kill you.

So could not concentrating, she told herself, feeling her mind trying to drift to other subjects. To one other subject, she amended. Matt Harrigan. As in trouble. She was irritated with herself. Usually she had the ability to shut out absolutely everything that was going on and simply apply herself to the gag at hand. But ever since he had kissed her in his trailer, Matt's rugged face had kept appearing in her mind at totally inopportune, unbidden moments. Like now.

She missed her footing and wound up landing on her rump.

Pepper leaped to her feet and ran over. "What's the matter?" she asked, looking concerned.

Chyna watched the way Pepper nibbled on her lower lip. The other woman was worried about this gag, she could tell. Well, it was a growing club, Chyna thought, not exactly feeling blasé about it herself. "It was just a misstep," she said, waving away Pepper's distress.

"You?" Pepper asked, wide-eyed.

"Me," Chyna laughed, trying to keep the situation light. "I'm not perfect, you know."

She saw the way Pepper eyed the mountain. "Maybe you'd better not try that gag," she suggested hesitantly.

Chyna swung off the trampoline and put a comforting arm around Pepper. "I'm not going to 'try' it," she corrected her. "I'm going to do it. 'Trying' will only get me fried."

In her mind's eye she saw the whole gag in vivid, breathtaking color. Sally was to look approximately brave for the camera, then step back as Chyna took her place, clutching a rifle in her hands. Taking a running leap, she was to clear a group of exploding gasoline tanks and land on a hidden spring ramp that would catapult her to safety. All very nice, very smooth—*if* it worked.

It would work, she assured herself. There was only one way to face the kind of work she did: with confidence based on the knowledge that she had done everything in her power to pull it off and insure her own safety. The rest was up to luck. And her luck had held for six years.

Pepper, usually so nonchalant about their work, looked unconvinced. "Maybe if you tell Dussault that it's too dangerous..." she began, her voice trailing off. "I've got a bad feeling about this, Chyna."

Superstition, Chyna knew, played a large part in the stunt world. "That's all he'd need to hear. He'd be more than thrilled to dump me for loss of nerve," Chyna said with a dry laugh, trying to kid Pepper out of her mood. She got back up on the trampoline. "Don't look so worried. If it wasn't so dangerous, I wouldn't be getting twenty thousand dollars for doing it. And the public wouldn't be clutching at their armrests for a second." That was about how long the shot was going to last on screen: one heartbeat. For that, her own heart was going to stay in her throat until the gag was completed.

Chyna swung back up on the trampoline and began the last part of her workout with renewed vigor, blotting out everything else.

Chyna's first gag was to be one of the action highlights of the movie, and it was one of the main reasons she had gotten hired. She thought about that as she lay on her cot, staring unseeingly into the darkness. It must be about three in the morning, she thought, listening to the sounds of the tropical night. Nothing moved except the mosquitoes in search of cooperative, dormant meals. She knew that it would be hours until the pearl colors of dawn would touch the sky. The crew would be up and around before then, setting up for her shot.

Chyna sat up, knowing that she was too keyed up to drop off to sleep again. An excited knot was taking over all the available space in her stomach.

"It's just another gag," she whispered to herself. Yes, just like Matt Harrigan is just another man.

The wayward thought made her eyes fly open. None of that, she chastised herself sternly. Not today. She decided to busy herself with the mechanics of getting ready.

After wrestling with the pump Chyna succeeded in generating a thin trickle of water. Cupping her hands, she waited patiently to capture enough to wash her face, or at least get the top layer of perspiration off.

That's what it's all about, she thought. Patience. And timing. "Lord, let the timing be right," she murmured. She had done all she could to perfect the routine. The rest was entirely up to her skill and the right conditions. And a little extra help. She closed her eyes and murmured a fleeting prayer she had learned a long time ago. Angels watched over fools and children, right? Which was she?

She had succeeded in bringing a smile to her own lips. A shower would make her feel even better, she decided, making her way through the dusky shack. She found a towel and slung it over her shoulder. At least she wasn't going to have to wait in line today, she thought blissfully, picking up a pair of shorts and a blouse that were lying nearby.

Because of the hour, she didn't bother changing out of her short nightgown. Instead she made her way quickly to the makeshift stalls. She was engrossed in going over the logistics of her stunt, which was why she didn't hear the water running or wonder why there was light showing beneath the large brown tent. She was too caught up in her own thoughts. Pushing the door open, she marched briskly in and stopped dead in her tracks, a gasp hovering in her throat.

Matt's startled smile greeted her. More than that, Matt's wet body greeted her. At least, the parts of it that weren't hidden by that partition did. There were three stalls in the tent, but Chyna didn't see past the first one.

He stopped what he was doing and came up close to the partition. "C'mon in," he invited sensuously. "The water's fine."

Behind him the steady stream of water from the showerhead continued, as if to reinforce his words.

"This isn't Japan," she heard herself saying. "Communal bathing isn't in."

"We could start a new tradition," he told her with the sexiest wink she had ever encountered in her life.

The knot in her stomach tightened. She began to retreat, then stopped herself. She couldn't keep running like this. It wasn't in her nature, and he'd think that he had succeeded in unnerving her. "What are you doing here?" she demanded.

"Taking a shower," he answered cheerfully, beginning to soap himself. As he bent down slightly, Chyna could imagine the path his hands were following. She felt herself getting warmer. As if she needed to be warmer!

"But it's three in the morning," she pointed out.

"You're up," she heard him answer from within the stall.

"I have a gag today," she said, resisting the urge to come closer and look in—just to be able to address his face, of course, she added.

Matt's head popped back up. He was frowning slightly. "I know."

Was he worried that something would go wrong? she wondered. Probably afraid she'd bring another suit against him if it did. "Don't you have a shower in that white-walled palace of yours?" she asked.

Her reference to his trailer brought back his smile. "Yes, I do," he acknowledged, continuing to lather himself. "But it's not working right. I'm going to have to get someone out to look at it," he told her. "I live in mortal fear of having the air-conditioning go out on me," he confided with a wink.

"Wouldn't want to see you enduring the elements like the rest of us," she murmured with a touch of sarcasm.

"You're welcomed to share my trailer anytime you

want," he said. His grin spread. "Anytime." He turned his back to her for a moment. "Do my back?" he asked.

Chyna stared at the bar of soap he held aloft for her. Not on your life, fella, she thought, making absolutely no move toward him. "Sorry," she quipped. "I don't do windows, or producers."

He shrugged good-naturedly as he turned back around. "My sweat-stained back is on your conscience," he said.

She nodded her head solemnly. "I'll try to live with it," she promised.

Matt returned the soap to its perch and angled his body beneath the showerhead, letting the fine mist dowse him. Chyna watched the water swirl around his feet, taking the white lather with it. She realized that he was watching her watching him, and a blush stung her cheeks as she raised her eyes back to his face.

Matt pulled his towel off the side partition and began drying himself off. "Sure I can't interest you in sharing these facilities with me?" he asked. "They say sharing helps you learn a lot about the other person."

"And what is it you'd want to learn about me?" she asked, knowing that her words sounded coy. Let him think she was playing along—at least for the moment.

"Well," he said brightly, rubbing the towel over his damp dark-blond hair, "I've already learned that you favor short nightgowns," he said, eyeing her. "And so do I—at least on you."

She had forgotten all about the fact that she was standing there in her pajamas. She tilted her head up, like a warrior in battle, refusing to retreat. "Would you mind hurrying up? I'd like to take my shower— alone," she emphasized.

"Your wish is my command," he said, beginning to swing the door open.

Quickly she turned her back. "I'll let you put your clothes on in private," she told him, not knowing exactly what he had in mind. This teasing, bantering Matt Harrigan was totally different from the man who had kissed her on the beach, the man who had apologized for taking advantage. The only thing that remained the same was the undercurrent of sensuality. He was an utter puzzle to her.

"Very decent of you."

Was that a touch of mockery in his voice? "One of us has to be," she retorted. Open mouth, insert foot, she thought. Oh, well, maybe her answer would put him off enough to make it clear that she wasn't interested in any games, and that she wasn't going to be bowled over by a naked, dripping man, even if he was gorgeous. Which he was. Very. Enough, Chyna, enough. You're reacting just the way he wants you to. Just the way he promised Dussault you would.

That did the trick immediately. Suddenly she was sane again.

She found herself growing impatient. He was taking too long. The silence mocked her, daring her to turn around. But she stayed where she was, studying the dull brown tent flap and trying not to let the fact that she was in close proximity to a compellingly handsome, naked man undo her.

Finally Chyna cleared her throat. "Are you finished yet?"

"That's a matter of opinion," Matt said. His voice

sounded almost too seductive for words. "I could say that I haven't even begun yet."

"Mr. Harrigan," Chyna said, "I—"

"Considering the circumstances, I think you could call me Matt."

"The circumstances would be a whole lot better if you got your clothes on," she said, hoping that she sounded sufficiently irritated. It was getting hard carrying on this conversation with a tent flap.

"That too is a matter of opinion," he said.

He was directly behind her. The scent of soap, mixed with his own very masculine essence, came wafting through the heavy air, filling her senses. The next thing she knew, his hands were on her shoulders.

Six

He turned her around slowly. "Your shower awaits, milady," he said grandly. There was a twinkle in his eyes.

For an instant she let her eyes roam over his well-developed chest. A few drops of water still clung to the fine layer of hair, glistening in the dim artificial light. Producers weren't supposed to look so enticing. Chyna took a deep breath. "Thank you," she said tersely. "Now, if you'll excuse me," she went on, using the most impersonal voice she could muster, considering the situation, "I'd like to take my shower before this area becomes the center of a crowd scene."

She saw that he was letting his gaze wander over her barely hidden curves. With a touch of satisfied pride she could tell that he liked what he saw. Pride? she thought, suddenly coming to. Chyna, get hold of yourself. It's three in the morning and you're standing in your pajamas in front of a very unsettling man.

"You're not moving," she pointed out. Wasn't he ever going to go? "You can't stay here while I take my shower," she insisted.

"I'm the producer," he told her. "I can stay anywhere I want."

He was having fun at her expense. Well, two could play that game, she thought. "Fine," she declared, turning away and heading toward the tent flap. "If anyone wants you, I'll tell them you're guarding the shower—which you wouldn't have to do if you had told the grips to build a separate one for the women."

Strong fingers clamped around her wrist, preventing her departure. Chyna turned to face him and saw that his expression was still mild, amused. "Then we would have missed this little encounter. Tell me, do you always get angry so quickly?"

"Only when I'm hot and gritty—and someone decides to withhold my water," she said, lifting her chin. He had made her lose her temper, and that made her even more annoyed. Usually she was extremely even tempered, but this weather was enough to drive anybody crazy. And now she had this half-nude producer bent on her seduction—or whatever.

Matt walked back over to the first stall and flipped on the faucet. "Your water," he said with a sweep of his hand. And then he walked out of the tent, shaking his head. "My father told me that if I became a producer, I could have anything I wanted...."

Chyna stared at the tent flap even after it had fallen back into place. She thought she had detected a self-mocking tone in his words, but she wasn't sure. All she was sure of was the word "want." She told her-

self again that it was all an act, all a silly little plan
to make her fall for him and keep her mind off watching Dussault. But there was an excitement building
within her that wasn't listening to any words. None
of hers, at any rate. It was feeding on the uncontrolled
tingling sensations that kept springing up each time
she was near Matt.

"You're probably allergic to him," she muttered
vehemently. In her extreme frustration, she said the
words aloud.

"I certainly hope not."

Chyna dropped her bar of soap as his voice came
floating through from the other side of the makeshift
tent.

She took the rest of her quick shower in utter silence.

Rubbing furiously, she tried to dry herself off. All
she succeeded in doing was getting rid of the heaviest
layer of water. The tropical humidity insisted on leaving a fine blanket of moisture on her skin. Chyna
struggled into the clothes she had brought with her.
The shorts refused to slide up her damp legs, sticking
to her skin every inch of the way.

"Damn this weather," she muttered impatiently,
then realized that the weather wasn't completely responsible for the way she was feeling. Hurriedly she
buttoned her blouse, only to look down and realize
that she had misaligned the buttons with the holes.
"Terrific. I'm supposed to do a death-defying leap
today and I can't even dress myself."

She half expected to hear Matt's voice offering to
do the job for her. When only silence met her comment, Chyna decided that he had tired of the game
and had gone back to the comforts of his trailer. So

when she hurried out of the tent and he stepped out of the shadows, she gasped and jumped back, nearly tripping on a large root.

He reached out in time to steady her. "I thought stuntpeople had nerves of steel," he commented.

"We do," she informed him, trying to shrug away his hands. She had no luck. "When it comes to our own stunts. As for Peeping Toms who leap out of the shadows..."

He laughed. "I'm a listening Tom, not a peeping one," he corrected. "And I'd hardly call stepping forward 'leaping.'"

Pulling back, Chyna managed to disentangle herself from his hold. "I don't have time to play word games with you," she said, trying to move past him.

She never made it. "What kind of games do you have time for?" he asked, his voice as low and lush as the dark green foliage surrounding them.

"The ones I get paid for—on the set," she added before he had any time to comment on *that*. "I thought producers were supposed to be busy people," she said impatiently.

"We are," he agreed. From the look in his eyes, it was obvious to Chyna that his mind definitely wasn't on the conversation.

"So what are you doing skulking around the showers at three in the morning?" she demanded.

"Waiting for you."

The words vibrated along her skin, raising the tiny hairs along her arm. Still, she tried to keep up the fight. "Why?" There, she had put him on the spot. Or so she hoped.

"Women who talk to themselves fascinate me," he teased.

He was undressing her with his eyes. She could feel it. It made her want to clutch at her clothes. Dummy, he's getting to you. And he was, damn him.

"Do you always talk to yourself?" he asked.

She lifted her chin slightly. "On occasion."

"What kind of occasion?" he prodded.

"On the occasions when sorting things out in my head doesn't quite do the trick," she said curtly. She wished he'd stop probing her this way.

The broad hint wasn't taken.

"So, I'm in your head now, am I?" he asked. Satisfaction was etched into every part of his handsome face.

This wasn't working out right at all. "Why shouldn't you be?" she asked, annoyed. She had walked right into this one. Now she'd have to get herself out. "You're the producer."

His eyes sparkled. He wasn't about to let her off the hook yet. "And do you always think about your producer when you're taking a shower?" The sensuous look in his eyes as they traced the path the water might have taken down her body made her hot despite all her attempts to dismiss his words as just so much empty banter.

Still, she managed to keep the fact that her pulse was racing a secret. "No," she told him, "this is a first. None of my other producers ever stood naked in front of me in a shower stall."

She had hoped to make him feel silly. He didn't. Not if that deep smile on his face was any indication of what was going on inside his head. "I'm glad," he murmured. Round two belonged to him.

Chyna breathed in deeply to buy herself some time. A lungful of stifling air didn't help the situation any.

"I've got my stunt to think about today," she announced, trying to get by him again. But as she moved he extended his arm, leaning it against the palm tree to her left. When she turned back his other arm went up, trapping her against the tree. And him. For a moment he looked very serious. And then, quickly, the look was gone.

"You smell good," he observed, lowering his head slightly and letting her wayward golden-brown hair caress his cheek.

"A shower can do wonders," she quipped, struggling not to give in to the sensuous feelings that were starting up in her again. Leave me alone, Matt Harrigan. I need an uncomplicated life. I don't need you in it, not like this. I know what you're up to.

All the logical thoughts in the world couldn't save her.

"No," Matt said softly, dropping the bars of her prison and slipping them around her instead. She felt more trapped than ever. "I think you have a natural perfume about you." The words were said against her neck. Wonderful sensations took wing as his breath stroked her skin. Chyna drew in another lungful of air. It did absolutely no good. She was quickly becoming intoxicated. But she tried again.

Matt looked at her, curious. "Careful," he warned, a smile tugging at the corners of his mouth. "You'll hyperventilate, and I'll have to resort to C.P.R."

Chyna felt her heart hammering against her chest. Here was the famous stuntwoman who leaped over exploding gasoline tanks getting weak-kneed because a man was holding her, she thought cryptically. "You don't give C.P.R. to a person who's hyperventilating," she informed him, her voice husky.

She saw his eyes sweep over the provocative swell of her breasts beneath the half-opened blouse. "I take my opportunities when they come up," he said.

As he spoke, she felt his hands go to either side of her waist, tunneling beneath her open shirttails. His fingers fanned out against her skin. She couldn't move, and her mind went blank. All she could do was watch his eyes. They were like liquid fire, shimmering in the faint rays of dawn. The slow, mesmerizing trail forged by his hands as they traveled upward, stretching, touching, tantalized her. She ached for more.

Chyna could feel her nipples hardening, peaking against the soft material of her bra as they yearned for the touch of a man. This man.

She was crazy. There was no other explanation for this moonlight madness on her part.

"Is there a full moon out?" she asked, her voice nearly lost in the recesses of her growing desire.

"No," he answered without looking up. "In fact, I think the sun's about to come up."

A fraction of a second later the tips of his fingers secured the crests of her breasts, and she gasped in response.

She was a full grown woman who had had a loving, satisfying relationship in her life. So why was the touch of a man who was almost a stranger reducing her to a quivering adolescent? she argued with herself. This had never happened to her before. It shouldn't be happening now, not with a man who was using his sensuality as a weapon to hold her in line. Skin touching skin, that's all it is, she told herself fiercely. But somehow her body wasn't getting the message. It was lost in the message that he was transmitting as his hands cupped her breasts.

It was an extreme effort for her not to gasp as she felt his hands close over her breasts, but she managed to keep silent. What she couldn't control was the look that came over her face as it softened. She was losing the fight, feeling herself slip into the vast, beguiling ocean of passion that was beckoning to her. Its waves lapped at her from all sides.

With slow, deliberate strokes Matt gently massaged her breasts, still leaving them within the cups of her bra. It was as if he were in no hurry, as if he were savoring this as much as she was. He kissed the side of her neck, igniting another rush of desire within her.

This wasn't going to lead to anything except problems, Chyna thought desperately as she tried to break free of the gossamer web of passion that was entangling her. Dragging out her last shred of self-discipline, Chyna pressed her hands against his chest, intent on pushing him back. What she felt stopped her for a moment. Beneath the tips of her fingers she felt the erratic beating of his heart.

It's all a sham, she insisted. He's trained his heart to skip at will. Get away. Now!

Swallowing, Chyna pushed him back to arm's length. "You need a shave," she observed, trying to sound unaffected as she spoke.

"That's not all I need," he whispered, but he didn't try to recapture her in his arms, much to her relief.

"Well, I don't know what else *you* need," Chyna said, avoiding his eyes, "but *I* need to get in a little more practice today if I'm going to pull off that stunt." She began to walk away, but her movements were slow, as if part of her was waiting for him to stop her.

"Chyna?" It was his voice that stopped her. There was something oddly serious about the tone.

"Yes?"

"Be careful." It wasn't an impersonal command. It almost sounded like a plea.

She gave him one more minute before she hurried away. "I always am," she assured him. "Don't worry, Mr. Harrigan. I won't sue if something goes wrong. I intend to check over all the equipment myself. If something happens, it'll be my fault. Besides, if it does, I won't be around to sue," she said cheerfully for what she assumed was his benefit.

To her surprise he didn't return her smile. His expression had turned solemn. "I know that."

His intonation puzzled her all the way back to her shack.

"A hundred and twenty in the shade and we're going to be lighting gasoline tanks," one grip muttered to another as they went about the task of setting up the shot. It had already been postponed twice that day because of unexpectedly capricious wind shifts that affected all Chyna's carefully thought-out calculations.

From where she stood on the mountain, she could see Dussault pacing impatiently. "Happy" was not a word that had applied when the stunt coordinator had gone to him the first time to say that Chyna wasn't going to attempt the gag until the winds died down. The second time the message was delivered, Dussault had looked as if he had murder on his mind.

That was okay, Chyna thought now. If he was in such an all-fired hurry, *he* could put on a dress and attempt the jump. She wasn't going to do it until everything was just right. She wanted to live to collect her twenty thousand dollars.

Chyna watched, almost unseeing, as the director turned toward the continuity girl and demanded to know if everything in the upcoming shot coordinated with the previous one. The bespectacled older woman nervously went over the checklist on her clipboard and nodded affirmatively.

Dussault turned toward Chyna again. Holding a megaphone to his mouth, he yelled. "Well?"

Chyna looked around. All was still. Cupping her hands around her mouth, she yelled back, "I'm ready."

Dussault dropped his megaphone to the ground and pretended to applaud her. Even from a distance, she couldn't miss his sarcastic intent.

"You mean she's finally ready?"

Chyna turned behind her to look at Sally, who was seated beneath a canopy, fanning herself. She had been sitting there for the better part of two hours, growing increasingly irritated. She was wearing an outfit that was identical to Chyna's. Even the strategically torn parts matched.

"Yes," Chyna answered crisply, "'she's' ready." She watched the makeup artist spring to life as he began to retouch Sally's makeup, restoring what nature had attempted to destroy with humidity.

"Well, it's about time," Sally said loudly as she shrugged the makeup man aside and moved to the top of the mountain.

Cameras closed in from all angles, recording Sally's touchingly heroic expression just before "she" leaped off the peak.

"Cut!" the assistant director cried. "Wonderful, Sally, wonderful," he enthused, stepping forward and taking the woman's hands in his.

Sure, Chyna thought humorously. Wonderful. All Sally had to do was stand at the top of the mountain. Standing wasn't very hard to do, even for Sally.

"Chyna?" the assistant called, looking over his shoulder toward where she was standing.

Chyna braced herself. Here goes nothing, she thought as she stepped up to the mark that Sally had just toed.

"Ready?" the assistant asked.

For a moment Chyna stood perfectly still, waiting for that inner signal she had come to rely on, the one that told her that it was all right. Yes, everything was ready. She gave a quick nod.

"Ready," she declared.

Out of the corner of her eye she saw the assistant director signal the ground crew below. She heard Dussault roar. "She's finally gonna do it! Roll 'em!"

It had begun.

Earlier, duplicate gasoline tanks had been filmed as they exploded. That was for use with Sally's close-ups. Merging the two shots would be a job for the film editor. Right now, new tanks were exploding, shooting flames in all different directions. Long, bright yellow fingers clawed their way up out of the inferno.

Poetry later, Chyna, she told herself. Jump now. With discipline that had taken her a long time to acquire, Chyna checked out everything in a matter of moments. Concentrating on nothing but hitting that vital spring ramp, she blindly looked over her shoulder at the Nazis who were supposedly chasing the heroine, and took a running leap.

Now!

The pit of her stomach leaped up to meet her throat as she sailed down, totally free, totally unhampered. The intensity of the heat rising up from the exploding tanks was tremendous. She came so close to the flames as she sailed by that as she felt her cheeks burning. The reassuring feeling of the spring ramp beneath her feet was one of the most fantastic things she had ever experienced. She came down with such force that she was catapulted back up and over onto the huge air mattress that was waiting to catch her.

A noise that she thought sounded something like "omffp!" came out of her as she sank into the air mattress. She resurfaced only to hear cries of, "Get that damned fire extinguisher!"

The fact that it was Matt's voice registered with her at the same time that she realized she was still the center of a commotion. One bright flame told her why.

She was on fire!

Two seconds later her legs were stinging, surrounded by the cloud of carbon dioxide that came shooting out of the extinguisher. Her dress had caught fire as she had sailed over the flames, but beyond consuming the bottom half of her outfit, the fire had done no damage.

"Did you get it?" she called out the head cameraman, searching him out in the crowd. She certainly didn't want to do that over again.

He gave her the high sign, looking as pleased with the shot as if he had done the jump himself.

Suddenly Chyna felt herself being scooped up by

a pair of strong arms, and she saw the look of mingled concern and relief on Matt's face.

Chyna was aware of the fact that she was sooty, bedraggled, and had definitely been more attractive in the past. "We've got to stop meeting like this," she cracked, breaking the tension for everyone.

"Back to work," Dussault bellowed without so much as one complimentary word tossed in Chyna's direction.

"You're welcome," she muttered audibly.

The bald man shot her an annoyed look. "Thank you," Dussault said sarcastically. "Thank you for earning your pay." He turned his back to her as a new detail took his attention. Chyna looked at Matt to see if Dussault's abrasive behavior had registered with him.

For the moment Matt wasn't interested in Dussault. "Can you walk?" he asked her, still holding her in his arms.

"You ask this of a woman who can fly off mountaintops?" she laughed. "Of course I can walk."

But he didn't set her down. Instead he attempted to walk over to the edge of the mattress so he could hand her down to someone else. All that happened was that he began to totter, and then they both fell onto the air mattress, with Matt landing on top of her.

Despite the fact that she had now disintegrated into peals of laughter over his failed gallantry, Chyna was more than a little aware of the firm imprint his body made on hers.

"Why, Mr. Producer, this is so sudden," she gasped mockingly, placing her hand to her forehead. Laughter punctuated every word.

"Not sudden enough," he said, and the look in his eyes made the laughter die in her throat.

"Need any help, Mr. Harrigan?" the stunt coordinator asked.

Matt's eyes didn't leave Chyna's face. "That remains to be seen," he said quietly, his words for her benefit alone. Before she could make any sort of retort, Matt rolled off her and climbed to the ground. Chyna was prepared to jump down unaided. But as she sailed off the seven foot mattress, Matt caught her in his arms.

"This is getting to be a habit," Chyna observed. She couldn't help smiling. The exhilaration of successfully completing a more than usually dangerous gag was still with her. Everything was perfect. The whole world was perfect, even Dussault and his perpetual frown.

"I certainly hope so," Matt said, but the words didn't sound as glib as she had thought they would, despite the fact that there were several people milling around.

"Are you all right, Mr. Harrigan?" Alex asked solicitously.

Matt looked at him with a touch of amusement. "Why shouldn't I be all right? I just climbed up on the air mattress. She's the one who caught fire," he pointed out, setting Chyna down.

The stunt coordinator grinned. "Great gag, Chyna," he said, clapping her on the back.

As if a signal had gone off, the other stuntworkers all approached, gathering around Chyna. Their voices mingled in hearty congratulation. She barely heard what they were saying; she was trying to keep track of Matt as the crowd grew larger. Their eyes met and held for a long moment, and Chyna was the first to break the contact.

"Well, I've got to get out of this lovely outfit and into a long, cool drink," Chyna said, making her way through the center of the crowd.

"The food trucks are having another refrigeration crisis," Pepper told her, striking a death knell over her hopes of refreshment.

"Aren't we all?" Chyna sighed. She wiped away a bead of perspiration that had followed a zigzag pattern from her temple down her cheek.

"My refrigeration's working," Matt offered.

And so is everything else that belongs to you, Chyna thought. Which is why I'm staying clear of you.

"No," Chyna said, shaking her head as the others went on about their work, leaving them standing alone. "I've decided to opt for just a shower."

"Need any help?" he asked, and then he smiled before she could answer. "No, I guess not. Anyone as capable as you are doesn't need any help."

Was she mistaken, or was there a hint of admiration in his voice?

"No," she heard herself murmur. "I don't need any help." With that she walked away, but she felt him watching her every step.

Seven

It was all well and good to tell herself that she wouldn't fall into his trap when she wasn't around him. But one look into his shimmering green eyes and she felt herself losing ground. So the most sensible thing, Chyna decided, was to stay far away from Matt.

That, however, proved to be impossible.

The next day's shooting schedule involved another gag, one she had nothing to do with, but she watched nonetheless. What she saw was a near-fatal accident involving a runaway car and a cameraman positioned too close to the scene for his own safety. During the commotion that followed the incident, Chyna turned toward Alex. He read her mind instantly.

"Nothing happened, Chyna," he said between gritted teeth.

This time, she thought angrily, watching him placate the head cameraman. The loud hum of mingled voices began to subside as Chyna walked away from the scene. Alex would never stand up for them, she thought, the fact bothering her twice as much because of their past friendship. She stopped walking for a moment, looking in the direction of Matt's trailer. He had told her to come to him with her grievances. She had felt at the time that he was only trying to mollify her, and nothing had happened to change her mind. But it was worth a shot. She had nothing to lose.

Her palms began to sweat as she raised her hand to knock on his door.

"C'mon in," she heard Matt call out. "The door's open."

He didn't sound very friendly, she thought. As a matter of fact, he sounded rather tired. This probably wasn't going to be the best time to approach him with a problem. But then, when would? She pulled back her shoulders and walked in.

She found him sitting bare chested at the desk, scowling. He didn't look up at first. Something was bothering him, and she couldn't help wondering what.

When he didn't hear anything, Matt looked up and saw Chyna studying him. He looked mildly surprised to see her. "To what do I owe this pleasure?" he asked. "Need another shirt?"

His scowl faded into a rather sad expression, even though he smiled at her, and Chyna felt something tug at her heart. As she moved forward she realized that he was holding his daughter's picture.

"Something wrong?" she felt compelled to ask.

A bemused smile met her question. "You came in to find out if something was wrong? I didn't know I frowned so loudly."

"Certain noises carry out here," she answered

drolly. "Dussault's scowls make the trees shake. He…" But she let her voice slip away for a moment. Suddenly she didn't want to talk about Dussault. Not just now. Something was bothering Matt, and she wanted to know what it was. In that moment Chyna realized that Matt *had* succeeded in at least part of his plan to keep her quiet. She was intimately involved with him despite the fact that they had done little more than kiss. There was something about him that stirred her, and it wasn't just physical. Maybe it had something to do with the fact that he had been the first at her side when she had caught fire. Whatever it was, she knew she cared about him, cared about what made him unhappy. She was going to have to watch her step to make sure that he didn't use her feelings against her.

Leaning across the desk, Chyna nodded toward the picture. "Is it about your daughter?" she pressed.

His eyes shifted from her face down to the photograph he was holding. He put it back in its place. "It's her birthday," he told Chyna.

"And you forgot it," she said. Typical man, she thought affectionately. Still, he did look disappointed.

"No, it's next week," he answered.

"Oh." She was at a loss as to why he looked so crestfallen. "Didn't you expect her to have one this year?" she asked, seeking recourse in a lighter tone.

"Not without me," he replied, his voice just the slightest bit annoyed.

She felt another tug at her heart as she realized that being separated from his daughter really bothered him. It made him seem more real to her, more human. She felt herself losing even more ground.

"Always been with her before?" she asked softly.

Just like her own father, she thought, when she was younger. He had always been there for her.

"Always," he answered, trying to sound brisk.

"Then why don't you fly out?" she urged. It seemed a simple enough solution, she thought.

But he shook his head. "Can't," he told her, pushing back his chair and getting up. He sighed. "I'm needed here. There's too much to do."

"That's what assistants are for," she pointed out.

"I did that once," he told her. He leveled his gaze at her face. "I think you'll remember the name of the picture."

He was talking about Neil's picture, she suddenly realized. Was he trying to explain away his part in it? Or make her believe that it had all been a mistake? She knew that. She knew he hadn't willfully tried to cause anyone an injury—or worse. Negligence was all she had ever charged him with. She tried to interpret the somber expression in his eyes. Did he feel responsible for the accident? Chyna pushed the thought away, not wanting to go over the past anymore.

She cleared her throat. "I wanted to talk to you about Dussault..." she began. And I wish you'd stop standing so close to me, she added silently. But she made no effort to back away herself.

"What about him?" he asked patiently.

"He's displaying a flagrant disregard for people's safety. This morning I saw a cameraman practically mowed down by an out-of-control car. If Dussault hadn't been so anxious to get the shot in one take, he would have let the man stand in a safer spot." *She* should be standing in a safer spot, she told herself, her thoughts drifting from the subject at hand. Being so close to him made her want him, made her long for things that had absolutely no place in this discussion. Her next words were said in a rush as she tried to beat back her feelings. "We also need a new insert car."

Her statement threw him. "What's wrong with the old one?" he asked evenly.

"Nothing, if you like having death as your co-pilot," she answered. "Dussault has them driving that thing at breakneck speed, and its center of gravity is far too high. I saw them careening around in it this morning. One of these days it's going to flip over when it's making a turn." The sobering words helped her quell some of the fire she felt inside. "There's a new prototype out," she went on. "It has every safety feature imaginable. Most insert cars are just stripped down pickups with some equipment loaded on. That's fine if you're a gardener on your way to mulch a lawn. It's not too terrific when you're practically flying around, trying to capture a wild chase scene."

He considered her words for a moment, but then he shook his head and her hopes dimmed. "Do you have any idea how much a new insert car would cost?" he asked her.

"A lot less than a man's life," she answered firmly. "Can you stand to have two lives on your conscience?" she asked, the words pouring out before she could stop them. Instantly she was sorry.

She saw the muscles of his jawline tighten slightly, and knew then that she had hit below the belt. He *did* feel responsible for what had happened. Whatever else he was doing now by trying to keep her away from Dussault, he did hold himself responsible for what had happened to Neil.

"I'm sorry," she said, her voice dropping.

"So am I," he told her. "I'll see what I can do."

With his softened words, the scene had turned intimate; something was pulling her toward him. This was just what he wanted, she thought. And yes, it was just what she wanted, too, heaven help her. She felt so drawn to him that it was almost painful.

"Well, that solves my problem," she said, her voice sounding stilted as she tried vainly to curtail the emotions she felt. "Now, what about yours?" she prodded.

His eyes made her think of a green flame. "I'm looking at it," he whispered, bending his head toward her.

If he kissed her now, she would be done for. As he put his arms around her shoulders, she pressed her hands against his chest. She meant to block his move. Instead she curled her hands around the sensuous, hard lines formed by his pectorals. The lure of his body grew.

'No," she said, her voice increasingly unsteady. "I meant your daughter."

He kissed her hair. "What about her?"

"If you can't go there, why don't you fly her out here for her birthday?" Chyna urged, her senses beginning to spin. Fine stuntwoman you are, she thought, getting dizzy just standing still.

Matt rolled the idea over in his mind. "Here?" he echoed, holding her back as he looked down into her face.

"Here," she repeated. His surprised expression amused her a little. "Have you been suffering from this hearing deficiency long?"

"I've been suffering from a lot of things since you

turned up," he told her softly, the words caressing her. "But I can't fly Meredith out here. She's only five—"

"She won't have to fly the plane, just sit in it," Chyna teased, feeling very close to him, emotionally as well as physically. She turned serious for a moment, setting aside her flippant humor as she thought of the girl in the picture. "Have someone come out with her. She'll appreciate the fact that her daddy thought enough of her to send for her. Nothing's worse than spending your birthday with strangers, no matter how well they're paid to take care of you." She put her hand on his arm. "You're going to be a busy man for the rest of your life," she pointed out, wondering how she was managing to make intelligent conversation when her insides had been reduced to the consistency of cotton candy. "You don't want Meredith to look at you in eighteen years and say, 'Hi, Stranger,' when you walk through the door, right?"

"Good point," he conceded. The space that existed between them shrank to nothing as he pulled her close again. "I've been noticing lately that you have a lot of good points," he murmured, his lips finally covering hers.

There was no way she was leaving. She knew that. He had successfully broken down every single defense at her disposal. She wanted him. Whatever his motives, whatever his reasons for bringing her to this moment, she wanted him. Every fiber in her body cried out for fulfillment. Being so close to him, having his body move lightly against hers, was sheer torture.

But some shred of pride forced her to at least try

to make an excuse, to try to leave just one more time. When his lips temporarily moved to assault her neck, Chyna said breathily, "I've got…to…practice…"

She felt his hands beneath her bustline, tenderly caressing the aching fullness of her breasts. His strokes echoed the rhythm of her breathing.

"You don't need any practice," he whispered, the words curling into the hollow of her throat just as his lips touched her. "I have a feeling you're letter perfect."

Slowly he encircled her throat with a ring of burning kisses. She was vaguely aware of the fact that he was now behind her, taking possession of the base of her neck. An army of throbbing sensation marched up and down her spine in answer to the machinations of his tongue.

"This tie is getting in my way," Chyna heard him say, half-teasing, half-serious.

"How…do you…generally…deal with…something that…gets in…your…way?" she asked haltingly, delicious sensations racing through her body.

"Usually," he said, his words hot against her neck, "I try to reason with it."

Or seduce it, she thought, receding into a misty haze. There was no turning back. No lifeline to grasp. She knew she wouldn't clutch at it even if one existed.

"But I don't think reason has any place here," he was saying. His words were separated by tiny, butterflylike kisses that captured her soul as soon as they touched her neck.

So, you're seducing it, just like you're seducing me, she thought, her eyelids getting heavy. She closed her eyes, savoring every scrap of emotion that she was experiencing. She was struck by the wonder of it. Fire and passion mingled in her veins, though so little had actually happened. What kind of an effect did this man have on her? Her head continued to spin.

The kisses stopped, and she felt the tie that held secure her halter top loosen. From the feel of his breath along the slope of her neck, he was undoing the tie with his teeth. She tried to stop a shiver from going through her at the same time that she felt her knees begin to weaken.

Chyna felt the front of her pink halter top begin to sag, but still he didn't turn her around. Instead Matt just held her against his chest, massaging her breasts and gently rubbing the palms of his hands against her nipples. Erratic signals made their way to her brain, foretelling both ecstasy and danger. She chose to ignore the second message. She had no choice, actually. All this had been preordained. She could feel it. It was almost as if her body were on automatic pilot. But he couldn't think that it was going to be so easy, her mind pleaded.

"Matt, I…don't think…"

"Good," he said, his lips meeting the rounded edge of her shoulder. It began to glow with his warmth. "Thinking's bad for you. Bad for us."

"Us?" she breathed. How could one word sound so lovely? Especially when she knew it wasn't true.

Matt turned her around. As he did so the fabric of her top slipped down further, hanging precariously across the hardened peaks of her nipples, displaying the swell of her breasts to his hungry gaze.

She saw the look in his eyes and feasted on it. It nurtured her own smoldering desire.

"Us," he repeated. "That signifies the presence of more than one person in a situation."

"Is that what this is?" she asked, her throat incredibly dry. This time she couldn't blame it on the weather. The air-conditioning in the room was giving her goose bumps. Who was she kidding? He was giving her goose bumps.

Slowly he ran his finger along her lips. "What?"

"A situation," she repeated.

"I certainly hope so."

Pressing his hand against the curve of her waist, he tugged on her top until it fell to her waist like the flag of a defeated country.

"Beautiful," he said, drinking in the sight before him.

Chyna was tempted to cover her breasts, but he was there before her, cupping them like long-sought-for treasures that had finally been attained. Chills ran all through her, clearing the way for another wave of molten fire. She had to press her lips together to keep a moan from escaping.

"I have to…go." But her body gave the lie to her words as she arched herself against his touch. His hands were stroking her, raising the fever within her higher and higher.

He lowered his head. Warm lips touched silken flesh. This time, the moan did escape. "No," he murmured, "you don't *have* to do anything." Raising his head again, he tilted hers back until their eyes met. "Not even stay here."

First he drove her out of her mind, then he told her that she was free to go. Free? She was no more free to walk away than a deep sea diver was free to strip himself of his oxygen tanks and swim away. Right now, he was her lifeline. What he had to offer her was more dear than the very air she breathed.

"You're making this very difficult," she complained, some of her senses returning to her—but diminishing none of her passion. "How can I tell myself you seduced me if you're giving me a way out?"

The smile she received made her heart beat faster with joy. Taking her face between his hands, Matt kissed her almost fiercely. She tasted all the passion, all the desire, that the smile had hidden from her. He wanted her. He wanted her as much as she wanted him. The realization increased the intense excitement she felt.

"We'll come up with some excuse for your conscience later," he promised, his smile answering the one that was growing on her own lips.

"Are you very good at excuses?" she asked as he picked her up in his arms. She put one of her own arms around his neck, cradling herself against the warmth of his chest. What excuse would he give her later? After this interlude was over and he wanted to go back to life as usual...back to business as usual.

"Yes," he answered honestly, carrying her into his tiny bedroom. From her vantage point, it looked like all bed and nothing else. But that was what she wanted right now—an endless bed where she could give herself up to the pleasures of loving him. "But I'm better at other things," he told her. It was a whispered promise.

She felt his velveteen bedspread against her bare back. It felt sultry, like his voice. She saw nothing but him as he filled the room with his presence. The yearning within her feathered out to every corner of her being. "What things?" she asked, her voice low.

He came to her on the bed, the length of his body touching hers. "Has anyone ever told you that you talk too much?" he asked, his hands tracing the valleys of her seminude body.

"Yes."

"Good, then it's not just me."

"Yes, it is," Chyna whispered, knowing her voice would crack if she spoke any louder. "Just you." He was making everything within her vibrate, playing her like a fine musical instrument, producing a melody from within her that she had never known herself capable of. The fierceness of her desire both surprised and excited her.

Matt seemed to understand the meaning behind her simple words and he pulled her to him, his eyes burning into hers. She saw the incredible amount of controlled hunger there, and her breathing became shallow even before his lips met hers. Over and over again, his mouth slanted against her, draining her of her very essence, taking everything from her and yet giving her something wonderful back in return. She felt more alive, more exhilarated, than she ever had before. It was as if she were building up to the longest chuteless jump of her career. His kisses had the same dizzying effect. They created the same whirling anticipation in her stomach.

Vaguely the fact that there was material sliding down along her thigh penetrated her consciousness.

"Lift, please." The sensual command caressed her ear.

"Hmm?"

"I'm trying to undress you," Matt said. "I need a little help."

Chyna opened her eyes, trying to pull the world

into focus. He was the only thing she could focus on. She raised her hips slightly.

"Like I said when I met you," she breathed. "I don't make waves."

"Oh, but you have. You have," he told her. His voice sounded tight, as if he were struggling not to reveal the emotions that were building inside him.

With long, caressing motions, he removed her white shorts and the tiny bit of lace that served as her underwear. She heard his sharp intake of breath.

Hold me. Love me, she wanted to cry out. But the words stuck in her throat as she watched him watching her. He was a portrait of restraint, and she was fast becoming a quivering mess. She wasn't sure if she could bear his sweeping touch any longer. There was just so much stoking that a fire could take before it rampaged out of control.

"Are you always this slow?" she murmured, trying to keep from sounding impatient.

"Thorough," he corrected. "The word is thorough. I want to savor every bit of you." But as he began to kiss her again, Chyna forced him back. If he was going to tantalize her, then she was going to give him back as good as she got.

"If you're so 'thorough,' how come you forgot to take off your own clothes?" she asked.

She saw the twinkle enter his eyes. "Why don't you do the honors?" he suggested. His teasing tone was back, even though she felt his heart hammering against her hand, which still rested on his chest.

She cocked her head, her hair fanning out against his pillow. "Is that a dare?"

He knew he had her then. "Can't resist one, can you?" he asked, rolling onto his back. He laced his fingers together beneath his head and watched her face, waiting.

He was right. More than that, she couldn't resist him. She wanted to shred the barriers between them with eager hands. Instead, she sat up and rocked back on her heels, slowly taking his belt into her hand and uncinching it. A gleam came into his eyes as she released the catch at the top of his trousers. Watching his face for every talltale nuance, Chyna slowly drew the zipper down. She felt him move against her ever so slightly as a flush came into his cheeks. Good. Let him feel what she was feeling. Let him burn the way she was burning.

"Don't stop now," he urged thickly when she paused. "You're coming to the best part."

"For whom?" she asked, wishing she didn't sound so breathless, wishing she could look as controlled as he did.

"For both of us," he answered.

He took her hands and placed them on either side of his muscular hips. Bracing his feet against the bed, he raised himself just enough for Chyna to finish what she had started. She didn't even see or hear the trousers hit the floor. She was too busy reveling in the new emotions that flooded through her as Matt pressed her hand against his hot flesh.

"One more article," he whispered.

Her bold mood left, but it was too late for her to back down, too late to run for cover.

They shed the last barrier together. She didn't even know if his hands were guiding hers, or if she had taken the lead again.

"Come here, Chyna," he called softly, opening his arms to her.

Gone was the woman who had wanted him to come to her. Gone was the woman who had wanted to teach him a lesson. She had been replaced by a woman who only wanted to be loved. Loved by this man alone. Later there would be time enough to worry about the consequences of her actions. Later she would plot a way out of her dilemma and make him love her. Right now was the time to abandon herself to the ecstasy that beckoned.

She felt his hands on her hips as he pulled her toward him, pressing her flesh against his. The fire roared, spreading its magic through her veins, igniting every part of her. This time there was no safety crew around to put it out. This was the most dangerous stunt of her career.

And she loved it.

Eight

She had no power to stop what was happening, nor any desire to. What she was feeling had the momentum of a jet and it was whisking her away into heaven, a heaven she had never dreamed of before.

When Matt shifted his weight and entered her, it was the most divine sensation she had ever experienced. As the depth of his kisses increased, Chyna closed her eyes and wound her fingers into his thick hair, wanting to pull him closer to her, wanting to absorb every sparkling emotion that he was awakening within her. Wanting to absorb him. Forever.

Dear Lord, did it happen like this? Did love just burst upon you? The only other time she had fallen in love it had happened gradually, like the long-awaited blooming of a spring flower, not like an exploding gasoline tank. Yet here it was, exploding all around her, engulfing her. And she couldn't do a thing about it.

She couldn't even think anymore, only feel. And what she felt was ecstasy.

Chyna opened her eyes to find Matt looking down at her. Part of her had been afraid of this moment, afraid that she would read triumph in his gaze, as if he had succeeded in his carefully planned conquest.

But there was no triumph on his face, only a very tender smile. She rallied slightly, even though she told herself not to rejoice just yet. After all, maybe he was just winding down from lovemaking. She wasn't exactly versed in what men looked like after they made love to a woman.

His smile was beautiful. *He* was beautiful. Steady, the game isn't over yet, Chyna. Now you have to be more cautious than ever. Now he knows your weaknesses.

He brushed her hair away from her face. When had she ever felt a gesture so incredibly gentle? "This might open up a whole new avenue of negotiations between producers and stuntpeople," he said softly, his eyes teasing her.

He had meant it as a joke, but Chyna stiffened, afraid of what he might be thinking. "I don't barter that way," she said, her tone deadly calm.

"I know."

And somehow she knew he did. She knew that he had learned more about her in this brief interlude than other people had in a lifetime.

She propped herself up on one elbow, a grin on her face. "But since you brought it up—what about the insert car?" she asked.

Matt began to laugh. It was a low, pleasure-filled

laugh that was replaced by a broad smile as he pulled her closer to him. "You remind me a lot of my father," he told her.

What an odd thing to say. But then, asking about an insert car after a passionate session of lovemaking wasn't exactly normal, either.

"Why?" she asked, curling up against him. "Did he ask you for an insert car, too?"

Matt began to slide his hand along the curve of her body, his gentle caresses arousing her again. She could feel the smoldering fires reigniting in her veins. "No, but he had the same kind of bulldog stick-to-itiveness that you seem to display."

"Sounds like a wonderful man," she commented. "What's he doing these days?" Did he hear the catch in her throat as his hand dipped lower? Breathing normally was getting to be very, very difficult around him.

"Not much of anything. He died five years ago."

"Oh."

His answer surprised her and momentarily freed her from the effect of his touch. "I'm sorry. Do you miss him?" she asked, peering up at his face. She was sure she had detected a great deal of fondness in his voice when he had mentioned his father.

He laid her flat on the bed, pinning her down with the weight of his chest. "Not right now."

"No, I mean really," she pressed, wanting to know about him. She suddenly felt a great desire to find out more about this man who aroused such inexplicably wonderful feelings inside her.

He sighed a little, and she could see a different, faraway look enter his eyes. "He was a terrific old man," Matt said. "Gruff, feisty. I thought the world of him."

And he said I reminded him of his father, she thought. The thought warmed her.

"Yes," Matt went on, looking down into her face, "I miss him. Any other questions?" he asked, a grin tugging at his lips.

"Yes, just one."

"Which is?" His forefinger curled along her cheek as he traced a slow path to her lower lip.

"When are you going to make love to me again?" she asked, her voice husky. She made no effort to hide her desire.

"Demands," he murmured, covering her mouth with his own. "Always demands."

Her demands were met beyond her wildest dreams.

"They're going to be wondering where you are," Chyna said as she lay in bed, cradled in his arms. Her tousled head rested against him, and she could feel the rhythmic movement of his chest as he breathed. The tiny hairs caressed her cheek. A warm glow still burned inside her, a warm glow she tried to hang on to, knowing it would be gone all too soon. The euphoria created by his lovemaking hadn't blotted out the words she had heard him say to Dussault.

Could someone make love like that and not feel anything? She knew she couldn't. But could he? Did he mean to hold her in check with chains forged of love? She told herself it wouldn't work, but there was a small kernel of doubt forming even now.

"I'm in heaven," Matt answered, making no movement to get up.

Chyna looked around the tiny bedroom. "Heaven's kind of cramped," she observed dryly.

He bent his head to kiss the top of hers. "That's what makes it heaven."

She glanced down at her watch. "It's four o'clock," she prodded. Part of her wanted to disentangle herself from him, literally and otherwise. But part of her wanted to stay, fearing that this joy could never be recaptured again, and she wanted to hang on to the blissful feelings just a little while longer. Even now they were fading away as reality impinged on the private world she and Matt had made.

"I didn't know they had a clock in heaven," he commented. She felt his chest rise and fall with a sigh. "But I suppose you're right. There are things I'm supposed to be looking into."

"Like the insert car?" Chyna laughingly reminded him, sitting up and looking around for her clothes.

"Like the insert car," he repeated, shaking his head in disbelief. "You never give up, do you?" he asked.

She had just put on her underwear, and she turned to look at him; she was a magnificent specimen of womanhood done up in a bit of lace. "No."

He had never thought that he could care for a woman who was wound up in her career, but Matt found himself admiring her spirited, independent quality. He liked the way she wouldn't back down. There were a lot of things he liked about her, this woman who had been all set to drag him into court a little less than a year ago. Life was full of funny twists, he thought.

She could see him fighting an urge to take her back into his arms. Maybe two could play at this game, she thought. Maybe she could turn the tables on him and make him as emotionally tied to her as she suspected he wanted her to be to him. Would their plans cancel each other out? Or would they give birth to something twice as strong? Her thoughts were getting jumbled, and she pushed them aside. Get dressed first, she told herself. One thing at a time.

"Yup," he said. She could see him retreating to his glib, easy-going mood. "Just like my father. We had a lot of arguments, too," he said casually.

Too? Were they having an argument?

"Who won?" she asked, reaching behind her back to tie her top.

He came up behind her, wearing only his slacks, and took the ties from her hands. She liked the feel of his fingers as they brushed against her back. "I plead the fifth," Matt said, turning her around to face him.

"Then there's hope," she said with a smile.

His eyes seemed to be searching for something, some sign in her face. It made her wonder. "I've discovered that there's always hope," he told her just before he kissed her.

She could feel the gossamer web beginning to rise around her again. If she weren't careful, it would grow strong enough to trap her. Was there no end to the passion he could generate in her? By all rights she should be an exhausted rag doll. And he...well, he should have been laid up for at least a day. But here he was, doing those magical things to her again.

Chyna wedged her hands against his bare chest. "You're incredible," she informed him, a bemused grin underscoring her words.

He rested his hands on her hips. "I've been told that once or twice," he teased.

"By adoring women," she concluded, attempting to appear nonchalant.

"I don't know," he said. "Are you an adoring woman?"

The question was far too probing. He was quick, she'd give him that. "I'm a woman in a hurry. I still have to practice," she said, breaking away. She walked back into the main living area. It was like stepping out of Wonderland into the real world.

See, Chyna, nothing's changed. His desk is still a mess. The sun is still streaming in through the window. Nothing's changed, she insisted.

But she knew she was wrong. Something had been irreversibly changed inside of her.

She reached the door before he could come up behind her. "I still say you don't have to practice," Matt said to her back. "What I found was absolutely perfect."

"Always room for improvement," she shot back gaily just before she left.

It would have been nice to get a lungful of invigorating air when she stepped out of his trailer, but none was available. The humid atmosphere made her want to turn around and march right back in. A lot of things made her want to turn around and march right back in. A lot of other things propelled her in the opposite direction. She was determined to get things under control before she faced him again.

"This woman's life is coming off like the *Perils of Pauline*," Chyna muttered the next day as she took

Matt's hand and got up from the ground. Her clothes were charred, despite having been thoroughly soaked with fire retardant chemicals. The heroine had caught on fire while fleeing a burning building.

A grip handed her a towel. As Chyna began wiping the soot off herself, she noticed a strange look on Matt's face.

"What's the matter?" she asked.

Behind them, Sally was preparing to take Chyna's place. Her melodic voice was raised, complaining about having soot applied to her perfect features. Chyna smiled wryly, wondering what the woman would be saying if she had to earn the dirty marks the way Chyna had just done.

But Sally occupied Chyna's attention only fleetingly, and then Chyna looked toward Matt and waited for an answer to her question.

"I've never watched someone I care for get set on fire before," he said simply. "It takes some getting used to."

"You should try it from this side," she cracked, draping the towel around her neck and letting it soak up the layer of perspiration that had formed there. Unconsciously she tensely gripped the two ends in her hands. He had used the words "care for." Well, what did she expect him to say? This was all part of his plan, wasn't it? He was a good-looking, intelligent man. He knew that one exciting afternoon of love wasn't going to render her permanently docile. His was a long range game plan that would require his participation until the picture was wrapped up.

But her logic still didn't prevent her from feeling a tingle of excitement at the words. He was turning her body against her, she thought in semidespair.

"No thanks," Matt said, turning down her "offer." "I don't have a death wish."

"Neither do I," Chyna said, turning serious. "Why are you so down on stuntwork?" she asked.

"I'm not down on stuntwork," he told her mildly. "I'm down on *you* doing stuntwork, I guess."

How honest he sounded, she thought. She could almost believe him. Almost. "Oh?" she prodded, wondering how far he would go. "Tell me more."

He took hold of her arm, pulling her away from the steady stream of grips and extras who were milling around, waiting for the next scene to begin. "Damn it, Chyna," he said, lowering his voice. It sounded all the more intense that way. "You're the first *real* woman in my life. I don't intend to lose you to some freak accident."

"Fine," she said, trying to keep the tremor out of her voice. He was acting. Only acting, she insisted. "Then keep the freak accidents from happening."

"I'm not God, Chyna," he said, looking somewhat annoyed.

"No, but you could do a few Godlike things," she pointed out. She was about to enumerate them when he cut in.

"I thought I already had," he said, his tone and mood shifting abruptly.

"O ye of little modesty, spare me." Chyna laughed despite the serious nature of the conversation.

"I don't intend to," Matt told her. She couldn't make heads or tails of the expression on his face.

He's just trying to confuse you, she told herself. See, he's turning the conversation away from your subject.

"What about getting the insert car?" she asked,

doggedly refusing to let him get away with his evasive tactics.

"I haven't looked into it yet," he said simply.

Well, at least he hadn't tried to lie and tell her it was on its way, she thought. "Why not?" she asked, knowing that she was putting him on the spot. Better him than someone's life.

"In case you haven't noticed, there aren't any phones out here," he said patiently. As he spoke he took her towel and trailed one end across her breast, managing to brush his fingertips against the high swell.

Chyna took a step back. She wasn't about to let him fog up her brain again. "But there are in Metro Manila," she countered. "I hear it's a nice place to visit."

With that she decided to let the subject drop. She couldn't very well engage him in verbal combat right here in front of everyone. And she had more than a sneaking suspicion that if she got him alone right then, they wouldn't wind up discussing insert cars.

Chyna hurried off to her shack.

She had hardly had enough time to wash her hair and put on clean clothes when a knock sounded on the door. She swung it open. Her visitor was Matt.

"Coming?" he asked.

She looked behind him and saw a Jeep. "Coming where?" she asked, bewildered.

"To Metro Manila. After all, it was your idea," he said brightly.

"What?" She felt as if they were engaged in two different conversations. This man had the ability to

muddle her thinking processes more than anyone or anything she had ever come up against.

"You said Metro Manila was a nice place to visit, so I intend to visit it. But I hate making trips alone."

"I'll bet," she quipped, but a smile was already forming on her lips. He was irresistible.

"So, will you come?" he asked.

"How can I say no to the producer?" she asked. Quickly she picked up her purse and took his arm.

"I'll keep that in mind," Matt said, putting his hand against the small of her back and guiding her to the waiting Jeep.

Metro Manila, Chyna found, was a bright collage of old and new, mostly new. The deeper into the city they drove, the more modern the surroundings became.

"I feel like we've just gone through a time warp. This looks just like Los Angeles," Chyna commented, absorbing the atmosphere. "Except that it's cleaner."

Matt grinned at her remark. "They haven't had as much time to litter it as we have. Damn."

"What's the matter?" she asked, looking around to find the cause of his irritation.

"I just missed the turn," he said, nodding off to the right.

"You sure you know how to get to wherever it is we're going?" she asked hesitantly, although the prospect of getting lost with Matt for the day *did* have its appeal.

"I'll have you know that I have wonderful homing instincts," he told her, taking a turn on the next block.

"Seems to me you must have left them home."

"You can dispense with the wry commentary—

unless, of course, you'd rather walk.'' He cast a mischievous glance her way.

Chyna raised her hands as she sank down into her seat. ''I surrender. I'll be good.''

''I know you will,'' he murmured under his breath.

Now just what did he mean by that? she wondered, almost afraid of the answer.

The steady flow of traffic eventually brought them back to the previous block. Matt stopped the Jeep before an imposing-looking hotel. The Manila Hilton, the fancy lettering on the awning proclaimed.

''What are we doing here?'' Chyna asked.

''I have a room reserved here,'' he told her, taking her hand and leading her inside. Chyna stopped short, throwing him off balance just shy of the revolving door.

''I didn't come for a tour of your room,'' she told him.

''It's not that big a room,'' he said with a laugh, leading her through the regular door next to the revolving one. ''But it does have a phone in it. You know, like the ones they use to make calls back to the States with.''

She pressed her lips together as she followed him into the lobby. He was laughing at her. ''Does that mean you're going to call about the insert car?'' she demanded.

''Could be.''

He was being so evasive, yet his words were the only thing she had to go on. She was no longer sure if he were just playing games or if she were beginning to wear him down. He was certainly beginning to wear *her* down. There was no question of that in her mind. He wasn't even touching her, and already she could feel herself responding to him, tantalized by the prospect of being alone with him in a hotel room.

And what a hotel room. The lobby was tastefully ornate, with gold carpets and plush chairs alternating with strategically placed marble statues. But the room itself made her think of something out of a magazine. It wasn't a room, it was a suite, with cream-colored walls accented by deep brown molding. The carpet was lush and brown, tempting her to kick off her sandals, which she did as she waited for Matt to finish his phone call.

As she watched him at the white French provincial desk, she tried not to let her thoughts wander in the direction they had seemed to favor ever since he had come into her life. It did no good to try to reason with herself, though. She knew what she was hoping for.

He's drawn you away from the set. He's done what he promised Dussault he'd do. And he's planning to enjoy himself in the process. Why are you being such a fool? She asked herself.

She had no answers, only churning feelings.

She wandered over to the window and looked at the bustling crowds outside. Who would ever have thought, a year ago, that she would be here, thousands of miles away from home, in a hotel room with Matt Harrigan, aching for him to love her again? Life was very, very strange.

"Yes, yes, I know it's short notice, Wanda."

Chyna turned back to him as his conversation floated into her consciousness.

"Wanda?" she echoed.

He covered the receiver. "My unflappable housekeeper," he explained. "There's nothing to be afraid of, Wanda," he said, returning to his conversation.

"Flying is safer than driving—especially the way you drive. Now, I want Meredith here on her birthday...."

The negotiations took a full ten minutes, but finally Matt managed to convince Wanda to come with the child in tow.

"Sounds like your unflappable housekeeper was doing a little flapping there," Chyna commented when he hung up.

"She hates to fly," he said with a shrug, sitting on the desktop. "Doesn't even like riding on ferris wheels."

"Sounds like a real daredevil," she quipped. "Well, what about your other phone call?" she asked, playing with the telephone cord.

"Oh, yes, that one," he said.

"Yes, *that* one." She wondered if he were going to come up with an excuse at the last minute, then try to throw her off guard by making love to her again. The thought sent shivers running along her spine.

Surprisingly, he said nothing at all. Instead he started dialing again. This conversation took a lot longer and didn't have the same result as the first one had. He came up empty.

"What happened?" she asked as he replaced the phone in its cradle.

"No dice," he told her. "They said they couldn't send one out. Too impractical, too expensive and too little time. They'll try to have one ready when we get back to the studio." He sighed and shrugged. "It's the best I can do."

Was it? she wondered. Had he even called the studio at all? For all she knew he could have placed a long distance call to the time lady and carried on his end of the discussion while a recording quoted the time to him every ten seconds.

"Well, you tried," Chyna answered, her voice a little stiff. What was she supposed to believe? Which inner instincts was she supposed to go with?

He slipped his arms around her waist. "Yes, I did."

She took hold of his arms as he held her from behind, and with a tug that surprised him, she pulled them away. "And you're trying again," she chided playfully. "But I said I'd heard that Metro Manila was a nice place to visit, remember?" she said. "So let's visit it," she urged.

But as she walked briskly past him, he surprised her by catching her wrist in his hand. It wasn't a hard grip. On the contrary, it was gentle, and it held her more securely for that very reason.

"I know a better place to visit," he said softly.

"Oh?" she asked, her voice higher than usual. "Where?"

"This room right here—with you."

Nine

Sorry, I'm not on the tourist map,'' she said, trying to sound blasé.

"I like things that are off the beaten path," he whispered, touching her hair.

Still she resisted. Or tried to. "You're going to love the volcano," she told him, turning with her wrist still in his hand and then leading him toward the door.

He laughed, going along with her. "I think I already do."

Was he trying to imply what she thought he was implying? All this inner conflict was beginning to really get to her. Just have a nice time, she told herself. Analyze it later.

But as he closed the hotel room door behind them, she felt just the slightest twinge of regret. She was definitely confused, she thought as they took the elevator back down to the ground floor.

The street outside the hotel was overflowing with people—tourists and natives alike. What caught Chyna's eye as they made their way to the Jeep were the street vendors with their carts of "untold treasures." They made quite a contrast to the executive types who were hurrying off to grab a cocktail or two at the end of the day.

"Bracelet, pretty lady?"

Chyna turned around to find a gnarled old woman tugging at her sleeve. She was holding up a green, wooden bracelet. Tiny mirrors were embedded around its perimeter, reflecting light in all directions.

"She looks like the wicked witch straight out of 'Snow White and The Seven Dwarfs,' doesn't she?" Chyna asked Matt, lowering her voice.

Matt was just about to get into the Jeep when he turned to look at the stoop-shouldered old woman. "I'd be careful if I were you, then." He chuckled, humoring Chyna. "The bracelet might be poisoned."

"If I remember my fairy tales correctly, it was a poisoned comb she tucked into Snow White's hair. And she fed her a poisoned apple. Poisoned jewelry was more Lucretia Borgia's territory."

"I love a well-read woman," Matt said, taking hold of Chyna's arm and trying to usher her to into the Jeep.

But Chyna wasn't ready to go just yet. "Matt, she looks like she could use the money," she insisted in a hushed whisper.

"So do a lot of other street vendors," he told her. "They're probably richer than you and I put together." But he saw Chyna's determination, so he released her arm and reluctantly followed, waiting patiently as she began to browse through the jumbled paraphernalia in the chipped wooden cart.

The woman smiled widely. "Want something, pretty lady?" she asked.

Chyna glanced at Matt. Yes, I want something, she thought. Something that's very bad for me in the long run.

Matt misread her look. "Okay," he said, reaching into the sea of glittering objects in the cart. He fished out a necklace and held it aloft. "You like this?" he asked Chyna.

The silvery chain seemed to sparkle. At the end of the chain swayed a shimmering purple stone. Chyna grinned and nodded her head.

"How much for this?" Matt asked the old woman.

"American?" she asked, cocking her head. The short, frayed kerchief slid back on her iron gray hair. Her hazel eyes glittered more than the stone.

Matt turned toward Chyna. "We've got a con artist on our hands. Yes, American," he said to the vendor.

"Twelve dollars," the old woman declared, putting out an incredibly wrinkled hand. Long nails hooked into her pal. Yup, definitely Snow White material, Chyna thought, looking to see if Matt would pay.

He took fifteen dollars out of his wallet. The woman snatched it, then appeared to look mystified as to how to make change.

"Keep it," Matt said, seeing right through her. The woman's grin spread, her face etched with satisfaction. "Your gift, milady," Matt said, presenting the necklace to Chyna.

She turned back to him. "Put it on, please," she instructed.

The leathery-faced old woman watched, beaming. "Bring good luck," she promised.

"Sure did," Matt commented. "At least to you." He turned Chyna around so he could admire the jewel. It nestled between the valley formed by her rounded breasts. "Lucky jewel," he murmured.

In a crowd of countless people Chyna felt suddenly very alone with him. For a moment she was afraid that he was going to trace the chain's path down to its resting place. But he only did so—though very effectively—with his eyes. She cleared her throat nervously, feeling her own thoughts drifting back to the hotel room. "I thought we were going to take in some sights."

"I am," he told her, looking up. The sparkle had returned to his eyes, teasing her. "I am."

"Different sights," she clarified, taking his arm and pulling him toward the Jeep.

"To each his own," he protested, coming in behind the wheel. "Okay, where to?" he asked.

For that she had no answer. "I don't know. Someplace terrific."

"We were just there," he told her, looking over her head at the hotel that loomed in the background.

"Don't you have a map?" she asked.

"I like feeling my way around," he answered, his voice low and teasing.

Chyna gritted her teeth. "Of Manila," she pressed.

"In the glove compartment," he offered, still watching her. He liked the way the sunbeams danced through her hair. He longed to reach out and touch the silky strands himself.

"Now we're getting somewhere," Chyna said,

reading the summary in one corner of the map citing the tourist attractions.

"I'm glad one of us is," Matt said quite audibly. But Chyna pretended not to hear. "Let's go here," she said, pointing to a spot on the map.

"Here" was the Ayuntamiento, the seat of the government during the Spanish regime and the early days of the American occupation. Along the border of the square was the Governor's Palace, known as the Palacio Real. It was in ruins, and Matt watched her as she picked her way through the crumbling rubble.

"And here we have the site of a gag that didn't quite come off," he said, using the voice of a tour guide as he followed her up an incline.

"Very funny," she retorted. But she couldn't suppress the smile that formed on her face. In front of them was the most breathtaking sunset she had ever seen. A multitude of colors swirled across the sky as the fading sun dipped down. The final rays washed over the ruins before they were eventually cast into darkness.

"There's nothing funny about the way I'm feeling right now," Matt said, joining her beside a crumbling wall that barely hinted at the beauty that had once existed here.

She knew she shouldn't say anything in answer to his words. She knew she would be better off just going on with her little tour. But a force stronger than her will made her ask, "And what are you feeling?"

Incredibly strong arms went around her, pulling her toward him. "Like if I don't have you soon, I'll take you right here in the ruins."

Steady. Keep your voice steady, she told herself. "It'd probably be the most exciting thing that's happened here in a long time." Did that sound as light as she wanted it to? It was hard to speak coherently when all your pulses were throbbing madly, she thought.

"You're driving me mad, woman," he said, his voice tight with controlled desire.

Each breath he took vibrated against her body as he held her close to him. When he kissed her, everything she had been holding back, everything she had thought was so well repressed, sprang forth like a winged fury. Her limbs were turned to liquid as she clung to him, her arms entwined about his neck, her lips sealed to his.

"You don't want to go on playing the eager tourist," he said softly. It wasn't a question, it was a statement, one she didn't have the energy to quarrel with. It was true. All she wanted was him.

Slowly she shook her head no. The sparkle in his eyes gave way to a look of devastating tenderness, and that was her final undoing. She let him take her hand and lead her back to the Jeep.

She didn't remember the trip back to the hotel. All she was aware of was his presence and the presence of a thousand excited sensations in her body, all waiting for fulfillment.

"Are you hungry?" Matt asked as he opened the door of the hotel room. It had been hours since they had eaten anything.

Yes, she thought, but not for anything that room service can bring me. Aloud she said, "No."

Stop looking at him like that, she ordered. You're going to make him think that his little scheme is working. You're going to make him think that you're even more eager than you probably look.

But she was eager, eager for the feel of his hands on her skin, his lips on hers, for the closeness they could share.

Matt put down the phone, room service and dinner temporarily forgotten. "Neither am I," he murmured, moving toward her. "The thing I like best," he said, beginning to slowly unbutton the front of her blouse, taking his time with each button, "about being in a hot climate is that there are so few clothes to put on. Or take off." His green eyes bore deep into her soul, holding her captive as she felt each button leave its hole, further parting the material that covered her breasts. The liquid within her limbs was turning into molten lava as she waited for him to finish.

When the blouse finally hung open he eased first one side and then the other off her shoulders. Ever so lightly, he ran his fingers along the swell of her breasts. Chyna was rapidly losing control of her breathing as the blouse fell to the floor. The situation became critical by the time he started working the catch loose on her shorts. He hastened their descent to the thickly carpeted floor with his hands, guiding the light material slowly along her smooth, tanned hips and caressing her thighs with it before he finally let the shorts fall. She stood before him dressed in underwear which displayed more than it covered.

"You look good in pink," he told her huskily, stroking the lacy pink bra, running his finger along the delicately scalloped edges.

He was playing with her, reducing her to mindless passion, and she couldn't do a thing about it.

"But you look even better without it." He whispered the words against the hollow of her throat as she tilted her head back, welcoming his kiss. Behind her, she could feel him releasing the clasp that held her bra together. Within a moment it didn't exist at all, and she felt the imprint of his chest against hers. His hands were on her hips, gently massaging them as he pressed them against his hardened frame. With each pass of his hand her underwear slipped a little lower, teasing the length of her thigh until that last scrap of lace floated away.

The fire grew as the refrain of an old song drifted into her head. "Black magic," she whispered as she curled her fingers along the ridges of his muscular back.

"What?" He raised his head, momentarily refraining from trailing further kisses in a sensuous path toward her breasts.

"That's what you practice," she told him, her voice thick with desire. She saw him through a haze, the light from the lamps in the room seeming to glow like candles.

"A guy's got to do something when he's trying to capture the attention of a fearless stuntwoman." His kisses, small, delicate and overwhelming, were creating havoc as they once again began to descend.

"You have my attention," she gasped, arching her back, inviting him to go on.

"Undivided?" he asked, a tender smile curving his sensuous lips.

"Undivided," she breathed, reveling in the emotions he was awakening within her.

Although he had taken his time undressing her, he wasted none on his own clothes. Before she knew it, he was as devoid of clothing as she was, and then he lifted her into his arms and carried her into the bedroom. The room was cocooned in the somber shades of dusk, but Chyna didn't care. She and Matt made their own light.

As he branded her trembling body with the hot seal of his own, Chyna felt a myriad of sensation exploding within her again. It was as if there were a secret trigger inside her that only he knew how to set off. And he could set it off with just a touch, just by the simple pressure of his body against hers.

The flames grew more intense, licking at her sides, consuming her and making her yearn for him with a force that frightened her. She tried to analyze her feelings, but she couldn't concentrate on anything. All she could do was feel, and the feeling was wonderful.

Lightning flashed through her veins as he molded her to him, pressing her buttocks with the flat of his hand. Vainly she tried to absorb all the heat his body emitted, collecting it inside of her. Unconsciously she was trying to store it against the day when all this would end. Even in her euphoric state, she knew that day would come.

Over and over and over again, Matt's mouth moved over hers, no longer gentle, no longer patient. He wanted her, wanted her as urgently as she wanted him. There were no more games, no more holding back. Paradise could be held at bay only so long.

"I've wanted you all day." Matt rasped against her mouth. "You were driving me out of my mind."

"Was I?" she asked as her breathlessness increased.

"If I couldn't have had you tonight, I would have been certifiably crazy by morning."

She felt his weight shift onto her, saw the smoldering need in his eyes. "I wouldn't want to be the one to shut down production,'' she whispered, moving to admit him.

"That's my girl,'' he murmured against her ear.

She had no time to explore the meaning behind his words, no time to wonder if what she was doing was sheer, wanton folly on her part and if she was playing right into his hands. All she knew was utter desire, utter love.

Off-key birds woke her the following morning. She turned her head and realized that her body was curled against Matt's. He was still asleep, a lazy, contented smile on his lips. The rising sun was sprinkling shimmering golden rays through the window, making his hair seem even blonder than it was. He looked like an innocent.

Some innocent, she thought. No innocent could do what he had done to her last night. Last night. The memory of it came back to her, bringing with it a fresh rush of euphoria. It had been wonderful, incredibly wonderful. She sighed and closed her eyes, sinking down into the pillow beneath her head. For a moment she let her feelings roam free, unhampered by cold facts. In the back of her mind she suspected that all this had been orchestrated. But somehow, emotionally, she hoped that perhaps he *did* care just a little, that some of the words he had said to her were true. It would be a start, she thought happily. A start in making him love her. That was all she really wanted.

The birds continued their cacophonous song, nudging her into consciousness. They had to be getting back. She hadn't meant to stay overnight. She had to practice. But then, she hadn't meant for a lot of things to happen, and they had. She shook his shoulder gently, thrilling to the cool, sleek lines of his body as it stirred against her.

"Hey," she said softly, "time to get up, sleepy-head."

One sexy eye opened. "I'm ready," he murmured, reaching for her.

"I didn't mean *that*," she laughed. "Don't you ever get enough?"

"Not lately," he said. "Not since you've entered my life. I feel like I'm insatiable."

How she wished she could believe him. But she was too much of a realist...or was she?

"Hey," Matt said, turning her attention back to him. He tugged the edge of the clinging sheet off her breasts, exposing them totally to his view. "Your neck is green."

"What?" Her hand flew up as she glanced down and caught light green track marks along the upper part of her chest. "It seems your gift has branded me," she said philosophically, digging into the hair at the base of her neck and searching for the clasp.

"Only my gift?" he asked, watching her. Her every movement aroused him.

She wanted to say a lot of things in answer to his question. She wanted to ask a lot of questions of her own. But she couldn't, not yet, so she hid behind a joke. "You don't leave green marks, if that's what you mean," she said, reaching to put the necklace on the nightstand next to her.

"No," he said seriously, pulling her back down and into his arms, "that's not what I mean."

The necklace fell from her fingers as Matt took what was already his.

"I thought you'd be gone longer," were the first words out of Dussault's mouth when Chyna walked past him, heading toward the site of her fight rehearsal. He was annoyed, and the words were seared into Chyna's brain. There, that's for all those castles in the sky you're trying to build, she told herself, searching for Alex. Taking you to the city was all just part of Matt's plan to keep your mind off the movie, nothing more.

Chyna felt a chill even though sun shone as brightly as ever.

The pace on the set became even more hectic than usual as the days passed. Dussault was determined to stay within the original tight schedule. He cajoled, prodded and screamed in order to get the most out of his actors. He went directly to screaming, bypassing the first two, when it came to the extras and the stuntworkers, Chyna observed. She tried to focus her attention on her work, but it wasn't easy concentrating. Her thoughts were constantly invaded by memories of the moments she had shared with Matt. He was infiltrating all her thoughts, both waking and sleeping. She found herself listening for his step, watching for his shadow to cross her path. She was, she admitted to herself, in love. In love with a man who probably just saw her as part of his job. She should have been indignant, or at least annoyed. But annoyance was the last thing on her mind whenever she was near him.

For one thing, it was difficult to be annoyed with a man who looked forward to his daughter's arrival with such anticipation. The glow that came into Matt's eyes when he talked about Meredith convinced Chyna that he was a warm, loving man. It gave her hope that everything that had happened between them wasn't just pretense.

"Meredith, this is Chyna O'Brien," Matt said, introducing his daughter. "She jumps over burning gasoline tanks for a living."

To Chyna's surprise, the little girl took the statement in stride, extending her hand solemnly to Chyna. She caught herself thinking that Meredith was the most solemn-looking five-year-old she had ever seen. She looked like a model for children's clothes and not a thing like a child who had just finished an exhausting plane ride, topped off with a bumpy trip in a Jeep.

Chyna flashed Meredith her widest smile and had it politely returned. She looked uncertainly over the child's dark head.

Matt beamed. "Great manners," he enthused.

Too great, Chyna thought, still smiling at the child.

And then Chyna saw Wanda, who was standing in the rear of the trailer. Now that she saw her, Chyna couldn't understand how she could have missed the woman, who looked as if she would have been more at home in a Wagnerian opera, wearing a horned helmet and metal breast shield. A very large metal breast shield. She stood like the personification of sternness regarding Chyna.

So this is what an unflappable housekeeper looks like, Chyna thought.

Chyna could see the dark brows narrowing as the

woman leveled her gaze at her. "I think I just flunked her appraisal," Chyna whispered, ducking her head so that Wanda wouldn't be able to read her lips.

"That's okay," Matt said, putting his arm around her shoulders. "As long as you pass mine."

"Well, Meredith, why don't you change into something more comfortable and I'll show you around," Chyna volunteered. The vanguard in the rear moved in closer. "You too, Wanda," Chyna added, forcing an inviting smile.

The face that looked back at her was stony. "I've seen enough sound stages to last me a lifetime," Wanda told her, turning her down.

"I take it that means no," Chyna said, turning questioningly toward Matt.

"Wanda used to be in movies," Matt explained.

Monster Madness in Manhattan, no doubt, Chyna thought. "Well, then, we won't bore you," she declared, then looked down at Meredith. "How about you?"

"Yes, please. If daddy can come, too."

"Daddy is most certainly welcome," Chyna said spiritedly. "It's his picture."

In response Matt grinned and nodded. They shared a tiny moment in private, despite Wanda's presence. She needed that, Chyna thought, heartened. How quickly she had become dependent on his smile. Addicting stuff, she told herself. So was his lovemaking. The more she got, the more she wanted. Enough, her wavering discipline pleaded.

"Don't you want to change?" Chyna asked Meredith, trying to pull herself out of the deep cauldron of emotion she felt herself falling into.

But Meredith shook her head. "I'll be fine, thank you."

"Isn't she terrific?" Matt asked, ushering them both out the door.

"Terrific," Chyna agreed. And restrained, she added silently. The children she encountered were never this reserved. And even when they appeared to be as polite as Meredith, there was always a hint of mischief in their eyes. No such hint existed here. She wondered what had happened to make the little girl that way.

But for the time being Chyna kept her questions to herself as she followed Matt and Meredith out the door.

"Damn it, man, if you were any more wooden, you'd be a prime candidate for Dutch Elm Disease!" Dussault spat, yelling at the leading man as Chyna and the others approached the shooting site.

"I see he took his happy pills this morning," Chyna commented to Matt.

Meredith looked up at Chyna. "They're not working," she observed quietly.

"You bet they're not," Chyna agreed, trying not to laugh out loud.

Dussault heard her voice—though apparently not her words—and whirled to face her, obvious disgust in his eyes. For a moment he didn't see Matt and Meredith. "I thought you were told not to hover around the set unless you were on call," he said nastily.

Chyna cast a glance toward Matt. He had never come out and told her not to "hover." No doubt he felt that actions spoke louder than words. And in her case, they had. But confronted with Dussault's haughtily condescending voice, Chyna was tempted to say something biting in return. She bit her tongue.

"She's not hovering, she's with us," Matt said, his voice sterner than she had ever heard it. She could tell he was annoyed with the way Dussault had spoken to her, and it made her feel warm and protected. She grinned at the silly notion, but hugged it to herself nonetheless.

She saw Dussault's expression change entirely. It became obsequious, although Chyna could have sworn that she detected an underlying layer of resentment, as well.

"Are we going on with this scene or not?" Beaumont called out impatiently. The actor stood with his doubled-up fists on his hips.

Dussault raised his palms upward in exasperated supplication. "The man's so bad, he doesn't even know when we've stopped working." His gaze shifted to Meredith. "And who's this little darling?" he asked, squatting down to Meredith's level.

"My daughter," Matt said needlessly. Chyna wondered if the director would have looked so fawning if Meredith had been her daughter instead of Matt's, then wondered why she'd bothered. She knew the answer to that one.

Her mind skidded to a halt. Her daughter? She slowly turned the unexpected thought over in her head. She looked at the little girl, her dark, delicate features so different from Matt's. She was the image of her mother, no doubt. Except for the eyes. The eyes were green and shadowed with lashes that looked almost too long for her small face. Matt's eyes. Matt's

lashes. Yes, she could have a daughter more about
this age. Except that hers would have smiled more.
A lot more.

As they went on Meredith appeared to be content
just to march along beside them, her hands at her
sides, a miniature adult, but Chyna reached out and
grasped her small hand anyway. It was a warm gesture and one that Meredith looked a little uncertain
about accepting. Chyna pretended not to notice. She
led the "tour" toward where she did her ritual morning exercises.

"What's that?" Meredith asked, pointing.

"That's a trampoline," Chyna said, dropping on
one knee to be on eye level with the girl. "It's kind
of like a big bed that you jump on—without the pillows. Want to try it?" she offered.

As far as Chyna knew, most kids would have run
right over her in their haste to get on. But Meredith
just stood there. "I don't jump on beds," she said
quietly.

"Wait here," Chyna said, getting back up. She
took Matt's hand and drew him aside. "Matt," she
said kindly, "what's wrong with her?"

She saw him stiffen slightly. "What do you
mean?"

Chyna spread her hands helplessly. "She's so reserved, so polite—it's like someone programmed all
the fun out of her. It's not natural."

Matt closed his eyes and sighed. "Laura didn't like
children very much, and she didn't keep it a secret
from Meredith. Meredith tried to do everything to
please her. When she left, Meredith thought it was
her fault." He looked over to where his daughter was

standing. Chyna could see the torment in his eyes. "She still does," he added quietly.

Chyna found herself profoundly disliking a woman she had never met. Without a word to Matt, she walked back to the little girl.

She lowered her voice as if she were talking to a fellow conspirator. "You're supposed to bounce on it. C'mon, we'll do it together," she urged.

The girl's green eyes opened wide as Chyna took her hand. "Really?" Meredith cried in surprise.

"Really," Chyna told her, lifting the girl up first, then climbing on herself. "Here. I'll hold your hands until you get the hang of this."

Meredith gave her an uncertain, grateful smile, placing both her hands in Chyna's. Matt just stood back and watched, marveling at Meredith's reaction to Chyna. Usually the girl hung back, intensely shy.

But Meredith was responding to Chyna just the way he had found himself responding to her at first. Warily, uncertainly, yet drawn in by her intensity and warmth. Chyna had more zest for life than anyone he had ever met. He hoped some of that zest could be transferred to Meredith.

"What did you do?" Wanda demanded when they walked back into the trailer. She cast a horrified eye at Meredith, whose formerly neatly-braided hair was now sticking out all over, while her bangs were plastered against her forehead, held in place by a large dose of perspiration. Her dress was rumpled and wilted.

"Had fun," Chyna said proudly, releasing Meredith's hand as she surrendered the girl to Wanda.

"Don't worry," she said cheerfully, "she's washable. We do a lot of sweating around here."

Wanda sniffed, but not quite as indignantly as she might have. Firmly taking Meredith by the hand, she marched the girl to the shower.

Matt took Chyna into his arms. "You're incredible, you know that?"

"Yes," she answered brightly, her eyes dancing. "I've been told so. It just took you a little longer than most people to find out, that's all. I'm making allowances for the heat."

"What heat?" he asked, tracing the outline of her lips. "Yours, or mine?"

"Nature's," she answered.

He kissed the tip of her nose, then worked his way down to her mouth. "Do you know what I want right now?"

"I think I have a strong suspicion," Chyna laughed, pushing him back slightly. "But you're going to have to be on your best behavior," she reminded him playfully, nodding in the direction Meredith had just taken.

"There's your cabin," he pointed out, tightening his hold around her waist.

"Shack," she corrected. "And Pepper's there."

"I'll fire her," he offered, kissing the point of her shoulder.

"You can't do that," Chyna protested teasingly. "Besides, I've heard that absence makes the heart grown fonder," she said, purposely running her finger along his chest and tracing a pattern around his heart.

"Maybe," he conceded. "But it's hell on the body."

"Daddy!" Meredith called from the bathroom.

"Wanda's probably scrubbing her skin off," Chyna guessed, taking the opportunity to step away from him. "Better go and rescue your daughter. I've got to practice anyway."

"The sky stunt," he remembered.

Chyna nodded, then saw that he looked concerned. Was that for show? Or was some of it real? "There's a plane involved," she assured him. "I don't just pop out of space."

"How do you practice something like that?" he asked.

"Very, very carefully," she teased, then became more somber. "You don't. Not from that height, anyway. You practice taking smaller jumps. You practice timing. You also practice praying a little," she added with a wink, leaving.

Was he really concerned about her? Had she gotten to him one-tenth as much as he had gotten to her? Had he fallen into his own trap? No, men like Matt didn't fall into traps. She was sure that his bad experience with Laura had colored the way he regarded women in general. And, after all, she had originally taken him to court. Not exactly the best foundation for a romance…or something more lasting.

It was up to her to change that, she thought as she headed back to her trampoline.

Work, concentrate on work, she ordered herself. Or else you're not going to be able to concentrate on anything. She found, to her relief, that she could still filter out all extraneous thoughts just before she undertook a gag. Doggedly she worked out her stunt, getting everything down to a science. Fear was the necessary ingredient that compelled her to triple-check everything before she started. But once that checking was done, fear was driven out. It had no place in the execution of her stunts. It could only cause her to freeze, something that could be fatal.

Chyna had set her equipment up near a hill that suited her specifications. After making sure that her knee, shin and elbow pads were fastened securely, she paused on the crest. From her vantage point she could see and hear the scene being filmed below her.

"Faster, damn it! Faster! Go faster!" Dussault roared, riding alongside the insert car. In answer to his orders, the driver accelerated even more.

That man was going to kill someone yet, Chyna thought angrily. She waited until the area was clear before she attempted her stunt, sailing down into the waiting air mattress. As she tumbled out of its recesses she saw that filming had come to a halt, and that two of the cameramen were walking by, grumbling audibly.

"You need a drink, kid," the older cameraman was telling his companion, who looked shaken.

"I need a safer profession," the other man answered. There was no missing the tremor in his voice. He ran his hand through a wayward mop of hair. "When we took that curve I damn near fell off."

"But you didn't," the other man said. "That's all that matters."

But it wasn't all that mattered, Chyna thought as she watched the two men walk away. It wasn't all that mattered at all.

Ten

Chyna thought of going straight to Matt to tell him what she had overheard, then changed her mind. Maybe she was overreacting to the situation. After all, by definition the stunts *had* to be dangerous. Maybe the cameraman she had heard complaining was just exaggerating.

Hold it. What was happening here? She was fabricating excuses for what she knew was going on. Was this the result of Matt's lovemaking? Was he succeeding in his attempt to "handle" the problem her presence generated? She pressed her lips together. A jumble of confused emotions warred within her, pulling her in two different directions. For the time being, she decided to hold her peace and go on practicing.

The sky above her turned an angry purple, then faded into an ominous gray. The sun had completely vanished. Rain, Chyna thought, deciding to cut her practice session short. Out here, she knew, it didn't just rain, it monsooned. Chyna gathered her equipment together. Overhead the wind's low moan grew into a bellow as it raked through the fronds of the palm trees. She passed the beach on her way to her shack and stopped for a moment, fascinated by the sight of the angry surf pounding white, foamy fists against the submissive beach.

It looked like it was going to be a big one, she thought.

Her mind shifted to Dussault. He was going to be furious if he had to stop shooting because of rain. The picture of a raging, frustrated Dussault brought a wide grin to her face. "Yes, Virginia, there is a Santa Claus," she murmured to herself as she began to run back to her quarters, trying to outrace the large drops of rain that had just begun to fall.

She had just made it inside when the large drops joined together to form pelting sheets of rain. Pepper barreled in right behind her, nearly knocking her over. Chyna jumped aside just in time.

"It's only rain, Pepper," Chyna said, laughing. "You won't melt."

"One way or another I keep getting wet out here. If it isn't perspiration because of the heat, it's rain," Pepper muttered, annoyed. Her dutchboy hairdo was plastered to both sides of her face. In a vain attempt to dry off she shook herself, mimicking the motions of a wet dog. Looking at Chyna as she hunted for a towel, she suddenly remembered something and said, "Oh, Mr. Harrigan's looking for you."

"Terrific," Chyna muttered. "He couldn't look for me before the rain started, right? Oh, well, when my

master calls..." she said loftily, looking around for
something to shield her from the rain. The last thing
in the world she had thought to pack was an umbrella.
After all who took am umbrella to a tropical paradise?
Or a safety net to a love affair? her inner voice whispered. She should have done both—and hadn't.

"Is he?" Pepper asked. She stopped peeling off her
wet shorts and looked quizzically at Chyna.

"Is he what?" Chyna asked absently, rummaging
through her suitcase. There wasn't anything there that
would do the slightest bit of good against the rain for
more than fifteen seconds, she thought, letting the lid
of the case drop back down.

"Your master."

Chyna caught the inflection in Pepper's voice. The
funny, crooked smile on the other woman's guileless
face matched it. "He's the producer, remember?"
Chyna said evasively. "That makes him *our* master."

"And that's all?" Pepper asked, cocking her head.
It was plain she didn't believe any of Chyna's protests.

Chyna didn't bother protesting any further. "Yes,"
she said firmly. "That's all."

With that she rushed out, bracing herself against
the pummeling drops.

Pepper's high voice followed her. "I don't believe
you," she singsonged.

"Neither do I," Chyna muttered under her breath
as she ran. The palm trees shielded her for part of the
way. The rest of the run was out in the open.

"This had better be good," Chyna announced
when Matt opened the door, letting her in. Rivulets
of rain ran down her face, and she pushed her water-

logged hair out of her eyes, wondering if she would ever feel dry again.

"My God," Matt cried, "you're all wet."

"Now I know why you're the producer. You have the gift of insight," she muttered, squeezing out the hem of her shirt. A puddle formed around her feet. "I look like a wet chicken."

"The most delectable wet chicken I've ever seen," Matt assured her, going in to another room for a moment. He popped back in with a huge, fluffy towel.

She took it from him. "How many wet chickens do you usually see in a week?" she asked as she rubbed the towel along her arms.

"You're the first," he said with a grin. "Why did you come out in this?"

She looked at him, stunned. "Weren't you looking for me?" If he wasn't, she was going to kill Pepper when she got back. When she swam back, she amended, listening to the rain. The metal trailer amplified the sound, making it seem as if the rain were attacking from all directions. Chyna wondered if the trailer could withstand the assault.

"Yes, but I could have waited. There was no need to try to drown yourself...or is that some inner compulsion you stuntpeople have?" he teased, watching the way the towel was gliding along her skin. Her blouse and shorts were plastered against her body, outlining every single detail. He felt an urge to follow the path blazed by the towel, but he held himself in check.

"No," she retorted, "but we're polite. When we're told someone is looking for us, we usually turn up." She began drying her hair, rubbing vigorously. She wound up with a tousled, wavy look. "Well, I'm here, so what's on your mind?'' she asked, running her fingers through her dripping hair, wishing she looked better.

"Lots," he murmured. The warm glow in his eyes pleased her. Maybe he liked wet women. "But I have to be on my best behavior," he said with a sigh.

"Ah, a first, no doubt," she laughed.

Wanda bustled in just then. There was no other word to describe the woman's entrance, Chyna thought. Wanda "bustled" everywhere she went, her huge hips swaying. "I've finally calmed her down," she announced to Matt.

"Meredith's afraid of storms?" Chyna guessed, looking up at Matt.

He nodded. "It's a new phase."

She thought of her own childhood and the time when she had been frightened of the loud noises that came rumbling out of the angry skies. She had always had a warm haven to retreat to. Her father always seemed to be there when she needed him, especially after her mother had died. Chyna's heart went out to the little girl in the next room as she thought of the times when Matt had been away and the only person Meredith had been able to seek comfort from was Wanda-with-the-iron-expression. The woman might be fond of the child, Chyna thought, but she was light years away from being warm and toasty.

"Is she asleep?" Chyna asked Wanda.

"No, but—"

"Excuse me," Chyna said, pushing past her. It was, she thought drolly, one of her more difficult stunts, given the narrow width of the passageway.

When she entered the room Chyna found Meredith in bed, her huddled body outlined beneath the blanket. She looked as if she were trying to pull herself into the smallest ball she could. Very quietly Chyna sat down on the bed. Meredith stuck her head out and looked at her.

"Oh," she cried, surprised. Her expression was uncertain, yet pleased. She looked, Chyna thought, relieved. Chyna had been right. She needed company.

"I've been out," Chyna explained, realizing that her appearance was a little startling. "Walking in the rain."

Meredith sat up. The pale face became animated, a conspiratorial glow entering it. "Weren't you afraid?" she asked, her voice hushed.

"There's nothing to be afraid of, except maybe catching a cold," Chyna told her, glancing at Matt, who was standing quietly in the doorway.

Meredith turned her face toward the window and watched the rain lash at the pane. The world beyond the room looked dark and foreboding. Another loud crash of thunder rocked the room. Meredith dove for the haven of Chyna's arms. "It sounds so scary."

Chyna pulled her closer. "When you get bigger you'll find that a lot of loud noises are only that— loud noises. If you stand up to them you'll see that there's nothing to be afraid of at all," she assured her, giving the girl a warm squeeze.

Meredith looked up into her face. "Were you ever afraid of storms?" she asked.

Chyna laughed. "Scared stiff," she confided. "I used to run into my daddy's study and crawl under his desk. And you know what he'd do?"

Meredith shook her head, solemnly waiting for the answer.

"He'd pick me up and hold me on his lap and tell

me stories until the storm was over—or until I felt brave enough not to be afraid." Chyna smiled at the trusting, upturned face. "Want me to tell you a story?"

The vigorous nod was all she needed.

She had nearly exhausted her entire repertoire of stories before Meredith finally drifted off to sleep. Gently Chyna eased her down and Matt tucked her in. He put his arms around Chyna's shoulders and they walked out.

"I'm not sure who enjoyed those stories more, you or Meredith," Chyna teased, her voice cracking a little. "I never thought I'd say this after my trek over here, but could I have a glass of water? My throat feels like the Mohave Desert."

"Anything for the master storyteller," he said lightly, going over to the sink. He handed a filled glass to her, his eyes smiling. "You're really something else, Chyna O'Brien."

She practically gulped down the entire glass in one swallow, then sighed, handing it back to him. "I thought you already knew that," she said wryly.

He put the glass down on the tiny kitchen counter behind him. "I've just taken a refresher course." There was a cough from the couch. They both looked in that direction. "She's asleep, Wanda. I won't be needing you anymore tonight."

Wanda rose. "If you want to be alone," she said in her no-nonsense voice, "just say so."

"I want to be alone, Wanda," Matt said, a degree of amusement and affection in his voice.

"She's really an ex-actress?" Chyna asked, looking over her shoulder as the full-figured woman disappeared into Meredith's room, where an extra cot had been set up.

"Absolutely," Matt confirmed, ushering Chyna over to the couch.

"Hmm, remind me to catch some of the old horror movies on the late show," Chyna muttered, sitting down.

"Wanda's all right," Matt assured her.

Chyna shrugged. "If you say so. Personally, I'd check her for fangs."

"And what should I check you for?" he asked, moving in closer. His thigh pressed against hers, stirring a response within her before she even realized it was happening.

"Sanity, for one," she quipped.

"Why?" he asked, his eyes glowing with some unidentifiable emotion. "Because you're beginning to feel something for me?"

She would have liked to have put him in his place for being so terribly sure of himself. Unfortunately, most of her wanted him to stay right where he was. She was feeling something for him, all right. More than just a small something, and it was clouding her vision. Recalling the conversation she had overheard between him and Dussault didn't remedy the situation at all. She was in love with him.

"No," she answered crisply. "Because I came out in this monsoon when Pepper said you were looking for me. What *was* it you wanted, anyway?"

"To ask you to Meredith's birthday party. I just mentioned it in passing to Pepper before the downpour started. I didn't mean for you to risk life and limb," he said, allowing his hand to roam leisurely along her thigh.

"Didn't you?" she asked meaningfully, struggling hard not to sway in her seat. Throbbing anticipation which she knew could not be fulfilled that night sprang up wherever his hand passed.

"Do all stuntpeople talk in riddles?" he asked, brushing aside her hair and kissing the sensitive area of her neck.

"It's one of our small pleasures," she murmured, momentarily losing some of the control she was trying so valiantly to exercise. He could create ecstasy for her so quickly.

"Name another small pleasure," he coaxed, following the line of her collar with light, tingling kisses. Desire began to bloom.

"It's not so small," she admitted, but refused to give it a name. "Not by a long shot. But you have to be good," she reminded him, pressing her hands against his chest. She had pushed harder in her lifetime, she thought.

But her action stopped him. "Parenthood," he decided, sighing heavily, "is not without its trials."

Chyna took two deep breaths before she went on, her voice still sounding a little shaky. "So," she said, trying to sound breezy, "what have you got planned for her birthday?" she asked.

Her question threw him. "Planned?" he asked, confused. "A cake. Candles. You know the usual."

"I thought you big Hollywood types threw outlandish parties for your kids, complete with rented circuses and things." She shook her head. "You're getting to be a big disappointment to me, Harrigan." Her eyes twinkled as she spoke.

"Am I, now?" The look he gave her warmed her to the very core. But then he laughed. "Maybe you haven't noticed this little fact," he went on, his hand still resting on her thigh, still stirring her, "but we're not exactly in L.A. at the moment."

"So that's why I haven't found the freeway!" she quipped, enjoying their lighthearted exchange, enjoying sharing a smile with him.

"Drink?" he offered, gesturing toward the compact bar in the corner.

"A screwdriver," she said slowly as an idea began forming. "Just because you've got a lousy work schedule," she said, getting up and walking over to him, "doesn't mean that you have to deprive her." Leaning her elbows on the counter, she watched as he poured orange juice into a glass, following it with a shot of vodka.

He handed her the glass, but rather than drink, she put it down on the counter. It immediately formed a ring around its base. She moved it around as she talked, making intersecting circles.

"Okay, just what is it you have in mind for my poor, deprived daughter?" Matt asked, eyeing her. "Or shouldn't I ask?"

"Sure you should ask," Chyna said. "How else are you going to find out?" Before he had a chance to comment about her talking in riddles again, she went on, her voice growing in momentum as she spoke. "You might not have a circus here, but you do have stuntpeople."

"How well I know that," Matt said, taking a long drink from his glass. The ice cubes clinked back down as he set his glass next to hers.

"None of your sarcasm, Harrigan," Chyna warned, "or I won't tell you my wonderful plan."

He wrapped his arms around her waist, pulling her

against him, and breathed in the sweet scent that was hers alone. The rain hadn't washed it away. "Just so long as you don't go away," he murmured. "Okay, and just what is this wonderful plan?"

"We can dress up as clowns and do tricks for her. Nothing overwhelming, just a few simple things. Something that would make a five-year-old's eyes grow wide," she told him, letting her own arms surround him. She liked the warmth he ignited within her. She just hoped it wasn't an illusion created by his own brand of special effects.

"Wanna make a thirty-two-year-old's eyes grow wide?" he asked, nibbling on her ear.

The sultry feeling of his breath against her cheek began to resurrect that by now familiar liquid sensation within her. "What is this, a test?" she asked. "Are you trying to see how long I can keep my hands off you?" She snuggled in closer. "If it is, you don't fight very fair."

"I never claimed to be a fair fighter," he reminded her. "Just a good one."

No, he had never claimed to fight fair, she agreed. And she was the casualty. "Well, I guess it's up to me to enforce the rules regarding your good behavior." She disengaged herself from his arms. "I've got to be going," she told him, backing away.

"But it's still raining," Matt said, pointing toward the window. "You'll get wet."

And if I stay here, I'll get burned, she thought. "That's okay." She shrugged. "I'm a wash and wear model," she cracked as she opened the door.

He caught her arm as she began to go outside. "And I'd like to wear it," he told her, holding her against him. The door flew completely open, pushed flat against the side of the trailer by the force of the wind. Sheets of rain began to come inside, but Matt didn't seem to notice as he kissed her fiercely. She felt the raw emotion that was churning within him rise to the surface.

It was all she could do to draw her lips from his and wedge her hands between them. "Not today," she breathed. "I'm not making love to a man who doesn't have enough sense to come in out of the rain."

And with that she fled into the downpour, though she turned back once to wave at him. He was still standing in the open doorway, the rain lashing at him. "What a mess," she muttered as she ran.

The rain stung her face, momentarily taking her mind off the dilemma she was in. Although Matt's feelings for her seemed genuine, Chyna couldn't rid herself of the fears created by the words she had heard him say to Dussault.

All right, even if it wasn't all an act, so what? People got close when they worked together. Once the movie was over, so was the romance. Matt was a busy producer. A lot of glamorous, willing women came his way. Why would he want to continue a liaison with a woman whom his peers viewed as a trouble-maker?

You think too much, she told herself as she reached the door of her shack.

The storm lasted into the next day, throwing the entire shooting schedule further behind than it already was. Because of their location, there was precious little for the cast and crew to do. For most, boredom set in long before noon. Felicia, the wardrobe mistress, however, found that she had no problem.

"Clown costumes?" she asked, staring at Chyna, who had just told her about the project for Meredith's birthday. "He wants five clown costumes by tomorrow?" she cried.

"He" was Matt. Chyna had known that she wouldn't get very far with the older woman if she said she was the one who wanted the costumes.

The plump wardrobe mistress stood surrounded by a variety of fabrics, buttons and other ingredients that could magically be converted into costumes at the right moment—after a great deal of muttering and snipping. Felicia spread her hands helplessly. "And just how does he expect me to do that?" she demanded.

Chyna shook her head in sympathy. Pepper, witnessing the charade, choked back a laugh. "You know how these producers are," Chyna said, "always demanding the impossible. But if anyone can do it, Felicia, you can."

"But I don't even know any sizes. I—" The wail turned into unintelligible sputterings as Felicia sifted through a large multi-colored heap of material.

"Medium," Chyna said. "Medium's safe," she assured the woman, despite Pepper's nudge to her own ribs. "If the costumes don't fit, so much the better. Who ever heard of a well-dressed clown, anyway?"

"It can't be done," the woman informed Chyna as both she and Pepper edged out of the room. But it was.

Chyna also managed to convince three other stunt-workers to join her and Pepper in acting out the half-formed scenario she had come up with.

"There's not going to be enough room to perform in the trailer," Scottie, one of the stuntmen, pointed out. "I don't sky dive too well from the top of a refrigerator."

Chyna remained undaunted. "The weather will clear up," she promised. And if it didn't, she'd come up with something else, she added silently.

"Do I have to put this on?" Pepper wailed the next day as she looked beseechingly at Chyna. Chyna sat on her cot, juggling a mirror she had purloined from the prop department and some foundation and blusher that she had gotten as a grudging gift from the makeup department. She glanced at the pot of white face-paint that Pepper was holding.

"You can't be a clown without makeup," Chyna told her, drawing in a broad mouth on her own white face.

"I'll start a new trend," Pepper said hopefully.

Chyna thrust the paint toward her friend. "It washes off," she promised.

Pepper frowned deeply as she sat down, following Chyna's lead. Outside, the sun was beginning to shine.

"Is there anything you can't do?" Matt asked Chyna later after she and the other clowns came tumbling out of Chyna and Pepper's shack, much to the glee of Meredith.

"Off hand," Chyna said, stepping out of the way as two clowns in blue went into their hastily conceived act, "I can think of one or two things."

"Such as?" Matt asked, his eyes on Meredith's beaming face.

Such as convincing myself that all this is real, Chyna thought sadly. "This is no time to get serious," she told him.

He caught her hand as she moved to join the others. "Remind me to get serious soon," he whispered.

She knew he didn't mean what she did, but she smiled beneath the painted-on red mouth. "I'll remind you."

"It's the very best party I've ever, ever had!" Meredith cried, wrapping her arms around Chyna's black-and-white checked waist.

It was Chyna's turn to beam with pleasure. The animated little girl before her was light years away from the subdued short adult she had met in Matt's trailer.

"Glad you liked it," Chyna said affectionately, ruffling the girl's hair. "Thanks, everybody," she called to the other clowns as they began to leave.

Murmurs of "Don't mention it," and "Happy birthday, Meredith," filled the air as they left. Matt came over to Chyna as Wanda began gathering up the litter left over from the party.

"Here," he said, offering the box of tissues he was carrying. "It's time for the fairy godmother to reappear."

"Is that what I am?" Chyna asked with a laugh.

He took a tissue out of the box and began to wipe away the red paint around her mouth. "You are to her," he said, nodding to Meredith.

The happy smile on the little girl's face confirmed Matt's words. "I need cold cream to get this off,"

Chyna told Matt, taking the smeared tissue away from him.

"Were you scared, Chyna?" Meredith asked.

The question came totally out of the blue. "When?" Chyna thought that the stunts she had done at the party were pretty tame.

"Daddy said you jumped over an exploding gas tank. He showed me the movie. Were you scared?" she asked again.

Chyna turned to look at Matt. "You have the rushes?" she asked. Normally the rushes were sent back to the parent studio the next day, and she had done the stunt a couple of weeks ago.

"I have a copy."

How odd, she thought. Then she realized that she hadn't answered Meredith's question. "No," she said, taking the girl by the hand and beginning to walk back to the trailer. "I wasn't afraid. There are a lot more frightening things in life than the stunts I do."

"What are they?" Meredith asked, unable to imagine anything more frightening than jumping over exploding tanks.

"Someday when you're older I'll tell you," Chyna said, turning for a moment to look back at Matt.

He was busy picking up Meredith's gifts and missed the solemn expression on her face.

Eleven

Work resumed at a fever pitch. Two days of filming had been lost, and Dussault was absolutely determined to make them up. He drove everyone relentlessly...not to mention crazy, Chyna thought, watching him from the sidelines as he readied everyone for the huge fight scene. Normally something involving so many stuntworkers would have taken nearly a week to rehearse and film. Each piece of the fight had to be separately choreographed, and camera angles had to be just so in order to fool the audience. More injuries were sustained during fight scenes than in any other stunt. Putting the sequences together to minimize risks took time and patience. Dussault had neither.

He was just as determined to get the fire sequence under wraps. Like the fight scene, it required the combined talents of all fifteen stuntworkers. Dussault ordered rehearsals for both scenes to be carried on back to back.

"Why not simultaneously?" Chyna muttered to Matt that night in his trailer. "That way we can swing and fight fire, swing and fight fire." She pressed her lips together in exasperation. "Matt..."

Matt raised his hands in defense. "Yes, yes, I know. He's getting a little out of hand."

"A little?" she cried. Was his phrasing just poor, or was he really blind to what was going on?

"The man is only trying to do his job," Matt pointed out. "Believe me, I know Phil. He's really not as bad as you seem to think he is. During filming he becomes a little obsessed at times, but there have never been any major accidents on his sets."

Chyna wondered just what Matt thought was a major accident, but she let him go on talking.

"And there won't be any on this picture, either," he told her when he saw the look of doubt in her eyes. He took her hands in his. "But if it'll make you feel any better, I'll talk to him."

"Promise?" she asked, eyeing him dubiously. Was this to put her off her guard? Or did he really mean it?

"I promise."

Matt sat down on the couch, pulling her onto his lap as he did so. It was clear that right then he had other things on his mind, but Chyna wouldn't let the matter drop. Still, she decided to put in the last words on the subject playfully.

"Remember," she warned, wagging her finger in front of him, "if you break your promise, I won't give you any peace."

"Is that a promise or a threat?" he teased.

"Take it any way you like."

He nipped her ear. Instantly Chyna was propelled into another world, a world populated only by the two of them. "I'll take it any way I can," he said just before he kissed her.

"Does that mean you like my daddy?"

The kiss ended abruptly. Chyna found it hard to kiss Matt when she was laughing. "Yes," she answered unabashedly, standing up, "I like your daddy."

Meredith had walked into the trailer, followed by her formidable escort. The child's next question was a little harder to handle. "Will you be going home with us?" she asked, her wide eyes hopeful.

Chyna ran her hand over the dark head, smiling fondly at the girl. "Nope. I have a film to make. And your daddy won't be coming home for a little while, either, I'm afraid. He's going to stay until we're all finished here."

For a moment the little face fell. But then Meredith considered the matter. "Will you take care of him?" she asked Chyna.

Chyna bit her lip, trying hard not to laugh again. She raised her right hand solemnly. "I'll take care of him."

"Okay," Meredith agreed. "I'll go home with Wanda." A yawn escaped her as she spoke.

"Time for bed," Matt instructed. "You've got a big day ahead of you tomorrow." Obediently Meredith went off to bed, with Wanda more than amply bringing up the rear. "I'll be there to tuck you in in a few minutes," Matt called after them.

"How about you?" he asked, turning back to Chyna and fingering the white lace tie on the front of her shirt. "Can I tuck you in, too?" he asked. The words were soft, sultry. Chyna could feel the familiar stirrings beginning.

But she shook her head. "I've got a big day tomorrow, too. Besides," she reminded him, her eyes shining mischievously, "there's no place for us to go."

"There's my room," he whispered into her hair as he drew her close to him. "You remember my bed, don't you? The site of our first meeting of the minds, so to speak." His words were teasing, but they were brimming with barely concealed desire.

"Meredith's in the next room," she protested, weakening despite her self. How long since she had last loved him? Too long.

"She's given us her blessing," Matt said, beginning to part the lacing down the front of her shirt. Flames ignited everywhere he touched her. The ache she felt grew nearly unbearable.

"She might have," Chyna agreed, "but Wanda is still in there with her. And I've no doubt that she's got ears like a bat." She felt herself melting against him. The separation had been too long, her body cried. Not long enough, her mind insisted. She was still unable to think straight around him.

Her internal war was forgotten as his kiss brushed against her lips.

"I promise to be very, very quiet. Wanda won't even know I've gone to bed. Only you'll know." It was a sensuous promise that did wild things to her pulse. So did the tiny kisses he was sprinkling liberally about her mouth.

Chyna let herself be led off without offering another word of protest. She was in no shape to protest anything, she thought as she followed him, her hand securely in his.

Her hand was the only thing that *was* secure, a little voice reminded her. Even though she appeared to fit so well into the little family scene that had been unfolding over the last few days, she was still plagued by doubts. Would she be a part of Matt's life once this movie was over? But her doubts weren't strong enough to keep her from loving him, from wanting him with every shred of her being.

Matt opened the door to his room and ushered her in. "There's something to be said for small places," he whispered softly against the nape of her neck, snuggling against her and teasing her with his body.

"Yes," Chyna whispered back, "they're maddening. Don't forget, you promised to tuck Meredith in," she reminded him.

His expression told her that he *had* forgotten. "You make me forget a lot of things," he told Chyna affectionately. "Wait right here."

And wait she did, although her common sense, slowly returning in the wake of his absence, told her to go. The more dependent she became on his lovemaking, the harder it would be for her later, but she couldn't help herself. She stayed, anxiously anticipating the glory of his touch.

She didn't have long to wait.

"Sorry," he murmured, kissing her temple. "Where were we?"

She reached up and took his face in her hands, moving his lips to hers. "Here."

He seemed to delight in arousing her. Her response grew with each caress, each kiss that touched a different part of her anatomy. He lingered over every part, branding it with kisses that alternated between soft and tender, and passionately urgent.

The undulations of her hips grew demanding as his tongue tickled her navel, circling it with kisses that were only half playful. Most exciting of all was the fact that his own breathing was increasing. She adored exciting him. But at this point she was beyond being able to do anything on her own. She was nearly numb with ecstasy.

"Matt..." She half whispered, half moaned his name, wanting him to come back up to her level, wanting to savor the taste of his mouth on hers.

"Shh," he chided. "Don't disturb the producer at work. This is a delicate project." His words warmed the sensitive skin of her inner thigh, his breath caressing it before his mouth did.

"Your...project...is turning into an...epic," she complained breathlessly.

"I don't believe in filming shorts," he said, pausing for a second before his tongue took intimate possession of her.

Chyna bit her lip hard to keep from moaning audibly. Her fingers buried themselves in his thick, blond hair. "Please," she pleaded. "Come to me." Before I scream out loud, she added silently, not knowing how much longer she could endure what was happening to her.

And then he was above her, a tender look in his eyes. A man like this had to be able to love, she thought. He just *had* to.

It was the last thought she was capable of as ecstasy pushed everything else out of her mind. As he took her, she joined him in the intimate duet that was theirs alone.

She pulled his mouth over hers to keep from crying out. And when it was over Chyna sighed, falling back against the pillow. Trying to steady her erratic pulse, she took a deep breath, hoping the air would clear her head. All she could smell was a mixture of cologne and body scent that was his alone. She smiled deeply, a feeling of incredible contentment spreading through her.

"You do good work," she whispered. "This was by far the greatest epic I've ever been in." She meant to sound light and teasing, but she didn't have enough strength to do anything except whisper the words.

Matt kissed her cheek tenderly, lying down next to her and cradling her in his arms. "When properly inspired, I can be a genius," he said. "And you're the greatest inspiration of my life."

Was she? Was she really? There were a million questions she wanted to ask him, but she was too tired. All she could do was hang on to the feeling his words had awoken within her. Some men did lie at times like this, she thought, trying to temper the joy she felt, but it refused to be dampened.

Reaching out, she ran her finger along his lips. He held her hand and kissed each finger lightly.

"I want to thank you," he said.

"For what?" she asked, puzzled.

"For the way you've been with Meredith. She's changed so much." He looked down into her face. "And it's all because of you."

Chyna shrugged his words away. "A person would have to be made out of stone not to respond to her."

Matt looked away for a moment, staring past her shoulder. "I was led to believe that gung-ho career women were too self-centered to care about other people."

She ached for him. He looked so vulnerable at that moment. Gently she touched his face, and he brought his gaze back to her. "Did she hurt you very much?" she whispered.

"Who?"

"Laura." She had no place prying this way, but

feeling the way she did about Matt, she couldn't help herself.

"I survived," he said, closing the subject. And then he kissed her forehead softly. "Survived long enough to discover something pretty precious."

"I wish I could go with you tomorrow," she said. "Will you be gone very long?" Suddenly, even a few hours was too long a time for them to be separated.

He nodded. "I'm afraid so. Besides putting Meredith on the plane, I've got to talk to the man at the government office...."

He let his voice trail off mysteriously. Chyna knit her brows together, waiting. "Why?" she finally asked.

"I need to extend the work permit," he told her. "We've lost two days. Or haven't you noticed?"

"You don't intend to make them up?" she asked, wondering if he were just pretending for her benefit, and hating being plagued by these doubts.

"Yes," he answered. "With two more days." For a moment the atmosphere became serious. "Does that answer your question?" he asked, looking at her intently.

"Yes," she said quietly. "That answers my question. And you'll talk to Dussault before you go?" she asked, still not able to believe totally that what she had hoped for in her heart was really true.

"And I'll talk to Dussault before I go," he said, parroting her words in a singsong fashion. "But right now I've had enough of words," he told her.

She saw the gleam that came into his eyes. "You're kidding," she murmured.

He shook his head. "Abstinence builds up strength," he told her.

"It certainly must," she whispered against his mouth just before he kissed her again.

But he didn't talk to Dussault before he left.

Chyna tried to keep her bitter disappointment from eating away at her. He was just in a hurry, she tried to tell herself. They had overslept, and he'd had only an hour and a half to get Meredith to the airport. He had tried to talk to the director, she reminded herself, but for once the man was nowhere to be found. Someone finally told Matt that Dussault was scouting another location with the cinematographer.

So much for words of caution, Chyna thought with a touch of fear. As she watched Matt and the others driving away, she could feel herself growing uneasy. She tried to tell herself that she was just being superstitious.

Chyna turned her attention back to the stunt coordinator, who was telling her what he wanted her to do during the fight scene. Sally stood at Alex's elbow, wearing a torn white dress. Chyna looked like a carbon copy of the actress, her hair disarrayed in the same manner, her dress torn in the same places. Both women had been carefully scrutinized by the makeup, wardrobe and continuity people for exactness of detail.

Dussault marched over to join them. Chyna quickly masked the involuntary frown that sprang to her lips. "Are you ready for a take?" he barked. Before Chyna or the other stuntworker had a chance to answer, Dussault was waving the cameras into the scene.

The positioning of the cameras was all-important for a fight scene. Chyna knew that she had to keep her back to the camera at all times. That way, the swing she took at the "villain" could miss by a country mile and still look effective on screen. It pleased Chyna to double for a feisty heroine. It also pleased her pocket. If the heroine hadn't been in danger all the time, Chyna's paycheck would have reflected that fact. She had arranged to be paid by the stunt rather than the customary five hundred dollars a day that many of the stuntworkers earned. So far, the total was adding up quite nicely.

"Okay, let's do it!" Dussault roared. After the appropriate commands the camera directly behind Chyna dollied in for a close-up of Sally.

"Cut!" Dussault commanded, and Sally willingly stepped away to let Chyna move in.

"Roll 'em!"

With that the fight was on. All Chyna was supposed to do was take a good swing at the villain who was running toward her, appearing to hit his midsection with the butt of a rifle. She checked her swing just in time, and the stuntman fell at her feet, doubled over, an appropriately dazed look on his face.

"Cut!"

She wasn't sure, but Dussault didn't sound very pleased. And he wasn't.

"I want you to come in closer when you swing," Dussault snapped at Chyna.

Was he crazy? "Any closer and I'll hit him," she protested, glancing at the stuntman, who was brushing himself off. He looked none too happy about the director's orders. "The camera—"

"I'll take care of the camera," Dussault told her coldly. "You just take orders. I want you to come in closer this time."

Chyna and the stuntman exchanged looks, then prepared to do it again. Chyna could feel the tension mounting.

Four takes went by before Dussault finally muttered something about that being good enough. He went on to another part of the scene, leaving Chyna free to rehearse her next stunt. This time, another stuntman was to come running from behind and tackle her, making her fall and roll in the dirt. It didn't seem very difficult, Chyna thought as the two of them began to practice.

She had taken exactly three falls before she noticed that the cameras were being set up nearby. She looked up, watching as Dussault began to browbeat the head cameraman.

This has the makings of a long, long day, she thought, getting up.

"Don't we get any more time to practice?" she asked. "It's still a little rough."

"You should have had the kinks out by now," Dussault retorted, overhearing her. "We're already two days behind. We're going to make them up. That means I don't have time to coddle nervous stuntmen."

"Matt said he was getting a work permit extension—" Chyna began. But her words were cut short by the look Dussault gave her. He seemed to be telling her not to be so gullible. Chyna pressed her lips together and fell silent, wishing she could be certain that Matt had been telling the truth. After all, the words would have been easy enough to say. And she wasn't going to see him actually apply for the extension. It would be easy enough for him to say that the extension had been denied for some reason or other.

"That's a nasty one," the makeup artist was saying.

"Yes, he is," Chyna muttered.

"No, I mean your bruise," the man pointed out, applying the appropriate shade of body makeup to the point of her shoulder where the dress was torn. It felt a little tender as his fingers brushed against it, and Chyna winced.

"I guess we're all just so anxious to please," she mumbled, "that we get carried away."

"I wish someone would carry him away," the makeup man said under his breath.

"You're not the only one," Chyna told him.

"Let's go, let's go!" Dussault yelled.

"Showtime," Chyna sighed, stepping back before the camera.

They broke for lunch right after the shot had been successfully completed. Dussault limited the break to half an hour, and told everyone to turn up for the fire sequence next. After she grabbed a sandwich, Chyna had only enough time left to change her costume.

At least this time she had pants on, she thought. The dresses worn by the heroine hampered her movements, and she still harbored bad memories of the time when she had caught on fire. She felt she had more of a sporting chance in pants. And the way Dussault was going, she was going to need all the help she could get. As she buttoned her blouse she wondered if Dussault was taking advantage of the fact that Matt had gone into the city. Or wouldn't it have mattered?

Chyna sighed. She had to put these doubts out of her head for the time being. She needed to concentrate on her gag.

"You ready?" she asked Pepper.

She glanced at her friend and saw that the woman looked uncharacteristically nervous.

"You okay?" she asked when Pepper made no answer.

Quickly a smile flashed across Pepper's face. "Sure, just thinking," she said as she walked out the door.

"About what?" Chyna prodded as she followed her out.

"About another profession." Pepper laughed. "God, that Dussault is a hell-raiser, isn't he?"

"I was thinking that hell was more where he belonged," Chyna quipped.

When they got to where the huge tent was set up, Chyna was surprised to see some of the special effects people getting ready to set fire to it. "I didn't know they were going to shoot the fire today."

Pepper merely shrugged in response. "Who knows what he has in mind?"

"Hey, you two, over here!" Dussault ordered, waving them over to the tight circle that had gathered around him.

Dubiously Chyna led the way, wondering what the director was up to.

"I want you all inside," he said, once the two women were within earshot. "We're going ahead with the fire scene. I've got the cameras all set up. If we do it right, we can get this shot in one take. Then we won't have to face the expense of burning two tents."

Chyna's mouth dropped open. What about the possible expenditure of lives? She looked at the startled faces around her. Wasn't anyone going to say anything? But she knew better. Protests didn't endear you to the men who made movies. Damn it, where was Matt when she needed him?

But would it matter if he were here?

"Okay, you, you and you," Dussault said, pointing to Chyna and two of the stuntmen as he consulted his storyboard for positions. "I want you—"

"No," Chyna said, not budging.

The other two stuntmen stopped walking, not daring to side with her, yet curious as to what was going to happen next.

Dussault's shaggy brows formed one straight, angry line. "No?" he echoed, surprised. "Did I hear you right?"

Chyna looked toward Alex for support. But the stunt coordinator didn't make a sound. He was watching warily. "We're not ready to film this," she said, measuring her words carefully.

She could see the color rising to Dussault's cheeks. "I say when you're ready to do something!" he informed her, barely suppressed rage in his words. "What is it? Aren't you brave enough to try it?" he taunted.

"No," she said, trying to keep her voice calm. "Just not stupid enough."

"Look," he said, jabbing a finger at her, "just because Harrigan wasted a little time on you and you did some tricks for his kid doesn't make you something special. You have no say in the matter—"

"Matt said—"

"The only thing Harrigan cares about is getting this picture done on time. His reputation is riding on it. One colossal money-eater could be a death warrant for his career."

She knew that what he was saying was true. In the movie business nobody cared about your past accomplishments. It was what you had done lately that counted with the studios. Failure took on much larger proportions than success did.

"I thought he was keeping you in line," Dussault snapped. "Obviously his methods don't work very well."

His words stung her, and she didn't hear what he said next. Just when she had been beginning to believe that Matt really did care for her... Had she been right all along? Had he been playing up to her just to keep her quiet?

"Now, you do this scene, or you never do another scene as long as you live!" Dussault threatened. She knew he could make good on his threat. He was important—and vindictive—enough to do just that.

Common sense told her to walk away from the set. What he was asking them to do would be dangerous enough even with adequate rehearsal. Without that rehearsal, Dussault was pushing for orchestrated suicide. But somehow that didn't matter to her right then. Matt's behavior toward her had been a game after all. And she had been a king-sized dupe.

"Well?" Dussault demanded impatiently, his hands on his hips.

"All right," she said hollowly. "I'll do your damn scene."

As she walked inside the huge tent, she heard Dussault laughing to someone. "They always come around when it means money."

Twelve

With raw determination, Chyna began to execute her stunt, which involved making her way along the inside wall of the huge tent and then actually rolling through the flames as she grappled with two assailants. She kept her eye on the flames at all times. When you were dealing with fire, you had to have a healthy respect for your co-star. It demanded your attention.

She wasn't exactly sure when or how it happened, but suddenly her co-star took over center stage. Whipping her head around, Chyna saw flames devouring their way to the top of the tent.

This wasn't in the script!

"Film it, damn you. Film it! This will look terrific!" she heard Dussault yell above the roar of the fire.

"My God, it's going out of control!" Pepper shouted, staring up as she backed away from the center of the tent. Everyone began scrambling for safety.

"Where are the fire extinguishers?" Chyna cried as she grabbed Alex's hand.

"Over there!" he shouted back as the noise grew louder. He pointed off to the right side of the tent, where several men were vainly attempting to douse the fire, which was spreading.

"But there should be more!" she insisted, scanning the area. It was hard to focus on anything as panic spread through the crew and smoke filled the air.

Alex pulled her back as a piece of the tent suddenly fell down in front of them, still blazing. "He's got them at the other location!"

He pushed her outside as the props and equipment that had been set up for the scene began to catch fire. They would be standing in an inferno in a matter of minutes if something wasn't done.

"Move the Jeeps," Alex roared, waving at the others, "before the gas tanks explode!"

Several stuntmen dashed toward the cars, and seconds later the sound of engines being gunned added to the general mayhem. The scene was a tangle of cables, equipment and fleeing people.

"Alex!" Chyna cried, pointing to the tent. The flames were searing through the top. They had to get the tent down so they could extinguish the fire before it spread to the surrounding vegetation.

"Way ahead of you." He nodded. "Find something sharp. Use anything you can, but start cutting that tent down! I'm going back inside to get that center pole down," he called. "I'll be back in two minutes."

"Pull up the stakes!" Chyna cried to one of the stuntmen. An extra ran by and she pulled his sword from the scabbard dangling at his side.

It wasn't very sharp, and she muttered an oath as

she hacked at the strong cord that attached the tent to the stake. After several desperate tries, she finally severed the rope, and the edge of the tent sprang free and collapsed toward the center. But the main support for the tent was still standing, and that meant Alex was still inside!

Dussault was standing nearby, frozen. He was staring in disbelief at the fire, oblivious to all the turmoil and noise around him. He looked horror stricken.

But she had no time to think about him. "Alex is still in there!" she cried to someone at her elbow. She turned and recognized Scottie. "We've got to get him out of there!"

This was just another gag, she told herself over and over again as she reentered the inferno. Just another gag. She held her frayed nerves together. There was no time for fear now. Later she could fall apart.

Smoke and fire were everywhere within the tent. It was far more devastating than anything that could be captured on film. Chyna's eyes swept the interior, looking for Alex. Scottie had followed her in, and now tugged at her sleeve and pointed overhead. Shielding her eyes, Chyna could just barley make out the figure of a man climbing up to the top of the center pole. When he reached the top, Alex began to frantically hack away at the rigging.

"Alex, get down from there!" Chyna shrieked.

If he heard her, he gave no indication, working at the ropes until one line finally tore free. The second, third and fourth followed suit in quick succession. That job done, Alex began to slide down the pole as the walls of the tent collapsed around him. He apparently didn't realize that the bottom five feet of the pole were engulfed in flames. Chyna stripped off her jacket and began beating at the fire, trying to keep the pole from collapsing until Alex made it down. Scottie joined in, but it was no use. Chyna heard a horrible crack and the pole began to go, severed by the fire. Alex leaped down, twisting his leg beneath him in the fall.

Chyna and Scottie rushed to him and each grabbed an arm to drag him away from burning canvas as it fell. When they got outside the area was swarming with more grips, who had come running with fire extinguishers. A cheer of relief went up as the threesome joined the bedraggled extras and crew members.

"He needs medical attention," Chyna told Dussault, who, though no longer frozen, still looked pale and shaken. He nodded and turned to the two nearest men. "Get him to the first aid station." He sighed, his breath rattling in his chest. "Okay, everybody get cleaned up. The excitement's over."

"Not by a long shot," Chyna declared, her voice stone cold. The fire in her eyes rivaled the blaze. All she could think of was that he had almost killed them all.

Dussault turned to look at her, stunned. "What's the matter?" He tried to regain his former verve, but it was obvious that he was shaken to the core.

"We're not working anymore. Not until you're taken off the picture," Chyna said defiantly, suppressing her rage. He had nearly gotten them all killed, and all he could say was that the "excitement" was over. She felt hysteria mounting within her and fought to keep it under control.

"What do you mean?"

"If you hadn't been pushing, if you had left us with enough time to rehearse this scene properly, if you hadn't had half the grips out working on another scene, then this wouldn't have happened." She gestured at the charred, smoldering remnants of the tent. "That makes you responsible! And no paycheck in the world is worth dying for." Her eyes narrowed. "I've got a lot of years ahead of me. I don't intend to let you make me lose them."

Dussault stared at her, knowing he had to do something to try to maintain control. He could see by the looks of the people around her that they agreed with her. "You're calling a strike!" he cried, licking his lips nervously. "You can't do that!"

"Call it what you like," Chyna said, rubbing away perspiration streaks with the back of her blackened hand. "It boils down to the fact that we won't work on an unsafe picture." The circle around her tightened, and Chyna knew that the others supported her. Finally. The hysteria within her abated a little.

"Do you realize what you're doing?" Dussault cried desperately. "You're jeopardizing Harrigan's picture!"

He was trying to get at her the only way he knew how, and for a moment uncertainty clawed at the pit of her stomach. What would Matt say when he found out what she had done? Would he feel betrayed by the woman he loved—or just furious that his attempt to control her had failed? But he wasn't there, and something had to be done until he got back. Dussault looked chastised, but how long would that last? No, Chyna felt that none of them could risk taking a chance. The next time might be fatal.

"No," she said softly. "*You're* jeopardizing Harrigan's picture," she said, turning away.

She was followed by the others, leaving Dussault to stare after them incredulously.

* * *

Matt returned an hour later, and he had been inside his trailer for exactly three minutes when the door burst open and Dussault stormed in, furious.

"She's done it, Matt. She's done it just like I warned you!"

"Sit down, Phil; you're turning red," Matt said calmly. He was tired from his trip, and in no mood for another outburst from Dussault. Although this time, he thought, looking closer at the man, he really looked strained. Matt moved toward the bar and began to pour himself a drink. He felt he was going to need it.

The scotch didn't prepare him in the slightest.

"She's called a strike," Dussault said, his voice trembling. He had never had his authority usurped before.

Matt's fingers tightened around his glass. "She's what?" His mind refused to register Dussault's words.

The director took the glass from Matt's hand, his own hand shaking as he took a long drink. "You heard me. She's called a strike."

"Chyna wouldn't do that," Matt said, his voice deadly still.

"Oh, wouldn't she?" Dussault asked, taking a second gulp.

"Why?" Matt demanded, numb. Had he been wrong about her all this time? Had he allowed his emotions to cloud his judgment?

"What does it matter why? She stood there in front of everyone and declared that they were calling a strike. She's got to go, Matt!" His bravado faded in light of the look in Matt's eyes. Dussault lowered his voice. "There was a fire. It got out of control. You know how those things can be."

He almost sounded as if he were pleading, Matt thought. It was totally out of character for the man. Tension formed in the pit of his stomach.

"You can't predict which way the wind goes, you know that," Dussault went on, rambling. He closed his eyes for a moment, trying to pull himself together. "She flew off the handle," the director continued, beginning to pace. "I warned you, Matt. I warned you," he repeated. "She's costing you money every minute we're in here talking."

"We're not in here talking," Matt corrected. "You are. I'm listening." *And hating what I hear.* "And I—"

He didn't get a chance to finish, for the door swung open again, banging against the opposite wall.

"Want to hear my side of it?" Chyna asked, afraid of what Dussault might have told him. What lies was she going to be up against? Dussault looked desperate. He'd say anything to downplay his part in the disaster.

Matt had never seen her so angry. She was still in her bedraggled costume, and she smelled of smoke. "Are you all right?" he asked, moving toward her.

Chyna nodded. "No thanks to him." All her previous doubts about their relationship came to a head as she turned to look at Matt. This would be the telling moment. What if Dussault had been right?

"We'll go over budget if—" Dussault began hurriedly.

"Chyna was talking," Matt said quietly, cutting the other man off.

Chyna couldn't read the expression on Matt's face. Undoubtedly Dussault had said that she had called a strike. A strike on *Matt's* set. Would that make him prejudiced against anything she had to say in her own defense? She turned squarely to face him.

"He tried to film two sequences today. We didn't have enough time to rehearse all the segments that went into the fire scene, but he went ahead with it anyway. There weren't enough special effects grips to control the fire. Suddenly it was everywhere." An involuntary shudder ran through her. "It was Alex who cut the tent down. If he hadn't, an awful lot of people could have gotten hurt. Instead, only Alex did. He broke his leg." She glared accusingly at Dussault who, in turn, looked at Matt.

"These things happen, Matt," he insisted. "You know that. It's not my fault," he declared adamantly.

"They don't *have* to happen if you take the proper precautions!" Chyna cried. She felt herself on shaky ground, but she couldn't stop. To back down now would be selling out her integrity. But was she giving up Matt's love instead? She tried to force the question out of her mind. Matt had to understand. He just *had* to.

Dussault struggled for control. "Matt, we can have another crew out here in twenty-four hours if this is the way they want to play it," he said, his brown eyes shifting wildly as he searched Matt's face for some sign as to whose side he was on. But Matt's face remained grim.

Chyna had no clue, either, and she wished that things hadn't come to a head this way. But she couldn't stand by and let Dussault go on doing what he was doing. Someone had to try to stop him. Someone had to go on record against him. Sure, he had looked stricken out there as they carried Alex away, but how long would that last? Chyna knew she couldn't live with herself if she turned a blind eye to the events that had just transpired. It would be tantamount to condoning Dussault's behavior.

The specter of Neil's accident hung over her, and she knew that the stand she had taken was the only one open to her. Otherwise she would be haunted for the rest of her life.

Matt looked from one to the other, knowing that his next words might forever change his life in one way or another. Studios didn't like rebels, even rebel producers. He couldn't just fire a known talent like Dussault. But if he gave Chyna an ultimatum, telling her to return to work or else, he knew he would lose her. He couldn't afford to do either.

As he attempted to come up with a compromise, there was a knock on the door. Relieved at the distraction, he called out, "Come in."

Alex, his arm draped around Scottie's shoulders, hobbled in, pain etched into his dark features.

"What the hell are you doing here?" Matt demanded, striding over to him. "I'll get someone to drive you to the city—" he began, looking at the makeshift splint that had been put on the man's leg.

Alex nodded, an unreadable expression on his face. "I'd appreciate that, but first I have to talk to you."

Matt's expression darkened. "If you're going to tell me about the fire, Chyna already took care of that," he said, giving her an enigmatic look.

"No, I don't think she did," Alex said. Chyna looked at him sharply. There was something about his tone that bothered her. "Not all of it." He shifted a little, and Scottie struggled to keep him upright.

"Stop playing martyr in my trailer, Alex," Matt said, his tone softening. "At least sit down." He tried to guide Alex to the sofa, but the stunt coordinator surprised him by waving him away.

"This isn't going to take long," he said, his voice devoid of expression. "The fire was my fault."

"What?" Chyna cried, stunned.

Alex looked at her, agony on his face. "It was my fault," he repeated.

"But how?...I don't..." Words failed her. Matt saw the utter confusion on her face and could only guess at what was going on inside.

"I came in here because I was afraid that Chyna would get fired. She stood up for us, for the whole crew," he clarified, "when she thought that the accident was Dussault's fault. But it wasn't." He measured his words carefully, even though they came out in a rush. It was, Chyna thought, as if he were trying to cleanse himself. "The assistant director was nervous about the shot. He asked me to cue the grips when to light the fire." He paused, licking his lips. "I miscalculated. I was premature. It was my fault."

The words had sounded hollow, but they rang over and over again in Chyna's ears. It was as if she had suddenly seen a ghost. She had been so concerned about safety, so concerned about the director taking precautions, that she had totally forgotten about the human factor. Numbed, Chyna sank down into a chair, unable to do anything except sit and watch Matt. What would he think of her?

His first concern was for Alex. "Scottie, get him into town and stay with him until they release him from the hospital. Take a driver with you." Alex and Matt exchanged a long look. "We'll talk about this later, Alex," Matt promised, his voice full of understanding sympathy. Alex's burden would be great enough without his adding any words to it now.

"As for our problem..." Matt began, turning back to Dussault and Chyna as the other two men left.

"There is no problem," Chyna said softly. She felt as if she were in a trance. She was only half-conscious of the fact that she had risen to her feet. "I'll save you the trouble of firing me," she told Matt. She turned to look at Dussault, who was still digesting what had just transpired. "I was wrong. I'm sorry. Something came over me. I guess I was still living with my husband's ghost." She took a deep breath. "I'll apologize to you in front of everyone before I leave if it will make a difference."

Before Dussault could answer, Matt cut in. "You're not going anywhere," he informed her. "We're not finished shooting here."

"But I—"

"Woman, would you please stop talking for once? You're one of the best stuntworkers in the business. I know that. Dussault knows that." He cast a meaningful glance at the director. The man forced himself to nod his agreement. "What happened here today should have taught us *all* a lesson. Maybe different lessons," he added, for Chyna's benefit. "But I'm not about to let hot tempers disrupt my set. *I* say who goes and who stays. And I haven't fired anyone." He fished a long thin envelope out of his hip pocket and threw it on the desk in front of him. "That's our extension. We have an extra week if we need it. No reason to hurry any longer. Studio money isn't everything. Once this picture is released, it'll earn back what was laid out here in a couple of weeks. I guarantee it. And I know my movies," he said firmly. "Now, get out of here, both of you," he said wearily, turning his back on them. "Tomorrow we'll all start fresh."

Dussault was quick to take his leave, but Chyna remained where she was, looking at Matt's back. Fear and uncertainty gnawed at her, feelings that were far greater than anything she had felt during the fire. Drawing on her last shred of courage, she reached out and touched his shoulder. "Matt, I—"

Matt turned around. His eyes appraised her for a long moment before he said anything. "Why couldn't you have waited until I got back before making that grandstand play?"

His words stung her. But he was right. Still, she wanted him to understand. "The accident brought everything back to me. I...I overreacted." She swallowed, trying to get rid of the scratchy feeling in her throat. She looked up toward the ceiling, hoping to keep her tears back. "I lost my head. I—" Abruptly she stopped, overwhelmed by the enormity of the situation.

Despite his own anger, Matt understood what she was going through, and he drew her into his arms. Nothing mattered right then, just as long as she was safe.

Chyna sagged against him, momentarily drained. "Oh, Matt, I was wrong, so wrong. All this time..." She sighed deeply. "It's like a rock's been lifted off my chest." She looked up into his face, "Can you forgive me?" The tears spilled out freely now, making tracks through the soot on her face.

He took out his handkerchief and wiped some of the dirt away. "I'll think about it," he said, a hint of warmth in his voice. "This is getting to be a habit," he commented, nodding toward his handkerchief.

"Poor Alex," Chyna murmured.

"I'll talk to him when he gets back. I'll talk to a lot of people," he added. "There should have been a way to prevent this."

"But Alex said—"

"I know what Alex said, but there should have been someone double-checking both of them. I'm not whitewashing Phil just because I didn't have him taken off the picture. He was wrong in rushing production. And I was wrong in not taking a stronger stand with him. And you," he said, touching her nose, "were wrong for putting me on the spot. Now we'll all do penance and be better for it."

He pressed her against him, stroking her hair. "I'll file a report when we get back," he promised.

"You'd do that for me?" she asked, knowing what such an action could mean as far as the studio was concerned.

"No," he said slowly, "I'll do it for me. You don't have a private patent on integrity, you know."

She couldn't believe it. "Do you really feel that way?"

"Would I lie to you?" he asked, searching her face for a sign of trust. She was so hard to read at times, so complex, so intense, yet gentle. What had life been like without her? Empty, he thought. Very, very empty.

"I don't know," she said honestly. "Why not? *I* lie to me. I spent all afternoon telling myself I didn't care about you...."

"And you were lying?" he asked softly.

"Viciously." Chyna kissed him soundly, lacking any other way to express her feelings of overwhelming gratitude.

Halfway through the kiss, Matt began to cough. "God, you smell awful."

"You would too if you just came out of a burning inferno," she informed him, a warm feeling beginning to spread all through her.

"Do you stuntpeople play with fire often?"

"Sometimes when we don't even know it," she said, running her hand along his shirt. She began to open the buttons.

"Well, you'll just have to take a shower before you come home every night. I like your natural smell much better—before you're hickory smoked."

Chyna stopped pulling out his shirttails. "Are you asking me to move in with you?"

"In a manner of speaking, yes." He urged her hand back into motion.

"But what will Wanda say?" she asked. His words had thrown her completely off balance. A glimmer of hope began to sparkle.

"Probably 'Good afternoon, Mrs. Harrigan.'"

She stared at him. "You're asking me to marry you?" Oh please, please say you're asking me to marry you.

"No," he quipped, "just to change your name. The space on the mailbox can't accommodate two names." He swept her closer into his arms, laughing. "Of course I'm asking you to marry me."

"But I just started a strike on your picture. I don't—" Confusion reigned supreme in her brain as logic and emotions ran into each other. He wanted to marry her. Nothing else in the world mattered. Stop trying to talk him out of it, dummy, she told herself. He loves you!

"And we've resolved that," he said, kissing her cheek. "What's the problem?"

"Nothing," Chyna laughed, feeling giddy. "Nothing at all."

"Glad to hear it," he answered. "Did you know I was superstitious?" he asked her suddenly.

"You?" The idea seemed impossible. He was far

too logical a person to hold with any superstitions, she thought.

He nodded, then paused to kiss the outer rim of her ear. A shiver slid down her spine. "Come here," he said, leading her to the couch. He gently sat her down and then began to work on her boots, pulling off one and then the other while he spoke. "I'm beginning to feel as if I need a good luck talisman to ward off any further problems on the set."

"A talisman?" Chyna echoed.

"Right. In the olden days ladies would send their knights off to battle wearing a scarf or something to act as a talisman. Got anything for me?" he asked. As he spoke, he was unhooking her trousers.

"How about a blouse?" she offered mischievously.

He slipped it off her shoulders and examined it. "Nope," he decided, tossing it aside.

"Trousers?"

They came off too. "Sorry, too dull looking," he told her, letting them join her blouse on the floor.

"Bra?"

"Worth considering," he agreed, taking it from her and rubbing the soft, lacy material against his cheek. She felt warmed by the glow in his eyes as he looked at her.

"Almost," he said, then sighed. "But not quite."

"Well," she said playfully, "all I've got left are my panties."

He snapped his fingers. "That just might do the trick." With that he eased the translucent blue material away from her body. "Yes," he whispered, not looking at the prize in his hand, only at her. "That just might do the trick."

He moved to cover her body with his own, unable to put up with the separation any longer.

"You're going to look pretty silly walking around the set with blue panties tied around your arm," she murmured against his lips.

"I'll chance it," he told her, beginning to explore her body. "After all, I'm the guy who took a chance on having a hell-raiser as part of my crew, remember?"

Wonderful sensations began to unfold all through her as anticipation took hold. "I remember," she said softly. "Matt?"

"Hmm?" The sound rippled against her taut belly, making it quiver. Matt raised his head. "You're interrupting my concentration."

"Do you love me?"

"You picked a strange time to ask," he said, pulling himself back up to look into her face.

"On the contrary, I think it's a very opportune time," she pointed out teasingly. "Do you?" She needed to hear him say it almost as much as she needed to feel his body against hers.

"Lady," he said, gently brushing the hair away from her face, "you've been walking through the shadows of my mind ever since I first laid eyes on you." Ever so tenderly, he kissed first one eyelid and then the other. "I don't think I'd really want to go on living if I couldn't have you. And in my book, Ms. Daredevil, that means I love you very, very much." He kissed her lips lightly. "Satisfied?"

"No," she answered, entwining her fingers through the hair at the nape of his neck. "But I think you'll see to that shortly."

The laughter in his eyes faded into passion. "You bet I will. Want to come back here on our honeymoon?" he asked.

"Not on your life!" she murmured feelingly, just before she brought his mouth down to hers and stopped saying anything at all.

* * * * *

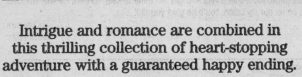

 **HARLEQUIN®**
Makes any time special™

 WIN A DREAM

In celebration of Harlequin®'s golden anniversary

Enter to win a *dream!* You could win:

- A luxurious trip for two to *The Renaissance Cottonwoods Resort* in Scottsdale, Arizona, or

- A bouquet of flowers once a week for a year from **FTD**, or

- A $500 shopping spree, or

- A fabulous bath & body gift basket, including **K-tel's** *Candlelight and Romance* 5-CD set.

Look for **WIN A DREAM** flash on specially marked Harlequin® titles by Penny Jordan, Dallas Schulze, Anne Stuart and Kristine Rolofson in October 1999*.

 FTD

RENAISSANCE. COTTONWOODS RESORT SCOTTSDALE, ARIZONA

 K·TEL

 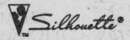